Before the
Cradle

Falls

James F. David

TOR®

A TOM DOHERTY ASSOCIATES BOOK
NEW YORK

This is a work of fiction. All the characters and events portrayed in this book are either fictitious or are used fictitiously.

BEFORE THE CRADLE FALLS

A Tor Book
Published by Tom Doherty Associates, LLC
175 Fifth Avenue
New York, NY 10010

www.tor.com

Tor® is a registered trademark of Tom Doherty Associates, LLC.

ISBN 0-765-34215-4
EAN 978-0765-34215-7
Library of Congress Catalog Card Number: 20010586109

First edition: June 2002
First mass market edition: May 2004

Printed in the United States of America

0 9 8 7 6 5 4 3 2 1

Acknowledgments

I can still remember the day I sat down at my keyboard and began my first novel. That day I had no idea that I would actually finish the novel, let alone have it published. Four novels later I can look back and say that it has been an amazing experience, both more work and more fun than I anticipated. Thanks again to Bob Gleason for his creative contributions and to my agent, Carol McCleary, whose suggestion about the opening was just right.

Thanks to my patient family who let me ignore them while I write and who read the drafts of my book over and over and over and over.... Gale, Abby, Katie, and Bethany, thanks for the editorial comments and all the suggestions for titles.

Acknowledgments

1

The Park

Sunday, 10:25 P.M.

Carolee and Carolynn Martin left Meaghan's house on the run. They had promised their mother they would be home by 10:30 P.M. and it was nearly that already. Their mother was strict and being even a few minutes late would get them grounded.

Carolynn led the way, jogging down the block along the park, following their usual path home. Carolee struggled to keep up. The Martin girls weren't identical twins and quite different in everything from physique to personality. Puberty hadn't run its full course yet but it was clear both would resemble their mother with slight figures—thin but not skinny. Carolynn had their mother's blond hair, and Carolee their father's dark brown. Both were pretty, but only Carolynn had found the courage to actually date a boy and then only to go roller-skating with his church's youth group. Nancy Martin didn't believe freshmen girls should date and approved the roller-skating trip reluctantly.

"Slow down, Lynn!" Carolee called to her sister.

Carolynn ignored her, keeping up her fast pace. Carolynn was the dominant twin, quick with ideas, creative, outgoing, and reckless. She took a risk now, angling across the street toward the park.

"We're not supposed to cut through the park at night," Carolee protested, still following her sister.

"If we don't, we'll be late, Lee," Carolynn shouted back.

The Martins had moved into an apartment near the park three years ago after their parents split up. It wasn't a divorce, exactly. The Martins were still married. Their father had simply left one day and never come back. Unable to afford their home on one income, Nancy Martin was forced to sell their house and moved herself and the girls into the apartment. Adjusting to the loss of space and privacy had been difficult. Eventually, the girls made new friends and with them explored the vast North Portland park, discovering its many secret places. During the day the park was a bright and active place with a swimming pool, playground, ball fields, and picnic tables. At night the park was dark and forbidding, full of shadows and a frightening silence. There had been problems in the park at night—fights and drinking mostly; teenagers using the dark to do secret teenage things. Carolee and Carolynn knew about night in the park but still here they were. Fearful of what hid in the park's shadows, Carolee ran harder now, keeping close to her sister's heels.

The park was sprinkled with mature fir trees that towered into the night sky, their canopy creating deep night shadows far below. There were open spaces too, and patches of shrubbery; large rhododendrons where children played hide-and-seek and other chase and catch games during the day. Deeper in the park was the playground, lit by one halogen bulb mounted high on the "rec-shack" where balls and jump ropes were handed out in the summer and where kids could buy gimp to make key chains and necklaces. As the girls approached the playground they saw movement. The merry-go-round was turning and in the dim light they could see three people riding.

Carolynn slowed, Carolee stumbling to keep from running into her.

"Watch it, Lynn," Carolee said.

"Quiet," Carolynn whispered back. "There's someone in the park."

The girls kept moving, angling away from the playground, trying to keep in the shadows. Carolee could see three teenage boys holding beer bottles. Empty bottles were scattered around the playground. Two more boys stepped out of the darkness, one of them pointing in their direction. Pulse already pounding from the run, Carolee's heart now thumped loudly. The merry-go-round stopped rotating, one of the teenagers standing, eyes locked on them. More boys came from behind the rec-shack, some staggering while they swigged from brown bottles. Something was shouted, the boys erupting in laughter. There was more talking now, some laughter, then shouting and cheers. Then, with a last round of laughter, the boys sprinted toward the girls.

"Run," Carolynn shouted.

Carolee ran faster than she ever had, discovering how fear can drive your body like no other emotion. She raced after her sister in a reckless run for home. Carolynn was pulling away from her at the same time she heard the pounding of feet behind her. She risked a quick look over her shoulder and saw the pack of boys spread out behind her, the leading edge only a few steps behind. She didn't have any more speed so she dodged around the trunk of the next tree, hoping the shadows would confuse them as she angled in a new direction. She lost sight of Carolynn when she did. Her quick move didn't fool the boys. Instead, the pack split, half the boys following her, the others continuing after Carolynn.

They ran her down a half minute later, the fastest boy coming up behind and pushing her sideways, tangling her feet and sending her into a tumble. The rest of the boys pounded to a stop as she got to her feet. Carolee found herself surrounded by a half-dozen teens, all breathing hard, some swaying from inebriation.

"Don't hurt me," Carolee said, backing in a circle, looking for a face she knew, someone to befriend her.

"We ain't gonna hurt you," one of the boys said, stepping

forward, taking charge. "We just want you to come to our party."

"I've got to go home," Carolee said, still looking for a friend. She vaguely recognized some of the boys from high school. She thought they were upperclassmen, two were on the football team. They had never spoken to her. Seniors were above noticing freshmen.

"What's your name, sweet thing?" the leader asked, stepping closer.

"Carolee," she replied, trying to sound calm.

The boy's speech was slightly slurred but his body steady. Most of the others were swaying.

"I've got to go home," Carolee said, pleading.

"Not now, it's party time," the boy said, stepping into her personal space.

Carolee could smell the beer on his breath and turned her head. Suddenly he grabbed he wrist, twisting her arm behind her and pulling her against his body. The pack cheered, howling and whistling approval.

"She wants you, Marcus," one shouted.

"Every girl wants me," Marcus said.

Carolee tried to push away with her free hand but now he held her with both, grinding his hips against hers.

"Please, let me go!" she pleaded.

A shout in the distance quieted the boys and Marcus released his bear hug, still holding her wrist. The other splinter group was calling and Marcus shouted back, telling them they had caught her. Helpless, Carolee was dragged toward the playground, the other boys trailing along, some stumbling along in a near stupor. There were a half-dozen boys circled near the merry-go-round now. When they parted to let Marcus drag Carolee to the center she saw her sister. Carolynn was on her knees, her blouse torn open, her arms across her chest. Her nose was bleeding and she was dirty. A boy towered over her, the others looking on in a mixture of horror and lust. Carolee pulled away from Marcus, dropping down

Rico lingered, even as the boys holding Carolynn ran.

"They'll tell," Rico said, looking from Carolynn to the approaching figure. Then to Carolynn he said, "If you tell anyone about this I'll hurt you!"

Then Rico ran after Marcus, quickly disappearing into the shadows. Now Carolee saw the man coming between tree trunks, wearing a long overcoat and a hat. Carolee crawled to her sister who was sitting up now, putting her torn clothes back together as best she could. Both girls were crying and they hugged each other.

"Get out of the park," their savior said.

Carolee helped Carolynn to her feet.

"I'm all right," Carolynn said. "Mamma's gonna kill me."

Carolee looked at the man who was moving into the light. His hat shaded part of his face but what she could see was a peculiar color.

"Thank you," Carolee said, but the man shook his head, dismissing the thank you.

"Give this to the police," the man said, handing Carolee a small piece of paper.

Carolee put the paper in her pocket and tried to thank him again.

"Go home!" the man said angrily.

Carolee didn't understand the man's anger but desperately wanted to be home. She wanted to shower and scrub every part of her body where she had been touched. This time Carolee led the way, running through the park even though her body was exhausted by the tension and her struggle against the hands that had held her down. For a change, Carolynn followed her, a few yards behind. Carolee thought of Rico's threat but planned to tell her mother what happened anyway. From the bruises on Carolynn's face and their torn clothes their mother would know half the story at her first glance and Carolee would fill in the rest despite her fear of Rico. Those boys would pay for what they had done.

A few minutes later Carolee broke out of the park onto

the street that led to their apartment complex. Nearly exhausted, she slowed to a walk. There were house lights across the street and a woman walking her dog and it made Carolee feel safe again. The park at night had been a surreal nightmare and she would never again enjoy the park the way she and Carolynn had as children. Then she realized Carolynn wasn't with her and she turned, waiting for her sister to emerge from the park. A minute passed and then another. Carolee called her sister's name.

"Lynn, where are you?"

Now panic returned. Lynn had been behind her. Carolee remembered looking over her shoulder at least twice, but how far back was that? Desperate to get out of the park, Carolee had lost track of her sister and now felt guilt for leaving her behind. Remembering the terror of the park's shadowy interior, she couldn't force herself to go back. Instead, she turned, fleeing for home.

2

Homicide

Monday, 1:58 A.M.

The ringing phone pulled Kyle Sommers out of a deep sleep, his hand lifting the receiver to his ear before he was fully conscious. He could hear a voice on the line but was too groggy to make sense of what was said. As Kyle became conscious, he became aware of his aching head and the thick saliva in his mouth. They were the familiar aftereffects of drinking himself to sleep. A practice he had adopted after the death of his daughter.

"What did you say?" Kyle said into the phone.

"I said I'm sorry to wake you," the voice said.

Kyle recognized the voice. It was Art Michelson. The sleep fog cleared slowly. Michelson was a homicide detective and should have gone off duty by now. Detectives worked three shifts, the evening and graveyard shifts being lightly staffed. If Michelson was still on duty, then something major had happened.

"You wouldn't call if it wasn't important," Kyle said, his tongue sticking to the roof of his mouth.

"Are you feeling okay?" Michelson asked.

Michelson asked about Kyle's health but what he really wanted to know was whether Kyle was drunk. Forcing his tongue to work, Kyle replied as clearly as he could.

"I'm fine, Art. I was deep asleep when you called. You know how it is."

"Sure, sure. It takes a minute to wake up."

Through bleary eyes, Kyle saw 1:58 A.M. on the clock radio.

"If you're up to it I need you to come out to Pier Park, Kyle. West end."

Kyle quickly agreed to meet Michelson. Since coming off medical leave Kyle had been deskbound by Captain Harding's orders. Michelson's call was an opportunity to prove he was ready for more than shuffling papers. Once the bureau "wunderkind," Kyle had been a star with a knack for creative problem solving. Other detectives had sought his help, appreciating his ability to think outside the box and bring fresh insights to their cases. The clearance rate of every detective in the bureau had improved because of Kyle, but that was the old Kyle, the sober Kyle.

Still dressed in yesterday's clothes, Kyle stripped, then pulled on jeans, a denim shirt, and running shoes. His weapon went in a belt holster. Then he filled his pockets with keys, wallet, and badge and pulled on a zip-front sweatshirt. Pausing in the bathroom, Kyle swallowed a small handful of aspirin, studying himself in the mirror as he did. He was tall at six feet three and the mirror had been mounted by a shorter person, so he had to duck slightly to see his entire face. His brown hair was mussed, his eyes slightly bloodshot, and there were bags under his eyes. Kyle ran a brush through his hair, splashed water on his face, and then left his apartment.

Kyle lived in Northeast Portland in a neighborhood of old stately homes. He rented the second-floor apartment of one of those homes, helping old Mrs. Pastorini who lived on the lower floor with yard work and home repairs. Kyle was supposed to get a rent reduction for the chores but he never took it, happy to have something to do when he was off duty.

It was a clear June night and the stars were bright. The cool night air helped clear Kyle's mind and as he looked at the sky he could see a faint sheen of color—the northern lights? Seeing the aurora borealis in Oregon wasn't impossible but it was unusual.

Kyle's pickup was parked at the curb and as he inserted the key there was a bright blue static spark. Suddenly, Kyle was struck by a powerful déjà vu experience. The 2:00 A.M. call, Michelson on the line, the taste of his mouth, the cool night air, the empty city street, all seemed familiar. Like a path he had taken once before, he had a vague sense of what might be around the next bend and he dreaded the trip. Shaking off the feeling, Kyle climbed into his pickup.

Kyle took Interstate 5 out to Lombard and then turned toward the suburb known as St. Johns. As a detective he knew North Portland well, since the lion's share of homicides occurred there. This time of night the streets were empty so he cut through the St. Johns business district into the neighborhood on the other side. Pier Park was nestled between the Willamette River docks and the St. Johns neighborhoods.

Kyle parked near the police barricade, fishing a flashlight out of his glove box. There was a crowd gathered, mostly neighbors in coats with pajama legs showing at the bottom. There were the usual police freaks too, who had picked up the call on their scanners. Kyle recognized a cherry '57 Chevy belonging to one of the freaks, then spotted the owner standing along the police line, staring into the park. This police groupie was thirty-five or forty, medium height and overweight, his gut flowing generously over his belt. He had pasty white skin and a two-day beard. Kyle had seen him at crime scenes before. Kyle flashed his badge to the officers keeping the crowd out, but avoided eye contact with the police freak who stared at Kyle like a groupie would a rock star.

Once over the tape, Kyle turned on the flashlight and was struck with another powerful déjà vu feeling. The police groupie, the crowd still in their pajamas, the flashlight in his hand probing into the dark ahead, all seemed as if it had happened just minutes ago. He'd had déjà vu experiences many times before but never this strong and never two this close together.

Kyle could see officers ahead and more yellow tape marking the crime scene. The tape surrounded a playground and a small building nearby. There were beer and liquor bottles scattered around the playground. In the distance he could see lights flickering through the trees. Kyle picked Michelson out of the officers near the merry-go-round. Even in the dark, his thick gray hair shone as if lit by a spotlight. Gray since his thirties, wearing thick glasses, Michelson was nearing retirement, the oldest detective left in the bureau. Slow talking and slow thinking, he was methodical and persistent, and ultimately effective. If Michelson made a case, it stuck, and he had one of the highest arrest-to-conviction ratios in the bureau. Kyle liked Michelson but his reflective cognitive style clashed with Kyle's impulsive tendencies and Kyle often found himself finishing the older detective's sentences for him. Michelson met him at the perimeter.

"Thanks for coming in, Kyle," Michelson began.

Michelson studied Kyle as he spoke. Other officers eyed Kyle too. They had heard the stories about Kyle and knew about his problems. Most could understand the drinking. It was the rumors about his other problems that made him a curiosity. Ignoring the furtive glances, Kyle went to work.

"You wouldn't have called if it wasn't important, Art," Kyle said. "What have you got?"

"Looks like it started here," Michelson said, indicating the playground. "Well, not here I guess, more like over there," he said, indicating with a vague nod toward a place in the trees.

Kyle waited patiently while Michelson reorganized his thoughts.

"Two girls were crossing the park on their way home," Michelson said slowly, planning each sentence carefully. "They were coming back from a friend's house and they live on the other side of the park," he said, pausing to point. "As they came through there," Michelson said with another nod into the dark, "they ran into a group of teenagers doing some serious drinking."

Michelson indicated the bottles scattered around the small lighted area as proof of his story. Polite to a fault, Michelson had called the boys involved "teenagers," when any other officer would have called them "punks," or worse.

"The boys chased the girls down and brought them back here where they proceeded to assault them."

"It was rape then?" Kyle said impatiently, grateful for Michelson calling him in, but wondering why he would have been called for a routine sexual assault.

"It was attempted rape but they were interrupted. Someone came out of the trees and scared them off. We're not sure which part of the park he came out of. The survivor just said he came out of the woods and the boys ran off."

The word "survivor" partially explained why Kyle had been called.

"The man who came out of the woods didn't give his name, he just told the girls to go home and so they took off running . . . that way," Michelson said, pointing toward the flashlights in the distance. "Let's walk over there as I finish filling you in.

"The girls are Carolee and Carolynn Martin—twins, but I bet you could tell that by the names. They live with their mother, Nancy Martin, in the Fircourt Apartments."

Kyle knew the Fircourt apartment complex from when he had worked the regional drug enforcement team. They had busted thirty Honduran illegals at the Fircourt five years ago, brought up to work the Old Town drug trade. They had been living crowded into three apartments along with wives and children. They took ten kilos of cocaine from the apartments that day, and a hundred sixty thousand dollars in cash. The owner had been sued by the other residents a month later and settled out of court by agreeing to sell the complex to a corporation. Kyle had heard the complex had been remodeled since then.

"Both girls were running to get out of the park, with Carolee in front," Michelson continued. "Carolee says she looked back at least twice and saw her sister behind her." Then in a softer voice Michelson said, "Carolynn's clothes had been nearly torn off and she might have slowed down trying to cover herself before they got out on the street. Anyway, when Carolee got to the edge of the park she discovered Carolynn wasn't with her. She was too afraid to go back in the park, so she ran home. Her mother called the police."

Michelson stopped by a big patch of rhododendrons. Yellow tape was stretched from tree to tree around the shrubbery like a shapeless connect the dot puzzle. Shorter, Michelson bent and went under the tape but Kyle waited and with his long legs easily stepped over.

"It took an hour to find Carolynn. Her body is in the shrubs here."

Michelson led him between the head-high plants to the center where there was an open area covered with bark dust. Two electric lanterns lit the interior, illuminating the body. The girl lying on her back in the bark dust looked fourteen or fifteen. Her blouse was torn open but she still wore her bra and pants. She was dirty but there wasn't any bark dust on her. There was blood caked under her nose and on the side of her head.

Michelson stood silently, letting Kyle take the scene in, assuming Kyle processed as slowly as he did.

"She still has her clothes on, so I doubt she was raped," Kyle said.

"The medical examiner doesn't think so either. She'll check when she does the autopsy."

"Art, it looks to me like the girls had the bad luck to stumble into some punks out for a little wilding but the good luck to have some neighbor out for a late-night walk interrupt what was sure to be a gang rape. The girls ran for home but one or more of the boys followed, catching one of them before they got to the street. She fought back and the boy, or boys, killed her during the struggle—except there isn't much evidence of a struggle," Kyle said again, playing his flashlight over the bark dust. "What we need to do now is find the boys, sweat them a little, and they'll finger each other."

"We've got the boys—at least the ringleaders. We'll pick up some of the others in the morning."

Kyle was impressed. The murder was only a couple hours old and the usually slow-moving Michelson had made arrests. Again, he wondered why Michelson had called him.

"Carolee—the one that survived—heard one of the boys called Rico and another Marcus," Michelson continued. "We talked to some of the neighbors who came out to gawk and they knew the boys. It's not like when I was a kid, Kyle. There were four Johns in my first-grade class, three Steves, and two Jims. There were two Arthurs in the class ahead of me."

Kyle understood Michelson's point. The ethnic mix, and tendency of parents to creatively name their children, had made identification easier. Instead of a high school full of Johns, Bills, Bobs, and Marks, teachers calling roll seldom called the same name twice and struggled to pronounce names like Enrico, Marcus, Grantly, Rioh'det, Putnam, and Mahallah.

"Rico and Marcus tell pretty much the same story. They admit the girls were at the party but they deny they tried to rape them. They say the party broke up when an old man threatened to call the police. They claim both girls were alive when they left. Rico wants us to think the old man killed Carolynn. We'll canvass the neighborhood in the morning to find him but if he's old I doubt he could chase down a couple of scared teenagers."

"Everyone over thirty looks old to teenagers," Kyle pointed out. "What they call an old man could have a gold medal from the last Olympics mounted over his mantel."

"Sure, but I don't think the old man killed Carolynn Martin."

Michelson reached into the pocket of his overcoat pulling out a plastic bag, handing it to Kyle. Kyle squatted, holding the bag to the light of one of the lanterns. Wrapped in the Ziploc bag was a blue baby rattle.

"We found it in her hand, Kyle, and the M.E. says she thinks the girl was suffocated."

Now Kyle knew why Michelson had called him. A chill ran down Kyle's spine as he realized the nightmare that was ahead for Portland. After coming back from medical leave, Captain Harding had sent Kyle to San Francisco for an orientation on a serial killer that had been working his way up the West Coast. Starting in San Diego, the killer specialized in murdering children, suffocating them in their own beds, and then leaving behind a child's toy as his signature. All the deaths appeared to be opportunity murders, with no motive, the only pattern being that the killer preferred young children. A tabloid had dubbed the killer "Cradle Robber" and the name had been picked up by the mainstream press.

"It could be a copycat," Kyle argued. "She'd be his oldest victim if it was him."

"Sure," Michelson said.

"I want to talk with the sister and the boys. The old man too when you find him."

"Sure, Kyle."

Kyle was taking charge of the case, knowing he would be officially assigned tomorrow. Harding had preselected a task force in case the serial killer continued north. Harding had selected Kyle to lead it as a way of easing him back to full duty. Sending him to San Francisco and then giving him time to review the voluminous case files kept Kyle out of harm's way while Harding evaluated his performance. No one had expected Cradle Robber to arrive this quickly and if he had taken another six months, Kyle suspected Harding would have replaced Kyle with someone else. But now that Cradle Robber was in Portland it was Kyle's job to stop the nightmare working its way up the West Coast.

"Let's go talk to the sister," Kyle said.

3

Evidence

The Fircourt Apartments looked much better than Kyle remembered. The paint wasn't peeling and the junk cars were gone. Most of the tall firs that had given the complex its name had been cut down, replaced by a swimming pool. Only three of the original tall firs remained, standing behind the complex. Several of the apartments had their lights on and there were neighbors outside the Martin door, gathered to comfort, console, and gossip. Those outside were mostly men, dressed in jeans or grease-stained work pants with sweatshirts or light jackets. The neighbor men parted for the detectives and inside were their wives and girlfriends. A dozen women were crowded into the small living room. It was a diverse group, Hispanics and Asians mixed with Caucasians. The women were all in their thirties and forties, most dressed in slacks with printed tops or sweatshirts. Two wore bathrobes, cinched tight around their ample waists. Nancy Martin was easy to pick out, sitting in the center of the couch in her bathrobe, the women on either side of her angled toward her, one with her arm around her shoulder. Two more women were in the kitchen, one spooning coffee grounds into a coffee machine, the other washing cups.

"Mrs. Martin, this is Detective Sommers," Michelson said. "I called him in on the case and I wonder if we could talk with Carolee again?"

"Leave the poor girl alone. Hasn't she been through enough?" the woman with her arm around Mrs. Martin said.

The woman's hair was rolled up in pink curlers but she had taken time to apply a thick coat of lipstick. Kyle had been at scenes like this before and knew the neighbors meant well. Like pioneers fearing attack, they had circled the wagons, gathering to provide strength through numbers. Each woman in the apartment played a different role. The women in the kitchen were hostesses, the women surrounding Nancy Martin were counselors, the woman in curlers had appointed herself bodyguard.

"Why aren't you out there catching whoever did this . . . this terrible thing?" the woman in curlers demanded.

"They already got the ones who did it," said the woman on the other side of Nancy Martin. "It was those boys—Marcus and Rico."

"They are persons-of-interest but we're following all leads," Michelson said.

"The best time to solve a case is right after the crime," Kyle added. "While the trail is still fresh."

Now the woman in curlers turned to Nancy for her decision. Eyes puffy from crying, face tear-stained, she said, "I think she's trying to sleep."

"I'm not sleeping," a voice called.

There was a short corridor leading back to two bedrooms. Carolee was standing in one of the bedroom doors wearing a pink terry-cloth bathrobe.

"I'll talk to you," Carolee said.

Kyle followed Michelson down the hall to the girl's bedroom. There were two beds on either side of the room, one neatly made, the other rumpled—Carolee sat on the rumpled bed, pulling her robe tightly around her. A desk was pushed against the far wall, and there was one dresser next to the closet. The room was small and the furniture filled it, leaving little floor space. Posters of rock stars covered the wall over the neat bed, a collage of pictures—mostly horses—decorated the wall above Carolee. Michelson pulled out the desk chair and sat on it, while Kyle closed the door and leaned against it. Both knew not to sit on the murdered sister's bed. If the Martins were like most victims' families, the bed would remain untouched for about a year, a memorial to a beloved daughter and sister. Then the family would move, the bed stored or sold, and a photo album would become the repository for their memories of Carolynn.

"This is Detective Sommers, Carolee," Michelson said. "I told him what you told me but he has a few more questions."

Carolee picked a tissue from the box on her nightstand, ready for tears.

"I'm sorry about your sister," Kyle began.

Carolee nodded and the tears began to flow.

"When you were running from the park—after you got away from the boys—did you see anyone following you?"

"No. Marcus and Rico left last and they went the other way. I didn't see anybody after the old man told us to go but I was running hard. I was so scared."

"I understand," Kyle said, waiting for Carolee to compose herself.

"Rico said he would 'kill you'?" Kyle probed.

Carolee closed her eyes briefly, remembering.

"He said he would hurt us," Carolee said. "I believed him. If you had seen his face—the look in his eye . . ."

"Sure," Michelson said.

"Did you or your sister have a baby toy with you—say a rattle or something like that?" Kyle asked. "Maybe a present for a relative's baby or something you might have picked up baby-sitting?"

"No," Carolee said slowly, puzzled.

"Would you know if your sister had something like that?" Kyle probed.

"Yeah, I mean why would she keep it secret? Is this important?"

"It's probably nothing but we check every possible lead.

Tell me about the man in the park. You said he was old?"

"Yeah."

"Old like me or old like Art here," Kyle said, smiling.

"Old like him," Carolee responded with a slight smile. "Nothing personal," she said to Michelson.

"I've still got my hair and most of my teeth," Michelson said, smiling.

"What did the old man look like?" Kyle asked. "Height, weight, scars, anything you can remember?"

"Well, he was shorter than you but taller than him," Carolee said, indicating Michelson. "He had on an overcoat—it was tan—with a belt that came around the front but the belt was tied, not hooked. Do you know what I mean?"

"I do," Kyle said.

"He had a hat on and it was pretty wide so it was hard to see his face. His skin was wrinkly, like older people."

"Was he white, black, brown?" Kyle asked.

"White, but with funny-colored skin—it was kind of blue."

Kyle and Michelson exchanged puzzled looks.

"Could be a circulation problem," Michelson said. "I knew a guy in the North Precinct who had a problem with his pump. He was blue just like she described, especially his lips and fingertips. He finally got a heart transplant and looked a lot better."

It could be a cardiovascular problem, Kyle thought, and if it was, then it was even less likely that the old man could chase down a teenager. Suddenly Carolee's eyes went wide.

"There's something else! I forgot. He gave me something to give you. It's in the pocket of my jeans."

"The old man gave you something for us?" Kyle asked.

"Yes. He gave me a piece of paper and told me to give it to the police."

Kyle looked at Michelson who was as surprised as Kyle.

"We bagged her clothes and sent them to forensics," Michelson said.

Sending notes to the police wasn't part of Cradle Robber's pattern. Whatever pathology drove his murder spree, the need to prove he was smarter than the police wasn't part of his psychological profile. If the old man was Cradle Robber, then his profile had changed and that could be the break Kyle needed. Kyle continued to question Carolee but his mind kept coming back to the piece of paper and what might be on it.

4

Killer

Killing the girl had done little to ease his pain. He hadn't realized how old she was until he had his arm around her neck, cutting off her wind, stopping her connection with this world, and liberating her from the pain that was part and parcel of life. When he placed the rattle in her hand—a reminder of the joy her life had once been—he saw through her ripped clothes that she wore a bra and he realized she had already reached puberty. Touching her body briefly he realized she was well into womanhood and his ministrations had come much too late. His heart ached for her and he wished he could have gotten to her sooner.

He had seen the girls come out of a house, jogging down the street and then into the park. He hadn't prepared for them but his need to help had been great, so he followed them into the park. When the boys had begun abusing them he felt their pain and more, since he could have prevented it if he had gotten to them first. Vicariously experiencing their suffering, he turned to leave, but then the other man had come. From his hiding spot he watched the old man drive the boys away. Then the two girls had come running toward him as if they were asking to be relieved of the hurt and humiliation while it was still an open wound. They were too far apart to get both, so he had taken the second one, separating her from the hurt of the world as quickly as he could, whispering apologies for the three minutes it took her to die.

Leaving a rattle in the girl's hand, he walked the three blocks to his truck before he heard a siren. He sat behind the wheel, reluctant to start the engine. He hadn't come for the teenager in the park and he had only managed to relieve her pain, not prevent it. There was little satisfaction in that.

The sound of the siren changed from a high-pitched squeal to a low drone and then was silent. The first of the police had arrived but he wasn't afraid. They wouldn't canvass the neighborhood for at least an hour. Turning on the radio he scanned the dial, still learning the Portland stations. He tried talk radio, oldies, smooth jazz, and country, but nothing distracted him from the thought of the little girl he had seen in the park two weeks before. "Wendy," her mother had called the cute little brunette. That day Wendy was dressed in blue corduroy overalls over a pink blouse. Wendy looked four years old—he had gotten good at judging the age of preschoolers.

Wendy's mother pushed her in a swing for twenty minutes, the little girl working her legs ineffectually, not understanding how to keep herself going. Not that it mattered, not with a mother engine to power the swing. Smiling wide with each arc, Wendy knew the joy of simple things like a swooping rush through the wind. Never would she be happier than she was that day in the park. When they left he followed Wendy and her mother home. They lived only a few blocks away from where he was now parked. It was Wendy he planned to visit, not the girl in the park. Now he couldn't stop thinking about pretty little Wendy, knowing that each step toward adulthood would bring her more pain. He wanted to save her from that pain. He needed to save her before the world sucked the joy from her.

He started his car and turned toward Wendy's house. There was little risk since the police were congregating many blocks away. Once they got the story from the girl who had gotten away, they would search the park, not the neighborhood. He had time for a quick visit with Wendy.

The streets of old North Portland were laid out in rectangles, not the confusing curves and cul-de-sacs of newer developments, making it easy to work his way up and down the blocks, circling in toward Wendy's home. The streets were empty, the houses dark except for the glow of occasional night lights, softening the darkness for a sleeping tot. Satisfied the neighborhood was sleeping, he turned down Wendy's street. Turning, his lights brushed the house on the corner, illuminating the shrubbery planted along one wall. Briefly he glimpsed a figure—a man in a hat. Someone was hiding in the bushes. He drove on, passing Wendy's house. A few seconds later he realized who the man in the bushes was—it was the man from the park.

Puzzled more than frightened, he continued out of the neighborhood, putting little Wendy lower on his list. Running into the same man twice on the same night was more than coincidence. Even stranger was the fact he was hiding in the bushes. He hadn't hidden in the park when he helped the girls, so why was he hiding now?

Checking his rearview mirror every few seconds, he drove toward the freeway, taking elaborate detours to make sure no one followed him. Knowing Wendy's suffering would have to continue for a time saddened him but with so many little ones out there to help, he couldn't risk going to Wendy tonight. Not with the man-in-the-hat watching. He would help another child instead. He had already scouted the city and knew there were many other little ones who needed his help. Putting the man-in-the-hat out of his mind, he selected another child from his list and began planning a visit.

5

Mac

The Portland Police Bureau was located in the Justice Center, a high-rise building in Portland's city center, with a view of the west hills on one side and majestic Mt. Hood on the other. Even the inmates had a mountain view from common areas joining cell blocks. Kyle took the elevator up to the bureau of investigations, where detectives worked in identical cubicles, each furnished with black metal desk, computer, filing cabinet, and a phone. Michelson's desk was tidy but Kyle's was like most of the others in the department, cluttered. File folders, forms, notes, and memos littered his desktop.

The department was short-staffed at night and it took three calls to discover the evidence from the Martin case had already been logged in. He and Michelson took the elevator down to find Sergeant Billings. Billings was responsible for receiving evidence and storing it securely. The evidence collected from the Martin case was in two boxes labeled with the case number, waiting to be secured in the evidence storage vault.

The procedures for collecting and storing evidence were well defined and to be followed religiously. Sergeant Billings was notoriously anal when it came to the procedures. Kyle's request to examine Carolee's jeans was logged by Billings, and Kyle, Michelson, and Billings all signed, noting the request. Only then was the bag with the jeans retrieved. When Kyle reached for the bag, Billings pulled it away, slapping a box of Safeskin disposable gloves on the counter. Only after Kyle and Michelson had the plastic gloves on did Billings hand the bag over, insisting the jeans be examined in his presence. Kyle pulled the pockets inside out. When he inverted the right front pocket a crumpled paper fell out.

Under Billings's watchful eye, Kyle smoothed out the paper wad. It was neatly typed in block format and looked like a photo copy of a page from a book or newspaper article. Kyle pushed the paper closer to Michelson so they both could read.

• Sunday, night: Twin teenagers, Carolee and Carolynn Martin, cut through Pier Park on their way back from a friend's house and stumbled into a group of drunken teenage boys gathered for a kegger and a little "wilding." By all accounts the primarily middle-class boys had limited their previous wilding to drinking and vandalism, but with Carolee and Carolynn the boys sank to new depths, raping and murdering the girls. Tried as adults, five boys served three to eight years for the crime. The ringleaders, Enrico Cortez and Marcus Jennings, were convicted of murder and executed by lethal injection after three years on death row. Nancy Martin, the murdered girls' mother, was present at the execution. Two days after Cortez and Jennings were executed for the murder of her only children, Nancy Martin was found in her bathtub, her wrists slit. A note taped to the bathroom mirror read simply: "I'm going to be with my babies."

Puzzled, Kyle read it again and then a third time when he realized Michelson was still working on his first read. When they were both finished he had Billings mark it and bag it, recording it as an addendum to the evidence log. After the paper had been examined by the forensics expert he would get a copy. For now, he invited Michelson for a talk. When they each had a cup of coffee in hand Kyle led Michelson to his cubicle, offering Michelson the victim's chair. The extra chair in their cubicles was called the "victim's chair" because it was most often used by those coming to the detectives to describe the horrible things that had happened to them.

Michelson sat like he spoke, slowly and methodically, taking his time getting comfortable, crossing and then uncrossing his legs. When he was finally settled Kyle asked him what he thought of the note the old man had given Carolee. Michelson took his time answering, Kyle drinking a third of his coffee while he waited.

"It doesn't make any sense," Michelson said, stating the obvious first. "It's written in the past tense, like all those things have already happened, but they haven't, and they aren't going to."

"Right. Carolee's not dead, Rico and Marcus don't look good for the murder of Carolynn, and I can't see Mrs. Martin killing herself and leaving Carolee all alone."

"She wouldn't," Michelson said.

"It's like a script someone wanted to be followed," Kyle said.

"The old man?" Michelson suggested.

"He's the one who stopped it before it went too far," Kyle said.

"Sure," Michelson said. "That's right. So if he wrote that scenario, why would he stop it?"

"Or, how could he know it would even get started—unless he knew Marcus and Rico?" Kyle said.

Kyle's mind raced from idea to idea. Absorbed by the problem, he was barely aware of the remnant of his hangover.

"What if he paid them to assault the girls and expected what was written there to happen as a result?"

"So why did he want us to see what he planned?" Michelson asked logically.

Kyle sorted through the possibilities again, looking for angles he had missed.

"Perhaps he thought both girls would die. Perhaps he botched the plan after he put it in motion?"

"Sure," Michelson said, his voice monotone, his mind struggling to keep up.

"Think of a kid standing dominoes on end, creating a long line that ends with one standing on the edge of a table," Kyle said. "With one touch on the first domino, they begin to fall into one another, setting in motion a chain reaction that ends with that last domino falling onto the floor. Maybe that's what this old man tried to do?"

"Sure," Michelson said again, sipping his coffee.

"Except," Kyle said, seeing the flaw in his own reasoning before Michelson pointed it out. "Except, Carolynn Martin had a baby rattle in her hand and that's the signature of Cradle Robber, not notes about what might happen after the crime . . ."

"Sure," Michelson said.

". . . and it only works if there's a connection between the old man and the boys."

"In the morning we'll try to find the old man and we can talk to the boys again," Michelson said.

Kyle picked up on the hint.

"Morning is fine. Let's get some sleep."

Michelson left then but Kyle stayed. He thought of getting a drink but for the first time in months he found his urge to drink was manageable. He had a reason not to drink. Cradle Robber had come to Portland and it was his job to stop him before another child died.

Kyle composed an E-mail to Captain Harding summarizing the Pier Park murder and Michelson's discovery of the baby rattle. Cradle Robber's signature explained why Kyle had been called to a murder scene for the first time since his return to duty. Kyle finished by endorsing Michelson's concern that Cradle Robber was in Portland and then recommended the Cradle Robber Task Force be activated. Kyle sent the message and then wrote his portion of the crime-scene report and sent it to Michelson. Michelson would have to fill in most of the details, but he was good at it, albeit slow. Kyle then spent the next hour and a half shuffling papers on his desk and answering e-mail, a part of his mind still pondering the strange note even as he caught up on his paperwork.

Near dawn he went to the nearest Starbucks for caffeine and the morning paper. He drank two cups of the overpriced coffee while he read. There was nothing about the murder in the paper but it would make the afternoon edition. Local television news would have it too, and then the calls would pour in—dozens of false leads, kooky theories, and false alarms.

He got back to the department before the day shift had arrived, heading straight for the McKenzie pool. He and Pat McKenzie frequently partnered on cases and had been good friends before Shelby's death. They were even closer since Kyle's troubles had begun. "Mac," as he was called, was one-of-a-kind, if any policeman with Irish heritage is one-of-a-kind. A Scotsman for a father and an Irish mother, Mac favored his mother, with red hair, ruddy complexion, and perpetual smile. Universally liked in the department, he had a disarming quality that worked equally well with friends and strangers. Walk into a restaurant twice, once without Mac and once with him, and you would understand Mac's knack for putting people at ease. A waitress who was merely polite on your first meeting would be joking and flirting when Mac was with you. Mac was lovable, generous, and sloppy.

It was Mac's sloppiness that was the basis for the McKenzie pool. Mac never made it through the day without spilling something on himself. Ink from leaking pens, coffee, jelly from donuts, ketchup from a hamburger—some substance from somewhere would stain his shirt or tie. The daily pool was for betting when the first stain would appear. A board was posted in the coffee room, divided into half hours. The board had been originally divided into hours but the pool had become so popular they had broken it down into half hours so more could participate. Mac feigned outrage when the pool was first created but then negotiated a deal with Kyle and the others. If Mac made it through a day without a stain, he won the pool. In the six months since they had been running the pool, Mac had never won.

Kyle selected "arrives with stain" and put his name on the board, dropping his money into the kitty jar. Mac was perpetually late and frequently spilled on himself on the drive into the city.

Kyle caught one of the forensic technicians as she arrived and asked her to take care of the paper they found in Carolee's pocket first, making Kyle a copy. She called back a few minutes later to say a copy was waiting for him. Kyle picked it up, reading it over and over as he came back up in the elevator. He was in his cubicle when he heard Mac arrive.

Mac lit up a room when he entered and the department was a different place when he was there. With Mac present the department was friendlier, noisier. Mac greeted everyone as he passed through, delighting whenever he found someone he didn't know. Gently chiding the reserved, sharing bawdy jokes with the outgoing, Mac adjusted his style to the person he met. Most astounding of all was his effect on women. Female officers and staff alike were completely at ease with him and he got away with audacious flirtation. If Kyle repeated half of Mac's bawdy comments to a secretary he would be charged with sexual harassment.

Kyle waited in his cubicle knowing Mac wouldn't pass without stopping. Mac had the secretary giggling now and a few seconds later came around the corner, plopping into the victim's chair.

"You won't believe what happened last night," Mac said.

Kyle studied Mac's shirt, noticing an ink stain in one corner of the pocket. It wasn't a winner—the stain had been there for a month. Mac only owned five shirts, and the permanent stains on each shirt were well documented. Kyle scanned the rest of his checked shirt, then his gaudy flowered tie—nothing there, and nothing on his jacket either. Disappointed, Kyle took Mac's bait.

"What happened last night?"

"You know my wife and daughter have turned vegetarian on me. We never have meat anymore, not even chicken. With my wife it's a health thing, but with my daughter it's her new religion. She tells me eating meat makes me an accomplice to murder, so they've had me on this vegetarian diet for months." Then with a brief pause Mac added, "The only good thing about all that lettuce is I've been as regular as Big Ben."

Kyle nodded and smiled. With daily reports, Mac kept Kyle up-to-date on everything from his marital problems to the frequency of his bowel movements.

"So last night I get home and there's no one there, just a note saying dinner is in the oven. I could smell something cooking that smelled oh-so-good," Mac said with animated facial expressions. "So I open the oven door and there's a meat loaf in the oven—a real, honest-to-God meat loaf. I thought I'd died and gone to heaven, Kyle. I was so grateful to Marilyn I decided I'd wait a whole week before I pestered her for sex again."

Kyle also knew all about Mac's sex life, or at least his version of it.

"There was a baked potato too, and of course six kinds of vegetables. So I set a place at the table, got out the butter—real butter, not margarine—sour cream, barbecue sauce—I even found where my wife hid the salt. Then I took that meat loaf out of the oven and put it on the table—I thought I was going to have an orgasm just looking at it. I fixed my potato first, slicing that puppy open and then filling it with butter, sour cream, bacon bits, and about a quarter inch of salt. When the potato was finished I cut myself a thick slice of that meat loaf and laid it next to my potato. I put some green beans on the plate too, just in case Marilyn came home while I was eating. I took my fork, cut off a big piece of that luscious-looking meat loaf, and took a big bite."

Mac's face froze, then reshaped into a grimace.

"It was a soy loaf," Mac nearly shouted, his voice an octave higher. "I wanted meat, real ground up dead animal meat, not some wussy vegetarian imitation. It tasted like puke. I could have cried."

"So what did you do?" Kyle asked.

"What could I do? I covered it in barbecue sauce and ate it anyway. Then when Marilyn got home I chased her all over the bedroom."

"That'll teach her," Kyle said.

"You and I are going to the Barbecue Barn for lunch," Mac said.

"Of course," Kyle said.

Mac overcompensated for his meatless suppers at lunch, defiantly wolfing down double beef cheeseburgers, sixteen-ounce steaks, and foot-long barbecued beef sandwiches. Finished with his morning story, Mac got up to leave but Kyle stopped him.

"Did you hear about last night?" Kyle asked.

"The body in Pier Park? I heard it on the radio on the way in. Are you in on that?"

"They found a baby rattle in the girl's hand."

Normally animated enough for two people, now Mac deflated, sinking back into the victim's chair.

"I hoped he would skip over Portland and head straight for Seattle," Mac said.

"Portland's a big league city now," Kyle said.

"There's no doubt it's Cradle Robber?"

"The girl was strangled and there was a baby toy," Kyle said. "She would be his oldest victim but Cradle Robber's signature was there. She was nearly raped by a gang of boys first so we have other suspects. Then there's this," Kyle said, handing over the copy of the note. "A man who broke up the rape gave it to Carolee, the sister of the murdered girl."

Mac read the note, then read it again.

"Are the names right in this?" Mac asked.

"Yes."

"It had to be written before the attack on the girls and before the murder."

"How else?" Kyle said.

"What do you know about the guy who gave this to Carolee?" Mac asked, tapping the paper.

"Not much. He wore an overcoat and hat. He was old and Carolee said his skin was blue."

"Blue skin?" Mac repeated.

"Michelson thinks maybe he has a weak heart. People with poor circulation look blue—not enough oxygen."

"The man who gave this to the girls has to be connected to the punks who attacked them," Mac said.

Working with Mac was much different than working with Michelson. Mac's mind worked as fast as Kyle's, but often with a quirky twist.

"We can check that out this morning," Kyle said.

"Tell me more about the boys," Mac said.

Kyle estimated the number of boys in the park for Mac and told him about the liquor bottles and other evidence of a party and then about the ringleaders, Marcus and Rico. When he was done Mac was shaking his head.

"It doesn't sound planned. If somebody hired you to kill two girls, you don't bring a dozen friends as witnesses and then get drunk before you do it," Mac said.

"So, where did this come from?" Kyle said, tapping the copy still in Mac's hands.

Now Mac hesitated, studying Kyle, reluctant to say what he was thinking.

"It's possible the guy who gave you this is psychic," Mac said.

Kyle tried to keep a straight face but he knew his feelings were showing.

"Hear me out, Kyle," Mac said, his voice dropping to a near whisper. "I'm not talking about the kind of thing that happened to you. That was just hallucinations."

Only a few people in the department knew that Kyle's alcoholism had reached the point where he had visions of his dead daughter, although there were plenty of rumors. Seeing those visions was rock bottom for Kyle and convinced him to get into a program.

"There's no such thing as a psychic," Kyle said.

"Really?" Mac said, waving the copy of the note in his face. "Keep an open mind, Kyle. I'm talking about someone with talent—not those sideshow hucksters that show up around here—someone with real ability! Maybe this blue guy got a flash that something bad was going to happen, typed it up, then showed up to stop it."

Part of Mac's quirkiness was his belief in the paranormal, including ghosts, poltergeist, precognition, and past life regression. It was standard operating procedure to point the local psychics to Mac whenever they turned up to help.

"But Carolynn Martin died," Kyle pointed out.

"But Carolee didn't and neither were raped. Maybe the vision wasn't clear."

If Kyle had a better explanation he would have used it.

"Let's invite Rita to lunch," Mac said.

"No," Kyle said.

Rita Morales worked the security desk in the lobby, checking visitors in and out, making sure no one got in without an identity badge. Rita was also the resident expert on ESP, channeling, reincarnation, and Eastern religions. She wore a crystal around her neck, slept under a pyramid, and performed foot massages to cure everything from migraines to the common cold. Mac had received several foot massages from pretty Rita, claiming he felt much better afterward, accenting his comments with wiggling eyebrows. Rita was attractive.

"Let's just talk to her, see what she thinks," Mac said.

"No."

"What else have you got?"

Kyle knew Mac would be relentless about inviting Rita to lunch and that he would eventually give in. Mac had stood by him through tough times and Kyle owed him.

"Fine, we'll go to lunch with Rita, but cancel the Barbecue Barn. Rita's a vegetarian."

"Noooooooooo!" Mac moaned, eyes wide. "I forgot."

"Maybe they'll have soy loaf on the menu."

"You've got a mean streak, Kyle. It ain't pretty when it shows."

With another loud moan, Mac stumbled out of Kyle's cubicle.

Shortly after Mac left, Kyle got a call from Captain Harding's secretary. Harding wanted to see him.

Captain Harding's office had a glass front and Kyle could see the captain behind his desk, glasses perched on the nose of his face, reading a report. When Kyle knocked, he motioned him in without looking up. A few seconds later he put the report down, took his glasses off, and turned to Kyle.

Captain Harding had been a friend to Kyle when he had precious few left in the department. It was Harding who had pushed the medical leave through and it was Harding that brought Kyle back to the department, easing him into his duties. Harding could have transferred him, demoted him, or even fired him, but instead Harding had given Kyle a second chance. Kyle didn't want to disappoint the captain, so he couldn't know that Kyle had been slipping back, obsessing about Shelby, drinking again.

Harding leaned back in his chair, drumming his fingers on the armrests. Harding was barrel-chested, with a short thick neck, square head, and short-cropped hair, graying at the temples. He had been a defensive lineman at the University of Oregon and could bench-press more now than when he was playing. Harding had an even temper, never shouting, but commanding attention with his size and his deep, steady voice.

"I read your e-mail. Do you have any doubt that it's Cradle Robber?"

"Plenty of doubt. The killing was outside. The girl was too old. There are other suspects. Only the baby rattle links the killing to Cradle Robber."

"But you want the task force activated?"

"Yes. It may be a copycat but we can't risk being wrong."

"I agree. I'll set up a meeting for this afternoon."

Harding sat still, watching Kyle, his fingers still drumming the armrest.

"I've been thinking about the task force," Harding said finally. "I'm not sure you're ready to lead it."

It was typical Harding. Straight to the point, pulling no punches.

"When I gave you this assignment, it was purely administrative. Select the best people for the task force, gather information from other cities, sift through the files, do all the prep work. I thought we'd have at least another six months if they didn't catch the bastard. By then I could have been sure about you. As it stands now you haven't been back long enough to make a judgment."

Harding paused, waiting for Kyle to respond.

"No one's complained about my work and I haven't missed a day since I've been back. I've stayed sober."

Harding held out a coffee cup. It said "World's Greatest Granddad" on the side.

"You ready to piss in a cup and prove that?"

"Yes," Kyle lied, holding out his hand.

Harding put the cup down.

"You've had soft duty, Sommers, doing the kind of administrative crap I'm buried in. You haven't been tested yet and Cradle Robber isn't the case to start you with."

"Because he's a child killer?" Kyle asked.

"Yes. It could trigger the hallucinations again."

"That was the booze. I've been sober for six months and haven't had that problem."

"I read the psychologist's report," Harding said, picking up the papers he had been reading. Putting his glasses back on he read, " 'Alcohol-induced psychosis compounded by clinical depression and debilitating guilt over his daughter's death.' " Putting the report down he said. "Sounds like more than just booze to me."

"You want your best detective leading this task force, don't you?"

"You *were* the best. That's why I brought you back. But this isn't about what you were."

Harding paused again, studying Kyle, his fingers drumming incessantly. He countered every one of Kyle's arguments yet he still hadn't taken the task force away from him.

"Three cities, three task forces, and no one has stopped Cradle Robber," Kyle said. "There are grieving families all along the California coast. I know something about grief, sir, I know it can destroy families and I know what it does to people. I don't want anyone to go through what I've gone through. What I'm saying is that there isn't a detective in this office more motivated than I am."

Finally, Harding's fingers stopped drumming and the captain leaned across the desk.

"Okay, you're in charge—for now. There was a time I thought you were the best detective I'd ever worked with. You had a knack for seeing what others couldn't. I just hope you have some of that gift left."

"I'll give it my best."

"It's day by day, Sommers. You can't slip up. I'll take heat for putting you in charge as it is, but I think you are still our best shot at stopping Cradle Robber."

Kyle left Harding's office relieved that he was still on the case but with a terrible burden.

6

Accident

Monday, 8:10 A.M.
To get her daughter to school by 8:35, Sandy Brown had to
have her out the door by 8:15. Having a schedule was one
thing, keeping Marissa on time was another. Marissa was
slow in the mornings, dawdling over her bowl of Cheerios
or sneaking into the family room to watch cartoons. This
morning was different, however. Marissa was ready for
school five minutes early, her "Special Person Poster" spread
on her bedroom floor in front of her. Making the poster had
taken up most of the weekend, Marissa carefully drawing
pictures in the corners and then coloring them with more care
than any pictures in her coloring books. Drawn in the top
corners were Marissa playing soccer and Marissa singing in
the children's choir. In the bottom corners were Marissa
playing with Mr. Fuzzy, her pet mouse, and Marissa's family. In the middle of the poster were pictures of her with
Minnie Mouse at Disneyland, her first pony ride, and a picture of her as a baby. There were lists too; her favorite foods,
beginning with pizza, her favorite television shows, and her
hobbies. Today Marissa's poster would be hung in the special spot reserved on the bulletin board in her class and Marissa would wear a button identifying her as Special Person
of the Week. It was her turn this week to be first in line for
lunch and recess and to carry the basket the class used to
hold the lunch boxes during recess. It was the first-grade

equivalent of being queen for a day. Marissa had waited all school year for her turn as Special Person, seeing each of her friends go before her, but today her turn had finally come.

"It's time to go, Marissa," Sandy said. As Sandy said it she suddenly felt as if she had said it before. Looking at Marissa bent over her poster felt like a memory, not like something happening here and now. Marissa had spent hours working on her poster over the weekend, so she had seen Marissa like this many times. But this felt different—unsettling.

"We have to go, Special Person," she urged Marissa.

"Help me roll it up," Marissa said.

Sandy knelt; carefully rolling the poster so there would be no creases and so the pictures would stay in place. Then she tied a ribbon around the roll to hold it together. When Marissa had her jacket on she took control of the poster, carrying it carefully with both hands like the precious treasure it was to a seven-year-old.

Picking up Marissa's backpack, Sandy opened the front door and pushed the screen wide. As Sandy touched the handle, she got a strong shock, her arm jerking reflexively. Sandy chided herself for touching the handle. For the last few days there had been a lot of static buildup and she had learned to push the wood frame of the screen.

"Careful," Marissa said, then waited for her mother to push the door wider.

Marissa's warning triggered the strange familiar feeling again, like Sandy was remembering what happened, not experiencing it. The feeling was mildly unpleasant but not frightening, and Sandy was fascinated by it. The feeling stayed with her as mother and daughter made it out the door and down the steps with the poster still in Marissa's hands. It was a short walk to school but they had to cross four busy streets and only the one closest to the school had a crossing guard. For once Marissa didn't lag behind, kicking at stones or petting neighbor's cats. Today she walked next to her mother, proudly carrying her poster.

Walking slowly, so that Marissa wouldn't drop her poster, Sandy noticed it was humid and the sky hazy, both unusual for Portland in June. When they reached the corner Sandy was reminded of why she walked Marissa to school. The traffic was heavy and the drivers impatient, jockeying with each other for position, each driver in a bigger hurry than the one ahead.

The light changed, but even with the walk signal Sandy hesitated, watching for the late-to-work driver who might run the light. When all cars had stopped, she led Marissa across and down the next block. Other mothers with kids were ahead, crossing at the next corner and more paralleled them on the other side of the street. Still, when she saw the man in the overcoat and hat she felt afraid. He was standing halfway down the block, leaning against the brick wall of the furniture store, hands in his pockets, head turned toward them. Sandy slipped her hand into her jacket pocket, palming the pepper spray canister she always carried, eyes on the stranger.

The stranger in the hat stepped away from the wall as they approached. His wide-brimmed hat partially obscured his face but Sandy could see his skin was a peculiar color. He was an old man but still a threat and Sandy nudged Marissa toward the curb to give him a wide berth.

"Mrs. Sandy Brown?" the man asked as they reached him.

"Keep walking, Marissa," Sandy said as the man stepped in front of them.

"You are Sandy Brown, aren't you?" the man said. "And you're Marissa."

Marissa looked nervous now and Sandy pulled her arm, trying to get around the man. In her pocket her thumb pushed the safety lock off the top of the pepper spray.

"I need to talk to you," the man said.

"I don't know you," Sandy said as the man stepped in her path again. Not today! Sandy thought. Not on Marissa's special day!

"You and your daughter are in danger," the man said.

Wide-eyed, Marissa stared, afraid of the stranger. Marissa had been an excited and proud little girl until the old man had stepped in their path and it angered Sandy.

"Get out of my way! Now!" Sandy ordered, but the man did not move.

"You're in danger . . ." he began.

Pulling the pepper spray from her pocket, Sandy's finger was pressing the trigger as she brought the canister to his face. The stream hit his nose first and then splashed up under the brim of his hat into his eyes. The stranger yelped with pain, his hands coming to his face. Sandy stopped the spray, keeping the canister aimed at the stranger's face. Tightening her grip on Marissa's hand she pulled her toward the corner.

"No, don't go," the old man pleaded, face flooded with tears.

"Run, Marissa," Sandy said, pulling her daughter along.

Racing to the corner she could see that the pedestrian signal read "WAIT." Slowing, she looked back to see the old man following, stumbling along, calling for her to stop. The traffic was thick in the intersection and if they waited for the light to change the stranger would catch them. Sandy decided to turn the corner hoping to find other parents walking to school. Suddenly, tires squealed and she looked to see a truck coming diagonally across the intersection. The driver was slumped sideways in the cab, the truck accelerating toward them. Cross traffic braked violently, the truck taking off the grill of one car, sideswiping another. Still the huge truck continued toward Sandy and Marissa, hitting the curb at the corner and caroming up onto the sidewalk. Dropping the pepper spray, Sandy shoved her daughter toward the street, the little girl falling with her poster off the curb. Sandy lunged sideways, rolling off the sidewalk into the street and onto her daughter, protecting her with her body. Narrowly missing them, the truck crossed the sidewalk, smashing into the wall of the furniture store with the sound of a wrecking ball demolishing a building. Then there was a brief eerie silence.

Commuters jumped from their cars, hands helping Sandy and Marissa to their feet. Sandy picked up Marissa, seeing the tears streaming down her face.

"Are you hurt?" Sandy said, wiping dirt from her little girl's face and knees, checking for injuries.

"It's bent," Marissa said, sobbing, holding up her poster. "And it's dirty."

Sandy pulled tissues from her pocket, brushing at the dirt caked to the poster.

"The dirt's on the outside, Marissa. No one will see it when it's on the wall."

"But it's wrinkled," she said, still sobbing.

Sandy returned the rolled poster to its round shape, knowing the crinkles would show when Marissa unrolled it.

"It's not bad," Sandy said, trying to reassure her daughter, while inside she was furious with the old man, blaming him for stampeding them into the path of the truck. Why couldn't he leave us alone? she thought. Angry that the old man had ruined Marissa's special day, she looked for the old man, but couldn't find him in the crowd. There were people gathered around the cab of the wrecked truck, someone inside helping the driver. At least three people in the crowd were on their cell phones, calling for help. Assured the driver was being helped, Sandy directed Marissa toward school.

"Why'd that old man chase us?" Marissa asked as Sandy dabbed at her tears and wiped the girl's nose.

"I don't know, honey, he's just some sad old man. Never talk to strangers like him," she said, throwing in a life lesson.

With a last look at the accident scene, Sandy led Marissa down the street, tears on her daughter's cheeks, the dirty and crumpled poster back in her arms.

7

Theories

"I know it was Marcus that killed that poor girl," the woman said.

Sitting in his cubicle, phone wedged between his ear and his shoulder, Kyle checked his yellow pad, struggling to remember the woman's name—it was Lincoln. Kyle wrote the name down so he wouldn't forget again.

"How do you know, Ms. Lincoln?" Kyle said.

Ms. Lincoln was one of the dozens who had heard about the murder in Pier Park and called in claiming to know something about the crime.

"I don't mind being called Mrs. Lincoln. I'm not one of those feminazis, you know."

"Mrs. Lincoln, how do you know Marcus killed the girl?"

"He never was any good. Even when he was little he was nothing but trouble. I know, I live right behind the Jennings family—"

"But, Mrs. Lincoln, what evidence do you have that Marcus killed the girl in the park?" Kyle interrupted.

"That's what I'm trying to tell you, if you'd let me talk. He never was any good. He used to climb over the back fence and steal apples off of my tree—pears too."

"Stealing apples has nothing to do with what happened yesterday," Kyle said.

"It most certainly does," Mrs. Lincoln insisted. "Once you

start down the slippery-slope of crime you can't stop."

Mrs. Lincoln was probably a lonely old woman with nothing to do but spy on her neighbors, tend her yard, and gossip with anyone who would listen. Kyle suspected Mrs. Lincoln was a regular abuser of the 9-1-1 system, and that the patrol officers assigned to her neighborhood knew her well.

"Thanks, Mrs. Lincoln, I took notes on everything you told me."

"But there's more," she said, sensing that she was being brushed off.

"I have more than enough for now. If I need more information I have your number."

Kyle said good-bye and hung up before she could protest again. Mrs. Lincoln wasn't the first person to waste his time that morning. The morning had been a series of fruitless phone calls and interviews. Kyle and Mac wasted half an hour interviewing Marcus and Rico. Their parents had arranged for lawyers overnight, and now the lawyers ran interference for the boys. The only statement that the lawyers would allow either of the suspects to make was that they didn't know the man who had "interrupted the party" in the park. Both vehemently denied they had tried to rape Carolynn and Carolee. Normally, Kyle and Mac would drive a wedge between the boys, trying to turn them against each other, offering a plea bargain to one to get him to implicate the other, but this time it wouldn't be necessary. Two other boys from the park had been found by Michelson and when they heard Carolynn had been murdered, they quickly cooperated. Terrified of going to prison, they identified the other boys at the party and confirmed Marcus and Rico were the ringleaders. Michelson made a list of names and sent officers to pick up the other teenagers. By the end of the day they would have a long line of boys anxious to blame everything on Marcus and Rico.

Kyle looked through his stack of messages, all from people claiming to know something about the murder of Carolynn Martin. He'd been proceeding in the order the calls had come in but now shuffled the stack, hoping by chance to actually find a witness.

"Detective Sommers?"

An officer stood outside Kyle's cubicle, an envelope in hand.

"I guess this is for you," the officer said, handing the envelope over.

On the front of the sealed envelope was a hand-scrawled "For the detective investigating what happened in Pier Park."

"Someone dropped it off downstairs."

"Thanks," Kyle said as the officer left.

There was no address or stamp. Kyle looked at the stack of messages, then back to the envelope and then at his watch. There was still nearly an hour before he was to meet Mac and Rita for lunch. Avoiding the monotony of the phone messages, he picked up the envelope and tore it open. Inside was a slip of paper like the one the old man in Pier Park had given Carolee. There were two paragraphs on the page. Kyle read the first one.

• Monday, early morning: The serial killer called Cradle Robber announced his arrival in Portland by entering the Janelle and Raymond Kirkland home in North Portland and suffocating their six-year-old daughter. Janelle Kirkland put Wendy to bed at 8:00 P.M., Wendy holding a stuffed Winnie the Pooh and listening to a Winnie the Pooh CD. Janelle Kirkland checked on Wendy at 8:30 P.M. Raymond Kirkland checked on Wendy at 11:00 P.M., as he went to bed. Wendy was a restless sleeper and her father remembers that he found Wendy sleeping sideways in her bed that night and had to turn her to get her head back on the pillow. Sometime after the parents were asleep, Cradle Robber cut through the double-pane glass of Wendy's bedroom window and entered. According to the medical examiner's report, something was pressed against Wendy's nose and mouth and Wendy was suffocated. The coroner estimated it took two minutes for Wendy to lose consciousness and another two to die. The next morning Janelle Kirkland found her daughter dead, a blue baby rattle resting in her hand.

When he finished, Kyle pulled a phone book out of his bottom drawer, looking up "Kirkland" and finding three names that could be Raymond Kirkland. Only one had a North Portland prefix. A woman answered on the third ring.

"Hello, this is Detective Kyle Sommers with the Portland Police Department, am I speaking to Janelle Kirkland?" Kyle said.

"Yes," a woman said warily. "Is something wrong?"

"Do you have a daughter named Wendy?"

"Yes. What's this about?"

"Is your daughter Wendy at home with you now?"

"She's playing in her room."

"And you can hear her?"

"What's going on? Who is this, really?"

"I'm sorry if this is scaring you, but would you please check on your daughter."

The phone crackled, telling Kyle it was a cordless phone and that Janelle Kirkland was walking through her house. A few seconds later Kyle heard the little girl in the background, her mother saying, "Just checking, honey." Then Janelle was back on the line.

"Wendy is fine. I don't believe you are with the police."

"I understand. I'm going to hang up and then I want you to call the police—look the number up yourself—then ask for Detective Kyle Sommers."

The line went dead almost immediately and Kyle slumped in his chair, studying the strange note, trying to make sense out of it. His phone rang a few minutes later.

"Detective Sommers," he said.

"It is you," Janelle Kirkland said.

"Yes."

"What's going on?"

"I'm telling you the truth when I say that I don't know, but it's very important for you to watch Wendy closely for the next few days."

"You're scaring me."

"I'm sorry. It's probably nothing but I found something with your names on it that suggested Wendy might be in some danger."

"Who would want to hurt Wendy?"

"I may have the wrong family but just to be safe don't let Wendy out of your sight for a while. Sleep in the same room with her."

"I will."

"It won't be for long."

"It doesn't matter how long it takes. I won't let anything happen to her."

"It's probably nothing."

"You'll call when you find out more?"

"I will."

Now Kyle regretted his impulsiveness—getting a mother on the phone without having thought out what he would say. He'd probably terrified her needlessly. Now he looked at the second half of the page, wondering whether he should take it as seriously.

• Monday, morning: Sandy Brown was walking her seven-year-old daughter, Marissa, to Tom McCall Elementary School when they were struck by a truck. It was the start of a big week for Marissa because she was going to be "Special Person of the Week," which meant it would be her turn to lead the class line to lunch and recess and to bring something for show and tell every day. On Friday, Marissa could bring a special guest, and at the end of Marissa's special week her father was coming to sit in the big rocking chair with the class gathered around and tell them stories about when Marissa was little. But Marissa's father never sat in the class rocker, or told the baby stories. While Marissa and her mother waited for a walk signal, a delivery-truck driver suffered a heart attack and lost control, running up onto the sidewalk, killing her mother and crushing Marissa. One of Marissa's legs was amputated that day but Marissa never knew since she never regained consciousness. Three days later she was declared brain-dead and her father made the difficult decision to end life support. Four days after the decision, her lips cracked and her tongue swollen, the body of the little girl who never got to be Special-Person-of-the-Week died.

Kyle reached for the phone book again, then he paused, reminding himself to be professional. He was impulsive by nature and his own daughter's death made him hypersensitive to the real or imagined plight of other children. His psychologist labeled it healthy overcompensation but healthy or not, it undermined his judgment. Not every child crying in a grocery store was abused, not every child with a dirty face was neglected. And telling the difference is all the harder when a man is intoxicated.

Kyle read the second half of the page again, noting the time and looking at his watch. This wasn't about a crime, it was about an accident that had already happened. Kyle called Cassidy Kellogg's number. She was the Public Information Officer but Kyle hoped to reach her secretary. Cassidy was a beautiful woman. She was a multiracial mix of African, Asian, and Caucasian, with dark oval eyes, almond-colored skin, and a slender figure. She modeled part-time for local department-store ads, took night courses in broadcasting, and was the public spokesperson for the department, showing up regularly on the nightly news. She had also just landed a weekend job on a local television station, doing the "Crime

Watcher's Notebook." The segment was popular with the male eighteen to thirty-five demographic. Kyle had dated Cassidy briefly before his medical leave and he had been making excuses not to get together again since coming back. Kyle winced when Cassidy answered.

"Cassidy, this is Kyle Sommers, I was—"

"Kyle Sommers?" Cassidy interrupted. "I once knew a Kyle Sommers. Used to be a nice guy. You know, the kind that would call a girl once in a while and let her know how he was doing and not leave her wondering what she did to piss him off."

"I was on leave—"

"You *were* on leave."

"It's been hard coming back," Kyle said. "Before I left, I did a lot of things I'm not proud of."

"You needed some help and you got it. You've got nothing to be ashamed of."

"It wasn't just the drinking. It was too soon after the divorce. It didn't feel right."

"Kyle, half the married men in the department have asked me out but I picked a guy who feels guilty for cheating on his ex-wife?"

"It wasn't so much my wife as my daughter," Kyle began, but again Cassidy cut him off.

"Kyle, I know what happened to Shelby hurt you badly, but you have to get past that too."

"I wasn't ready. I felt like I was using you and you deserved better."

There was a long pause.

"That's a sweet thing to say," Cassidy said. "Okay, Kyle, I'm going to give you one get-out-of-jail-free card. When you're ready to see someone you can use the card."

"You don't have to do that."

"I want to. Now, what did you call about?"

"Was there a traffic accident near Tom McCall grade school this morning around eight-thirty?"

Kyle expected Cassidy to access the database but instead she answered immediately.

"The driver of a Mustang Express delivery truck had a heart attack and ran through an intersection, smashing into the wall of a furniture store. The driver is in intensive care."

"That was fast," Kyle said.

"I heard it on the news. We don't have an accident report yet."

"Were any pedestrians hurt?"

"Three people were treated at the scene for minor injuries, but I think they were in cars. They didn't say anything about pedestrians."

"There was nothing about a woman and a little girl being hurt?" Kyle asked.

"If a little girl had been hurt it would have been in the report. I'll check for a precinct report if you like."

"I'd appreciate it."

"Are we going public about Cradle Robber?" Cassidy asked suddenly.

As Information Officer, Cassidy took reports from all the precincts, although she wouldn't necessarily be privy to evidence. The department routinely held back details of crimes to prevent copycat crime and so the information could be used for a "guilty knowledge" test. Keeping details secret helped separate real confessions from false. Only the baby rattle tied the Carolynn Martin murder to Cradle Robber and the fact that Cassidy asked about Cradle Robber meant officers were talking about the presence of the rattle. It also meant local reporters would know about the rattle by the end of the day.

"The task force meets this afternoon," Kyle said. "The captain will make the decision then."

"I should prepare, shouldn't I?"

"I would," Kyle said.

If there was a chance Cradle Robber had come to Portland,

they had to alert the city. Kyle would rather create a false panic than risk the death of a child.

Kyle thanked Cassidy again and managed to avoid promising he would call her. Now he read the note again, making sure he had the day and time right. There was no month or day, just simply "Monday," which could refer to any Monday but some of the details matched that morning's accident. There had been a truck accident, it was in the location described, and the driver suffered a heart attack. Like the other notes, some of the details were wrong.

The notes Kyle had received described five deaths, but only one had actually occurred. The timing of the last note with the two stories was different too. The first note had been delivered just after the attack, so it seemed like the note predicted the future. The last delivery, however, came long enough after the accident so that it could have been written and printed after the author had a chance to check the details. Kyle thought about the first note, realizing it had been delivered in the dark of the park and Carolee had not read it. It had then been stuffed into her pocket for hours. The note could have been switched before Kyle found it.

Kyle thumbed through the phone book, finding too many "Browns." Instead, Kyle found the school listings and the number for Tom McCall Elementary School. The school secretary answered on the first ring. Kyle could hear children in the background.

"This is Detective Sommers with the Portland Police Department, do you have a student in your school by the name of Marissa Brown? Her mother is Sandy Brown."

"I can't release any student information."

"I only need to know if she is enrolled there," Kyle said.

"I can't release any information," the secretary said. "I would think a policeman would know that."

What Kyle knew was that how much information you could get depended on who answered the phone.

"Who did you say you were?" the secretary asked, clearly suspicious now.

"Detective Sommers."

"Maybe if you told me what this is about."

"Does your school choose children to be Special Person of the Week?"

"Some of the teachers do that in their classrooms but we don't have a school-wide Special Person," the secretary said slowly, as if evaluating each bit of information for how it might be used.

"Thanks for your time," Kyle said.

Kyle hung up and then leaned back, thinking. He should be working through his witness messages, hoping someone had seen Cradle Robber, but was absorbed by the strangeness of the notes. Carolynn's murder barely fit Cradle Robber's modus operandi, however, the Kirkland family mentioned in the second note was exactly the kind of family Cradle Robber sought out. But if the notes were about Cradle Robber, then why include a traffic accident?

His phone buzzed and Kyle answered.

"Detective Sommers, this is Marian Packer from McCall school. I believe we just spoke."

"Yes, I was the one that called."

"You understand why I had to be cautious?"

"You did the right thing," Kyle said.

"We do have a Marissa Brown enrolled here and her mother is Sandy Brown. This isn't a custody case, is it?"

"No."

"Good. I know the Browns and they seem very happy.

"The children are at lunch now and I saw Marissa come by the office while we were talking. She was leading the line, so that means she is Special Person this week in Mrs. Bryce's first-grade class."

Mentally, Kyle checked details from the note off in his mind. The girl's name was right, the mother's name was right, the school name matched, the location where they lived was right, and the little girl was Special Person in her class.

"Marian, could you find out if Marissa brought a poster to school with her?"

"They usually do something like that but I can ask her teacher if it's important. Mrs. Bryce has lunch duty."

Marian left the offer hanging and Kyle knew she was waiting for an information exchange. A call from a detective had to be the most interesting thing to come into that school's office in quite some time and Marian wanted something for all she was doing.

"I don't know if any of this is important, but it could be helpful," Kyle said. "I got one copy of a report of a traffic accident that said Marissa and her mother were involved but another said they weren't."

"Someone filed a false police report?" Marian asked.

"Something like that."

"And they said Marissa and Sandy Brown were involved?"

"They said they were hurt."

"Why were you asking about the poster?"

"It was mentioned."

"Odd," Marian said.

"Yes."

"Let me talk to her teacher. Do you want to hold?"

Kyle said he did and the phone played classical music while he waited. Mac showed up a minute later, plopping down in the victim's chair, pointing at his watch, rubbing his stomach, and moaning like he was starving. Kyle studied Mac's shirt and tie but didn't see any stains.

"I'm back," Marian announced. "Mrs. Bryce said that Marissa did bring her poster to school but she was very upset. Her poster was dirty and wrinkled and her mother told Mrs. Bryce they had almost been hit by a truck."

Kyle checked two more details off his mental list, then handed the note to Mac.

"Does this help with your investigation?" Marian asked.

"It does. The more information I have, the closer I am to figuring out what's going on."

"Mrs. Bryce told me, that Sandy Brown told her, that an old man chased them. She said he almost chased them right into the path of that truck."

"An old man?" Kyle said, intrigued.

"Yes. Is that important?"

"It could be. Was that all Mrs. Bryce said?"

"I think so. Is that old man a pervert? Do we need to warn the kids?"

Now Kyle was even more confused. Cradle Robber didn't chase children down the street. He was nocturnal and stealthy. The old man couldn't be Cradle Robber but he didn't know what to tell the school secretary. If he had the parents and children of the school warned about a pervert it would hit the evening news and he'd be explaining himself to Captain Harding the next morning. Kyle decided on a half measure.

"It wouldn't hurt to remind the kids not to talk to strangers," Kyle said.

"I'll tell the principal. If I can be of any more help . . ." the secretary said.

"You've been great," Kyle said, then said good-bye.

Mac was reading the note and frowning.

"Did you check on this first one?" Mac asked.

"The little girl's fine. I scared the hell out of the mother, though. That little girl won't be sleeping alone for a while."

"Good," Mac said. "One safe, two hundred thousand to go."

"I just checked on the traffic accident part. There is a Marissa Brown and she and her mother were nearly hit by a truck."

"Nearly hit?"

"Marissa made it to school. Interesting, though, Marissa's mother said an old man chased them into the path of the truck."

"Doesn't make sense," Mac said. "If he was trying to kill them, how would he know the driver was going to have a heart attack at that moment?"

"The more I think about these notes, the more I think they're fake," Kyle said. "I got this a couple of hours after the accident. It was probably typed up afterward."

"Then why isn't it accurate?" Mac asked. "You said the old man chased the little girl—doesn't sound like someone on a list for a heart transplant. Was this guy blue?"

"I didn't talk to the mother and the school secretary didn't mention it."

"I would have asked," Mac said, "but then I'm always one step ahead of you."

"The only time you're ahead of me is in the lunch line."

"Speaking of lunch," Mac said, tapping his watch.

Rita was waiting in the lobby when Kyle and Mac got off the elevator. Rita hurried to Mac, giving him a full hug. There was no hug for Kyle, just a gentle smile.

"How are you doing, Kyle? I'm glad to see you back. Don't you let Harding work you too hard too soon. You've had so much bad karma—first your daughter, then your wife. I know someone who could help you. He changed my karma—that's how I got promoted."

"No thanks, Rita."

Rita was a small woman, barely five feet, but she was young and pretty with black hair and matching eyes. Even her security uniform couldn't hide her good figure and passing men turned their heads in admiration.

"You get the urge for a drink, you tell me, Kyle. I'll come by and give you a foot massage. I can work the neural nets so that you won't be thinking about drinking anymore."

"I can testify to that," Mac cut in. "When Rita rubs my feet I'm not thinking about booze."

"Mac, you're so bad. How come you never go to lunch with us anymore?" Rita said, slipping an arm around Mac.

Mac was popular with the women of the bureau and

lunched frequently with secretaries and female officers. Any day he wanted, Mac could meet a group of women for lunch, be hugged by them, have them take his arm on the way to the restaurant, and then spend an hour telling stories while they laughed and giggled.

As expected, Rita turned them toward her favorite restaurant, flirting with Mac as they walked, hanging on his arm. Kyle noticed the males passing, looking at Rita, and then at Mac as if they were wondering how a guy like him could get a girl like her. On the corner there was a street vendor selling polish sausage and Mac looked at the stand and then at Kyle, licking his lips and pretending to wipe away slobber.

The New Age Café was sandwiched between a camera shop and a stationery store, attracting an eclectic mix of customers, ranging from yuppies to middle-aged hippies still clinging to the counterculture days of the sixties. Rounding out the clientele was a smattering of younger people, vegetarian by choice or religion. There was a counter that faced the street, selling pitas stuffed with lettuce, guacamole, tomatoes, and your choice of cheeses. In the summer they sold frozen yogurt from the counter, the only menu item Kyle actually enjoyed. Inside there was a small eating space, packed with tables. They took one of the last two empty tables, Kyle and Mac squeezing into their chairs since there was barely enough room to pull them from the table without banging into the person seated behind.

"Are all vegetarians stick thin?" Kyle grumbled.

"A low-fat, high-fiber diet wouldn't hurt you two," Rita said.

"We've gone vegetarian at home," Mac said.

"You feel better, don't you?" Rita said.

"It's really amazing," Mac lied. "We've been off meat for two months and I've lost weight, I have more energy, and my cholesterol count is back in the safe range. I feel ten years younger."

It was all bull, Kyle knew.

"You look it too," Rita said. "Your color's better, and I thought you lost some weight. You should try eating healthy too, Kyle. You're pretty lean but your tissues are filled with poisons—some of that alcohol is still in there. Eat healthy for three months and it will clean all those toxins out of your system. You'll have thirty percent more energy and sleep twenty percent less."

"You'll be regular too," Mac said.

"Are you constipated, Kyle?" Rita asked, picking up on Mac's false trail.

"No."

"Don't be embarrassed," Rita said tenderly. "Regular bowel movements are as necessary as breathing."

"I don't have a problem in that area," Kyle said.

"Do you have daily movements then?" Rita asked.

The waitress interrupted the exploration of Kyle's regularity, saving him from further embarrassment. Kyle ordered a bowl of vegetable soup and a cheese sandwich. Mac ordered potato soup and a pita stuffed with cucumbers and cream cheese. Rita requested pasta with a mushroom sauce.

Mac flirted with Rita while they waited, commenting on everything from her hair to her figure, violating every departmental guideline on sexual harassment. She laughed at every ribald comment, even tossing Mac's hair at one point. When Kyle rolled his eyes at Mac, Mac simply responded by wiggling his eyebrows and making another suggestive comment.

The waitress brought lunch and beverages, water for Kyle, coffee for Mac, and herbal tea for Rita. After everyone had a few bites, Mac turned the conversation to the mysterious note.

"Rita, you're not just a pretty face to us," Mac said. "We wanted to meet with you to see if you could help us with something."

"One of your cases?"

"How did you know that, Rita?" Mac said as if he were surprised. "You must be a little psychic."

"Maybe just a touch," Rita said, flattered. "But my friend Natalie, she's the real thing. She knows it's me when I call even before she picks up the phone."

"Amazing," Mac said.

"Yeah, and she's good at finding things. If you ever need someone to help you find a lost child or something, I bet Natalie would help."

"Right now we've got something else you might help us with. Do you want to tell her about it, Kyle?"

Kyle declined, sipping his soup instead. It was good but would have been better with chunks of meat.

"You heard about the murder in Pier Park last night?" Mac asked.

"Oh, sure, my heart broke for that mother and the other sister."

"What hasn't been reported—you can't tell anyone this, Rita—is that the old man that saved the girl from the teenagers gave Carolee Martin a note to give to the police."

"Interesting," Rita said.

"Just wait," Mac said. Now leaning forward and speaking in a soft voice, creating a conspiratorial atmosphere, he said, "The note had some of the details of the crime right, but others wrong."

"Like what?" Rita said.

"The note said that Carolee and Carolynn were raped and murdered but neither was raped and only Carolynn was murdered. The note also said that two boys were convicted of the crime and executed and that Nancy Martin was at the execution and later killed herself."

"So, like this note is telling the future?" Rita asked.

"Not exactly, since only Carolynn died and the boys probably didn't commit the murder."

Rita was absorbed in Mac's story, her New-Age mind trying to make sense of the details.

"Let me see this note," Rita said.

Kyle had concentrated on his soup while Mac played detective with Rita but now Mac turned to him. He knew nothing good would come of the meeting, and sharing evidence with a security guard wasn't going to do his career any good. Still, he pulled the photocopy of the first note from his pocket and handed it to Rita.

"When you said note, I thought you meant handwritten. This looks like a newspaper article."

"Why do you say that?" Kyle asked.

"The font, the left and right justification, the spacing so perfect."

"A word processor can do that," Kyle said.

"Sure, but you have to have the right font and why go to that much trouble if you're just typing this up for the police to read? And why write it in such a narrow column?"

Rita was asking good questions. Kyle remembered when he first saw the page he also thought it resembled a newspaper article.

"I thought maybe someone had a premonition and wrote this up," Mac said as Rita finished reading it.

"That sounds reasonable," Rita said cautiously.

Kyle shook his head in disbelief. Mac smiled triumphantly.

"Whoever had the premonition then shows up and decides to stop it from happening," Mac continued.

"Couldn't happen that way," Rita said. "If it's a premonition of the future, then the future has to happen that way or it's not a premonition."

"But if you knew what was going to happen you could change it," Mac argued.

"If you changed it, it wouldn't happen, so how could you perceive something that isn't going to happen?"

"But it did happen in the future, it's just that the old man who had the note—article, or whatever—changed the future."

"So it didn't happen and that means it couldn't have been pre-perceived by the psychic," Rita said, as if that settled the argument.

Mac was frustrated, his face red, his Irish dander rising. Mac couldn't accept the laws that guided Rita's universe, but to Kyle they made as much sense as Mac's.

"Tell me more about the man in the park," Rita said.

Mac waved his hand at Kyle, needing a moment to cool down and to eat his pita.

"He wore an overcoat, a wide-brimmed hat, and was old—later fifties, early sixties," Kyle said. "He may have a heart condition."

"How could you know that?" Rita asked.

"His skin was blue, like his blood wasn't getting enough oxygen."

Rita slapped her hand on the table, startling Kyle and Mac and drawing looks from the diners around them.

"I should have known," Rita said. "No mortal has the power to change the future."

"No mortal?" Kyle asked.

"Don't you see? The blue color is the key," Rita said, black eyes bright with excitement. "Precognition, the power to alter the human time line, the blue skin . . ."

Rita let her words hang in the air, expecting Kyle or Mac to blurt out what she thought was obvious. Neither said a thing.

"It has to be a member of the Blue Jinn," Rita said loudly.

"Excuse me?" Mac said softly.

"A genie. It has to be a genie."

"Like from a lamp?" Mac asked.

"That's a gross distortion and the worst kind of revisionist history," Rita said. "Genies are meta-humans who are able to tap into the Universal Jinn—the energy flow that allows existence to happen. By making a slight adjustment in the flow, they can alter reality, whether it's the present reality or a future reality. Ignorant mortals call this ability magic because they don't know any better."

Rita looked back and forth between the detectives, her pretty eyes wide from excitement. Mac stared blankly, his mouth slightly open while Kyle kept a straight face.

"It's the only reasonable explanation," Rita said.

"Exactly," Mac said, stuffing the last of his pita in his mouth.

"Sure," Kyle said, tilting his bowl to get the last of his soup.

For another fifteen minutes they listened to Rita ramble on about the Blue Jinn, the Green Jinn, the Black Jinn, and the force called the Universal Jinn. Rita's lecture sounded like a cross between the theology of Star Wars and the story of Aladdin and the lamp. Rita was so serious that neither of them dared to smile.

When the check came, Kyle handed it to Mac who didn't protest. Paying the bill was penance for inviting Rita to lunch.

"That was really good, Rita," Mac said when they were outside, patting his stomach.

Kyle studied Mac's shirt looking for a stain. His sloppy partner had made it through lunch without spilling a drop on himself.

"Kyle and I have to meet someone, so we can't walk back with you," Mac said.

"Is it about the genie?" Rita asked.

"No, we're meeting a Polish guy—completely different case."

Rita hugged Mac, then waved at Kyle and left, Mac watching her bottom sway as she walked away.

"We're meeting a Polish guy?" Kyle asked.

"Wait," Mac said, watching until Rita was out of sight. "Come on."

Mac led Kyle to the corner street vendor.

"I'll take a Polish dog with everything including kraut," Mac said.

"You're a hypocrite, Mac," Kyle said.

"Yeah, but I got two hugs today and what did you get?" Mac asked.

The vendor handed over a bun wrapped around a thick sausage and covered with a mix of ketchup, mustard, onions, and sauerkraut. As Mac's mouth closed on the overloaded bun, an orange glob of condiments squirted from the end, splattering his shirt.

Kyle looked at his watch, noting the time. Someone had just won the McKenzie pool.

8

Task Force

Monday, 1:30 P.M.

Leadership came naturally to Captain Harding. Maybe it was his imposing size, or maybe it was his mellow temperament, or his firm voice, but whatever the reason, if he was in a meeting everyone oriented toward him. When the Cradle Robber Task Force gathered in the conference room, Harding sat at one side of the rectangular table with Kyle at his side.

There were fifteen people gathered in the room—the captain, Kyle, Mac, Cassidy, Michelson, and eight investigators drawn from the bureau and two from the Multnomah County Sheriff's Office. Most of the investigators were detective sergeant rank, but not all were experienced homicide investigators. One was a precinct detective, another an assault detective, and a third a regional drug investigator. Kyle had recommended their inclusion because of their interviewing skills or their people skills. Six of the investigators were men, four were women. Most of the detectives at the table had worked with Kyle, others knew him by reputation and rumor. All of them would have doubts about his ability to lead. Harding began the meeting.

"Last night a teenage girl was murdered in Pier Park. The killer, or killers, left behind a baby toy which is the signature of Cradle Robber."

Everyone around the table had been told that much when

they were called to the meeting, still, anxious murmuring spread around the table.

"As you know, Cradle Robber first hit San Diego, then L.A., then San Francisco. Three cities and three task forces just like this one and each failed to stop the killing. He's killing children and now it's our children he's after. It's time to stop him."

Heads nodded agreement around the table.

"The FBI will move their operation from San Francisco as soon as they are sure Cradle Robber has moved on but we're not waiting for them. Each of you was selected for this assignment because you are the best at what you do. Not all of you have homicide experience but all of you have special skills that we need. If you want to know why you're here, ask the man who put this team together, Detective Kyle Sommers."

Harding indicated Kyle with a nod of his head. Kyle leaned forward so that everyone could get a look at him. Kyle could see a lot of uncertainty around the table.

"Just as Detective Sommers selected you, I selected him to lead the task force because of his unique abilities. Detective Sommers will give you your assignments and interface with the FBI and local law enforcement agencies. If you have an idea, see him. If you have a suggestion, tell him. If you want to bitch about something, he's the man to see."

Harding paused as if he was daring anyone to object.

"All right, let's get to work. Detective Sommers, lay it out for them."

"Thank you, Captain," Kyle began. "As Captain Harding said, a girl by the name of Carolynn Martin was murdered last night and we found a baby rattle in the victim's hand. That is the signature of Cradle Robber but we haven't yet eliminated the possibility of a copycat crime. Besides the baby toy, the only other similarity is the fact the girl was smothered. But that's enough for us. Captain Harding and I agree that we're not taking any chances. Delaying a day could cost another child their life."

Again heads nodded in agreement all around the table.

"There is another peculiarity," Kyle continued.

"That murder of Carolynn Martin started as an assault by a pack of teenagers. They were drunk and the girls stumbled into their party. The assault was interrupted by a man who threatened to call the police. No such call was made. The same man then gave Carolee Martin a note for the police. The girls then tried to leave the park but Carolynn never made it. Someone grabbed her and smothered her."

"Was she raped?" Lucy Wu asked.

Wu was an assault detective. Wu was short and thick-waisted, with black hair and eyes. She had permanent worry lines around her eyes and the corner of her mouth and dressed in black slacks, white blouse, and black blazer. Kyle didn't know her well but her supervisor described her as "all business."

"We don't think so. She was fully clothed, although her blouse was torn open. One of the boys did that."

"What about the boys who initially attacked the girls?" Ken Danforth asked. "That's the place to start looking."

Danforth worked homicide with Kyle and was an ambitious climber who had the skills to make good on his boasts. Three years younger than Kyle, he was climbing faster than Kyle had but unlike Kyle, Danforth didn't care who he climbed over. Danforth wore a tailored blue suit, every brown hair on his head assigned a place and every hair where it belonged. Kyle could smell his cologne clear across the table. Danforth was a good detective but he was on the task force for only one reason—Harding insisted. Kyle asked Michelson to update them on the boys.

"We have four boys in custody," Michelson said. "Two of them are the ringleaders—Enrico Cortez and Marcus Jennings. We're holding two others that helped hold the girls down and we've talked with a half dozen more and released them to their parents. All of them except Marcus and Rico tell pretty much the same story. They grabbed the girls, Marcus and Rico were going to rape them, and it got interrupted by an old man. Then they all left. Two of them swear they met up with Marcus and Rico outside the park right after the old man scared them off. There wasn't enough time for either Marcus or Rico to chase down one of the girls, drag her into the bushes, then smother her."

"Maybe," Danforth said, but let the matter drop.

"You mentioned a note," Joanne Falk said.

Falk was from the Multnomah County Sheriff's Office and the first to speak up from outside the department. She was a big woman, middle-aged with light brown hair, wearing wire-rimmed glasses. She wore no makeup and her hair was pulled back in a bun. Like Wu, she wore a blazer, dark blue over a light blue blouse. The Multnomah County sheriff had highly recommended her. Kyle knew of her because of her work on the Regional Drug Task Force.

"Yes," Kyle said. "That's one of the oddities in this case. The old man left a note that contained details of the crime that had just taken place. It looks like whoever wrote the note knew what was going to happen—except some of what was described in the note didn't happen."

Explaining what was in the note was difficult, so Kyle passed out photocopies. After finishing the note, most of the detectives started reading it a second time. Danforth didn't bother to reread it.

"Whoever wrote that note had to be in on the attack on the girls or else he couldn't know the names of the boys when he typed this up," Danforth said. "That means it's likely the man in the park is Cradle Robber and we've got the first physical description of him on the West Coast."

When Danforth spoke he looked at Kyle but his eyes regularly flicked to read Harding's reaction.

Cassidy shifted in her seat, then cleared her throat for attention.

"There's not much in this note that matches what happened last night," Cassidy said. "Whoever wrote this missed key details and a lot of it concerns events that haven't happened and won't."

"I agree," Kyle said. "If the old man is Cradle Robber, then he's changed his pattern."

"It could be a red herring," Danforth said. "He might be feeling the heat and trying to throw the police off his trail."

Now for the first time Willie Baxter spoke. Baxter was the highest-ranking African American in the department. He was a big man but not as large as Harding, and softer-looking—more fat and less muscle. His head was hairless, except for a small fringe along the sides. Twice, smaller cities had pursued him for chief positions but Baxter had turned them down. Baxter detested administrative trivia.

"Cradle Robber is undoubtably psychotic," Baxter said. "Without treatment he is probably deteriorating. That could account for the changes in his profile."

"If it's Cradle Robber who sent the note," Kyle said.

"Who else?" Danforth asked.

"Take a look at this," Kyle said, passing out the note delivered to his office. "This one was delivered to me this morning."

Even Danforth read the note twice this time.

"Notice the first incident is about a Cradle Robber murder and the second about a traffic accident. I checked with the Kirkland family mentioned as the first Cradle Robber victims and their little girl is fine. As for the traffic accident story, there was an accident like the one described but the little girl and her mother weren't injured."

Puzzled murmuring filled the room.

"There's something else. A man fitting the description of the old man in the park showed up just before the truck accident and chased the mother and her daughter. That's when they almost got hit."

No one around the table could make sense of the notes—except Danforth.

"Whoever is writing these notes isn't Cradle Robber," Danforth announced. "He wouldn't talk about himself in the third person if he was Cradle Robber and Cradle Robber wouldn't make up these other stories. Why tip us off about the Kirklands if that's where he's going to strike? This is some kook who is yanking your chain and it's a dead end. We need to ignore the notes and concentrate on the forensic evidence from the murder scene."

Danforth ignored the fact he had fingered the old man as Cradle Robber earlier in the meeting. Those around the table split, some agreeing with Danforth, some holding back, unsure.

"We're going to consider all possibilities at this point," Kyle said, reasserting his authority.

"Does that include the genie theory?" Danforth asked.

The detectives didn't know what to make of Danforth's question. All eyes were on Kyle. Kyle stiffened when he heard Harding speak.

"What are you talking about, Danforth?"

"Rita Morales, who works the security desk, has been telling people that she's working with Detective Sommers on this case. She says that she was brought in as a consultant because she's an expert on genies. Based on the evidence that Detective Sommers shared with her, she concluded that there is a blue genie who is using magic and manipulating time."

Danforth finished, then leaned back, trying to hide a smirk. Kyle flushed, embarrassed and angry at the same time.

"Having lunch with Rita was my idea," Mac said.

Danforth hadn't mentioned Mac's name, only interested in discrediting Kyle.

"Kyle didn't want to go but I dragged him along," Mac said. "I know what she came up with sounds crazy but we didn't know what we were going to get before we met with her. It was worth a lunch hour, I mean if we keep looking for answers in the same places as the SFPD, the LAPD, and the SPD, then we're going to come up empty just the way they did."

Danforth was smart and knew it was time to back off. He had damaged Kyle's credibility and that was enough for now. If he pushed it further people would begin to question his motives.

"No one is to share evidence with anyone outside of this investigation," Harding announced.

Uncomfortable silence followed.

"There is one other detail that may be important," Kyle said to ease the tension. "The old man who showed up in the park and who may be the same man who chased the Browns may have a blue tinge to his skin. That's what Car-olee Martin reported. If it's true, then he may have a heart condition."

Kyle let the detectives make their own connection between the blue skin color and the blue genie theory.

"That's even more evidence that this isn't Cradle Robber," Danforth said. "Some of his killings were second-story jobs. An old man with a heart condition isn't going to be climbing onto roofs in the middle of the night. I still say the notes are a red herring. I'd save them for an obstruction of justice case."

Mumbled agreement spread around the table.

"We will concentrate on the most promising leads first," Kyle said, once again wresting control from Danforth. "You will all get summaries of the relevant case reports by the end of the day. I want everyone to know every detail. As soon as we have the FBI files and SFPD reports, we'll share those. I talked to Inspector Segal from the SFPD and she is coming up Wednesday to meet with us. We're still interviewing boys from the park and some of you will help with those. We haven't had any luck finding the old man from the park by canvassing the neighborhood, so we are going to expand the search to medical facilities in the north end. We also have a flood of tips on the murder of Carolynn Martin. Danforth, I want you to set up a team to sort through these. Separate the wheat from the chaff and follow-up anything that looks promising."

Danforth looked satisfied. He had a team to lead and cases were frequently solved through tips. Kyle made other specific assignments, then the meeting broke up. They had little to work with at this point, so most of the detectives would be reviewing case files. It saddened Kyle to know that the task force would be ineffective without clues and they would only get more clues if Cradle Robber killed again.

"There's one last question and that is whether we should warn the public that Cradle Robber may be targeting Portland."

The detectives talked among themselves briefly but this time Falk spoke before Danforth.

"There's little downside to notifying the media," she said. "If it isn't Cradle Robber we suffer a little embarrassment. If we don't warn the public and Cradle Robber kills again, we'll deserve all the condemnation we get."

There was general agreement around the table.

"I agree," Kyle said.

"I can get a press conference together in time to make the evening news," Cassidy said, turning to Harding. She was asking if he would be there. Harding nodded yes.

As the meeting broke up, Kyle caught Harding's eye. Harding said nothing as he left.

After the meeting Kyle thanked Mac for taking some of the blame for the Rita fiasco, then they took turns griping about Danforth. The rest of Kyle's afternoon was unproductive. He spent an hour on the phone with the FBI, talking to agents in San Francisco and in the local office. They weren't ready to shift their Cradle Robber efforts to Portland based solely on the Martin murder. Kyle did find out that there had been three other copycat crimes since the spree started—one on the East Coast.

Following up with other aspects of the investigation, Kyle found that officers had finished canvassing the neighborhoods around Pier Park, finding four old men with heart conditions, none with blue skin and none good suspects.

At three-thirty he called Inspector Ellen Segal who headed the San Francisco Cradle Robber Task Force, finalizing details of her trip north. Her relief that Cradle Robber had moved out of her city was mixed with compassion for the residents of Portland. Inspector Segal knew as much as anyone about the Cradle Robber killing spree and assured Kyle there had never been notes about the crimes and never a mention of an old man at the scene, with or without blue skin.

Rita called just before four, asking if they had any more information about the genie. Barely controlling his anger, Kyle reminded her that their lunch conversation was supposed to be confidential. She was apologetic but the damage had been done. At four Kyle swept all the paperwork on his desk into his top drawer, then laid the photocopies of the notes out on his desk. No matter what else he did, his thoughts kept coming back to the notes.

Kyle studied the print and layout, confirming the notes were the same font and spacing. Next, he cut the typed portions out, trimmed the edges neatly, then fit the pieces together in sequence. As Rita had observed, it looked like part of a newspaper or magazine article. Kyle took a blank sheet of paper and placed the clippings on the page. It looked even more like an article. Anyone with a word processor could produce something as neat, Kyle reminded himself, but why would they?

Kyle's eyes returned to the notes, dropping from segment to segment, noting the sequential order and the time notations that seemed to chronicle the crimes and accidents on a particular Monday—today, he realized. But there were only three listed and the last one had happened at 8:20 A.M. Eight hours had passed since then. Kyle thought of calling Cassidy to see what other accidents or crimes had been logged in that day, but worried she would interpret two calls in one day as romantic interest. Instead, Kyle pulled his phone directory from the bottom drawer, tearing out the listings for the Browns. With a last look at the pieced-together article, Kyle slid it into his middle drawer, seeing the wide white space below the incident with the Browns, wondering what would fill it.

9

Stranger

Mitch Nolan got home from work a little after six, kissed his pregnant wife, Lisle, on the cheek, then took the mailbox key from the hook in the closet. Lisle had a thing about mail and never picked it up herself. She would read letters addressed to her if Mitch pulled them out but never looked through the mail to find them for herself. She enjoyed Christmas cards as much as a child does Christmas presents but even in December she never made the short trek across the street to the mailbox to look for them. Instead, she would wait until Mitch came home from work and hand him the key, letting him separate the red and green envelopes, then snatch them from his hand and sit in her favorite chair, sipping tea and lovingly opening and then reading every line of every card and letter. Mitch never understood her mail phobia but tolerated the minor pathology because he loved Lisle.

As Mitch crossed the street to the mailbox, his neighbor's garage door opened, a minivan backing out. Mitch waved at Millie Sadler who waved back as she drove off. The Sadlers had two children, four and six years old, and one more on the way. Lisle was pregnant too so Millie had been ecstatic when she found out since it meant a playmate for Millie's new baby.

Mitch leafed through the envelopes briefly, seeing nothing to interest Lisle. Given the number of bills he wondered why he hadn't developed his own mail phobia. Turning back toward his house, he saw someone running up the street. Planning ahead for a family, Mitch and Lisle had bought into an established neighborhood, with large yards on a cul-de-sac. Mitch knew every car that belonged on their block and everyone that lived there. The man hurrying up the street was a stranger.

He wore an overcoat and a wide-brimmed hat that hid most of his face. As he jogged up the street, he looked at each house intently. When he reached the Sadler house, the stranger hurried to the front door. Keeping his eye on the stranger, Mitch walked back to his house. The stranger jabbed the doorbell a half-dozen times, then pounded on the door. There was a window set in the top of the door, and the man stood on his tiptoes trying to see inside, pounding all the while.

"Can I help you?" Mitch asked loudly.

Startled, the man turned briefly, then reached for the door handle, trying to get inside.

"I don't think anyone's home," Mitch said.

Now the man turned and Mitch could see more of his face. He was frightened and his skin was a funny color.

"Has she gone to the store?" the man asked.

"I don't know where she went but she left a few minutes ago."

"I've got to get in!"

"Are you a friend of the Sadlers?" Mitch said, now standing at the top of the Sadlers' walk.

"Nick and Christy are in danger," the man said.

The old man knew the names of the Sadler children, suggesting to Mitch he was a friend or relative. Still, he pounded on the door like a crazy man.

"Calm down," Mitch said. "What did you mean about Nick and Christy?"

Mitch thought back to Millie leaving in her minivan. He didn't remember either of the kids in the car. Mitch knew her husband, John, wouldn't be home for an hour yet. Was it possible Millie left the kids home alone for a few minutes? If the children were home, Nick was old enough to know the "home alone rules" and wouldn't answer the door for a stranger.

"They're getting in the hot tub," the man said, giving up on the door and walking to one of the front windows, trying to see through the closed blinds.

Suddenly the man kicked the window, the double-pane glass vibrating but not breaking. Mitch jumped him before he kicked again, wrapping his arms around him, pulling him back. Mitch had worked construction since he was a teenager and his upper body was strong from the hard work. Mitch held the old man easily.

"They're drowning," the man screamed.

Mitch pulled him away from the window.

"Calm down," Mitch said.

"Please believe me, they're drowning in the hot tub."

The old man reached for one of Mitch's arms, trying to pull it loose, and when he touched Mitch's hand it tingled like from a mild electric shock. Mitch looked to see part of his own hand and arm had turned blue.

"Calm down and I'll check on the kids," Mitch said. "You don't have to break a window, we can go around back."

"Yes. Please hurry."

Mitch let go of the old man slowly, ready to grab him again if he went for the window or tried to run away.

"Please hurry," the old man said again.

Mitch led him to the side gate, checking his arm as he did, seeing it was a normal color again. A six-foot cedar fence surrounded the Sadler and Nolan homes, with gates set on either side of the property line. Mitch reached over the top of the fence, feeling for the latch, one eye on the old man who looked near panic. Mitch released the catch and pushed the gate open, the old man rushing past, Mitch running to keep up.

The Sadlers had added a sunroom to the back of their house. The room resembled a small greenhouse and was decorated with a variety of large potted plants. There was also a spa surrounded by a small redwood deck. The old man reached the sunroom just ahead of Mitch, gasping as he did. Mitch's eyes went right to the spa as he turned the corner, horrified by what he saw. The children's legs were sticking out of the top—Nick and Christy had fallen in headfirst. Only one pair of legs was still kicking.

The old man was at the sliding door, trying to force the lock. Without hesitation Mitch grabbed one of the large planters that decorated the patio and threw it through the glass. Sparkling shards showered the tile floor, impacting, breaking into smaller pieces, and then rebounding into the air like raindrops. Kicking the glass away, Mitch stepped through. Time slowed as he did. Mitch stepped up onto the decking, eyes riveted on the flailing legs, reaching for them even as they stopped moving. Grabbing Nick by the ankles, Mitch lifted him straight up. The boy was limp. Mitch swung Nick over the edge of the tub, stepping aside as the old man reached for Christy. Making room, Mitch stepped off the deck, sweeping glass aside with his shoe, then gently laying Nick on the tile. Looking back once, he saw the old man lift Christy from the water, then perform the Heimlich maneuver on her, water gushing from the little girl's lungs. Quickly copying the old man, Mitch lifted Nick, folded him nearly in half, and pressed in and up just below his sternum. Water gushed from Nick's mouth and nose.

Watching the old man from the corner of his eye, Mitch copied his moves, placing Nick on his back, lifting up on his neck so his head was tilted back and his mouth open.

"Use your finger to make sure the tongue is out of the way," the old man shouted.

Mitch felt in Nick's mouth, finding the boy's tongue folded back, as if he had tried to swallow it. Mitch pulled it forward, unfolding it and tucking it to the side. Then he pinched the boy's nose, and placed his mouth over the boy's, blowing. He had no idea of how hard to blow. He remembered that blowing too hard could burst the lungs of children—or was that just a danger with infants? Out of the corner of his eye he saw the old man pumping Christy's chest and Mitch realized he had forgotten to check for a pulse. He pressed his fingers against Nick's wrist but felt nothing.

"Check his neck," the old man said.

Mitch pinched the boy's neck, trying to distinguish the pounding of his own pulse from the boy's—he thought Nick had a pulse, but the boy's skin was gray—he needed oxygen. Now Mitch put one hand on the boy's chest, pinched his nose closed again and blew harder into the boy's lungs, feeling his chest rise this time. Suddenly there was a crash and a gasp.

"No, no, no!" Millie Sadler screamed.

A gallon of milk had burst on impact, a spilled bag of groceries soaking up the liquid.

"Call 9-1-1," the old man ordered.

"Nick, Christy!" Millie moaned, stepping closer.

"Call 9-1-1," the old man repeated, switching from chest massage to pulmonary resuscitation.

Mitch blew into Nick's mouth again, seeing Millie turn from the doorway, heading for a phone. Another breath and suddenly Nick convulsed, liquid boiling from his mouth. Mitch froze, unsure of what to do, watching the little eruption of chlorinated water and vomit.

"Turn his head sideways," the old man ordered.

Quickly Mitch turned the boy's head and he convulsed again, vomiting out water and stomach contents. When he finished, Mitch turned his head back up, lifting his neck again to open his mouth. There was vomit around his mouth, and it tasted sour as Mitch pressed his mouth to the boy's, feeling the boy's chest rise. The taste was vile, but Mitch blew again and again. Millie came back, talking on a cordless phone, begging the operator to hurry. Again Nick convulsed, vomiting the rest of his stomach contents. When Mitch rolled him back over this time he could see the boy's chest rising and falling.

"He's breathing," Mitch said to reassure Millie.

Millie still held the phone, white-faced, staring at her prostrate children.

"I think Nick's going to be okay," Mitch said, not really knowing.

Now all attention was on the old man who alternated between pumping Christy's chest and breathing in her mouth.

"Help me," the old man said. "Do the breathing."

Mitch did as he was told, breathing once for every five pumps the old man performed on the little girl's chest. Mitch noticed that where the old man's hands touched Christy, she turned blue. As the man bent over his coat gaped and Nick could see a peculiar garment underneath.

While they worked, Millie knelt with Nick, wiping the rest of the vomit from his face, crying softly. A few minutes later there was a siren and Millie ran to the front door, urging the paramedics to hurry. There were three of them, one going to Nick, the other two to Christy. One of the paramedics pulled out a stethoscope, pushing the old man's hands aside and listening to Christy's chest. The other took over Mitch's job, using a plastic respirator to force air into the little girl's lungs.

"I've got a pulse," the first paramedic said. "It's very weak."

Mitch put his arm around Millie, comforting her. Then Lisle was there, taking Millie in a hug, crying with her. Police and firemen came, Millie and the Nolans pushed aside. Nick was loaded on a stretcher and taken out first as the paramedics worked on Christy. Only when she was strapped to a stretcher and rolled out to the ambulance did Mitch remember the old man. By then he was gone.

10

Survivor

Monday, 6:45 P.M.

Reaching the Tom McCall Elementary School, Kyle pulled into the parking lot, spreading the map out on the seat. Using the addresses in the phone book, he worked through the "Browns," checking the addresses to find one close to the school. There were two possibilities within walking distance, but only one of the addresses would take a mother and daughter walking to school past the furniture store where the truck had crashed. He drove to the most likely address.

Kyle was dressed in slacks and a square-cut shirt that covered the gun on his belt. Without a uniform, people were reluctant to believe that a strange man showing up at their door at night was a policeman, so Kyle held his badge out so it was the first thing Sandy Brown saw when she peeked through the window.

"Is something wrong?" Sandy Brown said as she opened the door.

"I'm Detective Sommers and I'm investigating an accident from this morning. I understand you and your daughter were witnesses."

Sandy Brown didn't ask him in or even open the screen door.

"Who is it, hon?" a man asked from behind her.

"The police. He's asking about the accident this morning," Sandy said over her shoulder.

The door was pulled wide now and Kyle could see the Browns. Sandy and Roger Brown were a matched set, like souvenir salt shakers, with gray eyes and blond hair—his was natural—both wore their hair cut short, both had slacks on and sweaters—his green, hers blue.

"Come on in," Roger said, pushing the screen door open.

The door opened to the living room, which blended into a dining room. A staircase sat against the far wall, leading to the second story. The room was neat, the furniture selected for comfort, not style.

"Coffee?" Sandy Brown offered, as Kyle sat in a rocker.

"No thanks. I only have a couple of questions."

A little girl came down the stairs, peeking through the railing at Kyle. She wore a button that read "Special Person." Kyle's stomach knotted and a chill went up his spine. For an instant, Kyle saw himself in his wrecked jeep, helpless, legs broken, looking through the seats at his own daughter, Shelby, seeing the blood spreading down her side, hearing her voice pleading softly for her daddy to help her. A droplet of sweat ran down his cheek.

"I understand you were at the scene of the accident?" Kyle said, wiping his face with the back of his hand.

"I was walking Marissa to school and this truck came right up on the sidewalk and crashed into a wall. It just missed us," Sandy said.

"The driver had a heart attack," Roger added.

"Someone said you were running down the sidewalk?" Kyle probed.

"Yes, that's right," Sandy said, her demeanor changing. Now she was angry. "Some pervert got in our way. I had to mace him to get by. Then he chased us down the block. He almost ran us right into that truck."

"You called him a pervert . . ." Kyle probed.

"He had on an overcoat, like a flasher would wear."

"Did he flash you?" Kyle asked.

"No, thank goodness. That would have been a pathetic sight, an old man like that."

"He was old?"

"Well, not old old. Late fifties, or early sixties."

"Better not let my father hear you call people that age old," Roger said, smiling at his wife.

"Did the man in the overcoat say anything to you?"

"He said he wanted to talk to us. He said we were in danger," Sandy said.

"Repent, the world was going to end," Roger said in a deep mocking voice.

Sandy giggled at her husband's joke. Kyle forced a polite smile.

"In danger from what?" Kyle asked.

"He didn't say. I sprayed him after that, then we ran down the block and the truck crashed. That's pretty much all of it."

"Can you describe the man for me?"

"Like I said, he was old," Sandy said with a smile at Roger, "he wore a tan overcoat and a big hat. I think the hat was leather."

"Anything else you can think of?" Kyle probed.

"Tell him about his color," Roger suggested.

"Oh, yeah. I know this is going to sound weird but he was blue. Really, and it wasn't makeup. His skin was light blue."

"Had you ever seen this man before?" Kyle asked.

"No, but if I ever do I'll spray him again!" Sandy said, holding up an imaginary pepper spray canister and saying "Pssssssss." Her husband laughed and pulled his wife close with an arm around her shoulder.

"She's a regular Clint Eastwood," Roger said, and hugged his wife again while she basked in his praise. Then she smiled and did her "Pssssss" routine again.

Kyle smiled, finding the Brown family humor painful but knowing the little girl on the stairs was lucky to have such parents. In Marissa's limited experience, all parents were like hers, devoted to each other, loving, and supportive.

Kyle thanked the Browns, waved at Marissa, and then left. He drove a couple of blocks, then parked, wondering what to do next. He had no family to go home to, no girlfriend, and his friends were family men. Even Mac, who complained daily about his wife, enjoyed her company, if for nothing else than the stories he could bring to work. He thought about Cassidy's second chance offer but knew he wasn't ready yet and didn't want to waste that chance. There were a couple of good cop bars, one favored by detectives but word would get back to Harding. There were other bars, though, and he knew them well but still Kyle hesitated.

Kyle had been up since 2:00 A.M. but knew he couldn't sleep yet. He was thinking about Shelby again and the depression and self-recrimination were back. His counselor had asked him to write a "self-talk" for when the depression set in and Kyle was supposed to recite the talk, a litany of all the good things he had done. He promised the counselor he would—one of many lies he told the counselor in order to get back to work. He'd tried the litany one time but his negative self-talk kept intruding. Liberal doses of alcohol did work, however. So Kyle had developed his own routine, joining a twenty-four-hour health club near his home—the club had a bar. He decided to go there now, promising himself he would only work out.

Kyle started his pickup, pulling into traffic, his mind coming back to the puzzle of the notes and to a little girl who might have been crushed by a truck but was now Special Person of the Week.

11

Suspicion

Monday, 8:30 P.M.

Whenever he bought the toys, he always bought diapers, baby powder, and canned formula. Buying just a baby toy would look suspicious. With his baby supplies in a handbasket, he looked over the toy selection. The rattles were the same in all cities and that was good, since if he bought one of the unique toys sold in a baby boutique a clerk might remember him. He preferred superstores like this one, where half the square footage was devoted to groceries and half to hard-lines and clothes and dozens of people waited in line at the checkout stands.

He had a boy in mind for his next visit, so he selected the rattle shaped like a baseball bat and dropped it in the basket, letting it sift down between the baby powder and the diapers. Then he searched out the pharmacy section, selecting a box of condoms, placing these on top of the diapers. Anyone looking in his basket would be amused by the juxtaposition of the condoms and the diapers and wouldn't remember the toy in the bottom.

He always used the "cash only" line, careful not to leave a credit trail. The woman in front of him was buying all vegetables and the man behind a gallon of milk and a dozen eggs. The woman ahead was absorbed by the tabloids display, reading the headlines, studying the pictures. The man behind had a newspaper in his hand and was reading the front page. When the woman took her turn with the checker, he faced the tabloid rack, keeping his basket between his leg and the checkout counter. When it was his turn he watched the man behind him from the corner of his eye. When the man flipped the folded paper over to read the rest of the front page, he could see it was a late edition with the headline "Cradle Robber in Portland." Then he heard the rattle as the baseball bat was pulled from his basket and run across the scanner. When he looked back he could see the man looking at the rattle, then flipping the paper back over to the Cradle Robber story, reading briefly, then looking at him again. He concentrated on getting his money out, feeling the man's stare. Paying the disinterested clerk, he took his bag and walked slowly to the nearest exit. The man from the checkout line followed him out, without his groceries. Walking directly to his truck, he dropped the bag in the back, using his peripheral vision to track the man who was circling around through the parked cars. When he opened his door he could see the man in the next row, writing down his license number. Starting the engine, he backed out slowly and drove down the aisle, turning away from the man. Two rows later he parked, seeing the man walk past his row heading back into the store.

His guns were under the seats, the pistol in a holster mounted under the passenger seat. His shotgun was there too but it was too big and even the small-caliber pistol was too noisy. Reaching deeper, he found his hunting knife. He kept the blade finely honed. He pushed the knife up the left sleeve of his shirt. Then he walked back to the entrance, looking inside. The man who had followed him was back in line, buying the groceries he had left behind and reading the Cradle Robber story. After checking out, the man came out with the paper under his arm, a paper bag in the crook of the other. Paralleling the man, he followed in the next row, ready to pretend to be getting into one of the cars if he was spotted. The man ignored him, stopping at a green minivan. Letting the knife slip into his hand, he hurried toward the man, timing it so he arrived just after the man leaned in to put his groceries on the passenger seat. As the man's head came up he slapped his hand over his mouth, turned the blade so that it could pass between the ribs and drove it deep into his back. A powerful spasm drove the man's head into the ceiling with a loud thump. Then, using the serrated edge of the knife, he sawed furiously, probing for the heart. With another spasm, the man went limp.

Jerking the knife free, he pushed the body inside, then stood, looking around. Two aisles away a woman pushed a cart loaded with bags. Another car was entering the lot, beginning the search for a parking spot. Other shoppers were coming and going from the entrance, none headed his way. Quickly he searched the man's pockets, finding an envelope from the gas company where his license plate number had been copied. He put the envelope in his pocket. The man's back was soaked with blood. He wiped his knife and hand on the man's shirt, then sat him up, leaning his head back. Taking the newspaper, he locked and closed the door. As long as no one looked too closely they would think he was asleep. Checking one more time, he saw no one who looked interested. Those nearest went about their business, loading groceries into their cars, tugging reluctant children along by the hand, searching for their cars. It would be hours before the dead man was found.

He read the paper as he walked back to his truck, noting with disgust the dire warnings the reporter had woven through the story. He wasn't a terror, he was a savior. If the children he had helped could speak, they would praise him as a protector, not a predator. But they couldn't speak because they were in a better place, a place with no cares and it was time for more to join them.

12

Puzzle

Monday, 11:00 P.M.

Exhausted from his workout and fresh out of the shower, Kyle stopped at the club bar, stumbling over his order. The men on the left were drinking beer, the women on his right white wine. When the bartender started to turn away, Kyle ordered orange juice with a creatine additive. There was a television mounted high on the wall and the local news came on, the station leading with Cradle Robber. A computer-generated image appeared in the corner above the female newscaster. It was an empty cradle with a rattle on the pillow where the baby's head should be. There was too much bar talk to hear the reporter, so Kyle picked up his juice, carrying it closer to the screen. Two women in exercise bras and shorts sat near the end of the bar and looked him over as he passed. The women were dressed for a workout but their hair was perfectly brushed and there was no sheen of sweat on their skin. Concentrating on the television he picked out the voice of the reporter and ignored the background chatter.

". . . Police spokesperson Cassidy Kellogg made the announcement," the reporter said.

Then Cassidy was on the screen, reading a statement filled with terms like "maybe," "strong likelihood," and "precautionary efforts." The statement was carefully crafted so that the public would be alerted but the police protected in case it was a false alarm. Kyle noticed that Cassidy was cool, professional, and beautiful.

The chief of police came on next with a speech reassuring the public the department was taking extraordinary steps to make sure that what had happened in California wouldn't happen in Oregon. Captain Harding was at the chief's shoulder. If Harding spoke at the news conference it wasn't included in the clip.

The reporter reappeared on the screen, the Cradle Robber logo once again in the corner. Now a list of ways to protect your children appeared, ranging from "Lock your windows and doors," to "Have the family dog sleep in the child's room." Kyle knew the same list had run in San Diego, Los Angeles, and San Francisco. Cradle Robber was more patient, more careful, and more random than any serial killer he had ever heard of. If they were going to catch Cradle Robber, it would take something extraordinary. Then he thought of the old man with the blue skin and what Danforth had said about him leaving false clues. Kyle's gut told him Danforth was wrong but the notes made no sense, not even as red herrings.

The Cradle Robber story ended and the camera switched to the co-anchor who led into a story about the unusual atmospheric conditions Oregon had been experiencing. A picture of the aurora borealis replaced the anchor, the reporter droning on about how unusual it was to see it in Oregon and a controversy among experts over whether the lights in the sky actually were a result of the aurora borealis. The next report was about the arrest of a man by the name of Nicholas Dawson for a road rage accident on Sunday that killed three teenagers and injured three more. Kyle had no stomach for stories about car accidents.

Kyle drained his glass of juice and left, thinking about the notes.

13

Drowning

Tuesday, 3:00 A.M.

Kyle couldn't sleep that night. Every time he went to bed he flashed back to the stretch of highway where Shelby had died. He still remembered every detail of the accident; the deer flashing through his headlights, the skid, the Jeep rolling down the embankment, the sound of shattering glass, Shelby's cries for help.

He gave up trying to sleep, pacing the floor instead, his mind alternating between memories of his daughter and fears of what Cradle Robber might be doing in the dark. The phone rang just after 3:00 A.M. and he jumped for the receiver, holding his breath as he picked it up. Only the department called this time of night.

"Is something bothering you, Kyle?" a woman asked.

It was Mrs. Pastorini, his landlady.

"Everything's fine here, Mrs. Pastorini, is there something I can do for you?"

"I know something's wrong from the way you've been worrying the floor. I've lived most of my life in this house and it speaks to me. Tonight my ceiling is telling me that something is bothering you."

Kyle had become used to the creaks and groans of the old wooden floor, forgetting it was just as loud below.

"It's just police business, nothing I can share," Kyle said.

"I'm sorry about the noise. I think I'm tired enough to sleep now."

"Would you like me to fix you a cup of warm milk?"

"No, I'm fine."

"Warm milk works wonders. It would be no trouble."

"I'll call you if I can't get to sleep."

"Call me anytime. I don't sleep much either and we could share a cup of milk."

It took three more assurances he would call before Kyle got Mrs. Pastorini off the phone. As he promised, he did try to sleep. Kyle dozed off around 4:00 A.M., startled awake when his alarm went off at six.

He had made it through the night without a call from the bureau but that didn't mean Cradle Robber hadn't struck. Parents of Cradle Robber's victims often didn't discover he had visited until 8:00 or 9:00 A.M. It would be an agonizing couple of hours as Kyle waited for parents to check on their children.

Kyle stopped by the McKenzie pool on his way to his cubicle, picking a time randomly. In his cubicle he went through the motions, shuffling papers, working on reports, reviewing the files they had gathered on Cradle Robber, but his eyes kept drifting to the digital clock, time slowing to an agonizing crawl.

Mac made his usual showy entrance just after eight, triggering laughter and giggles at every desk and cubicle he passed. Mac heard him showing off his shirt and tie to someone who had picked "arrives with stain" from the McKenzie pool. After a lot of exaggerated groaning and more laughter, Mac moved on. Mac didn't stop, waving at Kyle as he passed. He knew Kyle would be waiting for reports about child deaths.

Kyle's phone rang just before nine. Kyle answered it with a lump in his throat, his stomach knotting as he recognized Cassidy's voice.

"Relax, Kyle," Cassidy said, "nothing has come across my desk that might be Cradle Robber's work."

It was too early to relax, Kyle knew.

"I've got something else you might be interested in," Cassidy said. "There was a near drowning last night in southwest Portland. Two kids were home alone and somehow fell into a hot tub. They would have drowned for sure but a neighbor and another man pulled them out and revived them. The interesting thing is that the neighbor says the other man was a stranger but seemed to know the kids were drowning. The neighbor also says the man was wearing an overcoat and a hat. Sound familiar?"

"Could it be the same guy?" Kyle wondered.

"You're the detective," Cassidy said. "I'm only the lowly information officer."

Kyle asked Cassidy for the details from the report including the address.

"How are the kids?" Kyle said when he had the information.

"I knew you'd ask. The boy's fine. The girl is in a coma—she could go either way."

"Thanks, Cassidy."

"There's no expiration date on that get out of jail free card, Kyle."

Kyle said good-bye, then shuffled through his mail looking to see if another note had been delivered—none. Then Kyle spent half an hour calling and visiting members of the task force, checking progress. There was little to report. Even Danforth had nothing significant, although the number of tips had increased exponentially after the news of Cradle Robber was released. Satisfied there was nothing urgent, Kyle grabbed his coat and headed for Mac's cubicle.

"The man in the overcoat and hat was busy again last night," Kyle said. "He was in Southwest Portland and helped save two kids from drowning."

"What?" Mac said loudly. "We can't let this go on, Kyle! We can't have people running around stopping rape and murder and saving people from traffic accidents and drowning." Pulling his gun and pretending to check the load, Mac said, "To hell with the law! This guy's going down before someone else gets saved."

Kyle ignored Mac's routine. Mac would tell jokes at a funeral.

"Look, he was in the park with Cradle Robber when Carolynn was murdered. He might have seen something. Besides, no one can be in the right place at the right time three times—there's something kinky here."

Mac was still chortling at his own joke.

"Are you coming?" Kyle asked.

"Isn't there a Roakes Coney Island out in southwest?"

"We can stop by," Kyle promised.

"Then I'm on that dastardly do-gooder's trail," Mac said, putting his coat on.

They found the Sadler home on a cul-de-sac of well-maintained houses with neat, landscaped yards. There wasn't a rectangular lawn on the block but instead ovals and odd-shaped patches of green bordered by flowering shrubs and clumps of daffodils. Only five blueprints had been used in the development, the houses varying only in small details—double garage doors instead of single, shapes of dormers, the placement of brick accents. It was a cookie cutter neighborhood, popular with young families and signs of children were everywhere. Chalk drawings in the street, tricycles and jump ropes in the yards, a basketball hoop at the end of the cul-de-sac. It was the kind of neighborhood Kyle and Aldean had been raising Shelby in and memories came flooding back—Shelby coming home from the hospital, the sign Kyle had put in the yard declaring proudly "IT'S A GIRL," walking her in the stroller, watching her toddle up the block—many painful memories. Mac caught Kyle staring at a tricycle as they drove into the cul-de-sac.

"You okay?" Mac asked.

"Just checking addresses," Kyle lied.

There was a battered pickup truck in front of the Sadler home decorated with "Nolan Remodeling."

A side gate was open and they heard the sound of breaking glass in the back. Following the sound they found a man wearing jeans and a denim shirt, gloves, and a tool belt. The man had short-cropped brown hair and his face had the weathered look that comes from outdoor work. He held a large shard of glass in his left hand and a hammer in his right. Holding the glass over a garbage can he smacked it, the glass shattering. Kyle held his badge out as they approached, the man nodding in greeting.

"Are you Mr. Sadler?" Kyle asked.

"Mitch Nolan. I live next door," he said with a nod toward the cedar fence behind him.

"I'm Detective Sommers," Kyle said. "This is Detective McKenzie."

Kyle examined the hole in the glass wall that Nolan was working on. He had removed most of the shards from the frame. There was more glass inside the sunroom, pieces of a broken planter, and a lot of water. In the corner Kyle spotted the spa. Someone had chopped a hole in the tub, leaving the ax buried in the deck.

"Who did that?" Kyle asked.

"John—the kids' father—he went a little nuts last night," Mitch said.

"Are the Sadlers home?"

"They're at the hospital. Nick's coming home today."

"You're the neighbor that saved the kids?" Kyle asked.

"I did what I could. If only I had been quicker . . ."

Kyle understood his pain.

"Tell us what happened," Kyle said.

"I was out getting the mail and I saw this guy running up the street. He was jogging and looking at addresses. When he got to the Sadlers he ran right to the door and started ringing the bell and knocking. I'd just seen Millie Sadler leave, so I walked over and told him I didn't think anyone was home. Then he tried to kick in the window so I grabbed him. I thought he was nuts but he kept saying the Sadler kids were in danger. He knew their names and that the Sadlers had a hot tub so I thought maybe he knew them. I'd never seen him around before but I didn't know what else to think."

Nolan had been animated until now, but some of the energy left his speech as he related what happened next.

"I should have been quicker," Mitch said.

"He was acting crazy," Kyle said. "You handled it just right."

"I brought him around back through the gate and when we got back here we saw Nick and Christy were drowning. They were headfirst down in the spa, feet kicking. So I busted through the glass and we pulled them out. Millie got home while we were trying to revive them and called the paramedics."

Now, Mitch's face darkened and his voice became a whisper.

"Somehow this guy knew the kids were drowning but you can't see into the backyard from the front and not from the houses on the sides either. I checked. I can't figure out how he knew."

Mac and Kyle exchanged glances again, Mac lifting one eyebrow that Kyle took to mean, "There has to be a psychic involved."

"What did the man look like?" Kyle asked.

"He had on a leather hat and an overcoat. He was about my father's age—sixty maybe. His eyes were dark—probably brown. His face was thin and his chin a little pointy. There was something else about him . . ." Mitch said, his voice trailing off.

When Mitch hesitated Mac led him.

"Was his skin blue?" Mac said.

"Yeah," Mitch said, surprised. "Except I'm not sure it was his skin."

"What do you mean?" Kyle said.

"When I grabbed him, he touched my arm and my arm turned blue. When he let go the blue disappeared. The same thing happened with Christy. When his hand touched her she turned blue."

This was new and if Mitch was to be believed, whatever gave the man's skin its bluish tinge wasn't a circulation problem.

"I know that sounds crazy but it wasn't dark yet when it happened. Oh, and when he touched me I felt like I was getting shocked. It didn't hurt, it was more of a light buzz."

Mitch was a wealth of new information but even with the new pieces to the puzzle, Kyle couldn't put it together.

"He was wearing something strange too—under his coat. It was like a wet suit, but not like any I've seen."

"It was rubber?" Kyle asked.

"I don't know. I only got a glimpse."

"Wearing a wet suit and a coat in this weather?" Mac said.

"There's one more thing," Mitch said, taking off his gloves. "Come on over to my house and I'll show you."

Mac and Kyle followed him back through the gate and to the house next door.

"We've got visitors, honey," Mitch yelled as he led them in.

The kitchen was straight ahead and a woman appeared, wearing a loose-fitting dress that hung below her knees. The dress flattened against her as she walked to greet them and Kyle detected a slight bulge near her abdomen. Kyle thought she might be pregnant but would never ask. Mac, however, operated under a different set of rules.

"This is my wife Lisle," Mitch said. "This is Detective Sommers and this is Detective McKenzie."

"Nice to meet you," Kyle said, nodding.

"Hello, Lisle," Mac said, smiling sweetly, then looking at her abdomen. "You must be five months along."

Lisle smiled at Mac.

"Six months," Lisle said.

"Really, you hardly show," Mac said.

"It's my first," Lisle said, warming up to Mac as all women did. "They say you get into maternity clothes faster with the second one."

"It's easier to blow up a balloon the second time," Mac said.

Lisle laughed, then asked Mac whether he had children. With Lisle and Mac talking babies, Mitch led Kyle into the kitchen.

"I told you I was picking up my mail when I saw that guy at the Sadlers. When he started kicking the window I dropped my mail in their yard and forgot about it until the Sadlers left for the hospital. I picked it up and brought it home but didn't look at it until this morning—we were at the hospital with the Sadlers until late. When I got around to looking through it I found this."

Mitch pulled a slip of paper off his refrigerator held by a Domino's Pizza magnet. Kyle knew what it was as soon as he saw it.

• Monday, evening: Two children drowned in a freak accident when their mother left them alone to run to the store to get milk for dinner. While she was gone the children drowned in the family's spa. Police speculated the children were playing or fighting on the deck by the spa when they fell in. Six-year-old Nick and four-year-old Christy were found by their mother headfirst in water. The mother, Millie Sadler, and a neighbor tried to revive the children but they were pronounced dead by the paramedics. Four days later at the funeral for her children, Millie Sadler suffered a miscarriage.

"That old man took off when the paramedics arrived," Mitch said when Kyle had finished reading. "He might have stuck this in my mail on his way out."

"Probably," Kyle said.

From the living room he could hear Mac talking with Lisle about babies.

"Are you going to breast feed or bottle feed?" Mac asked.

"Breast feed," Lisle answered. "It's better for the baby."

"I agree," Mac said. "Breast milk is easier to digest and breast-fed babies don't get sick as much."

Kyle tuned out the conversation in the living room, seeing Mitch studying him.

Mitch tapped the paper in Kyle's hand.

"This describes what could have happened if that man hadn't come running up the street, not what did happen. But how could someone print something like this up and then stick it in my mail last night within minutes after it happened?"

"And why would they want to?" Kyle added.

"Exactly."

"I don't know," Kyle said honestly.

"You don't seem surprised by this," Mitch said, tapping the note again. "Did you get something like this before?"

"I can't discuss ongoing investigations."

"Sure," Mitch said. "It's as if that man knew what was going to happen and tried to stop it."

"It looks that way but if that was the case then why didn't he get here sooner?"

"I thought about that," Mitch said, then took a map off the top of his refrigerator, spreading it on the kitchen table. "This is Applewood Court where we live," Mitch said, pointing on the map. "If you look over here," he said, dragging his finger across the map, "there's another Applewood Court. I ran across it on a remodeling job I had a couple of years ago. If you look at the map index it only lists this other

Applewood Court. I always worried if we had a fire the fire department might go to the wrong place. I'll bet that guy in the hat made the same mistake."

Nolan's theory made sense but only if you believed the blue man knew what was going to happen before it did.

"This guy sure acted like he knew the kids were going to drown."

"It's not possible," Kyle said.

"Maybe he's psychic? I've been thinking about it all night and I can't explain it any other way. If you're interested, I know someone who knows about this kind of stuff."

"What stuff?" Kyle asked, making Mitch say it first.

"Prophecy, ESP, time travel, stuff like that."

"Psychics show up after every big crime, claiming they can help. They haven't yet," Kyle said.

"I didn't believe in any of that stuff before last night. Now I don't know."

Taking a business card from his wallet, Mitch wrote out an address and phone number.

"This is where you can reach my sister, Sherrie. She's into all this kind of stuff but she's not like what you're thinking. She did graduate work in physics at Caltech."

Kyle took the card.

"Thanks," Kyle said, knowing he wouldn't call.

"Don't let her scare you off," Mitch said. "She's got an attitude but just tell her I sent you. She'll talk to you."

Kyle thanked Mitch again, then collected Mac from the living room.

"Cloth or disposables?" Mac was asking.

"My mother signed us up with a service for the first month," Lisle was saying.

"Perfect," Mac said. "You get the benefits of cloth diapers without all the washing."

"But you usually have a week's worth of dirty diapers sitting around your house waiting to be collected," Kyle said.

The looks Mac and Lisle gave him told Kyle he wasn't welcome in their conversation.

"Time to go," Kyle said.

That set off a round of "So-nice-to-meet-yous" and "I-really-enjoyed-talking-to-yous" between Mac and Lisle. When they got to the door Lisle hugged Mac good-bye—a man she had met only a few minutes before.

"First hug of the day," Mac said when they were back in the car.

"While you were at your hen party, I got this," Kyle said, handing Mac the latest note.

When Mac finished reading the note, Kyle filled him in on the rest of the details he got from Mitch Nolan.

"Kyle, we need to talk to Rita again," Mac said.

Kyle turned to Mac, incredulous. After the embarrassment at the task force meeting he couldn't believe Mac wanted to meet with Rita again.

"Nolan said the blue came off of that old man," Mac said. "We need to find out if the Universal Blue Jinn can flow from a genie to a person."

Speechless, Kyle stared at Mac. If anyone saw Kyle with Rita and it got back to Harding, he would be back on medical leave. A few seconds later Mac burst out laughing.

"You should see your face," Mac said when he could control his laughter.

"Mac, you know I have a gun and know how to use it, don't you?"

Mac squeezed Kyle's shoulder, still grinning.

"You're just too easy, Kyle," Mac said, sobering.

Kyle pulled away from the curb, using the circle at the end of the cul-de-sac to turn around. Halfway down the block, Mac slapped his shoulder and shouted for him to stop.

"Oh, no, we have to go back!" Mac said in a near panic.

Kyle hit the brakes and stopped in the middle of the street.

"I forgot to talk to Lisle about what to do if her nipples get sore from breast feeding."

This time Mac couldn't hold a serious face and immediately collapsed into a laughing fit.

"You're pathetic, Mac," Kyle said, accelerating down the street.

"That's not what women whisper when they're hugging me."

There was coney sauce on Mac's tie when they got back to the bureau, making an intern from Portland State University the winner. Now others from the bureau gathered around Mac who was turning their stop at Roakes into a ten-minute story. Kyle left him to his fans, heading straight for his phone, checking for a message from Cassidy. None of the six messages were from her. Then Kyle called San Francisco to see if Cradle Robber had struck there—he hadn't. Next, Kyle made copies of the note he had gotten from Mitch and took the original to the evidence vault, logging it in with the officer on duty. Then he cut out the latest note and taped it below the story about the truck accident.

One of the phone messages was from Captain Harding whose office was just across the complex. Harding wanted an update. Kyle walked to Harding's office and found Danforth inside, talking with Harding. Kyle tapped at the door and Harding motioned him in. Danforth stopped talking as soon as the door opened. Danforth owned a dozen suits, each carefully tailored. He wore his gray suit today, looking like an account executive for a marketing company. Danforth stood as Kyle entered.

"Danforth was just briefing me on his progress sifting through the tips," Harding said.

"I'd like that briefing too," Kyle said, trying to hide his anger.

"I looked for you but you weren't in."

"I am now."

"Check your e-mail, I sent you a written summary."

"The bottom line is that we have no solid leads," Harding cut in to stop the squabbling. "Danforth, I appreciate the update but remember Detective Sommers is leading the task force."

"Sure, I understand," Danforth said. "I saw your door open, that's all. I didn't mean to take up so much of your time."

Danforth slipped past Kyle to the door.

"Keep up the good work, Danforth," Harding said as he left.

Kyle remained standing, wondering what Danforth's "briefing" had covered. Danforth had apologized for taking up "so much" of the captain's time.

"It looks like we made it through the night," Harding said, rocking back in his chair.

"Cradle Robber tends to kill in spurts. When he first reaches a city there is a rash of killings and then they slow down. The pattern makes sense because getting to victims gets harder for him. Parents get paranoid and the police shift resources into patrolling at night. He has to take bigger risks or move on."

"We're going to do the same thing here," Harding said. "If we can't catch him I want him out of town ASAP."

"To kill in Seattle?" Kyle asked.

"I want this bastard as much as you do, Sommers, but our first responsibility is to protect our people. We're not going to use our children as bait, not if we can force him to move on."

"I know, but I hate it."

"Besides, it might not have been Cradle Robber who killed Carolynn Martin," Harding said.

"Too soon to know," Kyle said. "He didn't kill any children in Portland last night but there weren't any child murders with his signature in San Francisco either. Until we have another signature killing, we won't know where he is."

"What about the old man in the park? Have you found him yet?"

Kyle hesitated, reluctant to go down this road.

"No. Lots of old men with heart problems, none that admit to being in the park that night. Most with solid alibis."

"That looks like a dead end," Harding said. "Too bad, he might have seen Cradle Robber in the park."

"The old man showed up in the suburbs," Kyle said reluctantly. "Same description as the man in the park—overcoat, hat . . . blue tinge to the skin."

Harding sighed heavily at the mention of the man's skin color.

"He helped save two children from drowning. He left when the paramedics arrived but he left another note."

Kyle put a copy of the note on Harding's desk, then sat down, waiting for the captain to read the note. Harding didn't move, eyes locked on Kyle. Then he slowly rocked forward, put his glasses on, and read. When he finished, he took his glasses off and leaned back in his chair again.

"You said the kids didn't die?" Harding asked.

"One's fine, the other is in a coma."

"So this note is wrong too?" Harding said. "Kyle, I agree with Danforth on this. This has nothing to do with Cradle Robber. It's damn strange, but it's a dead end. This old guy probably keeps a computer in his car and runs these notes off in a couple of minutes."

"How does he know where to be? He keeps showing up in the nick of time."

"You don't know that. You don't know what would happen if he wasn't there—you're starting to believe those notes. Sommers, a transient fell into the Willamette last night and drowned and a woman died in a car accident on the Interstate Bridge. That old man didn't show up in time to stop those. There weren't any notes mixing up fact and fiction. I can't explain how the old man—if it is one man— can be at all these accidents but I don't want you wasting your time on this. Keep it in the task force if you want but delegate it. Give it to McKenzie. He's so warped he might make sense of it."

Then and there Kyle decided not to tell Harding about what Nolan had seen under the man's coat or that the blue color could spread to another person.

"I won't let it distract me," Kyle said. "But since the old man was in the park with the Martin girls I want to keep looking for him."

"Fine," Harding said.

Kyle went over the rest of what the investigators had found, which was nothing, then left still wondering what all Danforth and Harding had talked about.

An hour later Mac came to get him for a late lunch but Kyle declined. The Coney Island from Roakes was still heavy in his stomach. Instead, he stayed at his desk, reviewing the files on Cradle Robber. He had two filing cabinets full of material sent from California. Kyle had read it all before and like the detectives in the other victims' cities could discern no pattern other than Cradle Robber's victims were usually young children.

Apparently Cradle Robber selected his victims randomly, stalking them, learning their patterns, and looking for an opportunity. When he saw his opening, he smothered his victims, leaving a baby toy in their hand. After four or five killings in a city, he would move on. There was precious little physical evidence—a shirt button, which may or may not be his and which was so common it was used on tens of thousands of shirts a year—footprints matching size eleven men's shoes, the sole of which belonged to the second most popular sneaker in the country—a few hairs, one blond, three brown for which there was no genetic match in the FBI's national DNA databank. There was no reliable physical description, unless you included the old man who showed up in Pier Park. Every clue had been explored exhaustively, leaving Kyle nothing to follow but well-worn trails. Then Mac showed up, plopping into the victim's chair.

"I have a theory about why the old man is leaving these notes," Mac announced.

"Great. Why?"

"He thinks he's the Lone Ranger."

"You want to explain that?"

"Didn't you ever watch the *Lone Ranger*?"

"I'm not that old," Kyle said.

"Me neither," Mac said quickly "My mother told me about it. Anyway, every week the Lone Ranger and Tonto would show up and help Ma and Pa save the farm from evil cattlemen or rescue a damsel in distress. Then at the end of the show he would sneak off before anyone could thank him. When they discovered he was gone someone always asked 'Who was that masked man?' and someone else would say, 'I don't know, but he left this,' and they would have one of the Lone Ranger's silver bullets in their hand."

"And your point is?" Kyle asked.

"Those notes are the blue guy's silver bullets."

"A signature?"

"Exactly," Mac said.

"So how does he know where and when a crime or accident is going to happen?"

"I figured out the note thing for you, now you want me to do the rest of your job?" Then after a pause, Mac added, "He's psychic, of course."

"Not a genie?"

"Don't be ridiculous, there's no such thing as a genie."

"But there are people who can see the future?"

"It's been done since Bible times," Mac said. "Remember Joseph who got thrown in jail because Pharaoh's wife had the hots for him? He got himself out of hot water with Pharaoh by telling the future."

"He was a dream interpreter, not a prophet, and it wasn't Pharaoh's wife, it was Potiphar's wife—he was captain of the guard. Besides, if Joseph had really been able to see the future, he would have known Egypt would turn his people into slaves and not brought them there in the first place."

"So I got a few facts mixed up. There are a lot more examples in the Bible," Mac said.

"How would you know?"

"Rita was telling me," Mac said, embarrassed.

"Prove it, Mac. Show me someone who can foretell the future and then I'll believe it."

Mac leaned forward, tapping on the notes Kyle had assembled on his desk.

"There's your proof. We just have to catch him."

"But if this guy really can see the future then he knows whether we catch him or not and if he knows how we catch him then he'll make sure it doesn't happen," Kyle said.

Mac leaned back in the chair, staring at Kyle.

"Good point," Mac conceded. "So if he can see the future, there's no chance of catching him."

"Not if he's all-knowing."

Mac was quiet again, reviewing his theory, looking for a way out of the corner he'd backed himself into.

"Try this," Mac said. "The old man isn't all-knowing or else he would have been on the right Applewood Court when he went to save the Sadler children. He should have also known that Carolynn Martin needed to be saved twice that night, not just once. He's fallible, just like people without the gift of prophecy. That means we can find him and use him to catch Cradle Robber."

Now Kyle leaned forward, speaking softly to Mac. With a cubicle, there was no door to close.

"Mac, six months ago I was one step away from being committed. The meds they had me on would knock out a Clydesdale. I can't take any of this to the captain. You saw how he reacted at the task force meeting. This kind of stuff sounds crazy to anyone but you and Rita. I can't use it."

"Does it sound crazy to you?" Mac asked.

Kyle didn't answer.

"Then don't take it to the captain, but until you get a break in the case follow the leads you have."

Mac was an unusual man, whom most would call odd. But he was gifted with exceptional interpersonal skills and a knack for thinking outside the box. Despite his comic persona, even Captain Harding valued his input.

"Sherlock Holmes once said to Watson, 'When you have eliminated the possible, whatever remains, however improbable, must be the truth,' " Mac said. "Don't be too sure what was impossible yesterday is impossible today."

Mac left then, leaving Kyle to his puzzle. Picking up the paper with the notes taped on them, he thought about what Mitch Nolan had said about "not believing in that stuff . . . prophecy, ESP, time travel" until the old man had come running up his street. Could someone actually know what was going to happen before it did? Kyle decided it was time to start eliminating the impossible. Picking up his phone book he flipped the pages to "Portland State University," looking to see if they had a physics department.

14

Peter

Tuesday, 3:35 P.M.

"Peter," his mother had called him when she brought him in for dinner. The boy was about six, redheaded and hyperactive, pulling two neighbor boys in a wagon up and down the sidewalk, twisting and turning, giving them a jerky ride that made them laugh uncontrollably. The boys riding in the wagon were possibles but Peter's joy made him stand out. Laughing and giggling, he played exuberantly, enjoying every moment, returning home only after repeated insistent calls from his mother. The little boy would never be happier than he had been that day and so his heart went out to Peter. The little boy had no idea of the pain ahead of him and the best thing for Peter was to never know. Like a ripe apple, Peter was ready to be picked.

Today he visited Peter's neighborhood one last time, finishing his plan. Peter lived in a new development, a mix of single- and two-story frame houses. The homes had two-car garages, red brick accents across the front, and were painted in one of four pastel colors. Half the homes had minivans parked in their driveways and there were tricycles, bicycles, basketball hoops, balls, and batting tees in yards up and down the street. It was a young neighborhood with young families and even the trees and shrubs were barely out of infancy.

It helped that Peter's family didn't own a dog and although

they lived in a two-story house—usually difficult to enter—it was on a corner lot and there was a back porch with a trellis on one end, making the second story accessible. Peter's room was in the back, he had seen the boy from the sidewalk, bouncing on his bed only his head visible from the street. The house behind Peter's was one story, so the neighbors couldn't see over the fence, and the house next door had no windows on the side facing Peter's house. He passed the house one last time, walking briskly through the neighborhood, looking for details he had missed. Peter was out again for some after-school play, this time throwing a Nerf football back and forth with one of the neighbor boys, dropping the ball more often than not. It didn't matter, the game continued, Peter as enthusiastic and confident after his twentieth drop as he had been when the game began.

It was a good last afternoon for a little boy.

15

Professor Lipke

Portland State University was hard to distinguish from the city that surrounded it since there was no real boundary to the campus, no open quads, and very few green spaces. Even the tennis courts were on the top of a high-rise building, making ball chasing as much exercise as playing. PSU was an urban campus and urban to excess, blending seamlessly into the city's core of office towers and retail complexes. Kyle was on the campus before he realized the buildings he passed were part of the university. He stopped five young people before he found a student who could direct him to the Physics Department.

The building housing the Physics Department was indistinguishable from the other forty-year-old buildings making up the core of the campus and the entire Physics Department took up only half of one floor including labs and office space. Business management was the most popular major at Portland State University, and physics merely a support department helping students fulfill general education requirements. There were only three physicists on faculty and they did triple duty teaching math and engineering as well as physics. Kyle knew nothing about any of the faculty, so he wandered the hall, stopping at the first occupied office. The tiny office was cluttered from floor to ceiling with copies of articles, books, files, and stacks of papers. There was a man at a desk typing on a keyboard, his back to the door.

"Excuse me, are you Professor Lipke?" Kyle asked, using the name on the door.

The man turned his head but his hands continued to type on the keyboard.

"What is it?" Lipke responded.

Kyle had come tentatively, embarrassed by what he planned to ask, but the man's attitude set Kyle off and he found himself reaching for his badge, flashing it in the professor's face. Now Professor Lipke's fingers ran their course on the keyboard and he turned to face Kyle. The professor was bald with a gray fringe of hair and a gray goatee. His head was lightbulb-shaped and he looked very much the part of a head-in-the-stars intellectual.

"I'm Detective Sommers and I have a couple of questions," Kyle said.

"If it's about one of my students I can't talk about them. Federal law protects student privacy."

"It's not about a student. These are technical questions. About physics."

"Physics? What would a detective need to know about physics?"

Kyle couldn't think of a preamble for his questions that made any sense, so he steeled himself and jumped in.

"What do you know about things like ESP and time travel?"

Lipke's face showed his disdain and his lips puckered before he spoke.

"Are you writing a book?" Lipke asked suspiciously.

"I'm not a writer. I'm trying to track down someone who may believe in these things and I thought the more I know the better chance I have of finding him."

Clearly Lipke didn't believe his story and he responded acidly.

"I get pestered with this kind of nonsense at least once a

month. Some would-be science fiction writer will poke his head in the door looking for free help to make his drivel more credible. I'll tell you what I tell them. ESP is pseudo-scientific crap and that's being kind. Psychics are charlatans and grifters, no better than the crooked carney working his rigged games at a county fair."

"But there are well-known psychics—" Kyle began.

"Nonsense. You bring one of those so-called psychics in here, under controlled conditions, and I'll expose them in ten minutes."

"And time travel?"

"Impossible."

"There's a lot of speculation about time travel. I've heard some credible people talk about the possibility."

"They're idiots. Look, the arrow of time is as much a part of the fabric of the universe as is entropy and gravity. The universe moves from the present to the future and the past does not exist except in physical record. You can't reverse the arrow and you can't move ahead of the arrow. Time is a constant like the speed of light and can't be altered, superceded, or bypassed. Like it or not all you can experience is the present."

Lipke spoke forcefully and finished with a glare, daring Kyle to ask another stupid question. When he didn't Lipke said, "Do you want to ask me about faster-than-light travel? That's impossible too."

"No, but thanks for your time."

Lipke turned back to his keyboard and was typing again before Kyle was out the door.

Walking slowly through the streets, Kyle tried to find a logical explanation for the notes the man-in-the-hat was delivering. He stopped in Pioneer Square, buying a cup of coffee and sitting, watching the passersby. The usual crowd of street kids were gathered on one side of the square, sitting under the fake Greek pillars. A boom box played a loud mix of twang, screech, and unintelligible vocalization. Their clothes were loose and black, their skin decorated with tattoos, their bodies pierced in multiple places, their hair dyed. He recognized a few of the teens, knowing their street names—Boxer, Pinky, Razor, and Willow. They had been busted before, mostly for drugs, but also for disorderly conduct and assault. There were two or three kids in the group he didn't recognize, their bodies the least mutilated. In six months the new ones would be indistinguishable from the rest.

Kyle had never worked the juvenile gang unit but knew the frustration of the officers who did. Most of the public believed street kids were fleeing abusive homes but in fact the abuse in most homes amounted to parents who expected their children to be home at a reasonable time, not use drugs, and to limit the number of holes they poked in their bodies. Preferring a life of no restrictions and no responsibility, these kids fled their homes, dropped out of school, and now lived on the street, supported by teen shelters that provided food, toiletries, medical care, clean needles, and the occasional abortion. The police who patrolled the square often complained the shelters did more harm than good. If the support for their street life dried up, the teens would either move to a city that would support them or go home, either of which would be better for Portland.

A shoving match broke out now, Razor squaring off with one of the new teens. Kyle stood, ready to intervene before it escalated but then saw two uniformed officers enter the square. Immediately the fight ended. The boom box was turned off, their few belongings gathered, and the teens melted into the crowd. The officers followed the teens onto the street, making sure they moved on. Kyle thought about the scuffle and the man-in-the-hat and wondered if Razor had pulled the weapon that gave him his street name, would the man-in-the-hat have shown up just in time to stop the fight? Or weren't the street kids worth his help? Were there limits on how good this Good Samaritan was?

Finishing his coffee, Kyle walked slowly back to the station, then circulated between the task force detectives, encouraging, problem solving, collecting information—nothing useful. Danforth was civil but reserved, forcing Kyle to dig for information. Finally, Kyle was back in his cubicle, clearing his e-mail. Then Kyle started through the Cradle Robber files again.

"Go home, Kyle, I've seen healthier-looking people in the morgue," Mac said, leaning into Kyle's cubicle.

"Inspector Segal will be here tomorrow, I want to be up on the files."

"You know her files better than she does. Go home and get some sleep."

Kyle wanted to keep working, but knew Mac wouldn't leave until Kyle was out of the building, so Kyle gave up. If he couldn't sleep, he would come back later.

Mac mothered him to the elevator, making sure he didn't take any files with him. Once out of the parking garage, Kyle turned toward the gym but found himself thinking about the obnoxious physics professor. Lipke was rigid and dogmatic, lacking the creativity needed to be a good detective or, Kyle suspected, a good researcher. Lipke was probably good at coloring within the lines but give him a blank page and he wouldn't know where to begin. Kyle needed someone to help him draw on that blank page. Remembering his conversation with Mitch Nolan, Kyle pulled the business card from his pocket for the address of Mitch's sister.

16

Sherrie Nolan

Tuesday, 6:07 P.M.
Mitch Nolan's sister lived in Northwest Portland, a short
drive from the Justice Center. It was an old neighborhood,
saved from the urban decay when it became popular with
yuppies and the gay community. Faddish specialty restaurants and boutiques had replaced the Coast to Coast Hard-
ware, Coronet Five, Ten and Twenty-Five Cent Store, and
Rexall Drug that had been the core of the business district
thirty years before. Many of the old homes had been remodeled into specialty stores selling upscale clothing. The reju-
venation had saved this particular subcommunity from
oblivion but the renewal wasn't as thorough as it looked on
the surface. The neighborhood had the second-highest violent
crime rate in the city. Assault and robbery were common and
the burglary rate was nearly twice the city average. Worse,
a serial rapist had been working the northwest side for the
last six months. It was a neighborhood fighting for its life,
the outcome still undecided.

The nearest parking space was two blocks from Sherrie
Nolan's home, Kyle enjoying the short walk although the air
quality was poor. The air was thick with haze, as if a grass
fire were burning through the city. The sun was still bright,
but the blue sky was tinted brown. Nolan's neighborhood
had a welcoming feel. The trees were stately—eighty years
old he guessed—with late-spring foliage. The sidewalk was

uneven with heaves created by the massive roots burrowed underneath. The homes on both sides of the street wore fresh paint. There were no garages. The Rose City Trolley was still running when these homes were built and no one then would have owned a car when they could ride the trolley for a nickel.

Sherrie Nolan's house was in the middle of the block and was a two-story like the rest, although it was bigger than average, the queen of the block. These weren't the cookie cutter houses of her brother's neighborhood, each house here was an individually designed home. Going up the short walk, Kyle saw part of the porch had been removed and a ramp installed that zigzagged down from the entrance level to the sidewalk level. Kyle used the steps, ringing the bell and then knocking when no one answered. Kyle repeated the doorbell and knocking routine a couple of times, then walked back toward his car. He was halfway up the block when a woman in a wheelchair came around the corner, moving fast.

The wheelchair was bright red, built low, with the back wheels toed in at the top. The woman driving the wheels had no lower legs, the amputation on both legs just above the knees. She wore a white tank top over a gray sports bra and her arms were muscular with the definition of a bodybuilder. Her cheeks were red from exertion, her skin deeply tanned. Her eyes were dark and she wore her black hair cut short in a severe look. Sweat plastered her shirt to her body and Kyle found himself admiring her breasts, then suddenly feeling embarrassed that he would look at a handicapped woman that way. The woman turned her wheelchair down Sherrie Nolan's walk. Kyle caught up to her as she wheeled her chair up the ramp.

"Sherrie Nolan?" Kyle asked, holding out his badge.

"What do you want?" Sherrie snapped with all the friendliness of Professor Lipke.

"I'm Detective Sommers and I wonder if I could ask you a couple of questions."

"No. I don't know anything about my neighbors that I'd tell you and if it's about that asshole raping his way through the neighborhood you don't have to worry about me. I'm not his type—I'm a cripple."

Sherrie Nolan's tongue dripped acid and she couldn't have been any colder. Kyle wanted to tell her there were rapists who specialized in every type of woman—over eighty, amputees, obese—but knew she wouldn't listen.

"Your brother Mitch gave me your name."

Sherrie finished unlocking her front door with a key she wore on a chain around her neck, then turned back to Kyle.

"How do you know Mitch?"

"I met him after he helped save the Sadler children from drowning."

"Mitch saved someone from drowning?"

She was honestly surprised and it took a little of the edge out of her voice. Then with a shrug she said, "You can come in if you want, but you'll have to wait while I shower."

Kyle followed her in, surprised by the interior. The door opened into a short hallway with a closet. The hallway opened to a living room on one side and a dining room on the other. The rooms were furnished like the interior decorator was someone's grandmother, not a young woman. There were knickknacks on the mantel over the fireplace, overstuffed furniture with doilies on the arms of the chairs and sofa, and more doilies on the end tables. The lamp shades had fringe and there was a grandfather clock in the hall. The look reminded Kyle of his aunt's home. Straight ahead were stairs that made a sharp angle right after four steps. The bottom steps were covered with a platform and a more traditional wheelchair was parked there. Sherrie rolled to the platform, turned her chair sideways, and dropped the side of the wheelchair. Then she slid onto the platform, and using her arms to lift herself step by step up the stairs, disappeared up to the second floor without another word. Soon Kyle heard the sound of a shower.

Kyle wandered around the first floor, looking at the knick-knacks, noticing those above chest level were dusty and those below were not. The dining-room table was covered with a crocheted tablecloth over a blue liner, a well-polished silver tea set in the middle. The kitchen table was chrome and Formica with matching chairs, something that hadn't been manufactured since the 1950s. The only anachronism in the house was in the living room where there was a thirty-five-inch television in an entertainment unit. Speakers from a surround sound system were mounted on the walls of the small living room. There were stacks of DVDs and video-cassettes on one side of the unit and Kyle opened the glass door, looking through the titles. There were exercise videos, a few *National Geographic* specials, and a handful of animated Christmas cartoons. The bulk of the videos were musicals and the collection was impressive. *Oklahoma, Gigi, Singing in the Rain, Blue Skies, Grease*, and two dozen others were packed in the unit. Kyle put the videos back as he'd found them, then sat on the flowered couch to wait.

After a few minutes the shower noise ended and soon he heard a blow dryer. After another few minutes he heard Sherrie Nolan thumping down the stairs. Kyle stood as she hand-walked to the edge of the platform, then pushed the racing chair out of the way and pulled the other wheelchair next to her. After she climbed into the chair, she rolled to the kitchen without a word to Kyle. He heard the refrigerator open and close. Then she was back, a bottle of Snapple in her hand. Her hair was dry, but unkempt, like she'd combed it with her fingers. She wore a pair of shorts, her bare legs ending in the scar tissue where her lower legs had been removed. She wore a T-shirt and no bra and again Kyle was embarrassed when his eyes were drawn to her body. Sherrie caught him looking so Kyle pretended he was looking at the drink in her hand.

"No thanks, I don't want anything," Kyle said.

"I didn't ask you here," Sherrie said. "You're only here because my brother sent you."

"Fine, I'll get to the point."

"First, tell me about my brother and the children he saved," she ordered.

Sherrie's persona was as hard as steel and Kyle's every word like flint, striking sparks. He told the story of the near drownings hoping to get past Sherrie's impenetrable exterior. Sherrie listened attentively, sipping her Snapple—it was Black Cherry. Kyle stopped the story before he mentioned the note her brother found in his neighbor's mail.

"You want to know how that old man knew the kids were drowning," Sherrie said when Kyle finished.

"There's more but what I'm going to show you is confidential," Kyle said, taking a copy of the latest note from his pocket.

Since Harding had decided the notes were unrelated to Cradle Robber, Kyle could argue they didn't need to be confidential. Still he could get fired for sharing evidence.

"We think the man left this for your brother to find."

Kyle handed her a copy of the note, watching her eyes light up as she read.

"You should know that this same man has shown up two other times—at an accident and at the scene of a rape—he left similar notes."

"And what happened was different than what is written in these?" Sherrie asked, holding up the note.

"Yes."

"What are your questions?" Sherrie asked abruptly.

Embarrassed, Kyle said, "Your brother said I should ask you about ESP or time travel."

Now Sherrie smiled but she wasn't laughing at him, she was enjoying his embarrassment. Kyle decided to get it all on the table.

"Someone else said a genie might be doing this."

"Really," Sherry said, amused. "Why is that?"

"They said that only genies have the power to alter the human time line. Something about the Universal Blue Jinn. That's another thing you should know. Witnesses who have seen the man who's dropping these notes say his skin is tinged blue."

"Blue?" Sherrie repeated, now serious.

"And when he touches people the blue spreads to them."

"That's interesting," Sherrie said, eyes wide, her face softer.

"Your brother also said his arm tingled where he was touched by this blue man."

"Curiouser, and curiouser," Sherrie said. "It can mean only one thing."

"What?"

"It's time to order Chinese food."

"I just need a little information—" Kyle started.

"You came to me for help," Sherrie said sharply. "I need to know everything you know."

"I can't talk about an ongoing case," Kyle said.

"Then get out!" Sherrie snapped, completing the mood shift from tolerant to angry.

Kyle locked eyes with Sherrie, his own anger rising in response to hers, but giving anger for anger wouldn't get him anywhere with this woman.

"I like sesame chicken," he said finally.

"Add some fried rice and chow mein."

"Egg roll?"

"Of course."

"I'll buy," Kyle said.

"You got that right," Sherrie said. "The number's on the bulletin board by the phone in the kitchen."

The phone was baby blue with a rotary dial. When Kyle got back from ordering the food Sherrie was upstairs again. She came down fifteen minutes later, her hair combed, wearing makeup and in different clothes. She wore a blouse now, and stretch pants that covered her stumps. Kyle also noticed she was wearing a bra and was disappointed until he remembered her legs and then silently cursed himself for his insensitivity.

Kyle was answering Sherrie's questions about the Carolynn Martin murder when the food arrived. Kyle expected to eat in the kitchen but Sherrie directed him to bring the food into the living room, sliding out of her chair onto the couch, then down to the floor, sitting with her half legs straight out, her back against the couch. Kyle put the food between them, then retrieved plates from the kitchen and a fork for himself, then sat next to her. Sherrie used the chopsticks that came with the food, expertly serving herself generous portions of rice and chow mein.

"Get me another Snapple, will you?" Sherrie said.

Kyle got up again, finding one refrigerator shelf filled with various flavors of the drink. Kyle grabbed two, an Iced Tea–flavored Snapple for Sherrie and a Black Cherry for himself. Back in the living room Sherrie was in front of the entertainment unit putting in a videotape. Then she dragged herself back to the couch with the remote in her lap. Kyle settled in next to her, putting the Iced Tea Snapple next to her on the floor. Holding his drink out where she would see it, he opened it and drank noisily. She ignored him, a slight smile marking the corner of her mouth. Then she turned on the television, powered up the surround sound system, and started the videotape.

The movie was *The Unsinkable Molly Brown* and started with a raft accident, the only survivor an infant that toddled out of the river. They ate in silence watching the movie, Kyle impressed with Sherrie's appetite as she finished her first helping and then reloaded her plate. Kyle had never seen the movie before and found Debbie Reynolds's overacting amusing and her voice outstanding. Molly Brown's husband had just burned all their money in a stove when Sherrie decided they had eaten their fill and turned off the video asking Kyle to continue his story.

Putting the rest of his food aside, Kyle finished with the Carolynn Martin case, describing the old man, his color, and the subsequent murder. Sherrie listened attentively, asking questions like a detective. When she ran out of questions he moved on to receiving the notes that described the murder of the Kirkland girl that never happened, and the truck accident that missed the Browns. He then went on to the incident with the Sadler children where Kyle had met Sherrie's brother. Kyle described Mitch's role in heroic terms, not needing to exaggerate.

"Let me see the other notes," Sherrie said.

"I didn't bring them."

"Fax them to me," Sherrie said sharply.

Kyle felt as if he were being dismissed, the little warmth Sherrie had shown while she listened was gone, the steel exterior slowly being pulled across like a jewelry-store security gate at closing time.

"You want me to go downtown and fax you evidence I shouldn't even have told you about?" Kyle said, making it sound as inconvenient as possible.

"I can see why they made you a detective."

Sherrie wasn't smiling, her security screen in place again.

"Your place isn't much out of my way. Why don't I just drop the copies by?"

"I need time to research this."

"The library is closed," Kyle said.

"Ever hear of the Internet?" Sherrie snapped.

Sherrie lifted herself up onto the couch and then into her wheelchair, the pleasant living-room picnic clearly over. Kyle stood, finding he was reluctant to leave. At her warmest moment she had merely been tolerant of Kyle and occasionally amused by him. Her demeanor had never approached "friendly" so he didn't know why he wanted to stay, except that he had no place else to go.

"Give me your fax number," Kyle said reluctantly.

Kyle wrote the number down in the notebook he carried,

then noticed two fortune cookies in the bottom of the bag the food had come in. Kyle picked them up holding one out for Sherrie. Suddenly her cheeks reddened and her chin trembled. Snatching the cookie from his hand she crushed it in her fist, the pieces filtering through her fingers.

"I know my future," Sherrie said through clenched teeth. "It's to have my butt parked in one of these damn chairs for the rest of my life!"

By the well-healed scars he'd seen, and her expertise with the wheelchairs, it had been years since Sherrie had lost her legs, but she was still bitter.

"You'll get the fax within an hour," Kyle said.

Sherrie nodded, staying parked in the living room when he walked to the door. He heard the sound system turn on and Debbie Reynolds wailing about the burned money as he closed the door.

17

Used Car

Willie Mendez kept the stolen Lexus in the right lane and at
the speed limit, like his brother taught him. He was sandwiched between two semis heading north on I-5, five miles
from the safety of the Washington border. The Washington
police would impound the car if they caught him but the
state of Oregon wouldn't pay the extradition costs of a car
thief, so at worst he would spend a night in jail and miss a
day of school. He knew that, because it had happened to his
brother and his friends many times.

Willie passed the Killingsworth exit, counting down the
exits to go—Portland Boulevard, Lombard, Marine Drive.
Willie fought the urge to accelerate, cutting around the trucks
and racing to the state line. His brother had given him the
drill many times. "Not too fast, not too slow, and keep your
eyes on the road. You watch how people drive. They don't
go looking around all the time. They just drive and listen to
the radio—that's what you do."

The Lexus had a fine sound system, but the CDs were all
classical. Music—any noise—just gave Willie the jumps
anyway, so he drove in silence; the silence of a luxury car.
He was coming up on Hayden Island now and the Interstate
Bridge was just ahead. The cops worked this stretch of freeway, Willie's brother had told him, so watch your speed.
Willie checked the speedometer again, seeing he had drifted

up to sixty. He was keeping pace with the trucker ahead who was speeding now. Willie slowed slightly, seeing the other truck coming up behind, following too close. The sight of the truck looming in his rearview mirror unnerved him, so Willie changed into the center lane. Checking his mirror again he saw a car behind him with a police light bar mounted on the roof. Willie's foot twitched and he had to fight to keep from flooring it and racing to the bridge.

Willie wasn't like his brother, Alberto. Willie hated stealing cars. He hated being afraid all the time—afraid of the cops, afraid of being caught by an owner when he was boosting their car, afraid of Alberto's friends in the Brotherhood of the Rose and of their enemies. Willie liked school, he was good at math and thought about going into business or accounting. On career day there had been a speaker at school who was a certified public accountant and he talked to Willie about accounting. "People make jokes about accountants, Willie," Mr. Steiner had said, "but it's a good living. The CPAs in the big Portland firms are all making six figures and that doesn't include bonuses. You've got to start at the bottom, of course. In my firm young men like you have to travel quite a bit at first."

Mr. Steiner came to campus in a Mercedes and wore an expensive suit with a silk tie. He smelled slightly of cologne but to Willie it was the smell of money.

"I like to travel," Willie said.

"Wait until you spend a week in Walla Walla, then tell me that," Mr. Steiner had said and laughed. "Fairbanks in February is as bad as it gets in our region but then our territory includes Hawaii too. Here's what you do, Willie. You finish high school and then get into an accounting program at one of the local colleges. We've got a work-study program for minorities and you could work for the firm part-time and in the summers. Then if you've got what it takes you can go full-time and start working on passing the CPA exam."

"You serious, man?" Willie had said.

"Understand I'm not offering you a job, I'm offering you a chance to earn one," Mr. Steiner said.

Mr. Steiner took one of his business cards out of his pocket and wrote "A promising young man," on the back, then signed his name and gave it to Willie.

"If you graduate, and your grades are as good as you told me they are, then you bring this card and your transcript and you come see me in June. Then we'll talk seriously."

Willie kept Mr. Steiner's card hidden behind his dresser in his room. He never told his brother or mother about Mr. Steiner or of wanting to be an accountant. He thought his mother would be proud of him but she would tell Alberto and Willie didn't want his brother to know—not yet. Alberto had been good to him, taking him into the gang and into his business, looking out for him like a father would, but Alberto wanted him to drop out of school. Education was a dead end Alberto argued to his brother. Why keep your nose in a book when there is easy money to be made? Willie just couldn't follow his brother's path.

Now seeing the police car behind him he worried his dream of walking into Mr. Steiner's office with the business card would end with an arrest. Would anyone hire an accountant who was a thief? Whispering a prayer to the Virgin Mary, he promised her that if she protected him that this would be the last stolen car he ever delivered. Somehow, he would find the courage to tell Alberto he was finished. A light flashed in his rearview mirror and his head snapped to the mirror. It was the blinker on the police car. The cop was changing lanes, heading for the Jantzen Beach exit.

"Thank you, Mary," Willie prayed, "I will keep my promise."

Willie was on the bridge now, the Columbia River flowing beneath him, jets approaching Portland International Airport above. The water was black, reflecting the lights of the restaurants and motels lining the banks. Then he was across and into Vancouver, passing the "WELCOME TO WASHINGTON" sign. Willie took the Fourth Plain exit, driving to the warehouse where the cars were delivered. The warehouse door was open and the yellow light was on in the window telling him it was safe to enter. Willie pulled into the garage, the door closing behind him immediately. There were three other cars in the garage, one being disassembled, two being readied for painting. Montoya was there to meet him, as usual, and Willie got out quickly, anxious to hand over the keys.

"Tell your brother he still owes me two Cherokees," Montoya said, handing Willie an envelope filled with twenty-dollar bills.

Willie thumbed through the bills like Alberto had taught him. You didn't count the money in front of Montoya, that would insult the man. But you did a quick estimate. There was about four hundred dollars in the envelope, the going rate for a Lexus.

"Want a drink, man?" Montoya said.

"No, I got a history test tomorrow," Willie said.

Montoya laughed, then shouted to the other men in the garage.

"He's got a history test."

Everyone laughed. Willie stuffed the envelope in the pocket of his jacket and left, hurt by the laughter. It was two blocks to where Alberto had parked the car he would return in. Willie hurried. He was ready for the test but he wanted to get a few hours of sleep so he would do his best. Math grades were the most important to Willie, but colleges expected good grades in all subjects. Willie had never gotten less than a B and he didn't want his history class to be his first.

Willie was walking in an old neighborhood now, with rundown houses and overgrown shrubs. It was like his neighborhood, bordering on a commercial district and slowly decaying.

Willie saw the 1968 Chevy Impala. It had been red once, but now had patches of primer gray. It was the kind of car police expected someone like Willie to drive so he would have no trouble getting home. Willie inserted the key in the lock. Suddenly there were sounds around him. Men were coming—three or four. Willie twisted the key, pulling on the door handle. The door opened but as he hurried to get in, someone hit him in the kidney, the pain dropping him to his knees. A pillowcase was shoved over his head and then he was being kicked and punched from all sides. Curling into a ball to protect his face and genitals, the beating continued until he was nearly unconscious. When the pounding stopped he was left with throbbing pain. He was only semiconscious but he felt warm and wet. During the beating he had lost control of his bladder and wet himself. Now his hands were pulled behind him and taped together and he was lifted and thrown into a car. He could tell it was his brother's Impala because of the smell and the sound of the engine.

"Are you the police?" Willie asked when he could control his breathing.

They laughed at him.

"You got the wrong guy," Willie said, struggling not to cry.

"Shut up," a voice said, followed by a blow to his ribs.

Too scared to talk and hurting from head to toe, Willie kept quiet, terrified of what they were going to do to him. He wanted to pray again but he had been granted one favor that night—would asking for two be blasphemous? Terrified, he risked it and prayed that he would live through the night.

After an eternity the car slowed, then made several sharp turns. Then the sounds of the car changed like they had driven into a building. Willie was dragged from the car and the tape on his wrists replaced with rope. There were many hands on him and many voices. The air had a familiar stench he couldn't place and there was a constant hissing sound.

"Which one did you get?" someone asked.

"Is it Alberto?" another asked.

"Wait and see," said a voice close to Willie's ear.

Willie could hear the sounds of several people around him. Then Willie was lifted into the air, hanging by his hands, his arms taking the full weight of his body. His ribs ached; at least two broken.

"Please, don't hurt me anymore," Willie begged.

Suddenly the pillowcase was pulled from his head and Willie could see. There were six men in the room, ski masks covering their faces. He was hanging from a hoist in a garage, his feet six inches off the ground. The weight of his body made it difficult to breathe and when he did his broken ribs sent daggers of pain through his lungs.

"It's Alberto's brother," one of the men said.

"Look at that, he pissed his pants," another man said, pointing at his crotch.

The men laughed at him and then one spun him around.

"Let's see if he crapped them too," the man said.

Willie was spun around and around the men laughing and taunting. As he spun he saw there was a propane burner behind him and on it was a five-gallon can filled with a steaming black goo. Now he recognized the smell; it was tar.

"You're Psychlos," Willie said as they let go of him, letting him twist back to face them. "I know you're Psychlos. I never did nothing to you."

A big man in a black ski mask with red circles around the eyes and mouth stepped forward and punched Willie in the solar plexus. Willie gasped, unable to breathe. Then using Willie's body like a punching bag the man beat him from chest to groin. Willie was barely conscious when he finished.

"Now you listen and don't talk," the man said. "Tell Alberto that the Brotherhood is out of the used car business! Do you understand?"

"Please don't hurt me anymore," Willie managed to whisper.

Responding with a punch to Willie's broken ribs, the man said, "Do you understand?"

"Yes," Willie gasped. "No more stolen cars."

"Good boy," the man said, patting his cheek. "Now all we've got to do is wrap you up and return you."

Another man came and put duct tape over Willie's mouth and then the man with the red eyeholes nodded to the others who produced switchblades, coming at Willie. Willie tried to scream through the tape. The men cut at his clothing, stripping him to his underpants and then stopped, laughing at the wet front.

"I'm not touching those," one man said.

"Me neither, I don't want no greaser's piss on me," another said.

The man in the black ski mask stepped forward and slid his knife along Willie's hip into his underpants and cut the side. Then he cut the other side and the underpants dropped to the concrete floor.

"Give me the brush," the man in the black ski mask said.

One of the men produced a large paintbrush and handed it over.

"Turn him around, we'll start with the front."

They turned Willie toward the bubbling pot and the man dipped the brush in the tar, stepping in front of Willie's naked body.

"Remember, the Brotherhood is out of the used car business."

Willie struggled but hands held him. Then the brush with the liquid tar was slapped on his chest and his bruised and bloody body contorted with pain.

18

Peter's House

Wednesday, 1:37 A.M.

He drove through Peter's neighborhood twice, but thirty minutes apart so no one would notice the same car passing twice. He parked two blocks away, then walked back, wearing a blue-and-yellow windbreaker, trying to look like a middle-class insomniac out for a night walk. No cars passed him and the houses he passed were dark except for occasional dim night-lights. He passed Peter's house, then turned sharply, hoisting himself over the fence and dropping to the other side. He waited there, listening. Ten minutes had passed before he was sure he hadn't been seen. No neighbors had come to investigate or called to alert Peter's house and there were no distant sirens. He took off the windbreaker, dropping it by the fence. Now he was dressed in black jeans, black running shoes, and a black sweatshirt, all purchased at Kmart.

Keeping low and close to the wall of the house, he was nearly invisible and moved confidently to the back porch and the trellis. He would be exposed when he climbed and while on the roof but the happy redheaded boy sleeping inside was worth the risk. He climbed quickly, glad the trellis was relatively new, the thin slats still strong enough to support his weight. Once on the roof of the porch he hurried to Peter's window, pressing against the wall, studying the neighboring homes. The few windows facing him were dark.

Using a razor blade, he cut the nylon fabric out of the screen and then examined Peter's window. It was double-paned—they all were in the newer neighborhoods—and the slide lock was in place, the rod down into its slot in the frame. There was no alarm system. Fabric curtains decorated with rocket ships were drawn. Through the space between the two curtains, and in the soft glow of a night-light, he could see Peter in his bed. Taking a suction cup he attached it to the corner of the window, then cut the glass with his cutter making a hole a little bigger than his fist. His glass cutting was well practiced and the outer pane came out on the first try. Placing the glass on the porch roof he made sure it wouldn't slide and then put the suction cup on the second pane, cutting a slightly smaller section. It took two passes with the cutter this time, but then he had the glass free and pulled it straight out, placing it gently next to the first piece.

Now he reached through the hole and pulled the curtain aside, creating a larger gap so he could study the room. Peter was still sound asleep, the door to his room half closed, no light coming from the hall. Reaching through he lifted the slide lock. Then using a ruler, he put his arm in, reaching the latch with the ruler and pressed, pulling on the window at the same time. The window slid open a few inches. Now he paused again, checking on Peter to make sure he still slept. Then he leaned in and looked straight down to see what he would be stepping on. Like most of the children's rooms he had entered, the floor was cluttered with toys. Peter also had a small fish tank sitting on a table under the window. Sliding the window open wide now, he stepped in, careful to clear the fish tank and table. Carefully, he pulled his other leg through the window, then stepped over a Tonka dump truck to the side of Peter's bed.

The little boy was snoring softly, lying on his side, turned toward the wall. Pulling a piece of clear plastic from his pocket, he stroked the side of the sleeping boy's face. Peter turned in response, rolling onto his back. There was an angelic quality to sleeping children and he enjoyed these moments. For a few precious seconds he flashed back to watching his own son sleep.

Peter stirred, ending the moment. The sleeping boy smacked his lips a few times and then began to roll to his side. Quickly he pressed the plastic to Peter's face, holding it tight. The plastic sealed Peter's nose and mouth, freezing him in his angelic look. Like the others, Peter's eyes popped open in surprise and then in terror. He never looked at their eyes when they were like this. Sitting next to the boy now, pressing his body close, keeping his eyes averted, he ignored the boy's feeble efforts to push the plastic from his face. Peter clawed at the plastic but it was thick and his small fingers couldn't puncture it. Now Peter slapped and clawed at his head but he kept low. The children always fought and he took the minor pain stoically. They didn't understand the gift he was giving them.

"It will be over soon, Peter," he whispered. "It's better this way. They'll never be able to hurt you now."

Peter was a strong boy and struggled long and hard. He winced when the boy found his hair and turned his head to protect his eyes when Peter probed for them. Still he kept the plastic tight and the breathing passages sealed. Now the boy's flailing became unfocused and weaker. He was losing consciousness.

"Go to sleep, Peter. Go to sleep."

Suddenly the doorbell rang, over and over, nonstop. Then he heard voices from another room. Now there was pounding from downstairs and shouting.

"What is going on?" he heard a man mutter nearby and then the sound of someone walking down the stairs.

Peter was nearly gone, but his legs and arms were still twitching. He needed a few more seconds with the boy. He held the plastic tight, trapped between his need to help Peter and the importance of not getting caught so he could help others. Then he heard a gasp behind him.

Peter's mother launched herself with a fury, screaming as she charged. Reflexively he released one side of the plastic, swinging his elbow up and back to meet the charge. Peter's mother took the elbow in the face, breaking her nose and stunning her. She collapsed to her knees, giving him the few seconds he needed with Peter. It was too late. Peter had pushed up one side of the plastic, and was gasping for air, about to cry. He didn't have another three minutes to save Peter. Peter's mother was screaming for help, getting to her feet, her nose bleeding profusely. He leapt for the window and was climbing out when he heard heavy footsteps pounding up the stairs.

He hurried to the edge of the porch, then paused. In the distance he could see flashing blue lights. The police were already on their way but he didn't understand how. Peter's parents couldn't have called them. Not this quickly.

He squatted and jumped, catching the gutter with his hands to slow his fall. He rolled when he hit, coming up running, vaulting Peter's back fence and racing through the next yard. Thankfully, there was no dog, only a cat that slithered under a bush. He jumped the next fence and then ducked behind a bush as a car passed. Then he was out onto the sidewalk and running. If he saw car lights he would cut into a yard but he could make better time on pavement.

He saw no one in his sprint to his truck but as he climbed inside he saw the flashing blue of the police car. He flattened on the front seat, reaching underneath for his guns, hand resting on the shotgun. The police car was coming silently, as if they didn't know he had been in another child's room. Suddenly the siren came on, the police car accelerating. Alternating blue and red lights lit up the interior as the car passed. He hid until the car was dark again, then sat up and started the engine. Pulling away from the curb slowly, he fought the urge to race to safety. It was only a few blocks to a feeder street and then a few more to a freeway entrance. There would be traffic there, even at this time of night.

Two blocks later he came to a four-way stop, a car coming from the right, reaching the intersection before him. With barely a pause, the car crossed in front of him. The driver wore a large hat, triggering a memory. He had seen the man before—first in the park when he had ministered to Carolynn Martin and then again outside Wendy's house. Could it be the same man? It couldn't be a coincidence.

Reaching under the seat, he pulled out the pistol and put it in his lap. Then he turned left, following the man-in-the-hat.

19

Witnesses

Wednesday, 2:12 A.M.

After faxing copies of the notes to Sherrie, Kyle went to the gym, lifting weights for an hour and then running the tread-mill for another thirty minutes. He skipped the bar afterward, afraid he would add vodka to his orange juice instead of creatine. He was home by eleven and staring at his cracked and peeling bedroom ceiling by midnight. He would rather be pacing the floor but knew it would bring another call from Mrs. Pastorini. She might even make a rare trip up the stairs with a cup of warm milk.

Sleep was increasingly elusive for Kyle. Tonight he split the blame for his insomnia between worrying whether Cradle Robber would strike and the puzzle of the old man and the notes. He also found himself thinking about Sherrie Nolan and the way she had looked in her sweat-soaked tank top. Then he would see the scarred stumps of her legs and alter-nating waves of revulsion and guilt would sweep him.

By one he had dozed but then a peal of thunder woke him. Getting up he looked out. The night was sultry, a few stars showing feebly through the haze. A few minutes later he heard another boom, seeing a flash of light but no lightning bolt—sheet lightning? He went back to bed, staring at the ceiling, listening for the patter of rain on the roof. He fell asleep waiting for rain that never came.

When the phone rang he was ripped from deep sleep to

consciousness. He was holding the phone to his ear before he was coherent enough to say "Hello." His stomach knotted as his mind cleared. He knew the phone call would be about Cradle Robber. The clock glowed 2:12 A.M.

"Sorry, Kyle, it's Art Michelson. I promise I won't make a habit of waking you like this."

"Is it Cradle Robber?" Kyle said impatiently.

"Yes," Michelson said.

Kyle pulled the phone from his ear, holding back the tears that welled up. With a deep breath he put the phone back to his ear and heard Michelson still talking.

". . . anyway, he survived and we have a witness."

"Say it again, Art. I didn't hear what you said."

"Which part."

"Everything."

"I said Cradle Robber attacked a little boy but his mother caught him in the act and stopped him. The little boy survived and got a look at Cradle Robber. I'm afraid he's too young to give much of a description—just six years old. The good news is that the mother saw him too."

Kyle was at once relieved and elated. For the first time Cradle Robber had failed to kill his victim and they had witnesses.

"Give me the address," Kyle said.

Michelson did and then said, "That's the Benchlys' home address but if you want to talk to them right away they're at Emmanuel Hospital. I'm heading there now."

"I'll meet you," Kyle said, hanging up before Michelson could say good-bye. Jumping into his clothes, he hurried to his truck. A blue spark shot from his key to the lock as he inserted it, this one powerful enough for Kyle to feel. Kyle paused, looking at the sky. A glowing band of light was clearly visible now, even through the hazy sky. There was a rumble in the distance, but no lightning. On another night he might have taken time to enjoy the unusual sky.

Michelson was standing outside the emergency entrance

when Kyle arrived, turning toward the door to fall in next to Kyle as he hurried through the entrance.

"They're waiting for us," Michelson said. "The mother's name is Rhonda and the father is Larry Benchly. The little boy is Peter. The doctor has released them to go home but they're too scared. They're going to his mother's house for the night. He says he won't move back into their house until they have security grates on the windows."

"Good," Kyle said.

A uniformed officer stood with the couple and their son, the boy sitting on the exam table with his mother, head in her lap. He wore blue pajamas, the kind with feet in them. The mother had on a long coat and he could see the collar of a pink nightgown poking out the top. There were bloodstains on the collar. The father was dressed in slacks and a sweatshirt. The mother was redheaded like the boy, the father with advanced male pattern balding. The mother's nose was bandaged and one eye was swollen and purple. Her lip was puffy and split, the seam crusted with a thin line of blood.

"Thank you for waiting for me," Kyle said, holding out his badge. "I'm Detective Sommers and I'm heading up the Cradle Robber Task Force."

The Benchlys were polite but reserved. Peter sat up and wrapped himself around his mother, glancing furtively at Kyle.

"I know you've spoken to other officers but would you mind telling me what happened?" Kyle said kindly. "Sometimes when you tell a story over you remember more details."

"My wife will have to tell most of it. I never saw the sonofabitch," Larry Benchly sputtered. "But if I ever get hold of that sonofabitch I'll kill him."

Larry was a pudgy man, soft-looking, despite his righteous anger.

"Larry, watch your language," his wife scolded, indicating Peter was listening.

"Sorry," Larry said, still seething.

"We were sound asleep when someone started ringing the doorbell and pounding on our front door," Rhonda said.

Kyle's heart beat a little faster. Michelson hadn't said anything about someone waking the Benchlys up. Kyle looked at Michelson who shrugged his shoulders.

"I went down to see who the hell it was," Larry said, his wife wincing at the mild profanity.

Clearly swearing wasn't normally part of Larry's vocabulary. He was trying to sound street tough. The swearing didn't help.

"I looked through the window and there was some maniac pounding on the door yelling at me," Larry said. "Then I heard my wife scream and I went tearing up the stairs. When I got there she was holding Peter and the sonofabitch was gone. She'll have to tell you the rest."

"When Larry went to answer the door I went across the hall to check on Peter," Rhonda said, squeezing the boy closer as she remembered. "I opened the door and there was a man on top of Peter holding plastic against his face."

Kyle looked to Michelson.

"We have the plastic and a coat we found in the yard," Michelson said.

Kyle's heart raced. This incident was a treasure trove of evidence.

"I screamed and I ran right at him," Rhonda said.

"She would have killed the sonofabitch," Larry cut in.

"But he hit me in the face and knocked me down," she said, touching her nose gingerly. "He broke it."

"Loosened a tooth too," Larry added, stroking his wife's head.

"Then he climbed out the window," Rhonda said.

"Can you describe him?" Kyle asked.

Shaking her head sadly, she said, "It was dark and his back was turned. I only got a glimpse of his face before he hit me."

"Sundstrom is on her way over," Michelson said, referring to the department sketch artist.

"Can you give me a general description?" Kyle asked. "Height, weight, hair color, clothes, distinguishing marks?"

"He was wearing all black, even his shoes. His hair was dark—black or brown—there wasn't enough light. I don't know about eye color. He was maybe thirty, about six feet tall, and very strong. He knocked me down like I was a feather!" she said, her hand going back to her nose.

Kyle wished Mac was with him, working his magic on Rhonda. The way her hand kept going to her nose he knew she worried about being permanently disfigured. Mac would make some comment about crooked noses looking sexy and put her at ease. Kyle didn't risk it. Instead he made a mental note to have Mac interview her later.

"Mr. Benchly, tell me about the man who was pounding on the door," Kyle said.

"Huh?" Larry said, caught by surprise by the sudden switch.

"What he was wearing, what he looked like," Kyle prodded.

"He was about my height and wearing a hat," Larry said. "I didn't really get a good look since I came running when my wife screamed. I just wish I could of gotten my hands on that sonofabitch!"

"What kind of coat was the man wearing?" Kyle asked.

"I don't know . . . a long one, like an overcoat. What difference does it make? He's not the one that was smothering my boy."

"Larry," Rhonda scolded. "You're scaring Peter."

"Sorry," Larry said sheepishly.

"This man didn't give you anything, did he?" Kyle asked.

"How could he? I didn't even open the door. The police were pounding on the door a couple of minutes later. Ask them. They must have seen him."

"Someone called 9-1-1 with a tip about a prowler on the

roof of the Benchlys' house," Michelson said. "It wasn't the Benchlys. Dispatch sent a unit as soon as they could but Cradle Robber and the man at the door were both gone when they arrived."

"They sent a single unit?" Kyle asked, angry that they had missed an opportunity to stop the killer.

"Dispatch was flooded with calls last night," Michelson explained. "Cradle Robber was spotted in dozens of neighborhoods. We were lucky to get a unit to the Benchlys as quick as we did. When the officer on the scene realized it was the real deal, she called it in and we flooded the area, setting up roadblocks. They're doing a house-to-house search now."

"Cradle Robber's gone," Kyle said. "The old man too."

"Sure," Michelson said.

"Get the 9-1-1 tape as soon as possible," Kyle said.

"Sure," Michelson said.

Sundstrom arrived then, sketch pad in hand. Kyle asked the Benchlys to wait, then asked Sundstrom to make three additional sketches besides the one using Rhonda's description. Then Kyle asked Michelson to wait and show the sketches to Peter to see if he could pick the one created using his mother's description. Kyle had used sketch lineups before to judge their accuracy.

Kyle drove to the Benchly home using his badge to pass through the police cordon. The street was filled with police cars and vans, the Benchly home getting the fine-tooth comb treatment by forensics. There were more squad cars than necessary, every officer on the force knowing the Cradle Robber case could be broken tonight and wanting to say he or she had been there. As Kyle had expected the attention was focused on the backyard, porch roof, and Peter's room. Kyle found Mac on the front walk talking to Cassidy. Both of them had been dragged out of bed in the middle of the night but only Mac looked like it. Cassidy looked like she had been awake for hours, hair in a neat bun, makeup perfectly applied, uniform neatly pressed. She smiled involuntarily when she saw Kyle, then put on her business face.

"I expected to see Mac, but it's a little early for you," Kyle said to Cassidy.

Suddenly Kyle was hit by a powerful déjà vu feeling. The house, Mac and Cassidy standing in front of it, the flashing lights from the police cars—all familiar—except it should be daylight. The feeling quickly faded.

"Someone tipped one of the local stations that this was a Cradle Robber attack. There's a news crew on the way," Cassidy said. "I heard there's a witness."

"The mother got just a glimpse in the dark and the little boy is only six," Kyle said.

"Should I mention the witness?" Cassidy asked. "We could scare Cradle Robber out of town."

"Might as well," Kyle said. "The media will have it by morning anyway."

"Anything else you want to get on the air?"

"Just feed them the usual," Kyle said.

"All steps are being taken, every available officer is on the case, everything that can be done is being done, the mayor and the chief of police are monitoring the situation, yadda yadda yadda," Cassidy said in her television voice.

"You're on, Cassidy," Mac said, pointing down the street to an approaching van, a dish antenna mounted on the top and "CHANNEL 7 ACTION NEWS" painted on the side.

"At least this time I have good news," Cassidy said, moving to intercept the television crew pouring out of the van.

"Mac, the Benchlys said they were awakened by a man pounding on the front door," Kyle said when she was gone.

"Don't tell me he was a blue guy wearing a hat and overcoat?" Mac said.

"Hat and coat for sure. Do you know if anyone's found one of his calling cards?"

"No silver bullets that I know of. Except for a piece of plastic and a coat, they haven't gathered even a hair. You say he was at the front door?"

Kyle followed Mac to the front door where they used their flashlights to examine the porch, walk, and the surrounding bushes—nothing. The front door was closed but unlocked and they opened it examining the entry hall and again found nothing.

"A dozen officers have come in and out this door," Mac said. "They could have tracked it anywhere."

Splitting up, Mac headed into the dining room and Kyle to the living room. A minute later Mac gave a shout. Kyle found him slipping a piece of paper into a plastic bag.

"Looks like someone stepped on it with a wet shoe," Mac said.

"So much for crime-scene protocol," Kyle said.

Holding it under his flashlight beam Mac and Kyle read.

• Wednesday, early morning: Cradle Robber found his second victim in Peter Benchly, the six-year-old son of Rhonda and Lawrence Benchly. Like Cradle Robber's other young victims, Peter was found the next morning, smothered and holding a toy baseball bat. The second Cradle Robber murder hit the city hard and the public lost faith in the police. After the Wendy Kirkland murder the public prayed that the police could stop Cradle Robber but after the Peter Benchly murder a feeling of helplessness set in and the parents were reduced to hoping the murder spree wouldn't touch their own families.

"This blue guy is starting to spook me and I believe in all that paranormal crap," Mac said. "Kyle, if this guy knows when and where Cradle Robber is going to hit next, then why doesn't he stop him?"

"He might have tried, Mac. He called 9-1-1 and told them where to send the police, then he waited to make sure nothing happened to the boy. When the police didn't get here in time he beat on the door to wake the parents."

"He nearly waited too long," Mac said. "That boy almost died."

"I think he wanted him caught in the act, not scared off."

"So why doesn't he just tell us when and where?" Mac asked. "I swear he can't make up his mind whether he wants this killer stopped or not."

Kyle thought about that. In some ways he felt the same way about the old man. He wasn't sure he wanted the old man caught.

"He could have gotten the mom killed too," Mac said. "If our blue friend won't call us and let us do it, he should get a gun and do it himself."

Mac had a good point but he thought like a cop. Civilians talked tough about facing off with Cradle Robber—especially men like Larry Benchly—but they had no idea what it took to shoot a human being, even a ruthless monster like Cradle Robber. Give Larry Benchly a loaded revolver and put him ten feet from Cradle Robber and Kyle would bet that Cradle Robber would get away and Larry Benchly would be lying on the ground, shot dead with his own gun.

Then the news team turned off the lights and started toward Kyle. Seeing them coming, Kyle tried to walk away.

"Detective Sommers, can I ask you a couple of questions?" the reporter asked.

She was tall and blond with heavy television makeup. She wore slacks and a yellow windbreaker with "ACTION NEWS 7" stenciled across the chest. She held a microphone with a square top that had a red "7" painted on each side. Kyle hated interviews, managing to avoid them most of the time. Kyle looked at Cassidy who shrugged.

"I'm busy," Kyle protested.

The television lights were turned on, aimed at his face, and then the cameraman brought the camera to his shoulder, pointing it at Kyle.

"Just a couple of questions, Detective Sommers," the reporter said, thrusting the microphone forward.

"Just a couple," Kyle finally conceded.

"You are leading the Cradle Robber Task Force, correct?"

The reporter snapped the microphone back and forth holding it close to her mouth when she spoke and close to Kyle when he spoke.

"Yes," Kyle said.

Kyle deliberately kept his answers short. If you were a terrible interview the media would look somewhere else the next time.

"Is it true that you just recently returned from a medical leave?"

Alarms went off in Kyle's head.

"Yes," Kyle said softly.

"Weren't you on leave for alcoholism?"

"That's not relevant," Kyle said defensively.

"And you had hallucinations where you saw your dead daughter?"

"None of your damn business," Kyle snapped, then turned to walk away.

The man holding the lights and the cameraman cut Kyle off, then backed up in front of him. The reporter fell in next to Kyle.

"Is it true you believe a man with blue skin is involved with Cradle Robber?"

"I can't discuss details of the case," Kyle growled, walking toward his truck, the camera and lights still on him.

"Isn't it also true that you believe the man with blue skin is a genie?"

When the reporter put the microphone in front of Kyle's face, he grabbed it and shoved it away, crushing the plastic top with the "7"s painted on it as he did.

They kept the cameras on him as he got in his truck and drove away.

20

Hideaway

Wednesday, 2:15 A.M.
As patient as a fox on the hunt, he had followed the man-in-the-hat at a distance, just keeping his taillights in sight. He couldn't risk getting closer since there were few cars on the roads this time of night. The man-in-the-hat led him to the freeway, where there was enough traffic so that he could follow a car behind. The man-in-the-hat drove through the city center, then took U.S. 26 over the west hills, leaving Portland. Once past the zoo and through the hills he continued west on the Sunset Highway through Beaverton and west toward the coast. The cars traveling the Sunset Highway were few and far between but the road was straight as an arrow and he followed the taillights.

As they reached the far edge of Portland's suburbs, the taillights drifted right, and then exited. He mimicked the move, but slowed, letting him reach the light at the top of the exit ramp and turn before he took the exit. At the red light he paused, studying the interchange, noting where the freeway entrances were and that there were businesses to the left—a strip mall, 7-Eleven, and Chevron station. To the right, where the man he was following had gone, there was a blizzard of signs advertising new housing developments. Farther down the road he could see the first of these developments, half filled with homes in various stages of construction. The taillights of the man-in-the-hat passed the first development, disappearing around a corner.

Turning right, he followed what once was a country road that wound through developments with names like Meadowlark Valley, Castle Hills, and The Evergreens. As they continued away from the freeway the projects thinned and were fewer and farther between.

Suddenly the man-in-the-hat's lights disappeared. Slowing only slightly so it wouldn't look suspicious, he searched both sides of the road looking for where the man had turned. He feared he had lost him but then spotted a car driving into one of the developments. The man-in-the-hat had turned his lights off, not the behavior of a man returning to his own home. Continuing past the turn, he noted the man-in-the-hat had turned into the Pumpkin Court development. A quarter mile down the road he turned around, switched off his own lights, and drove back to the entrance, stopping just outside. Under the large "PUMPKIN COURT" sign was a plot map showing the land divided into lots varying between one and three acres. He drove in slowly, parking just inside the development, studying the layout. Pumpkin Court was a loop and the man-in-the-hat couldn't get back out without going past him.

He waited, his gun nestled in his lap. Minutes passed but the man-in-the-hat did not come back. He waited five more minutes but still no one came back out of Pumpkin Court. Curious now, he put his knife in his belt, and took his pistol, leaving the car. Quietly he followed the edge of the road. The land was wooded with thick underbrush and only a few of the lots had been cleared. A mound of woody debris was piled in the middle of a lot being prepared for construction. There were no houses on the lots he passed, just foundation work. He came to a lot that had been scraped free of vegetation and he paused, afraid of exposing himself. He studied the perimeter of the lot and the pile of debris in the middle, seeing no one. When he was sure the man-in-the-hat wasn't hiding in the shadows, he trotted to the pile. The car he had followed was hidden behind the debris. He watched the car for a minute, seeing and hearing nothing. Finally, he was sure the car was empty unless someone was lying on the floor. He crept to the car, gun pointed at the side window, then looked in. There was no one in the car. Now he crouched in the shadow of the car, trying to figure out where the man-in-the-hat had gone. Ahead he spotted a dim light coming from the only completed house in the development. He moved toward it, keeping to the deepest shadows, pausing often to look and listen. The light was coming from the rear. Running to the house, he flattened against the wall, trying to hear inside—nothing. There were no windows along this side so he moved to the corner and peeked around. There were patio doors in the back and they were glowing softly. Creeping to the edge of the first door he leaned out carefully, looking inside with one eye. The interior was dimly lit but he could see there was no carpet or furniture. The walls looked freshly painted. He was looking into a family room. To the right he could see into the kitchen. The cabinets had been installed but the appliances were missing and where the stove would go a man was sitting with his back against one wall, his legs across the opening where the stove would slide in. The man's overcoat and wide-brimmed hat were on the floor and he could see the man's face clearly now. He was in his late fifties, hair graying, face weathered, or maybe careworn, with the creases of a perpetual frowner, a man who had lived a hard life.

Now his eyes took in new details and he looked closer at what the man was wearing—nothing like anything he had ever seen. It resembled a wet suit, one piece and gray, patches of black across its surface that appeared plastic. The surface was studded with nodes that coated him from head to foot. He was still trying to understand the strange suit when the man picked up a long cord. On one end there was a three-pronged plug designed for a 220-volt outlet. The opposite end terminated in a round plate. Now the man in the strange suit removed a small cover from the plastic plate on his chest and attached the round end of the power cord. Next he plugged the other end into the outlet prepared for the stove. Then the man in the suit leaned back against the cabinets and closed his eyes.

Stepping back, he squatted next to the house, looking at the gun in his hand and thinking. The man-in-the-hat didn't know he had been followed home. He could kill him anytime but he was of two minds. The man-in-the-hat was a threat to his ministry and there he was on the floor, helpless, an easy victim. But he never entered a house without scouting it thoroughly and he knew nothing about this house. The neighborhood was new, the house probably empty, but he hadn't survived as long as he had by taking unnecessary chances.

More important was his curiosity. How had this man found him? Was he working alone? How did he keep showing up at the houses of the children he selected? And what was the strange suit he wore? Since he knew the man's nest, he decided to learn more.

He retraced his steps, keeping in the shadows, pausing frequently to look and listen. Finding his truck where he left it, he started the engine but left the lights off. Pulling to the edge of the highway, he paused. There was an intersection to the right and he turned toward it, then left across the highway. The shoulder was wide and he turned the car around, pulling over and parking where he could see the entrance to Pumpkin Court. Turning off the engine, he waited.

The man-in-the-hat left just before dawn. He let him go. He waited only a few minutes, then drove back into Pumpkin Court, parking behind the mound of debris where the man-in-the-hat had hidden his car. The doors to the house were locked but no one is careful to secure an empty house and he found a kitchen window unlatched.

Inside, there was no sign the man-in-the-hat had been there—no hat, no coat, no power cord. He searched the house first, stealthily creeping from room to room on both levels. The rooms were empty. Returning to the kitchen he searched the cabinets, finding the power cord in one over the space for the stove. It wasn't as if the cord were hidden, simply put away in a cabinet. The cord was six feet long with a standard 220 plug on one end and a round plastic plate on the other. Turning the plate over he could see the bottom looked like a circuit board covered with a dozen tiny gold squares. In the cabinet he also found canned juice, fruit, granola bars, a city map, and papers. He opened the map finding circles drawn here and there. One of the circles was near Pier Park where he had planned to minister to Wendy. Next he checked for Peter's block finding a circle there too. Intrigued now, he checked other circles finding four marking the homes of the children he had planned to visit. It was as if the man was reading his mind. The other circles meant nothing to him. How could this man know so much? It made no sense. Certainly he wasn't working with the police. Police don't hide out at night in unfinished houses. Turning to the other papers he found, he read, confused. Reading them over and over he slowly came to understand what it all meant and he was amazed. Now that he understood he knew the man-in-the-hat had to be stopped and he regretted letting him go earlier. It didn't matter. He knew the man's hideaway. Tonight he would come back and kill him.

21

Writer

Wednesday, 6:00 A.M.
Kyle was awake when the Channel 7 morning news came on. The station's Cradle Robber logo appeared over the anchor's shoulder as soon as the theme music ended. The logo was a silhouette of a man and a woman placing flowers on a child's grave. Kyle tried to ignore it. The anchor began with the news of Cradle Robber's attack and that for the first time the victim had survived. The Benchlys were shown from a distance and then the sketch of Cradle Robber filled the screen. An interview with Cassidy followed. Then came the part he dreaded—the ambush interview.

They ran it all, the questions about his alcoholism and hallucinations, the blue man and the genie theory. Then they showed Kyle crushing the top of the microphone. The report ended with the blond reporter holding the microphone with the broken top asking whether a man with a history of alcoholism and hallucinations should be leading the most important task force in Portland's history. Kyle's phone began ringing as soon as the report ended. He didn't pick it up.

Kyle was in Harding's office at 7:15 A.M., detailing what they had learned from the night before. Kyle didn't mention the Channel 7 report. As Kyle spoke Harding was reserved, almost withdrawn. Kyle showed him the sketch of Cradle Robber, the first ever, and yet he didn't respond. Kyle told him about the sheet of plastic, the jacket, the footprints found in a neighbor's yard, and Harding listened passively.

When Kyle finished Harding said, "I've had three additional phone lines dedicated to handle the tips. We'll need more help screening the calls."

"I'll assign more officers to Danforth's team," Kyle said.

"No, Sommers, you won't," Harding said bluntly. "The chief called me. The press has been hounding him all morning about you. The bottom line is that he wants you replaced."

Kyle had expected it but it still hurt.

"I'm putting Detective Danforth in charge of the task force."

"Who do you think leaked the genie story to Channel Seven?" Kyle asked.

Harding ignored the question.

"Sorry, Kyle, but once the press got hold of your history there was no way I could keep you in charge."

"Am I still assigned to the case?"

"For now but you've got to keep a low profile."

Now the only sound was Harding's fingers drumming the arms of his chair. Harding didn't dismiss Kyle and Kyle didn't make a move to leave.

"Was it the same man at the door?" Harding asked finally.

"Same description," Kyle said.

Harding's fingers drummed some more and he shifted in his chair.

"What do you make of him?" Harding asked.

"You don't want to hear what I'm thinking," Kyle said.

Harding took it the way he intended.

"Danforth thinks he might be working with Cradle Robber," Harding said. "Maybe a lookout. Or maybe Cradle Robber is really two killers working in coordination."

"That doesn't fit many of the facts," Kyle said.

"No, but it doesn't involve a genie or ESP."

Kyle reddened but didn't say anything. More uncomfortable silence followed.

"I'm going to tell Danforth to leave you alone," Harding said finally. "Follow any leads you think are relevant."

"Thanks," Kyle said.

Kyle stood to leave.

"Sommers?"

Kyle stopped at the door, turning back.

"Let's keep the . . . the exotic theories between you and me."

Kyle understood. Harding had gone out on a limb by putting him in charge of the task force and had paid for it. He wouldn't risk more career damage.

Kyle's phone was ringing when he got to his cubicle. It was Rita, calling from the security desk.

"I'm so sorry I told people about the genie," Rita said. "People are so close-minded."

Rita had seen the news.

"Forget it," Kyle said.

"You forgive me?"

"It's all right, Rita. It's not your fault."

"Thank you, Kyle. There's someone here who insists on seeing you. She won't talk to anyone but you."

"Who is it?"

"Sherrie Nolan."

"Send her up."

Kyle walked to the elevators, most of those he passed avoiding his eyes. If they hadn't seen the Channel 7 news they had heard about it. Within an hour everyone would also know about his demotion. Kyle ignored the sideways glances and the pitying looks.

Kyle was waiting at the elevator when Sherrie rolled out, pushing her way through those in front, rolling over their feet and banging them with the stumps of her legs. Kyle found himself amused by her pushiness and smiled a greeting. Sherrie fought to stay impassive but Kyle detected a slight smile flash across her lips. Sherrie wore another pair of stretch pants and a black top with a low neckline that drew stares from passing men and women. Kyle had seen only a small part of Sherrie's wardrobe but it was all revealing as if Sherrie was compensating for the unattractiveness of her legs.

"This way," Kyle said, leading her toward his cubicle.

Sherrie rolled along behind him, looking around, curious, taking in every detail. When Kyle got to his cubicle he plopped in his chair, automatically indicating the victim's chair as he had done so often. Sherrie glared at him from the doorway and then at the vacant chair. There wasn't enough room for her wheelchair and the victim's chair. Before Kyle could move Sherrie reached out, picked up the victim's chair with one arm, lifted it over her head, and then threw it down the hall. Then she rolled in, smiling at Kyle.

"I think your blue man is a time traveler," Sherrie said bluntly.

Kyle winced, knowing the cubicles were poor sound dampeners. Before Kyle could respond Mac appeared, picking up Kyle's chair and setting it against the outside wall. He had come to commiserate but stopped when he saw Sherrie. Kyle saw Mac look at Sherrie's cleavage as he leaned in the cubicle, giving her his phoniest smile. Kyle looked forward to what would happen next, confident Sherrie would be immune to his charm.

Pointing at the chair he had just set back up, Mac said, "I told them when they designed this place there wouldn't be enough room for the differently abled."

"I'm not differently abled, I'm a cripple!" Sherrie said sharply, voice cold as ice. "Don't ever call me differently abled or physically challenged or any of that other PC bullshit. They took me to the hospital and put me to sleep and chopped my legs off—they didn't ask me if I wanted to be a half woman, they just played God and decided half a life was better than none. Well it isn't!"

Mac was surprised at the outburst, eyes wide. Kyle was pleased that Mac had finally run into a woman he couldn't charm. Several long seconds of uncomfortable silence followed with Sherrie's eyes locked on Mac's, daring him to speak. Just when Kyle thought Mac was speechless, he had a comeback.

"Well, halfling, from what I can see of what's left of you it was for the best. If your legs were as beautiful as the rest of you it would just be too much for mortal man."

Sherrie held her cold stare for another few seconds and then to Kyle's disappointment her facial features softened.

"My legs were my best feature," Sherrie said.

"I wish I'd seen them," Mac said.

"You can. They're in a glass case in the Smithsonian between Lincoln's stovepipe hat and Dorothy's ruby slippers," Sherrie said.

"Well what's left of you ain't half bad—no pun intended," Mac said.

Sherrie smiled.

"Are you free for lunch?" Mac asked. "I promise I won't play footsie with you under the table—whoops, I can't believe I said that."

Mac and Sherrie laughed together. It was the first time Kyle had heard Sherrie laugh and he liked the sound. It was a soft laugh, just louder than a giggle and infectious.

"Can't do lunch," Sherrie said. "I'm meeting my editor."

"Editor?" Mac probed. "You're a writer?"

"Science fiction and fantasy. I'm P. G. Turner when I write fantasy, and Natasha Quark on my SF books."

"You're P. G. Turner?" Mac said, shaking her hand as if he'd just met her, his voice syrupy. "My wife and I are reading the Gem Wizards series—I thought *The Ruby Wizard* was wonderful. My wife liked *The Emerald Wizard* better but then my wife's not normal. I can't wait for *The Diamond Wizard* to come out."

"It will hit the bookstores in July."

Kyle listened to Mac and Sherrie chatter about her books, realizing she was a fairly well-known writer. He was also losing confidence in her. He didn't need fiction, he needed fact.

"Why do you use a pseudonym?" Mac asked.

"I was doing graduate work in physics when I published my first novel. You can't write science fiction and be taken seriously as a physicist. When I branched into fantasy my editor asked me to use another name so she could promote me as a first author again."

"Why P. G. Turner?" Mac asked.

"I wanted to use Paige Turner but my editor wouldn't do it, so we compromised."

"If I ever write a book I'm going to use U. R. Thayer," Mac said.

"Ima Writer was my second choice," Sherrie said.

Mac won a punning contest in college and Kyle knew he wouldn't let Sherrie get the last word in.

"Sherrie's here to see me, Mac," Kyle said, interrupting. "Maybe you two could pick this up later?"

"It was so nice meeting you," Mac said, his voice honey sweet. "Let's do a book discussion lunch sometime."

"Love to," Sherrie said, taking Mac's hand again.

Mac squeezed Sherrie's hand with both of his and Kyle was sure she would have stood and hugged him if she'd had legs.

"Nice man," Sherrie said when Mac was gone.

Kyle nodded agreement. Now that he had Sherrie's attention again he wasn't sure he wanted to hear what she had to say.

"You said the blue man is a time traveler?" Kyle asked anyway, picking up a pen and a yellow pad.

"I was up all night trying to explain it another way," Sherrie said. "I know it's hard to believe."

"Ever write a story about time travel?" Kyle probed.

Sherrie's face reddened and her emotional armor closed around her.

"Yes, I wrote a book about time travel, so does that disqualify me? Does having an imagination make me just another kook that wanders in here with crackpot conspiracy theories? You came to me for help, Detective, and now you will have the courtesy to sit there and listen to me!"

Her voice was loud and aggressive and an officer walked slowly past Kyle's cubicle, checking to make sure everything was under control. When he saw Sherrie in her wheelchair he relaxed and kept walking, dismissing Sherrie as a threat. The officer underestimated Sherrie. Kyle had faced off with two-hundred-pound murderers who didn't intimidate him as much as this handicapped woman.

"I'm listening," Kyle said.

"Here are the facts. This man has shown up three times where crimes or accidents were happening as if he knew they were going to happen—three times we know of. After each incident a description of what might have happened is found and in each case the outcome is different."

"Four times," Kyle said, passing Sherrie a copy of the note Mac had found at the Benchly house.

Sherrie's eyebrows went up and she took the note, reading.

"He knew Cradle Robber would be there," Sherrie said when she finished reading. "This is terrible."

"In what way?" Kyle asked.

"The blue man gambled last night that Cradle Robber would be caught and he lost. Cradle Robber is a compulsive killer so the murders won't stop, but because of last night he'll probably repress his urges for a few days or a week or even a month—he'll change the pattern. The blue man won't be able to predict when and where he'll strike again."

"If he really was a time traveler why couldn't he just update himself on where and when Cradle Robber kills next?"

"He's not hopping back and forth in time—the energy requirements for a single trip are staggering—not to mention the difficulty of accurately displacing that much mass in time and space. No, I'm sure it was a onetime trip back."

"If someone sent him back in time to stop Cradle Robber,

then why didn't they send a younger man? Why not send a cop? And if they want him stopped, why not just tell me who he is?"

"He wasn't sent," Sherrie said emphatically. "If time travel becomes possible, then it would be absolutely prohibited. Imagine the moral dilemma of deciding who would live or die?"

"There's not always a dilemma," Kyle argued. "If you kill Hitler before he comes to power, you save six million Jews from the death camps."

"That's what everyone thinks but it's not that clear that killing Hitler would help. Let's suppose someone did go back and kill Hitler as a child. Hitler doesn't come to power and Germany remains weak. But what about Stalin? Stalin still comes to power in the Soviet Union and instead of Hitler rolling across Europe, it's Stalin. Did you really save six million people by killing Hitler or have you traded the lives of six million Jews for six million Poles, Italians, and French? Tinkering with time is too unpredictable. It would never be allowed."

Sherrie talked with certainty about something most people thought impossible.

"So if we have a time traveler he's a renegade?" Kyle asked.

"It's an illicit trip, that's for sure. He's come back for something and he's got one shot at it."

"To stop Cradle Robber?"

"Maybe," Sherrie said, biting her lower lip, looking doubtful. "But if that's why he came then he would have started in San Diego three months ago. It's more likely he's here for another reason and doing good deeds on the side. It would be hard to just stand by and let a child die when you know you could stop it," Sherrie said.

Kyle tried to stay impassive but Sherrie picked up the flushing of his cheeks. Then Kyle was hit with a sickening realization.

"Cradle Robber is never caught," Kyle blurted out. "That's why the blue man can't just tip the police. Cradle Robber is another Jack the Ripper."

"How so?" Sherrie asked.

"Jack went on a killing spree in London, eviscerating six women. The police were baffled by the case and had no good suspects. Then just as suddenly as he started killing he stopped, never to kill again. No one knows why he stopped and the case has never been solved. That must be how the Cradle Robber case ends—he's never caught. Maybe one day Cradle Robber is hit by a car or maybe he dies of a heart attack, but somehow, someday, he stops and the murders are never solved. Nothing we do will make a damn bit of difference!"

Kyle was flushed and breathing hard. Embarrassed, he fought to regain his composure. Sherrie gave him a few moments to collect himself, then spoke in a soft voice, a tone he hadn't heard before.

"That was before but the time traveler has changed things."

"Changed the pattern, but not the outcome," Kyle said.

"There's no way to know how it will play out now."

If the notes the blue man left were to be believed, Sherrie might be right. Some events had turned out differently, although the new endings weren't all that happy. Carolynn Martin still died and Christy Sadler was in a coma. Still, if Sherrie was right, there was hope of changing things and that made him think of his own daughter.

"I posted messages on a dozen chat rooms around the country," Sherrie said. "I should have more information tonight. Show up around dinnertime and I'll let you know what I have."

"If I can," Kyle said.

"You can!" Sherrie said forcefully. "Bring a large pepperoni pizza with you," she said, rolling out of his cubicle.

Sherrie ran into Mac outside and the two of them greeted

each other warmly, Mac walking her to the elevator. Kyle stayed slumped in his chair, thinking about what Sherrie had said about changing the course of life events. Certainly he never would have met Sherrie if the blue man hadn't connected them through Mitch Nolan and that meant every moment he spent with Sherrie was time he would have spent with someone else or doing something else. Sadly, he realized, most of the time Sherrie had used up would have been spent at the gym or in a drunken stupor. Memories of Shelby bleeding to death in his wrecked jeep came back then, and he heard Sherrie's words repeated in his mind. "It would be hard to just stand by and let a child die when you know you could stop it." Kyle wanted to believe time travel was possible and he desperately wanted to find the blue man.

22

Drive-by

Wednesday, 7:45 A.M.
The girls would come by soon. Alberto and his friends took
their positions, posing for them, trying to look casual. Alberto sat on the steps of his house, one of the last two homes
remaining on his block, the rest displaced by businesses—a
body shop on one corner, a Plaid Pantry on the other. A
beauty parlor and a secondhand store filled in the rest of the
block. The walls of the businesses bore the red and white
spray paint tag of the Brotherhood. Like wolves pissing on
rocks and trees to mark their territory, they sprayed their sign
on walls to warn off other predators.

Carlos sat next to Alberto on the step, and Luis, Juan, and
Paco leaned against Luis's car. They all wore their colors;
jackets with a rose dripping blood stenciled on the back.
Alberto and his friends were the core of the Brotherhood of
the Bloody Rose, although there were many wanna-bes who
occasionally hung with them. The Brotherhood was tight and
exclusive and Alberto was the unquestioned leader.

Like the girls they waited for, Alberto had once walked
this street on the way to high school but he had dropped out
three years ago and now made a good living in the used auto
parts business—that's how he described his business to his
mother. He was good at "finding" parts and had two dozen
of the bright green "The Clubs" in his garage, removed from
steering wheels by cutting through the plastic steering wheel

instead of the steel club. With car theft only a misdemeanor in Oregon, the Bloody Rose gang stole their cars in Portland and then drove them across the Interstate Bridge to Vancouver, Washington, where they were sold. Some ended up in Mexico, many more were disassembled for parts.

Alberto, Paco, and Luis had all been caught in stolen cars on the way to Vancouver but the police had merely ticketed them and sent them on their way. Paco was legendary among the Brotherhood for being pulled over in a stolen car and walking away with his ticket in his pocket, only to walk around the block and resteal the car before the police tow truck could arrive.

The girls were coming now, the seniors, Lucinda, Amber, and Lawanna leading the way. All would graduate this year—even Lucinda who was five months pregnant with Paco's baby. Behind them came younger girls, freshmen and sophomores and then little brothers and sisters who would be dropped off at the day-care center in the church on the next block. There were promising buds among the freshmen but Amber took all of Alberto's attention.

"When you going to go out with me, Amber?" Alberto called.

"When you gonna ask?" Amber said, pushing her long black hair out of her face.

"I asked you plenty of times," Alberto said. "Didn't I, Carlos?"

"Yeah, I heard him. He asked you yesterday," Carlos said.

"Yeah, yesterday," Alberto said.

Amber stopped now, holding her books to her chest, smiling at Alberto. Lucinda drifted over to talk with Paco who looked nervous, unsure of what to say to the girl who was carrying his baby. Now Linda, one of the sophomores, spoke up shyly.

"Where's Willie this morning?" Linda asked.

Alberto knew Linda had a thing for his little brother, Willie, the youngest member of the gang. Willie was still going

to school despite Alberto's constant ragging to run full-time
with the Brotherhood. Willie was usually with them now,
waiting for the girls and then walking to school with them,
keeping close to Linda. As he thought about it, Alberto wondered where Willie was. He hadn't seen his little brother
since the night before. They had picked up a Lexus in the
Lloyd Center parking lot, then partied until near midnight.
Willie was the only member of the Brotherhood who was
sober, so Alberto had sent him to Vancouver with the car.
The police hadn't picked him up, he knew, because Willie
hadn't called.

"He had some business last night," Alberto said. "I think
he's sleeping late."

Linda looked disappointed. Turning back to Amber, he
said, "So, you gonna go out with me?"

"My mother would kill me if I went out with you," Amber
said.

"What? I'm offended. I've got standing in the community.
Everyone respects me."

"Everyone's afraid of you," Amber said, still smiling.

"That's what I said, everyone respects me. Your mother
don't have to know. Tell her you're going over to Lawanna's
house. Lawanna would cover for you, wouldn't you, Lawanna?"

"What would I get out of it?" Lawanna asked, talking to
Alberto but looking at Carlos.

Carlos was about to answer when a stranger approached,
dressed in an overcoat and a hat. He hadn't crossed the street
to avoid the gang, so Alberto knew he wasn't from the neighborhood. Alberto had the urge to teach the man a lesson
about crossing Bloody Rose turf but Amber was there and
being friendly. He decided to let the man pass, nodding to
the others to ignore him, but the man stopped at the edge of
the group.

"Get off of the street, you're in danger!" the man said.

He was an old man, Alberto could see, although part of his face was hidden under the hat.

"Do you know who you're talking to?" Alberto asked, getting up and stepping to face the man.

"Hurry, get off of the street! They're going to shoot you. Get the children off the street!"

The little children had been milling around, waiting for their older sisters to continue the walk to the day-care center but now they were listening, the littlest ones drifting to their sisters' legs and wrapping their arms around them. Amber's sister came to her, leaning against her leg, watching the old man.

"You're the one that's in danger, old man," Alberto said, his anger growing. He didn't want to drop the old man in front of Amber and the others but there's only so much disrespect a man can take.

"The Psychlos are coming," the old man said.

Alberto and his gang exchanged looks, Paco and Luis looking up and down the block. The Psychlos were an Anglo gang that competed with the Brotherhood for the stolen car market. There had been a lot of posturing and threats between the two gangs but no open warfare.

"What are you talking about, old man?" Alberto asked.

"We better be going," Amber said, taking her little sister's hand.

"Don't let him scare you," Alberto said, still hoping to get Amber to agree to go out with him. "He don't know nothing about the Psychlos."

"Please believe me, they are coming," the old man pleaded. "You need to get the children off of the street. Take them into the house or into the backyard."

"How do you know this?" Carlos said, shoving the old man back a step.

"I can't explain it, I just know—please believe me," the old man said, and then turned to Amber. "Please get the children out of here."

Alberto slapped the old man across the face, catching part of his hat and knocking it askew. "You don't talk to her, you understand?"

The man staggered back a step, then pulled his hat back tight onto his head and down over his face. Alberto had gotten a good look in that instant and saw his skin had a strange color.

"This looks bad!" Paco said suddenly.

Two cars were coming down the street, a black Pontiac Firebird in the lead. The windows of both cars were rolled down on the street side and Alberto could see the cars were full of men.

"Get down," Alberto yelled, pushing Amber and her sister to the ground, then reaching for a little boy who was frozen from fear. Paco pulled Lucinda down behind his car, and the other members of Bloody Rose grabbed girls or children, pulling them to cover. The old man herded three children against a car and then covered them with his body.

The Psychlos saw them ducking for cover and opened fire with pistols and a shotgun. The air was filled with lead pellets, shattering glass, puncturing tires, and whining off of concrete and brick. Alberto's house was peppered with slugs, the two front windows shattering, the weathered siding splintering from dozens of impacts. The children screamed. Two of them bolted down the street, crying for their mamas. The gunfire continued as the second car passed, and then the car stopped and a door opened, the gunfire slowing only slightly. Then the door slammed and the firing picked up again. There was little glass left to shatter and now the sounds were of splintering wood, the whine of ricochets off of concrete, and the dull thump of lead puncturing steel. Then suddenly it ended, the cars roaring off with the sound of three-hundred-horsepower engines.

No one moved for a few seconds, fearful the shooting would begin again. Then, as one they moved, Alberto and the others jumping up and cursing the fleeing Psychlos. Amber, Lucinda, and Lawanna checked the children, looking for injuries and trying to calm them. There were cuts and some of the children were bleeding, but miraculously there were no bullet wounds. Then Linda screamed.

"It's Willie!" Linda wailed. "What did they do to him?"

Linda was pointing into the street where a body lay. Alberto hurried to find his brother lying naked, tied hand and foot, duct tape across his mouth. Willie had been stripped and coated in tar from head to foot and then sprinkled with feathers as the tar hardened on his skin. Tarred and feathered, like some medicine show huckster run out of a frontier town. Willie's eyes had been spared and they were open, tears running from the corners telling Alberto his little brother was in agony. When Willie saw Linda and the other girls come into the street, he rolled to his side, trying to hide his nakedness. Alberto knew the pain of shame would be worse than the pain from his burns. Alberto took off his coat, covering Willie's middle, the coat with the bleeding rose emblem immediately ruined by the tar. As Alberto carefully peeled the tape from his brother's face he whispered to him.

"They'll pay for this, Willie. I swear a solemn oath to God they will suffer for what they did to you."

23

Inspector Segal

Inspector Ellen Segal was five feet three inches, stocky and wore her dark hair in a tight bun. Despite the severe exterior, she was cordial and shook Kyle's hand warmly. She had come from San Francisco to brief Portland's Cradle Robber Task Force, but now had as many questions for Kyle as he had for her. In one night the Portland Police had collected more evidence than all three previous police departments had in nine months.

Inspector Segal had asked for Detective Sommers when she arrived at the security desk downstairs. Kyle had hurried down to greet her. He didn't tell her he wasn't in charge anymore. Once Danforth got hold of her Kyle would never see her. Kyle ushered her to his cubicle.

Segal listened to Kyle describe the evidence they had collected, taking occasional notes. She was impressed but realistic.

"Unless forensics can get something off that jacket you found, I'm afraid you're not much better off than we were."

"The jacket doesn't have a surface we can lift prints off of and it's one of the best-selling men's jackets in this region—Mervyn's, Fred Meyers, Kmart, many of the chains carry it," Kyle said. "We've lifted dozens of prints outside and inside the house but the witness now remembers Cradle

Robber was wearing gloves so we're probably wasting our time. One hair was found on the jacket. We've sent it out to be DNA typed. We'll run it through the DNA database and try and link it to the hairs you found."

"How accurate is the sketch?" Segal asked.

"The boy picked the sketch out of a sketch lineup, so we know the key features are right—shape of the face, eyes, nose, amount of hair. I've got one of our detectives going through your suspect files and using the sketch to weed the suspect pool."

Segal was shaking her head before he finished.

"We eliminated almost all in that pool as suspects too but it won't hurt to go through it again."

"I don't think he's on your list," Kyle said. "To be honest, I think you've got the profile wrong."

"We got the male part right," Segal said, looking intrigued and not offended.

"The suspect pool is filled with child molesters, abusers, rapists, flashers, pornographers, and other assorted perverts who specialize in children," Kyle said.

"Three psychiatrists independently concluded that Cradle Robber has a hatred of children," Segal argued.

"There's no evidence that any of the children were sexually abused in any way—no evidence of penetration, no genital bruising, no abrasions, no semen or other bodily fluids, and all the victims were dressed when they were found."

"The psychiatrists call it sublimation," Segal said. "Cradle Robber's sexual urges are being fulfilled through the death of the children."

"Why sublimate when the victim is at your mercy and available for the real thing?"

"Cradle Robber's id, ego, and superego balance is out of whack," Segal said. "The superego has insufficient strength to suppress the sexual urges of the id but is strong enough to pressure Cradle Robber's ego to redirect his sexual urges into a form less repulsive to his superego. If you want evidence that these crimes are sexual you should be checking Cradle Robber's pants, not his victim's."

"Very Freudian," Kyle said. "Do you believe it?"

Now Segal smiled, indicating she shared the suspicion most detectives had of psychiatry. Psychiatrists and psychologists were useful for controlling suspects once they were captured but they were little better than psychics when it came to telling the police what to look for.

"Let me hear your theory," Segal said.

"None of his victims were molested, and he doesn't abduct them and kill them somewhere else. Most of the children have been killed in their own beds—the place they are most comfortable. Those in their beds are tucked in and when they're found they look to their mothers like they are sleeping. In their hands he puts a toy—one last gift. I know it sounds bizarre but he's gentle with his victims, almost loving."

"Pimps are loving to their whores too, at least when they're not whipping them with a coat hanger for not turning a dozen tricks a night," Segal said. "He's killing them, Sommers, and there's nothing gentle about murder."

"Of course it's violent but he doesn't use a knife or a gun or anything that would pierce the body. He rarely leaves bruises. I know the plastic over the face is horrifying but only carbon monoxide poisoning would be less invasive."

"A gentle killer? What would be his motive?"

"Maybe he's putting them out of their misery."

"I don't know the boy he attacked in Portland," Segal said, "but the murdered children in San Francisco, Los Angeles, and San Diego were anything but miserable. There was no evidence of parental abuse and if there's a common denominator among the children it is that they were cheerful and outgoing."

"We can't see through his eyes so we can't know how he sees these children," Kyle argued. "I've heard that manic depressives use the mania stage—where they are overly optimistic and cheerful—as a dam to hold back their depression. When you see the mania you know depression is on its way. Maybe he sees these children that way and their cheerfulness is a sign of bad times ahead."

Now Segal looked thoughtful, mulling Kyle's theory.

"What about Carolynn Martin?" Segal asked. "She had been assaulted before he killed her. She certainly wasn't happy when she was killed."

"She's hard to explain," Kyle admitted.

"If you're right, how do you develop a pool of suspects?" Segal asked.

"Look for someone who has a reason to fear growing up. Maybe it's someone who was abused as a child or unpopular, or maybe they had a child that suffered as they grew up. Maybe from illness. Whoever it is thinks he is helping these children."

"It's too general," Segal said. "You have to narrow it down."

"There might be another angle," Kyle said. "If Cradle Robber is moving from city to city he has to be supporting himself somehow."

"Walk into any McDonald's and they'll hire you on the spot," Segal said.

"Sure, but why the four West Coast cities?"

"He likes the Pacific Ocean?" Segal said. "He's working his way up I-5? Maybe he has family in the West?"

"Maybe he has a job that takes him to these cities?" Kyle said.

"Well, he's working his way north with the seasons—he spent the winter in southern California and then started up the coast," Segal said, warming to the theory. "I'd say it was some kind of crop work except he's been working the big metropolitan areas."

"He may be a broker or wholesaler. Strawberries are in season here—maybe he works for one of the canneries. I'll assign a couple of detectives to check into it and see if it leads anywhere."

As he said it, Kyle remembered he didn't have the power to assign anyone.

"Would you do me a favor? They've assigned Detective Danforth to lead the task force," Kyle said.

Segal didn't ask why and Kyle appreciated that.

"I'm still assigned to the case but it would be better if you brought up the idea of Cradle Robber being a seasonal worker of some kind."

"It's nice to know your department is as political as mine," Segal said.

Now Kyle paused, indecisive, wondering whether to tell Segal about the blue man. There was nothing like it in any of her reports. Kyle found he didn't want to discuss the blue man with her or anybody in the department, and instead he walked her to Danforth's cubicle. Dressed in an immaculate blue suit, Danforth took charge of her immediately, dismissing Kyle. Later, in the task force meeting, Kyle had to sit passively while Segal shared Kyle's thoughts on the killer's motives and that he might be following the crops up the coast.

Danforth was a micro-manager, requiring each detective to report in excruciating detail instead of summarizing. The only significant development was the recording of the person who called 9-1-1 to report Cradle Robber. Danforth assumed it was a neighbor, although a canvass of the neighborhood hadn't turned up the caller. The tip wasn't as important as the new evidence, however, and Danforth quickly forgot it.

As the meeting dragged on Kyle's thoughts drifted to Sherrie Nolan and her unconventional theory. By the time the meeting ended he had decided he needed another visit to Professor Lipke before he saw Sherrie again.

24

University

Professor Lipke was in his office just as before, back to the door, typing on his keyboard. Kyle had come sheepishly the first time but this time Kyle rapped sharply on the door frame. The professor jumped.

"This better be important!" Lipke said as he turned.

Seeing Kyle, his face fell and his lips tightened.

"What is it this time?"

"You said that time travel was impossible. Do you mean impossible given current technology or absolutely impossible?"

"As I tried to tell you when you interrupted my work yesterday, time travel is a theoretical impossibility. Like the speed of light, the arrow of time—by that I mean that time moves only from present to future—is part of the fabric of the universe. The speed of light cannot be exceeded and it is impossible to travel back in time."

Kyle heard someone behind him and he turned sideways letting a man slip past him into Lipke's office, handing Lipke a photocopy of an article.

"I wouldn't say time travel is impossible, just unlikely," the new arrival said.

"Don't encourage him," Lipke said angrily.

"I'm George Murooko," the man said, offering his hand.

"Kyle Sommers," Kyle said, shaking Murooko's hand.

Murooko was a Caucasian-Asian mix, six feet tall, black hair and eyes, and a firm handshake. His face was smooth, showing none of Lipke's frown wrinkles. He looked to be about Kyle's age.

"Don't mind Professor Lipke," Murooko said, smiling, "he's part of the old guard in physics and a bit of an intellectual snob."

Kyle looked at Lipke who seemed unperturbed by Murooko's comments.

"A snob who will judge your application for tenure," Lipke said.

"And do so in an unbiased fashion," Murooko said, smiling at Lipke. Turning back to Kyle he said, "There are three possible methods of traveling backward through time. The first would require a black hole, which is essentially a collapsed star with a gravitational field so powerful not even light can escape from it. The gravitational power of black holes bends time and space so either by passing through a black hole or near one, it is theoretically possible to move backward in time."

"Anyone passing near a black hole would never escape its gravitational field," Lipke said.

"But if they had sufficient velocity—" Murooko said.

"Light has insufficient velocity to escape and nothing can travel faster than light," Lipke countered.

"Let's use our imagination," Murooko said.

"There's a difference between imagination and fantasy," Lipke snapped.

"Yes, but you have to have an imagination to tell the difference," Murooko shot back, then turned back to Kyle. "The second method of traveling through time would involve strings of dark mass left over from the Big Bang. Like black holes this matter is incredibly dense and distorts time and space. Unlike a black hole, the amount of dense matter is small enough that a spaceship could pass nearby and still escape its gravitational field. If you could find two strings near enough to each other, you could loop the strings in a figure-eight pattern, hopping between the two distortions in space-time and move backward in time."

"Would you like to prove that to me," Lipke said, holding up a piece of chalk and indicating a chalkboard mounted on one wall of his office.

"It's just speculation," Murooko said. "More of that imagination stuff."

"What's the third method?" Kyle asked.

"There is some evidence that tachyons—a kind of subatomic particle—will shift backward in time. Under certain experimental conditions tachyons occasionally arrive at an instrument before they have been released—that's true for some other subatomic particles too," Murooko said, flashing Lipke a smile.

"Those results are spurious," Lipke said, now stroking his goatee. "Strict adherence to experimental protocols would eliminate that kind of error."

"Those experiments have been replicated," Murooko said.

"Replicated error is still error," Lipke said.

Listening to the two physicists argue, Kyle wondered what their department meetings must be like.

"Does this help you?" Murooko asked Kyle. "Is it for a book?"

"I'm not a writer, I'm a detective with the Portland Police."

"Those aren't mutually exclusive categories," Murooko said.

"I'm working on a case where one of the suspects believes in time travel," Kyle lied. "I thought if I knew more about it, it would help with the case. But I don't think we're dealing with black holes or strings of dense matter and that last method is for microscopic particles."

"Subatomic, not microscopic," Lipke corrected.

"Right," Kyle said.

"If you need more help, feel free to come back. Better ask for me," Murooko said, smiling.

"Yes, ask for him," Lipke agreed.

Kyle left discouraged but after walking two blocks he realized he had started out like Lipke, believing time travel was impossible, but had just learned from Dr. Murooko that it was theoretically possible in space and had been demonstrated at a subatomic level. It made him wonder why if time travel was possible with spaceship-sized objects and subatomic particles, why it couldn't happen with objects in between—something the size of a man? With that realization, Sherrie Nolan became much more credible.

25

End of Shift

Amazingly, Mac's clothes were still clean when he stopped by Kyle's cubicle just before their shift ended. Mac had his coat on like he was quitting for the day.

"I'm sorry I talked you into the lunch with Rita, Kyle," Mac said. "You never had anything to do with that crazy genie theory. How do you think Channel 7 got hold of it?"

"Danforth," Kyle said. "He leaked it to them. He leaked everything; the drinking, the hallucinations."

"I never told him about that part," Mac said defensively. "I never told anyone about the visions."

"They were hallucinations, not visions," Kyle said. "I know you didn't leak it, Mac. He probably got it out of my records."

"If it's any consolation, some of the detectives are already complaining about him taking over the task force. He's got them spending as much time documenting the useless as the useful. He's more bureaucrat than detective."

"Then he'll be chief someday," Kyle said.

Kyle looked at his watch, then at Mac's coat.

"I must have missed the notice," Kyle said.

"What notice?" Mac asked, sitting in the victim's chair.

"The one telling us the union negotiated a shorter work-day."

"You're only working one case and you're criticizing my

workday? Harding didn't clear my desk when he put me on the task force. I'm doing my work and most of yours too."

"Who had the highest clearance rate last year?" Kyle asked.

"You only worked half a year," Mac pointed out. "If you can stop being a smart-ass for a minute, I came to ask if you want to visit the Psychlos with me. Harding seems to think they need a stern talking to."

One of Mac's assignments was to a special unit that dealt with Portland's street gangs. There were two major gangs and a half-dozen sprouts. The police pruned the sprouts as often as they could to keep them from growing. Even the two larger gangs were small by East Coast standards but they were well rooted and had bigger aspirations.

"What's up with the Psychlos?"

"This morning someone did a drive-by through Bloody Rose turf, turning Alberto Mendez's house into Swiss cheese. A couple of children were injured. Nothing too serious, mostly a whole lot of poopy pants. Whoever did the shooting also dumped Alberto's brother, Willie. He'd been tarred and feathered. Honest to God, they coated him with hot tar and sprinkled feathers on him."

"Can a person survive that?" Kyle asked.

"He did, although it was close. He's been burned from head to foot but nothing worse than second degree. The assholes that did it to him got the tar too hot so he was burned worse than he should have been but what nearly killed him was skin suffocation. They stripped him naked and did a thorough job of it. Skin has to breathe and the doctor said they coated too much skin with the tar."

"Is anyone ready to finger the Psychlos?" Kyle asked.

"Worst case of mass amnesia and temporary blindness I've ever seen," Mac said. "Alberto's doing his cock-a-doodle-doo I'm-cock-of-the-walk routine, making a lot of noise about revenge. Alberto's been the father in that family and he's very protective of his brother. He's not bluffing about getting revenge. I talked it over with Harding and he agreed I should drop by and put the fear of God in the Psychlos. We need to get them to lay low until the chest thumping dies down. Besides, slapping the Psychlos around is better than sitting around and plotting revenge against Danforth."

"Let's go," Kyle said.

Kyle agreed to go because Mac had asked him. If Mac wanted Kyle at his back when he confronted the Psychlos that was enough for Kyle.

"It won't take long," Mac said. "The wife called and we're going to an estate auction tonight. There's nothing I like better than buying dead people's stuff. I called Michelson too, he's coming on shift and will meet us at the Psychlos' hangout."

Mac stood, holding open his coat.

"Notice my shirt? My tie? Finally, I'm going to win the pool."

"Your shift's not over," Kyle said. "As I remember it, the Psychlos hang out in a garage—grease, oil, grime."

"I'll just have to be careful," Mac said.

26

Scout

Willie was in the hospital with second-degree burns over most of his body. Amber and Linda had been to see him but Alberto wouldn't visit his brother until he could tell Willie that the Psychlos had suffered for what they had done to him. Alberto took another swig from the whiskey bottle, then passed it to Carlos who sat behind the wheel. They had stolen a 1980 Cadillac Eldorado for the job. There was plenty of room in the car for four men with guns and the engine had the power they needed when the shooting was over. They had picked an older car because any cops they passed would wonder about four Hispanic teenagers in a new car. The Cadillac wouldn't raise any suspicions. They were parked four blocks from the Domino Garage where the Psychlos hung out in the evening. The garage was owned by the brother of Nick Bletson, the leader of the Psychlos. Nick and his friends used the garage after hours to work on their cars or to drink and get high. Alberto knew they would be partying tonight.

"Here she comes," Carlos said.

Alberto could see Sky coming down the street. "Sky High," was her street name. Alberto had never heard Sky's given name. He doubted even she could remember it. A skinny black girl, Sky had lived on the street since she was twelve, renting her body on Martin Luther King Junior Boulevard until rotten teeth and runny eyes took away her livelihood. Now she drifted from one drug rehab program to another, living on government or church handouts, getting her drugs any way she could. With her addictions no one would trust her to deal for them, or even work as a mule, so Sky was a thief, shoplifting, stealing from unlocked cars and the shelters where she lived. Arrested several times for petty theft, so far she had avoided serious jail time. Oregon was a "three strikes and you're out" state, and there wasn't enough room in the jails for all the rats of the city, so an annoying gnat like Sky had little to fear as long as she was never caught with more than two rocks of crack on her at a time. She came straight to Alberto's side of the car, leaning on her arms, her face inches from Alberto's. Her rotting teeth made her breath foul and Alberto leaned back.

"They're in there," Sky said. "You got my stuff?"

"How many?" Alberto demanded.

"Six or eight, I don't know for sure. I walked fast like you told me. Let me have my stuff."

"Are the garage doors open?"

"How else could I see," Sky said, starting to whine.

"Both doors?" Alberto asked.

"Yeah, both doors."

"Are the hoists up or down?"

"Huh?" Sky said, confused.

"The things they lift the cars up and down with. Are they sticking up or in the floor?"

Now Sky closed her eyes, trying to see through a thick drug-induced haze.

"They's down," Sky said.

Alberto looked at Carlos to make sure he was satisfied and then handed Sky a plastic bag with two rocks of crack— forty dollars' worth of high that wouldn't last her the night. Sky grabbed the bag, stuffing it in her jeans pocket as she hurried off. When she was gone Alberto reached over his head, Luis handing him the shotgun. Keeping it below the window, Alberto pumped a shell into the chamber and released the safety. Carlos checked his nine-millimeter pistol and in the backseat Luis and Paco checked the loads on their M-16s.

"For Willie," Alberto said.

"For Willie," the others echoed.

Then Carlos started the engine.

27

Shootout

Wednesday, 6:50 P.M.
The Domino Garage was built to be a full-service gas station back when gas stations gave service. The pump islands were still there, the pumps long since removed. Weeds grew in the cracks around the concrete islands, and the original Exxon sign had been replaced by a hand-painted picture of a domino, six dots on one end of the domino, one dot on the other. "Domino Garage" was painted below that. Kyle and Mac drove by the garage seeing the Psychlos gathered inside, then continuing around the block. Michelson was parked around the corner, moving from his car to the backseat of theirs.

"Bletson's in there," Mac said to Michelson as he got in.

"Yeah, I saw him," Michelson said.

Nick Bletson led the Psychlos but wasn't as charismatic as Alberto Mendez, the leader of the Brotherhood of the Rose. Where Alberto impressed the members of his gang with his wit, charm, and intelligence, Bletson dominated his gang with his ruthlessness. Like a medieval warlord, he kept his position only as long as the others feared him. At twenty years old, Nick Bletson was the oldest member of the gang. Bletson had done juvenile time twice, but was smart enough to form a gang to insulate himself from the law, getting younger and dumber members to take the risks. Bletson was brutal by nature, and Kyle knew he would have been part of the shooting. Kyle was also sure Bletson had two or more of his flunkies ready to give him an alibi for the time of the shooting. There was no doubt that Bletson had dreamed up the tarring and feathering. It was the kind of sadistic thing he would be into.

"Are we looking for evidence or just getting their attention?" Michelson asked.

"Just a friendly visit," Mac said. "A search warrant was served on the garage this afternoon but they found nothing— no guns, no tar. The cars they used for the shooting are in pieces by now. We'll have to dredge the Willamette River if we want to find the guns. The best we can hope for is to put a little fear in them."

"Fear of the law?" Michelson asked doubtfully.

"Fear the Brotherhood will be gunning for them," Mac said.

All they really could accomplish here today was to keep the Psychlos from clashing with the Brotherhood of the Bloody Rose until Alberto and his gang cooled down. There would be retribution at some point but Alberto and the Brotherhood might settle for less than murder if Willie Mendez had time to get out of the hospital.

They left the car, walking around the corner to the garage. The Psychlos on the sidewalk watched them from the moment they came around the corner, then sauntered into the garage to warn the others. With Mac in the lead they turned into the garage and found themselves facing eight gang members who milled about, most putting down beer bottles. Everyone in the garage was under the legal drinking age. Through a window they could see two more Psychlos in the garage's small office. The boys in the office looked nervous and guilty. They hurriedly put something away in an overhead cabinet. Kyle could smell marijuana in the air and half the boys in the garage moved with a drug-induced nervous energy. Two visits from the cops in one day had caught them by surprise but without a warrant and no cause to search them again, they would ignore the drug signs. Nick Bletson was sitting on a workbench, a hammer in one hand, a beer bottle next to him. He sat regally like a king on a throne, staring derisively at the cops, the hammer his scepter.

"That your beer?" Mac said to Bletson.

"Naw, it belongs to my brother. All this beer was left by my brother and the guys who work for him."

Mac walked deeper into the garage, Michelson following. Kyle stayed by the door, making sure none of the Psychlos got behind them. The Psychlos drifted toward the walls, eyes alternating between Mac and Bletson.

"So we won't find your fingerprints on the beer bottle?" Mac said.

"I had to move it so I could sit down."

"What about the rest of the bottles?" Mac said.

"My friends and I were just cleaning up. We're expecting a few ladies to come by."

Now Bletson slid off the workbench, stepping close to Mac. Slowly Mac let his eyes drift toward the hammer in Bletson's hand. Then Mac touched his coat where he wore his gun. Bletson rolled his eyes, then tossed the hammer back onto the workbench. When the clatter from the hammer died, Mac dropped his hand to his side again. Bletson was a head taller than Mac and built like a linebacker, with wide shoulders and narrow hips. The sleeves of his sweatshirt were cut off, and he wore a tattoo of a spaceship on his beefy arm. Bletson had gotten the name "Psychlos" out of a science fiction book he had read. Kyle made a mental note to ask Sherrie about the name and the book. It might give him some clue about what motivated Bletson.

Bletson was posturing, hands at the side, chest out, coming into Mac's personal space trying to intimidate him. Bletson was underestimating Mac. Despite his pudgy look, Mac was strong and quick and had taken down bigger men than Bletson.

"You came down here to hassle us about some beer?"

Bletson said. "Man, if you don't have better things to do with your time, I do."

"You've got some tar on your finger," Mac said.

Bletson looked at his hand, then caught himself, now smiling at Mac.

"Funny. Hey, your zipper's down," Bletson said, the Psychlos laughing nervously.

"We have a witness who puts you in one of the cars that did the drive-by," Mac bluffed.

"I wasn't there and you got no witness or else you'd be cuffing me, not boring the shit out of me."

The Psychlos forced another laugh but it had a hollow guilty sound.

"The witness is in the hospital," Mac said, making it up as he went along. "He's got some bad burns but he's going to make it and when he finds out you were shooting at his brother and girlfriend, I think he's going to be real cooperative. There were little children there too."

Bletson kept his smile but it was forced now.

"What kind of coward shoots at a four-year-old?" Mac asked.

Bletson reddened, his fists clenched, knuckles white. Mac was trying to goad Bletson into taking a swing at him. If he did, they could get Bletson off the street. With him in jail the rest of the Psychlos might be smart enough to hide out for a few weeks, giving the Brotherhood of the Rose time to cool down. Then Kyle heard the roar of a car engine.

Turning, he saw a Cadillac racing into the garage at full speed. Kyle jumped left to get out of its way, seeing guns come out the window as he hit the concrete. Then like *Old Ironsides*, the Cadillac fired a broadside. The Cadillac had pulled into the stall farthest from the office, the windows of the office imploding from a shotgun blast, the chests and faces of the two boys inside peppered with lead pellets and shards of glass. They went down, disappearing behind the half wall that divided the garage from the office.

The gunfire from the Cadillac was steady and deafening, a mixture of shotgun, pistol, and rifle fire. Caught unprepared, the Psychlos were like ducks in a shooting gallery with nowhere to hide. Kyle rolled out the door of the garage, pulling his weapon as he did. Mac and Bletson were down, Mac lying on his back, drawing his weapon and shooting over his feet. Bletson was lying on the concrete, a halo of blood forming around his head. Michelson was in a crouch, weapon in hand, but as he returned fire he took a shotgun blast, his head suddenly flopping sideways, his body collapsing. Kyle fired at the man holding the shotgun, two, three, four times, seeing the shooter's head jerk with two impacts, the shotgun slipping from his hand clattering to the concrete floor. Then Mac hit one of the riflemen in the backseat just as Kyle put four more rounds into the back of the Cadillac, silencing the other gun. Now the Cadillac went into reverse, tires squealing as the driver tried to escape. Kyle was up and in front of the car as the tires spun on the oil-slick floor, smoke boiling from the rear wheel wells, the car moving slowly backward. Kyle released his clip, pulling his spare from his coat pocket, then took aim at the driver's window.

"Police, stop the car!" Kyle shouted.

Suddenly the tires caught clean pavement and the Cadillac shot backward. Kyle jumped out of the way, letting the Cadillac pass. In the garage Kyle had seen the face of the driver but as the Cadillac shot past him into bright daylight, the glare obscured the driver's face. Kyle fired into the driver's window, head high. The first round punctured a hole in the windshield, sending cracks spider-webbing in all directions. Kyle's second round imploded the windshield, the next three shots passing through an empty frame. The Cadillac continued backward, crossing the street and crashing into a parked car on the far side, coming to rest, the engine stalling. Cars coming from both directions screeched to a stop, then there was the scream of metal on metal as one of the cars was rear-ended. Then everything was silent.

Kyle ran to the Cadillac, gun pointed at the open driver's side window. As Kyle came along the side he could see the driver was slumped over the steering wheel. Kyle could see where one of his bullets had exited the back of the boy's head. There were three other boys in the car, one in the back still alive. He had a hole in his sternum and a head wound, but was conscious and holding his hand to his chest, trying to stem the bleeding. He was terrified.

"Help me," the boy begged.

"Keep pressure on the wound," Kyle said, collecting the rifles in the backseat and tossing them into the front.

A crowd was gathering and he saw a woman punching on a cell phone.

"Is that 9-1-1?"

The woman nodded.

"Tell them there's been an officer-involved shooting and two officers are down."

The woman nodded, speaking to the dispatcher even before Kyle finished. Kyle hurried back to the garage. Three Psychlos were still moving, only one had escaped injury and he was huddled in a corner in shock, eyes wide at the horror in the garage. Kyle checked Michelson first, seeing the shotgun had hit him at throat level and at the short range the pellet spread had been minimal, ripping out most of his throat. He left Michelson, hoping Mac was in better shape. Mac was conscious but blood was soaking his right side and his face was pasty white. Mac's short breaths came as rapid as machine-gun fire. When he saw Kyle he took a deeper breath and Kyle heard a liquid sound.

"It was over!" Mac said.

Kyle ignored him, pressing his hand into Mac's armpit, trying to stem the bleeding.

"This doesn't count," Mac said.

"Shut up," Kyle said. "Lie still, the ambulance is coming."

"They shot me after shift!" Mac insisted.

"Yeah," Kyle said. "You're off duty."

Now Mac smiled, raised his left hand, touching his bloody shirt.

"Then this doesn't count. I win the pool."

"Yeah, you won it, Mac. I'll tell them you made it through the day without a stain."

Mac smiled weakly, then slowly his eyes sagged closed.

28

Knowledge

Wednesday, 9:28 P.M.
He knew the future now, or at least a small part of it, and it gave him a sense of power. The police hadn't caught him yet, nor even come close and now he knew they never would. He knew this because of what he read in the papers he found in the man-in-the-hat's hideaway. He also knew the man-in-the-hat's name. He was Robert Sinclair. Sinclair had done him a great favor, because now he could continue his mission confident he wouldn't be caught. He would be careful; that couldn't change. But if he was as careful as he had been, they would never catch him. No one could, except Sinclair. So Sinclair had to be dealt with. His ministry could go on; it must go on. But there was another reason to stop Sinclair. He knew why Sinclair was here and what he intended to do and he couldn't let Sinclair succeed.

After reading the papers he put them back in the cabinet, returned the power cord to its place, then left. He knew Sinclair wouldn't be back until after the construction crews went home. He returned to Pumpkin Court at 7:00 P.M., hiding in the brush of an uncleared lot, watching Sinclair's hiding place.

Sinclair cruised slowly into the development at nine-thirty, parking behind the debris pile again, walking quickly to the house and around back. Moving to a new position where he could keep Sinclair in view, he watched Sinclair open the patio doors and enter. He waited in hiding, letting Sinclair get farther inside, then he crept to the back wall of the house and to the door as before, looking into the kitchen. Sinclair took off his coat, revealing the strange suit he wore. Opening the cabinet where he had hidden his food and papers, Sinclair suddenly froze, staring inside. Now agitated, Sinclair looked around, panic in his eyes. Suddenly he ran from the kitchen out of view.

Flattening against the wall, he realized he hadn't been careful about putting the papers back in the cabinet. His carelessness had tipped off Sinclair that someone had been riffling through his stash. He saw Sinclair come back into the kitchen, a gun in his hand. He turned and ran.

Keeping low, he made it to the brush and kept on going, picking up the pace when he heard the patio doors open. He had killed before but always unarmed men or women and always by surprise. Sinclair was an old man and in a fight he would beat Sinclair. But guns had a way of equalizing physical differences. There were too many uncertainties about shooting it out. Did Sinclair have weapons training? How steady was his aim when his life was threatened?

He was committed to stopping Sinclair but there was a less risky way. He would have the police do it.

29

Breakfast

Thursday, 5:20 A.M.

Sherrie's house was dark but Kyle rang the doorbell anyway. Then he rang it twice more, stepping away from the door. A few minutes later the porch light came on and Sherrie peeked out the living-room window. He expected her to be angry but she nodded at him and a few seconds later swung the screen door open and rolled her chair back to let him in. She was wearing only a T-shirt but showed no embarrassment.

"You said to come by after work," Kyle said.

"I said with a pepperoni pizza."

"Damn, I forgot it."

"I don't eat pepperoni pizza at five in the morning anyway," Sherrie said. "How's Mac?"

"Alive. He came through surgery fine and they saved his lung. The next few days will tell the story. If he doesn't develop an infection, he'll be okay."

"What about the other officer?"

"Art is dead. He was a short-timer, just months from retirement. His wife will get the pension and the insurance but she'll have no one to spend it with."

"Did you know him well?"

"Yes. He had this slow way of talking that irritated the hell out of me but I never once wished anything like this would happen to him."

"Of course you didn't. What about the gangs? On the news they said there were survivors."

"Three of the Psychlos survived; one without a scratch. One of the Psychlos is paralyzed from the waist down, the other was back in surgery when I left. It didn't sound like he was going to make it. None of the shooters survived."

"I'm sorry about Mac," Sherrie said. "Do they need people to give blood?"

"Half of the force has already been in," Kyle said.

Sherrie's face had lost all its hard edges, the defensive attitude temporarily put away like storm windows in the spring. Now Kyle could see the person she had been before the accident. He liked what he saw.

"Go fix us some breakfast while I get dressed," Sherrie said.

"You don't have to dress for me."

Sherrie stared briefly, as if she was trying to judge whether Kyle had just hit on her. Kyle quickly apologized.

"Sorry. It's been a tough night and I've got something I need to know."

"Fix breakfast," Sherrie ordered. "I'll be down in a minute."

Kyle turned toward the kitchen, resisting the urge to watch legless Sherrie thump up the stairs in her T-shirt. "Kyle, you're a pervert," he whispered to himself.

There were eggs and bacon in the fridge and Kyle pulled these out, starting eight strips of bacon frying and then a pot of coffee. Bacon and eggs would have been enough for Kyle, but he remembered Sherrie finished two-thirds of the Chinese food they had ordered. She had the appetite of a trucker. Kyle searched the cabinets until he found Bisquick and a bowl. He noticed that everything was in the lower cabinets. Kyle mixed up pancake batter and then found an electric griddle. The eggs were cooking in the bacon grease when Sherrie came in, now dressed in a University of Oregon sweatshirt, the most conservative thing he had seen her wear.

"I like mine over easy," Sherrie said.

"Health regulations require eggs to be cooked until the yolk is solid," Kyle said.

"If you cook them hard you can't sop up the runny yellow stuff with your pancakes," Sherrie said.

"Good point."

Kyle flipped the half-dozen pancakes he had on the griddle.

"Didn't they teach you about nutrition in school?" Kyle asked.

"Yeah, and I used to be part of the tofu and bran fiber crowd," Sherrie said. "I ate five helpings of fruit and vegetables a day, exercised, refused to eat red meat, and drank in moderation. Then one day I woke up in a hospital and my carefully cared for legs were gone and now I don't give a damn what happens to what's left of my body and I eat what I like."

Kyle knew that wasn't completely true. Sherrie's wardrobe was selected to be revealing and she exercised to exhaustion nearly every day, allowing her to eat like she did and still keep her body firm and her arms muscular. She was proud of what was left of her body.

"What did happen to your legs, Sherrie?" Kyle blurted out.

"Well you waited longer to ask than most."

Sherrie rolled to a lower cabinet and pulled out plates and then silverware from a drawer, setting the table as she spoke. Then she filled two coffee mugs.

"Do you really want to hear this or do you want to talk about what happened to you today? I heard they took the task force away from you. Then one of your friends was killed and another wounded. Don't you want to talk?"

"I've been talking about it all night. People were coming and going. I talked about it over and over."

"Going over the details isn't working through it," Sherrie said.

"There was some of that too. What I need now is a break from talking about it," Kyle said. "I want to know about you."

Kyle scooped up two of the eggs and put them on a plate in front of Sherrie, the others on his own plate. Sherrie rolled to the table, picked up her fork, and tasted the eggs, pronouncing them "Not bad."

"I dated a few guys in college but all they wanted was to get me in bed. They would take me out three or four times and when I wouldn't put out they would dump me. My friends thought I was nuts since some of the guys I dated were considered hot. Most of my friends had a three dates before sex rule but I grew up conservative," Sherrie said, indicating the furnishings in her home. "I wanted the guy I went to bed with to want more than that from me."

"Like a wedding?" Kyle suggested, scooping up the pancakes and adding them to the plates.

"An engagement ring would have been enough," Sherrie said honestly. "I didn't get it, at least not from anyone I wanted. Anyway, I went to graduate school and met a guy who said all the right things."

"And gave you an engagement ring?" Kyle asked, sitting opposite Sherrie, then pouring syrup on his pancakes.

"No, just a promise, but he said it so sincerely," she said with a smile. "His name was Tom. He'd inherited quite a bit of money and owned a condominium and drove a Corvette. I moved in with him three months after we met. My mother cried when she heard I was living with someone. She wouldn't call me after that, I had to call her. We were pretty happy for about six months and then one night we went to a party—one of the professors threw these great New Year's Eve parties. We did a lot of drinking. When we left for home we were both drunk—it took me a year to admit it, but we were drunk."

Sherrie paused, nibbling on bacon and sipping her coffee. Her face was blank, her eyes staring at nothing.

"Car accident?" Kyle asked.

"Not like you're thinking. Tom kept telling me he wasn't too drunk to drive and I was too drunk to know better. By some miracle we made it home without killing ourselves or anyone else. We were sitting in the driveway and he asked me to get out and open the garage door. I was standing in front of the car when his foot slipped off the brake and hit the gas. The impact drove me through the door. I woke up when the firemen lifted me onto a stretcher. I didn't know it then but I left one of my legs on the garage floor. They cut the other one off a couple of hours later. I didn't wake up for three days and when I did it was just like a scene out of that old Ronald Reagan movie. You know the one where he wakes up and finds out his legs have been amputated and starts yelling, 'Where's the rest of me? Where's the rest of me?' I wasn't that coherent. I just screamed. They kept me tied down and sedated for a week after that.

"Tom came to see me twice in the hospital. The first time he couldn't stop staring at the sheet covering my legs, like he didn't believe they were really gone. I finally threw the cover off and showed him the stumps—he turned green and left. The second time he showed up to tell me he was dumping me. He brought a suitcase of my clothes and a key to a storage locker where he'd moved my things. He claimed he had been planning to tell me before the accident and it didn't have anything to do with me being a double amputee. I lost it again then and crawled off the bed after him, screaming that I was going to kill him. They had to tie me down again and it was two weeks before the psychiatrist would let me sleep without restraints. Even then the nurses came in every fifteen minutes."

Kyle realized he was smiling and was suddenly embarrassed. Sherrie smiled back.

"If you think that's funny, you'll love what happened next," Sherrie said, enjoying her own story. "I sued him. I sat in the courtroom with the stumps of my legs bare and pointed at the eight women and four men on the jury. I ended up owning his condominium and half of everything else he had. His wages are garnished and I get a check every month and I will until one of us dies. I would have killed myself long ago except I won't let Tom off the hook that easily."

"So there is justice in this world?" Kyle said.

Sherrie's smile faded.

"No, he was my one and only lover and I'll never have another. I passed up all those other boys and now no one worth having wants me."

Kyle felt she wanted to be contradicted, to be told she was desirable, but he couldn't lie to her. Despite the way he felt when he looked at her face and upper body, he couldn't ever forget she was an amputee and that horrified a part of him. Instead, he gave her generalities.

"Other people have lost limbs and have lovers, marry, have children."

Sherrie's face clouded and he knew he was on thin ice.

"I guess I don't want the kind of man who would want a cripple," Sherrie said. "I don't want a co-dependent, I want someone capable of healthy love—someone to want me the way Tom wanted me before the accident."

There was no comforting her and Kyle didn't try. He respected her pain, the way he wished others had respected his. They ate in silence for a few minutes, then Sherrie rolled to the counter, getting the coffeepot off the warmer, and refilled their cups.

"Mac told me you lost a daughter," Sherrie said.

Sherrie left the comment hanging in the air, expecting Kyle to fill in details. As he began to talk, he realized he wanted to tell her and shared details he had never shared with anyone else.

"The accident occurred a couple of years ago in early September at the end of a long drought. I was at my mother and father's place out in the country. We call it 'Grandpa's Farm' but it's really their retirement home. They keep a horse, a few sheep and chickens, to justify their tax status as a farm, but my father's no farmer. He was a lawyer. Shelby loved going there. She would feed the chickens, ride the horse, and swim in the pool. I'd just sit on the deck with my father looking at the view, watching the seasons change, and telling him about my cases. My dad specialized in contract law. He was a partner in one of the big Portland law firms when he retired. He made a good living but he grew to hate his job—it bored him. That's why he loved hearing about my work—domestic disputes, drug busts, homicide cases—even shoplifting intrigued him. He couldn't get enough.

"Aldean—my wife—was working late that night so Shelby and I stayed out at the farm until after ten. It was hot and Shelby was having fun in the pool, so why go home? We didn't leave until Aldean called asking where we were.

"I buckled Shelby into the car seat in the back of our jeep just as the storm reached the farm. It was starting to sprinkle as I drove away. Shelby fell asleep before we reached the end of the driveway. The storm front was coming from the west and heading toward Portland, the same direction we were going.

"It was raining hard as I turned east on the highway and the road was slippery—the first rain after a drought brings up road oils. I'm not sure how fast I was going. I know that stretch of road so well I don't even think about what I'm doing.

"A few miles down the road a deer jumped in front of my jeep. The visibility was so bad I didn't see it until it was too late. I hit the brakes and swerved but hit the deer anyway. My left fender caught the deer, spinning it around. The antlers shattered the windshield. The jeep skidded across the road and over the embankment. I heard Shelby scream as we went over the side. I don't remember what happened next but they tell me the jeep rolled over at least twice. When I came to we were at the bottom of a gulley. The windshield was gone and the roof was crushed. Shelby was crying."

Kyle paused, sipping his coffee. The next part was the hardest to tell.

"I was sideways on the seat with my legs under the steering wheel. My legs were broken and I was bleeding from a head wound. The doctors pulled a dozen pieces of glass out of my skin. Shelby was conscious, calling for me to help her. I released my seat belt but the roof was crushed nearly to the headrests. I could barely move. I finally managed to twist around so I could see her and saw she was still in her car seat. She looked fine except that she was bleeding. I tried to reach her through the seats but I could barely touch her. I couldn't get pressure on the wound.

"She stopped crying when she saw me looking at her. I guess she thought I was going to help her. I remember her saying, 'We had a crash, didn't we, Daddy?' The jeep was so mangled I couldn't get to her between the seats, so I pulled myself out through the windshield onto the hood. My legs were useless and I was nearly unconscious from the pain. It was still raining hard and the hood was slippery so it was easy to slide off, but when I hit the ground I passed out from the pain. When I woke up I heard Shelby calling for me again. I couldn't stand and couldn't get enough leverage to pry the door open so I told Shelby I was going to get help. She begged me not to leave her but what choice did I have? She was slowly bleeding to death and there was nothing I could do except get help.

"I dragged myself up the embankment to the highway. There wasn't much traffic along that road and I lay at the top a long time. I was unconscious when a car full of teenagers spotted me. When I woke up my head was in the lap of a teenage girl. There were two guys with her and one of them was on a cell phone. I told them about Shelby and they ran down the hill to help. They tried everything but couldn't get in the car either. They were still trying when the firemen arrived. They had to use the Jaws of Life to get Shelby out of the wreck.

"The paramedics put splints on my legs and then strapped me to a stretcher and called in the Life Flight helicopter. They were putting me in the helicopter when I saw them bring Shelby up the hill on a stretcher. They had her covered in a blanket. She was dead."

Kyle rocked back in his chair, careful to avoid Sherrie's eyes. He didn't want her to see the tears welling up in his own.

"It must have been hard on your marriage."

"Yes, it was," Kyle said. "Do you really believe the blue man is a time traveler?" Kyle asked.

Sherrie paused, startled by the abrupt change in topics. Sensing that Kyle wasn't ready to share more, she let it go.

"I do," she said.

"Do you believe it's possible to go back in time and change things to make them come out differently."

"I believe that's why the blue man is here," Sherrie said, "and I believe he has changed some events."

"So it's possible to alter history."

"Within limits, Kyle. I've been getting responses from all over the world to my Internet request for information on time travel. Ninety percent of it is from flakes but when you weed out the Trekkies, New Agers, and ufologists, there are a respectable few who not only believe time travel is possible but believe that it happens all the time on a micro level."

"I can't believe it's common," Kyle said.

"At the micro level it might be, Kyle," Sherrie said. "Think of any system—a car engine for example. In order for an engine to operate its parts must meet certain narrow specifications, yet even as the engine ages and friction wears the parts below factory specs, it continues to function. Every system has elasticity built into it. Physical systems, like car engines, have the least elasticity and biological systems, like you and me, have more. Psychological and social systems have the most elasticity of all. It's reasonable then to assume the universe has elasticity too."

"Aren't physical laws absolute? Like the speed of light?" Kyle asked, hearing Lipke's words in his head.

"Yes, but the universe is a fabric made up of many such laws all woven together and that creates flexibility."

Suddenly Sherrie rolled from the table and opened a drawer, returning with a handful of pencils. She dropped the pencils on the table, then picked one up, holding it tight in her fist.

"This pencil represents one physical law like the speed of light. Try to push it out of my fist."

Kyle pushed down on the pencil, but it wouldn't move. Then Sherrie picked up the rest of the pencils, holding a dozen in her hand.

"All these pencils represent the universe which is made up of a number of physical laws. Now try pushing a pencil out."

Kyle pushed on one of the center pencils and it slid down.

"Any system has to have a certain amount of give to it. Concrete highways have expansion joints to allow for the heat of summer and the cold of winter and steel bridges are designed to flex in high winds. As the most complex system of all, the universe should have the most elasticity."

"So where does the time travel come in?" Kyle asked.

"Remember the automobile engine example? Sometimes engines misfire—the car chugs a couple of times. Perhaps something similar happens with the universe and it hesitates, resetting itself ever so slightly."

"Wouldn't we notice?" Kyle asked.

"I think we do. Haven't you ever had a déjà vu experience? The feeling that you've experienced the exact same event before?"

"Yes, a couple of times recently."

Sherrie's head was nodding before he finished.

"Me too," Sherrie said. "I had several very powerful experiences but they stopped when I met you. I think meeting you changed the trajectory of my life."

Sherrie paused now, looking at Kyle with her soft side

showing. It unnerved him. Standing, he started clearing the table, putting the dishes in the dishwasher.

"Kyle, when I saw you on the news they mentioned the man with blue skin, but they made it sound like a joke. They mentioned the genie theory."

"Another detective leaked that story to the media."

"There wasn't much said about the blue man. Why is that?"

Kyle rinsed the bowl he had mixed the batter in.

"He isn't Cradle Robber. Some of the detectives think he's a false lead left by Cradle Robber to keep us off his trail."

"What about the notes?" Sherrie asked.

"Same thing—false trail. Besides, not all of those notes are about Cradle Robber."

"Does your captain know that he might be a time traveler?"

"No, and he doesn't want to hear it. No one would believe it except Mac and he's in the hospital."

Kyle finished cleaning and relaxed against the counter, studying Sherrie. Her brow was furrowed and she looked concerned.

"I better get to work," Kyle said.

"You're thinking about your daughter, aren't you, Kyle," Sherrie said.

As if he had been struck, Kyle's body tensed.

"You can't do it, Kyle."

"I've got to get to work," Kyle said, leaving the kitchen abruptly.

"Talk to me about this," Sherrie said, rolling after him. "You know why he's leaving you those notes, don't you?"

Kyle paused, hand on the doorknob.

"He's leaving the notes to establish credit, Kyle. He's saving those children to justify something he's going to do and whatever it is it's dangerous—not just to him, but to all of us. He's disrupting the space-time continuum."

"It's elastic, remember," Kyle said.

"The elasticity isn't infinite, Kyle, and I think what the blue man is planning is going to push past the tolerances. You have to find out why he's here and stop him, not help him."

Kyle walked out the door, Sherrie rolling to a stop on the porch, shouting after him.

"We need to talk, Kyle!"

Kyle drove away without looking back.

30

Phone Calls

Thursday, 7:45 A.M.

"I've been thinking about jobs that would keep Cradle Robber on the West Coast," Segal said over the phone. "I've got a couple of ideas."

Inspector Segal had called in from her hotel before the start of the day shift, knowing Kyle would be in early.

"You should talk with Danforth," Kyle said.

"I will when he gets in but I need someone to brainstorm with first."

Kyle had come straight to the bureau from breakfast at Sherrie's house. He hadn't bothered to try to sleep. He spent the early morning hours writing a report on the killings at the Domino Garage.

"Last night I saw an ad on TV for *Les Misérables*," Segal said. "It's playing in Portland next week and it was in San Francisco a few weeks ago. I got to wondering if Cradle Robber might be with one of the touring companies? They usually work the big metropolitan areas on the coast."

"True, but they tour all across the country and the West Coast is usually the last stop," Kyle said. "The murders didn't start until San Diego. I suppose it's possible Cradle Robber joined the company late in the tour."

"Or something happened in San Diego that set him off," Segal suggested.

"It's a good theory. Be sure to mention it to Danforth," Kyle said.

"I have another idea too. Don't you have some sort of festival coming up pretty soon?"

"The Rose Festival," Kyle said. "It starts this weekend."

"There are vendors that work festivals. They follow them around the country."

"You think Cradle Robber's selling curly fries?"

"Or scones, or maybe he's a ride operator," Segal said. "He could have worked the Pasadena Tournament of Roses in January, then moved to San Francisco—we've always got some festival or another going in the valley. Same with San Diego."

The more Kyle thought about Segal's idea, the more he liked it. If he was following the festivals, after Portland's Rose Festival he would move to Seattle for the Seafair.

"The Fun Center opens this week," Kyle said. "Most of the vendors are already setting up in Waterfront Park."

They brainstormed a few more ideas, then Segal hung up to try to reach Danforth. The phone rang as soon as she hung up.

"Sommers," Kyle answered.

"Talk to me or I'll come down there," Sherrie said.

Kyle almost hung up but knew Sherrie wouldn't make an idle threat. She would love to come to the station and make an ugly scene.

"There's nothing to talk about," Kyle said, stalling, trying to think of a way to pacify her.

"You need to know what you're getting into," Sherrie said.

Kyle didn't answer.

"I'm coming down," Sherrie said.

"No," Kyle said sharply. "I'll come by after shift."

"Meet me for lunch or I'll be there in twenty minutes."

"All right. Meet me at noon in Waterfront Park across from the Firehouse Museum."

"Be there, Kyle, or I'll pay a visit to Captain Harding."

Sherrie hung up without a good-bye. Kyle felt like he was being blackmailed but saw no way out. He would have to meet Sherrie.

Just before eight, Cassidy wandered into his cubicle, slipping into the victim's chair. Cassidy was a beautiful woman and kept her uniform starched and pressed and her badge polished. She was camera-ready twenty-four hours a day. Her hair was pulled back in a bun today that highlighted her high cheekbones. As beautiful as her face was, Kyle found himself glancing at her legs, even though she was wearing pants. Cassidy seemed to notice, and slowly crossed them, then folded her hands in her lap and leaned forward, speaking softly.

"I called the hospital and they said Mac is conscious. He can have a few visitors. I'm going over tonight and wondered if you would like to ride along?"

Cassidy spoke with concern, as if she thought visiting a hospital would be traumatic for Kyle. Like others, Cassidy thought Kyle might associate the trauma of Shelby's death with a hospital. But Kyle never visited Shelby in a hospital. Shelby died strapped in her car seat. She was buried before he got out of the hospital.

"Maybe, Cassidy. Let me see how the day goes. With the Cradle Robber case and the shooting last night . . ."

"Sure, Kyle. If you want to come along, just give me a call."

"What's Mac's condition?" Kyle asked.

"Serious, but not critical. He's a tough old Texas bird. He'll pull through."

Cassidy stood, smiling at Kyle and showing flashes of her nearly perfect teeth.

"Call me," Cassidy said, then left.

Kyle leaned out of his cubicle, watching her walk away, eyes drifting to her legs.

At nine-thirty an envelope was delivered, marked "To Detective Kyle Sommers." Heart pounding, Kyle tore it open, finding another of the notes:

• Wednesday, morning: After a night of car thieving, members of the Brotherhood of the Rose gang liked to gather in front of Alberto Mendez's house to flirt with the neighborhood girls on their way to school. It was this moment that members of the Psychlos chose to deliver a message to their rivals for the Portland stolen car market. Eight gunmen in two cars opened fire while they dumped the body of Willie Mendez. Willie, Alberto's brother, had been tarred and feathered. Drunk and reckless, the Psychlo gunfire cut down one of Mendez's gang members, Paco Nobles, as well as a teenage girl, Linda Roquet, a four-year-old boy, Kelly Grant, and a three-year-old girl, Teresa Nunez. The attack set off a gang war in which four more innocent bystanders would be gunned down as well as Willie Mendez and most of the Brotherhood. The war ended six months later when Alberto Mendez killed rival gang leader Nick Bletson, wiping out the last of the Psychlos. Alberto Mendez is serving three consecutive life sentences.

Kyle didn't bother to put the note in a plastic bag because he wasn't going to log it in as evidence. Instead, he copied the note and cut the text out, pasting it below the Benchly note. He read the pieces from the beginning again, sure now they were part of a larger piece. He wondered how many more of the notes he would receive and what other tragedies might still be waiting to happen. Sherrie had said the man with the blue skin was helping people in order to build up credit against something he was yet to do. If you could believe the information that the blue man had left so far, he had saved at least eight children, not including the teenagers from the Bloody Rose drive-by shooting. If he felt he needed that much justification for what he was going to do, then what he was planning must be terrible indeed.

At ten, Kyle met with the task force. The meetings were much different with Danforth in charge. There was an agenda now and a secretary to take minutes. Each detective reported in turn, Danforth doing all the questioning and directing further work. There was still little real progress but Danforth insisted on reports anyway. The sketch had brought hundreds of tips, but none had panned out yet.

With the loss of Mac and Michelson, two detectives would be added to the task force. Danforth already had two names, both detectives that Kyle approved of. Until the additional detectives were reassigned, the rest of the task force had to split the extra work. Danforth divided the work evenly, skipping Kyle. Everyone noticed and avoided Kyle's eyes.

When Danforth reached the end of his agenda, Inspector Segal got his attention, offering new theories about why Cradle Robber was working up the coast. Danforth was skeptical but assigned Joanne Falk to pursue the fruit broker idea and Willie Baxter to look into the theater road company theory. Danforth was about to assign someone to look into the festival vendor idea when Kyle interrupted, volunteering. Danforth paused, studying Kyle. Harding had ordered Danforth to let Kyle go his own way, which he had. Now Danforth was wondering why Kyle wanted the assignment. The answer was complex. Partly it was because Kyle thought it was the best of the new theories, but partly it was because of the way Danforth treated him. Kyle wouldn't be ignored.

"Fine, Sommers you can investigate the corn dog theory."

Danforth smiled but no one around the table laughed. Danforth knew he had stepped over the line and quickly moved to bring the meeting to a close. Before he could, Randy Cummings spoke. Cummings had been assigned from the Multnomah County Sheriff's Office and looked like an accountant, wearing slacks, a white shirt, and bow tie.

"I've got a brother-in-law in the shipping business," Cummings said. "He suggested Cradle Robber might work with one of the container shipping companies. They barge those containers up and down the coast. They bring them down the Columbia to Portland too. Cradle Robber might be working for one of those shipping companies or even one of the oceangoing tugs. I'll look into it if you want."

Danforth agreed, then reviewed assignments and set the next meeting time. Kyle left for his cubicle, thinking about how to find Cradle Robber if he was part of the Rose Festival.

The festival was held in June, a month on the cusp of the rainy season in Portland. The Grand Floral Parade was held in rain as often as in sunshine. The long-range forecast had predicted another rainy festival this year but a high pressure system had formed unexpectedly, creating unusual June weather. The air was humid yet there was a lot of static electricity. Dry electrical storms, rare in Oregon, had plagued the Willamette Valley. There had been several grass fires. The air quality was poor, the skies hazy, creating spectacular sunsets. The night sky was bright with the aurora borealis. The strange weather was better for outdoor activities than rain, and the directors of the Rose Festival were ecstatic, predicting record crowds. The festival lasted three weeks and included three parades, car racing, an air show, a rose show, a carnival, and many other activities. That was the problem. How to find Cradle Robber in the crowds.

It was already seventy degrees when Kyle left to meet Sherrie for lunch. Too warm for his jacket, Kyle untucked his shirt so that it would cover his gun. Kyle walked to Waterfront Park, making sure he was on time since he knew Sherrie wouldn't wait more than a couple of minutes. He spotted Sherrie while he waited for the signal in front of the Firehouse Museum. Sherrie was rolling back and forth impatiently, paying no attention to the passersby forced to dodge her chair. Sherrie spotted him at the same time, picking Kyle out of the crowd of office workers going to the park for lunch. Sherrie rolled to the curb, parking herself at the edge of the crosswalk, forcing pedestrians to flow around her like a rock in a stream.

Sherrie wore a white polo shirt with a Nike swoosh over her left breast and a pair of blue Nike shorts over black stretch pants sewn closed to cover the scarred stumps of her legs. Kyle noticed the men staring at Sherrie's breasts, then their eyes taking in her legs. Two men in business suits in front of him eyed her, one whispering, "What a waste," as they passed.

"Let's eat first," Kyle said as he reached her, making sure their conversation stayed private.

"Nice day for a picnic," Sherrie said, turning to roll next to him into the park. "But you're not carrying a picnic basket."

"We're going to eat the way our forefathers did," Kyle said.

"Forage for roots and grubs?"

"Eat at a hot dog stand."

Kyle stopped at a silver cart with a large striped umbrella, lining up behind a half-dozen office workers. A transient walked down the line, palm up, asking for change. He was dressed in mismatched clothes: work boots, dress slacks, sweatshirt, and tattered overcoat. He had a three-day beard and was missing two front teeth. Those in the line shied away from his hand, most turning away, ignoring him. When the transient reached Sherrie he gave her a quick pitying glance, then held out his hand to Kyle.

"Spare some change for food."

Suddenly Sherrie's hand shot out gripping the man's wrist, pulling it down to her lap, and holding it there. The man struggled to get free, but Sherrie held him tight, stronger than the transient. Reaching with her other hand into a purse hidden between her hip and the side of the chair, Sherrie pulled out a twenty-dollar bill and slapped it into the man's hand, then shoved him back. Now he stared at the money, surprised by his sudden windfall.

"Thanks, lady, thanks a lot," the transient said.

Then the transient hurried away, rubbing his wrist.

"He's going to buy booze with that money," Kyle said.

"I know."

"With that much money he could buy enough rotgut whiskey to kill himself."

"That's his choice."

"He's an alcoholic, Sherrie, it's an addiction, not a choice."

"Bullshit! He chose to take the first drink and he makes the same choice every time he reaches for a bottle. He can walk through the door of the Salvation Army Rescue Mission any day he decides to make a different choice but he won't, because it's easier to stay drunk and not face life than get sober and see what you really are."

Kyle doubted kicking an addiction was as simple as that but didn't argue.

Sherrie ordered two hot dogs with mustard, a bag of Sun Chips, a chocolate chocolate-chip cookie, and a Classic Coke. Kyle ordered one hot dog, a bag of sour cream and onion chips, and a Diet Coke. Kyle knew Sherrie's eating habits now and knew he couldn't match her calorie for calorie. They found room on one end of a bench facing the walk that ran along the Willamette River, Kyle sitting, Sherrie parking at the end of the bench next to him. There was a steady parade of joggers, office workers, and panhandlers passing by, but enough of them so that they felt alone. Sherrie finished her two hot dogs in the time it took Kyle to eat one and was eating her chips when she opened up on him, her usual blunt self.

"You can't use this man to save your daughter, Kyle."

Kyle almost choked on the last bite of hot dog. He'd never been that honest with himself. Kyle looked over at the two women who sat at the other end of the bench, listening to their conversation to be sure they hadn't heard Sherrie. To his relief he heard, "Of course she was sleeping with him, that's how she got promoted to district manager."

"Just what do you think I'm planning to do?" Kyle said.

"I think you're going to try to get our time traveler friend to go back and save your daughter."

"I can't even find him," Kyle said evasively.

"That's what you're planning, isn't it?"

"I don't know," Kyle said, "but let's say I do catch him and it is possible to go back and save my daughter, then why shouldn't I? You said yourself that the universe is a complex system with built-in elasticity. The life or death of one little girl couldn't be more than a grain of sand in the works of the great universal machine."

"You're using the wrong analogy. Saving your daughter is more like someone swallowing a fragment of glass. You'll get a lot of bloody discharge for sure and the whole body might die."

The mention of bloody discharge ended Kyle's appetite and he crumpled up his bag of chips and shot it like a basketball across the walk and cleanly into the trash can on the other side. Then he turned to Sherrie and spoke low but firmly.

"I don't want to live in a universe that demands the death of babies to keep running."

"The universe doesn't demand anything, events just happen."

"And they can happen differently!" Kyle said. "The blue man has proved that."

"Yes, but only to a point. It's not saving your daughter that scares me, Kyle, it's the price you'll have to pay for his help. The time traveler is here for a specific purpose and he's not going to give up on that to save your daughter."

Kyle noticed the women next to him had stopped talking and were watching them. They looked away when Kyle caught them looking.

"Let's walk, Sherrie."

"I'm still eating," she said, putting another chip in her mouth. "I can't eat and roll the damn chair."

"I can push you," Kyle offered.

Sherrie's face clouded and her lips tightened. Kyle had never seen Sherrie accept any kind of help or accept any kind of pity. Then her face softened.

"You can push me, just don't push me too far," she said.

Kyle finished his Diet Coke, dropped the empty can into a recycling bin, and then merged Sherrie into the crowd strolling the waterfront. They walked with the river on their left, the beginnings of the Rose Festival Fun Center on their right. Rides were being set up and tents pitched that would house the midway games and side shows. Farther down he could see many of the food trailers were in place and beyond that the big tents that would house the arts and crafts vendors, selling everything from summer sausage to silver jewelry, to horoscopes. Kyle focused on the men setting up the rides, studying their faces, looking for someone who matched the sketch of Cradle Robber. There were many possibles, too many.

Sherrie shoved the last of her cookie in her mouth and washed it down with the last of her Coke. Then she mimicked Kyle's garbage can shot, tossing the chip bag and then the Coke can into a passing garbage can. Both shots were as clean as Kyle's. A transient stationed by the garbage can quickly dug for the Coke can, adding it to a net bag tied to his waist, already half filled with empty cans. Sherrie immediately took control of her chair, letting Kyle walk next to her.

"Kyle, how did you think you were going to get the time traveler to help you?"

"I never said—"

"Don't lie to me, Kyle."

Kyle held his tongue. Lashing back at Sherrie was pointless.

"He's helping other children, why wouldn't he want to help my daughter?"

"Because it means another trip back in time, Kyle, and I doubt he'll be able to get away with another."

"I'll just have to make sure he comes back."

"How?" Sherrie asked. "If you stop him from doing whatever he came for, he has no reason to help you. If you stop him and then let him go so he can come back from the future again, he won't come back to help your daughter, he'll come back to complete whatever he failed to do this time. Once he's back in the future you lose control over him. The only hope you have of saving your daughter is to gain his loyalty and to do that you have to help him do whatever he came to do. But helping him is the one thing you can't do."

"If he's here to save the president from assassination, you're right, I can't help him without dramatically altering the future, but what if he's here to save his dog from being hit by a car? I think we can risk altering the future of dogdom," Kyle said.

"Don't be too sure. Let's say he saves his dog from getting hit by a car and whoever killed the animal in the other time line now has no reason to feel guilty. Since they don't feel guilty about the accident, they don't go into veterinary science and don't discover a cure for the simian AIDS virus which means the human equivalent isn't discovered and millions die from AIDS."

"That's far-fetched," Kyle said. "You could make up an infinite number of those scenarios and I could make up just as many which would end up benefiting mankind."

"Humankind," Sherrie corrected. "You're right, but there's a bigger risk."

They were passing the food vendors now, Kyle still studying the faces of the workers. The trailers parked there were mini-restaurants with picture-covered menus advertising Texas Bar-Be-Que, Sausage on a Stick, Raspberry Scones,

Snow Cones, Pronto Pups, and Auntie Sarah's Fried Ice Cream.

"Kyle, what if you help this man and he does whatever he came for?"

"Then he'll help me save Shelby."

"But if you take away his reason for coming to the past, then he won't have a reason to come back in the first place."

"But he did come back to change things," Kyle argued.

"But he won't if he doesn't have a reason and that's the danger. If he doesn't have a reason to come to the past, then all those children he saved will die."

Kyle thought of Marissa Brown who was enjoying the fourth day of being Special Person, Nick and Christy Sadler saved from drowning, and Peter Benchly who he'd last seen clinging to his mother's leg in the hospital.

"Worse yet, if he does change the past and takes away the reason he came back, then there will be a temporal paradox," Sherrie said. "Do you know what that is, Kyle?"

Kyle didn't.

"Imagine the blue man comes back and accidentally kills the younger version of himself. Then he could not grow up to be the man that came back and killed himself as a child. It's an unresolvable paradox and there isn't enough elasticity built into the cosmic system to accept that, Kyle."

"You're talking about the end of the universe?" Kyle asked. "I don't believe it."

"Not end of the universe, not even end of the planet, but something that could kill a lot of people. The universe will go on but there has to be a correction and cosmic corrections tend to be violent. You may think you're saving Shelby but in reality you are killing her all over again and yourself too. Think, Kyle, if you prevent the car accident, and Shelby lives, then you and Aldean and Shelby are a happy family again. Then when the time traveler comes back again and takes away his reason for traveling back in time, the paradox is created and has to be resolved. The energy differences between the alternate time lines needs to be balanced. The correction will be explosive."

"You don't know that," Kyle said.

"I know the universe won't tolerate a temporal paradox. What I don't know is how violent the correction will be. It's hard to know how to put numbers to something like this, but think of the energy that it took to send a man back against the tide of time and then add the energies of all the life paths he's altered—especially those he's saved. If that energy is liberated all at once, it would have to be the equivalent of a fission weapon, or a small fusion bomb."

Kyle wanted to say, "Subtract Michelson's energy," but didn't. Sherrie didn't know the blue man had been involved in the Psychlo-Brotherhood shootout and he didn't want to fuel her argument.

"That energy is building up every time he saves someone anyway," Kyle said.

"True, but he's being selective in where he intervenes— it's exclusively with children. There were three murders in the Portland area this week that didn't involve children, and he didn't show up at any of them. There was a trailer fire in Clackamas that killed two old women and a car accident on I-5 that killed the most prominent heart surgeon in Portland. He didn't help them, Kyle. He's selective because he knows the danger. Knowing people will die that you could save must be a terrible burden but once you start where do you stop? Why is it fair for anyone to die from an accident or a crime or even an illness? Life and death is based on luck, Kyle, not fairness."

"And whether someone is crippled or not?" Kyle said.

"Yes, like being crippled. Don't you think I'd get my legs back if I could? I'd give almost anything to be able to walk again, Kyle, but I won't sacrifice a city of people for my legs."

They continued in silence, Kyle forgetting to scan the

faces around him for Cradle Robber. He was disturbed by Sherrie's argument but not persuaded. He wouldn't give up hope easily.

"There must be a way to avoid the temporal paradox," Kyle said.

"He wouldn't have come back in time unless he was obsessed, Kyle. You can't simply talk him out of what he came to do."

They were past the last tent so Kyle and Sherrie cut across the park, walking back on the city side, Kyle once again scanning the workers.

"You have to stop the time traveler, Kyle, he's a bigger threat than Cradle Robber."

"I can't find either of them."

"Come to dinner tonight. Maybe we can figure something out together."

"I'm going to see Mac after shift," Kyle said.

"Come to dinner and we'll go together," Sherrie said.

Kyle agreed and they finished walking the length of the park in silence. When it was time to leave, Kyle found himself lingering, looking down at Sherrie who made no move to roll away. Sherrie had made a scene with the transient and berated Kyle, but now he felt like a teenager seeing his first date to her front door, trying to get enough nerve to try for a good-night kiss. He didn't want to kiss her, but he found that he would rather spend an unpleasant hour with Sherrie than lunch with anyone else.

"See you for dinner," Sherrie said with a smile, then turned and rolled up the block.

Watching her roll away, Kyle wondered what would have happened if he had tried to kiss her.

31

Rose Festival

Thursday, 12:22 P.M.

He'd set up his booth so many times his routine was automatic. He put the screens up first, using them to mark off what would be his stall. In the back he put the table where he would work. Creating his art in the back of the stall helped sales since it drew customers in. While parents and children watched, he would cut pieces of colorful plastic into fantastic shapes and fit them into a frame. When finished, his creations were hung along the sides of the stall, priced between twenty and two hundred dollars. Out front he kept a bin of five-dollar pieces. They were simple works, usually with only one or two large dragons or mermaids. The little ones liked those and would paw through the stack, smiling at one discovery after another.

If the rain didn't keep the customers away he would gross five thousand dollars in the two weeks of the fair, enough to keep him in Portland for another few weeks so he could finish ministering to the children he had selected. He always selected the children before the fairs began, since he couldn't scout while he worked. He did his ministering at night, after the fair closed.

Unloading the last of his tools, he picked up two emptied boxes, heading for his trailer. As he turned to leave the tent he saw a couple walking along the riverfront. He'd never seen the woman in the wheelchair before but he recognized the man from television—he was the police detective who had been on the news lately. He had been deposed as head of the Cradle Robber Task Force because of a history of alcoholism and crazy theories about a genie. He shrank back inside the tent watching the couple pass. As they passed, the detective studied the vendors setting up their wares.

He turned away, returning to his stall, thinking. He decided it had to be a coincidence. Police headquarters was only a few blocks from the park and half the city center came to the park for lunch in nice weather. Still, watching the detective study the faces of the vendors worried him. Was it just coincidence that he was here? They had a sketch of him now broadcast on every newscast and printed on the front page of the *Oregon Chronicle*. It was a poor likeness but gave them something to work with.

He also thought about the news reports about Detective Sommers. They detailed his past, including the death of his daughter, the breakup of his family, and his alcoholism. The detective didn't understand what a gift his daughter's early death was. Most disturbing were the stories of the detective's interest in bizarre theories about Cradle Robber—genies and ESP were mentioned. As he straightened his workbench, he thought about the detective and about Sinclair and how to take care of both of them.

32

Tip

Kyle began his afternoon on the phone, first contacting the
Rose Festival Association and then tracking down Sheila
Torres who was the Fun Center director. It was the worst
possible time to call her and she returned his call from her
cell phone while she supervised the setup of the Fun Center.

"What can I do for you, Detective Sommers?" Torres
asked politely.

"I need some information about the vendors working the
Rose Festival."

"I only handle the Fun Center, the parade vendors are li-
censed through the parade committee."

Kyle could hear the sound of hammering in the background, and the voices of men and women.

"I'm looking for someone from California who might be
one of your vendors."

Torres laughed, then said, "We have over three hundred
vendors and at least a third are from California, not to mention our ride operators. Enchanted Amusements operates out
of Oakland and half the floats were designed and built by a
company in Pasadena."

"The man I'm looking for might have recently lost a child
or gotten divorced."

"A divorced man from California, that hardly narrows it
down. Look, I can have my assistant fax you a list of the

vendors but I don't know anything about their personal lives."

Kyle gave her a fax number and then started to hang up but Torres stopped him.

"There's an old couple by the name of Santini that sell novelty redwood items—you know, your name carved in redwood, redwood boxes, redwood toys, that sort of thing. They're in their seventies and have been working fairs for twenty years. They know everyone on the circuit and all the gossip. If anyone knows about the personal lives of the other vendors it would be them."

Torres promised him the fax that afternoon, then said good-bye. A minute later his phone rang.

"Sommers," Kyle answered.

"It's Rogers," a voice said.

Officer Lee Rogers was assigned to the tip line, taking calls from citizens claiming to have relevant information. Young, eager, bright, and African American he was a rising star. Kyle had worked briefly with Rogers running drug stings. Rogers worked undercover making drug buys for six months until word spread among the dealers. He had impressed everyone who worked on the operation.

"I've got an insistent citizen on the tip line who won't talk to anyone but you," Rogers said.

"Is there something special about this caller?" Kyle asked.

"He says he was in the park when Carolynn Martin was killed but then so have fifty others I've talked to," Rogers said.

"Tell him Danforth is in charge now. If he wants to talk to the man at the top, it's not me."

"I already told him," Rogers said. "He insists on talking to Detective Sommers."

There were always callers like this, insisting on talking to specific detectives or even the chief of police.

"I'll tell him you're not in," Rogers offered.

"No, it's okay," Kyle said. "Put him through."

"Detective Sommers," Kyle said when the connection was made.

"Thanks for talking with me," the voice said.

"What's your name?"

"I don't want to get involved. I just want to do my civic duty."

"Your civic duty is to get involved."

There was a moment of silence, then the man spoke rapidly, like he thought the line was being traced.

"I was in the park the night the girl was murdered. I saw a man in the park. He was wearing an overcoat and a big hat. I'd never seen him before and I walk in that park almost every day."

The voice was male and sounded young—twenties or thirties. It wasn't the man who had called 9-1-1 about Cradle Robber.

"I never thought I'd see the man again but I did. I saw him in a car so I followed him out the Sunset Highway to Cornell. He drove into a new housing development called Pumpkin Court."

Kyle was taking notes as he listened.

"It was the middle of the night and he went into an empty house through the back and sat on the floor. He was wearing a strange suit and he plugged it into the wall. His skin was blue."

Kyle was suddenly interested.

"Where is this again?"

"Pumpkin Court. I checked for him during the day but he only seems to be there at night. The house isn't finished and I think he's avoiding the construction workers and hiding there at night. If you want to catch him you better go after midnight."

Kyle was suspicious. Why would someone who didn't want to get involved follow a stranger in the middle of the night.

"What did you say your name was?" Kyle asked.

"I'm just trying to help," then the line went dead.

Kyle hung up. The caller had told Kyle where and when to find the man from the park and gave him details he knew would intrigue him—blue skin, some sort of suit, being plugged into the wall. It was as if the caller knew what he wanted to hear. His instincts told him it was a trap.

Kyle wished Mac were well. His long-time friend would go with him to Pumpkin Court, no questions asked. The others in the department would want to know too much. Kyle didn't blame them. Why should they blindly follow someone with his history? It was risky to go alone but it was better. When Kyle found the blue man he wanted time alone with him.

33

Identified

Kyle was studying a map, locating the Pumpkin Court development when Harding called him to his office.

"We've got a lead on the man in the park," Harding said, handing Kyle a fax.

The FBI logo was printed at the top and Kyle recognized it as a response to a fingerprint ID request. The bureau had matched the fingerprints found on the note given to Carolee Martin. The fingerprints belonged to Robert Sinclair, Ph.D. The FBI had cleared Sinclair for a low-level security classification last year when a software company had subcontracted him for work on a CIA code-breaking program. A California address was included and a phone number for his office at UCLA.

"Check his age," Harding said.

He was thirty-two.

"He's too young," Kyle said.

"Exactly. And what would a young professor from UCLA be doing wandering around at night in a park in North Portland?" Harding asked.

"And show up in all those other places?" Kyle added.

"Check him out," Harding said.

Kyle hesitated. Harding should have given this to Danforth, not Kyle. Harding saw his hesitation.

"If it leads anywhere, take it to Danforth. If not, report it as a dead end in the next task force meeting."

Harding was giving him a chance to redeem himself. A chance to make a meaningful contribution to the investigation.

"I'll follow up on this right away," Kyle said.

Kyle hurried back to his desk and got on the phone, confirming the listing for a Robert Sinclair living in Pasadena. Kyle dialed the number and got an answering machine. A little girl's voice came on the line.

"We can't talk now 'cause we're busy," the little girl said. "You can give us a message when the phone beeps at you."

A tone signaled it was time to leave a message and he hung up. Next he called the number for Sinclair's UCLA office asking for the professor's extension. He was connected and listened to the phone ring again. When the university voice-mail system picked up the call, Kyle hung up. Then Kyle dialed the university information number and asked which department Dr. Sinclair worked in.

"Dr. Sinclair is in the mathematics department," he was told.

Kyle thanked the operator and hung up, thinking. He doubted Sinclair was Cradle Robber but it was possible he was the blue man—the age difference even made sense. The fact Sinclair was a mathematician didn't fit. Mathematicians were theoreticians. They didn't build time machines.

Kyle called Sinclair's home and office off and on all afternoon, getting no answer. It was difficult for Kyle to think through the implications of time travel, but if Sinclair had come back from the future, then Kyle doubted he would be in contact with his younger self.

At four in the afternoon Kyle called to see how Mac was doing and his wife answered, telling Kyle Mac was sleeping but could have visitors. At five he gave up calling Sinclair and left for Sherrie's house. Pizza seemed a little too ordinary, although he knew Sherrie would eat almost anything. Instead he drove to a deli in Northwest Portland not far from her house. The deli specialized in sandwiches thick with meat. He ordered one pastrami and one turkey sandwich and coleslaw. While he waited for the sandwiches he studied the desserts on display. There was a seven-layer chocolate cake, cinnamon rolls the size of a loaf of bread, apple strudel, and other luscious desserts. The sandwich and coleslaw was enough for Kyle but he guessed Sherrie wouldn't be that easily satisfied. When the sandwiches came Kyle added a slice of the chocolate cake and a piece of apple strudel to his order.

On the drive to Sherrie's house he used his cell phone to try the Sinclair home again. Again he got the answering machine with the little girl's voice.

Sherrie opened the door before he knocked, rolling backward and inviting him in. She wore a short-waisted blue V-neck sweater and a pair of slacks, folded where her legs ended. This time when she caught him admiring her figure he didn't try to hide it.

"You didn't have to get dressed up for me," Kyle said.

"I didn't. I put this on for Mac."

Kyle held up the bags of food.

"Are we eating at the table, or do we finish *The Unsinkable Molly Brown*?"

"We eat in front of the TV, but I finished *Molly Brown*. Tonight we're watching *Paint Your Wagon*."

"Isn't Clint Eastwood in that?" Kyle said.

"Yes, and he sings. Lee Marvin too. It's almost too much to stand."

Kyle followed her into the living room. Napkins were already piled on the floor and there were two bottles of Snapple on ice. There was nothing fancy about eating with Sherrie, although Kyle suspected her love of food meant she would enjoy a gourmet meal at a nice restaurant as well as she did hot dogs in the park. Although he also imagined that if the restaurant wasn't handicapped accessible, Sherrie would fling dining-room chairs across the room to make way for her wheelchair.

Sherrie maneuvered herself out of her wheelchair, again sitting on the floor, her back to the couch. Kyle sat next to her and took out the sandwiches while she started the VCR with her remote.

"What are we eating?" Sherrie said.

"Deli sandwiches. Turkey or pastrami—your choice," Kyle said.

"Why choose? I'll take half of each."

That suited Kyle and they split the sandwiches and watched the movie as they ate. It started with a covered-wagon accident and a young Clint Eastwood being taken in by a grizzled old miner played by Lee Marvin. Calling Clint's character "Pardner," the two were well bonded when Lee Marvin's character bought a wife from a passing Mormon. The woman was beautiful and Eastwood's character was attracted to his partner's new wife. Kyle could see the trouble coming and was actually enjoying the story when Sherrie stopped the VCR.

"What's in the other bags?" Sherrie said.

Kyle passed them over, letting Sherrie look inside while he gobbled down the rest of his sandwich and coleslaw.

"I'll take half of each," Sherrie said.

Kyle retrieved plates and a knife from the kitchen and cut the cake and the strudel in half, the two half desserts nearly filling a dinner plate. Using a plastic fork from the deli, Sherrie took a bite of the cake and started the movie again. Five minutes later she had finished the cake and the strudel while Kyle was only halfway through his desserts and too full to continue.

"Would you like some more?" Kyle said, offering his plate.

"Thanks," Sherrie said, taking his plate and eating without taking her eyes off the movie.

Ten minutes later Sherrie stopped the movie, turning slightly toward him, ready for a discussion whether Kyle was or not. It was like that when they were together. She determined when and what they ate, where they ate it, what they watched, what they talked about or didn't talk about.

"Have you thought about what I said?" Sherrie asked. "About the potential for a time paradox and the importance of stopping the blue man from doing what he came for?"

Relaxed, full of rich food and enjoying the movie with Sherrie, Kyle was reluctant to spoil the feeling.

"Let's talk on the way to see Mac," Kyle said.

"I'll drive."

Kyle almost blurted out, "You can drive?" Instead he said, "Fine."

Sherrie owned a handicapped-equipped van with a lift built into the side door. She didn't use the lift, though, rolling to the driver's side and using her powerful upper body to pull herself into the driver's seat. Once behind the wheel, she ordered Kyle to put her chair in the back. Kyle rode in the passenger seat watching Sherrie work the hand controls that allowed her to operate the throttle and brakes without legs. The van operated more like a motorcycle, with squeeze brakes and throttle.

Mac was at Emmanuel Hospital on the west side of the Willamette River but the drive from Sherrie's southwest home to the hospital was short. Knowing she would have little time to work on Kyle, Sherrie started as soon as she pulled away from the curb.

"Kyle, you can't help this man create a causality paradox. I've been on the Internet with a couple of physicists I know and they agree that it could be catastrophic. They estimate a broad spectrum energy release roughly half that of the bomb used on Hiroshima—and that's based on the disruptions we know he's caused. The longer he stays and the more changes he makes the more energy there will be to release."

"What is a broad spectrum energy release?" Kyle asked, the warm feeling he'd had back at Sherrie's gone.

"It's an explosion, Kyle."

"Sherrie, if we do have a man who has found a way to come back to the past to change the future, then wouldn't he know something about physics? And wouldn't he have thought about the implications of what he was doing? Anyone that intelligent wouldn't risk an entire city to do whatever he came to do. Your friends don't really know what could happen, do they?"

"No one does, Kyle."

"But someone from the future would know," Kyle insisted.

"You don't know the man, Kyle. You don't know his frame of mind. Even sane people do insane things. Remember, Kyle, I told you that whoever this is, is helping people because he's trying to build up credit to pay the costs of what he is really here for. I think he knows he's going to create a causality paradox and he's doing penance in advance."

"Sherrie, I don't know what I will do if I ever catch up to this guy. If he's really a time traveler then . . ."

"Then he can save your daughter," Sherrie finished for him.

"Yes, and why not?" Kyle snapped. "Shelby didn't deserve to die. If there is a way to save her I owe it to her to try."

"Kyle—" Sherrie began.

"But I won't do anything unless I'm sure it will do more good than harm," Kyle said, trying to head off her argument.

"You can't make that decision, Kyle. It's too personal for you."

"There isn't any decision to make," Kyle said.

"Talk to me before you do anything."

"That may not be possible," Kyle said.

"Promise me you'll talk to me first?"

Kyle studied Sherrie, wondering why she would ask for his promise. She didn't know whether a promise meant anything to him.

"I promise," Kyle said, unsure he would keep it.

Now they rode in silence, Sherrie expertly guiding her van through traffic. Sherrie was an assertive driver and more than once drew glares and honks from other motorists. After a brief but exciting ride, she parked in the hospital's visitors lot.

Mac was in Emmanuel Hospital on the fourth floor. He had already been moved out of Intensive Care. As they came to his room Kyle could see Mac's wife, Lenore, sitting by his bed talking to him. Lenore was a tiny woman, with delicate aristocratic features, but according to Mac there was nothing delicate about her. She was a strong-willed, domineering woman. Also according to Mac—a source prone to exaggeration—she was slightly nuts. As they entered Mac's room Kyle saw Cassidy there, sitting on the far side of the bed. Cassidy wore a khaki-colored skirt with a matching jacket over a white blouse. The skirt was short, showing off her crossed legs. She stood as they came in, her eyes immediately going to Sherrie and then running down her body, pausing briefly at her missing legs.

"Halfling, nice to see you again," Mac said to Sherrie.

An IV was plugged in Mac's arm, and a bag of fluid hung by his bed. Mac's face was pale and his voice raspy and weak. Only his head shifted when he looked at Sherrie and Kyle, like he was trying not to move the rest of his right side. There was a hospital tray on a table in front of him, the food half eaten. Kyle noticed there was food in Mac's beard and a yellow stain on the front of his gown.

Kyle introduced Sherrie to Lenore and Cassidy. Cassidy came around the bed to shake Sherrie's hand. The two women sized each other up like a couple meeting for a blind date.

"This is good timing," Lenore said. "Cassidy and I were

just going down to the cafeteria to get some dinner. You can keep Mac company while we're gone."

Cassidy followed Lenore to the door, reluctantly, eyes on Kyle and Sherrie, then paused at the door.

"Why don't you come down and join us for dinner after you've visited a few minutes?" Cassidy asked.

"Kyle and I have already eaten," Sherrie said, smiling sweetly.

Cassidy hesitated another second, then said, "Some other time then."

"Roll over here, Sherrie. It hurts if I have to turn my head too far," Mac said.

Sherrie rolled close to the bed and took Mac's hand.

"Any breaks in the Cradle Robber case?" Mac asked. "What about our Good Samaritan friend, has he been up to his no-good good-deed doing again?"

"Lenore wouldn't like it if I talked department business with you," Kyle said.

"Kyle, I make the rules in my house and I don't give a damn about what Lenore wants or doesn't want. So you just go ahead and tell me what's happened and be quick about it."

"Quick so I'm done before Lenore gets here?"

"Exactly," Mac said, laughing.

"I can't talk about department business in front of a civilian," Kyle said, indicating Sherrie.

"Really, then why does she know about the blue man?" Mac asked. "Those cubicles in the department aren't designed for privacy. Now hurry up and tell me the latest before Lenore gets here."

Kyle filled Mac in on the search for Cradle Robber, telling him about the possible traveling show and Rose Festival connection but leaving out the tip Kyle had received about going to Pumpkin Court. He didn't want Sherrie to know. Thankfully, Sherrie didn't tell Mac about the danger of a causality paradox. They were still talking about the possibility that they were dealing with a time traveler when Lenore came back without Cassidy. Mac switched topics in midsentence.

"—and that was the longest home run I've seen since back when the Mariners played in the Kingdome. Too bad he's a free agent next year," Mac said.

With Lenore in the room, Sherrie let go of Mac's hand. The conversation dried up a minute later, and Kyle and Sherrie excused themselves. Sherrie drove them back to her house, parking the van in a handicapped zone. Kyle brought her chair around for her, then walked her to her front door. There was an awkward moment at the door. Sherrie unlocked the door, then pushed it open. Then she looked up at him and their eyes met. Kyle bent and kissed her, Sherrie responding, placing one hand on the back of Kyle's head and holding him in the kiss. When they broke, Kyle felt as embarrassed as Sherrie looked.

"Would you like to come in?" Sherrie asked.

Kyle hesitated. He had to get to Pumpkin Court but the person who tipped him told him to arrive after midnight. Kyle intended to be there before midnight and was estimating when he needed to leave. Sherrie misunderstood his hesitation.

"We could finish the movie," she quickly added.

"Sure, as long as Clint doesn't sing 'I was born under a wandering star' again," Kyle said.

Sherrie took her position on the floor by the couch again and Kyle sat next to her but closer than before. Sherrie started the movie but Kyle couldn't concentrate on the story. Sherrie's presence had him aroused and he wanted to be even closer to her, to feel the warmth of her body against his. He was wondering if she felt the same when she scooted closer and leaned toward him, Kyle lifting his arm and putting it around her. They snuggled together like that until the end of the movie. Kyle couldn't remember half of what happened in the rest of the movie, his senses clouded by the feel of Sherrie next to him.

When the movie ended Sherrie reached for the control, turning it off. Now she looked at Kyle. Kyle pulled her close and kissed her, deeper than before and she responded. When the kiss ended she wrapped her arms around him and tried to pull him close but sitting sideways as she was it was awkward. Now Kyle lowered her to the floor, lying next to her on his side and then pulling her body next to his. Sherrie pulled herself tight against him and he could feel her breasts flatten against his chest.

Aroused, Kyle rolled Sherrie to her back, running his hand up her side. When she responded with another kiss he slid his hand onto her breast, her body shuddering involuntarily with pleasure. Then Kyle moved his leg over to place it between Sherrie's legs but when he did his leg dropped off the stump of her left leg. Suddenly all Kyle could picture was the scarred stumps of Sherrie's legs. His body went stiff and Sherrie sensed his sudden coldness. She kissed him again, trying to bring back the passion but Kyle's arousal was gone. Sherrie released him and he sat up.

"I'm sorry . . ." Kyle said, his voice trailing off. He was about to make an excuse but cut himself off. Sherrie was brutally honest with others and expected others to be that way with her.

"Get out," Sherrie said, tears filling her eyes.

Saying nothing, Kyle got up and put on his coat. As he did, Sherrie sat up and dragged herself to the TV, ejecting *Paint Your Wagon* and putting in another tape. Kyle let himself out, making sure the door latched behind him. Kyle remained on the porch, reluctant to leave. Thunder boomed in the distance but there were no clouds in the sky. Above him he could see the aurora borealis, bright enough to be seen despite the city lights. Now he heard music coming from the living room. He listened for a minute but couldn't pick out the musical but from the thump of the sub woofer he could tell she had the volume cranked all the way up. Reluctantly, he left for Pumpkin Court.

34

Robby

Thursday, 11:05 P.M.
Pumpkin Court was dark, the construction workers long gone. He had arrived two hours ago, bringing a submarine sandwich and a six-pack of beer with him. He picnicked in the dark, watching the house where Sinclair hid. He wanted to be there long before Sinclair and Detective Sommers arrived. He had his shotgun with him, cradling it in his arms like he had once held his little Robby. He ran his hands along the barrel, feeling the cold of the steel. He was ready.

He had spent an hour in a public library, learning about Detective Sommers. The more he learned, the more he believed that Sommers was as big a threat as Sinclair. If Sommers didn't come for Sinclair, he would kill him. If Sommers did show up, he would make sure they both died. His ministry must go on.

He understood himself well enough to know that ministering to the children wasn't just a desire, but an addiction. Just like an alcoholic, he could go weeks without helping another child but then the nightmares would come again. His son Robby was in those dark dreams, coming home from school in tears, telling his papa all the terrible things that had happened to him that day. He relived his own childhood through Robby, the teasing and the jeers of his peers. Robby and he were so alike. They weren't unattractive as children, weren't too smart or too dumb, and they didn't bully other children. All he, and later his Robby, had wanted out of childhood was to fit in, to be one of the gang, but for some unfathomable reason they were rejected. At school Robby wasn't asked to join in play at recess, he was picked last for games, getting to play only when the teacher forced the other children to accept him. He understood Robby's pain. He had lived the same childhood.

He watched his son change from a happy outgoing preschooler to a sad withdrawn child. Soon Robby was staying in at recess to help the teacher, something he had done himself, finding more joy in dusting erasers than watching other children play. After school Robby would come straight home, walking alone, no friend to race from the bus stop. With no mother to greet him, Robby was a latchkey child and would fix himself a snack and watch TV alone, waiting in the empty house for his father to come home from work. While Robby sat in front of the TV the other kids would be in the street, playing kickball or football, laughing and shouting. Robby could hear them play but they would never ring his doorbell, asking him to join in. In grade school, even children who had played with Robby in preschool began ignoring him.

"Why don't the other kids like me, Papa?" Robby asked one day.

"I don't know," he answered honestly, "but I love you and that's better than having all the friends in the world."

It wasn't true of course, the other children were loved by their parents and had friends too. He talked to Robby's teachers about his son's isolation and they tried to get the other kids to include him but the fixes were always temporary. When he saw a school counselor about Robby she had little to offer other than a label.

"Robby's what we call 'neglected,'" the counselor explained. "It's not that the other children don't like him, it's just that they are indifferent to Robby. It could be worse, he could be what we call a 'rejected child' and actively disliked by the other children."

"Being hated is better than being ignored," he told the counselor. "There isn't anything worse than being nothing to other people, to be just another piece of furniture."

He knew that from his own experiences and knew how terrible life was for his Robby.

When Robby turned eight he signed him up with the Boy Scouts and his son was assigned to a den. It did little to help Robby make friends. When he would pick his son up from the den meetings the other boys would be running and playing together while Robby sat on the porch by himself waiting for his papa. Robby didn't ask to join the scouts again the next year and no one from Robby's den, or the pack, called to see if he was going to continue. That angered him, since he thought the Boy Scouts should care about one of their members. One night after Robby had gone to bed he stuffed his son's scout uniform into the bottom of the trash can.

Summers were the best times for Robby, since he wasn't forced to spend his days with children who ignored him. On weekends in the summer he would take Robby along when he traveled to fairs to sell his art. Robby helped to set up his stall and then helped to sell the colorful three-dimensional scenes his father created.

"I'll teach you to make these someday," he promised Robby, anxious to pass on his skills to his son.

By then there was little of the old joyous Robby left and his son simply nodded, seeing no future for himself. The happy joyful three-year-old who hugged his papa every night when he came home from work, and kissed his cheek at bedtime, was gone. He tried everything but soon he lost hope of bringing the old Robby back.

For Robby's tenth birthday he invited all the boys in his class for a surprise party, promising in the invitation cake, ice cream, and pony rides. The ponies were there for the birthday but no guests arrived. Robby cried in his room all afternoon, younger neighbor children riding the ponies before he sent them back. It was the last time he remembered seeing Robby cry. When he came down for dinner that night his eyes were red, his cheeks puffy, but there was something else about his eyes. They had lost the quickness that comes with an inquisitive, open mind. From that day on Robby's eyes tracked slowly, reluctantly, as if nothing held interest for him.

Robby started skipping school after that and while he disapproved, he understood. He had skipped school too when he was young like Robby, hiding behind the community center in the bushes, reading comics until school was out, and then mingling with the other children walking home. He tried to keep Robby in school but Robby would leave for the bus stop and then sneak home after he had gone to work. They fought over going to school and he regretted that since Robby had no friends except for his father and it must have seemed to Robby that even his father was turning against him. Then one day he had come home from work and found Robby lying on the floor in front of the TV, empty pill bottles all around.

He was in a coma for four days but the doctors gave him no hope that his son would recover. A get well card arrived for Robby from his class at school. Every child in Robby's class had signed it. He tore it up.

Robby died in the afternoon of his fourth day in the hospital, his father by his side. The nurses let him sit with his son through the afternoon but come evening one came, gently telling him that the bed was needed for another sick child. They transferred Robby to a cart then, covering his face with a sheet. They took him to the loading dock where he was transferred to a hearse from the funeral home. When he visited Robby in the funeral home his son's face was set in a frown and it pained him. Robby had been happy once and he wanted to see his son happy again. He asked the funeral director to shape his son's face into a smile but the mortician couldn't capture his son's natural expression from the old photos he had provided. Robby went to his grave with a phony smile fixed on his face.

He couldn't work after that, coming in late, missing days, and finally losing his job. He drank a lot after the funeral, sitting in the house and looking at pictures of his son. In the afternoons he would sit on the porch watching the children play in the street, getting angry, blaming them for killing his son. He had never been a vengeful person but he did believe in justice and it wasn't fair that the children who had driven his son to kill himself should go on with their lives as if they were blameless. In a just world they would get a taste of the pain they had caused his son.

He bought a gun, the first he had ever owned. It was a pump-action shotgun. He took it to the country and practiced with it, finding satisfaction in the explosive power of the weapon. He became an expert with the weapon, pumping shell after shell through the firing chamber, and soon could fire and reload unconsciously.

One day he bought four new boxes of shotgun shells and cleaned and loaded his gun. Then he checked the school schedule to be sure classes were in session. He would start with the children in Robby's class, the ones who wouldn't come to his birthday party, then move on to the other classrooms until there was only one shell left. That one he put in his pocket and it would send him to be with his son.

His plan was simple. The surviving children would understand suffering, as would the parents and teachers. The press would spread Robby's story and people would become sensitive to the "neglected" children of the world. They would get friends. They would have someone to walk to school with and to giggle with during sleep-overs. Thinking of children like Robby having friends made him happy. He could make Robby's death mean something.

The day before he was going to visit Robby's school

something happened that changed his plan. It was a Sunday evening and he had spent the afternoon cleaning his shotgun, making sure the mechanism worked smoothly. Now he was on his porch, a can of beer in his hand, watching the neighborhood children play. A new boy had moved into the neighborhood and he had begun to join the games in the street. Slowly the new boy had been accepted and then became a leader much to the dismay of the boy who had led the pack before. Every day the two boys jockeyed for leadership. Today a shouting match erupted over a call at second base. The former leader of the pack, Willy, insisted he was safe. The new boy insisted he was out. From his porch seat he had seen the play. Willy was clearly safe. The two boys were deadlocked, neither willing to budge. Suddenly the new boy shouted, "How many say Willy is out?" All the hands of the children went up. Devastated, Willy found he had fallen from the top of the mountain to the bottom. Hurt, he left the game, walking up the street, head hanging.

Even after the children went in for the evening, he sat on the porch thinking about what he had witnessed. By the time he went in to bed he had decided to delay his trip to the school. For the next week he watched the children in the street even more closely, coming to realize his son and he weren't so different from others after all. He realized that the joy of childhood ends for everyone at some point. For some it comes in grade school, like it did for Robby. For others it comes in high school when the prom invitation never comes. For others it happens when they can't find anyone to love and marry or when they fail in college or their careers. He realized then that pain was inevitable.

Over the next few weeks he sat on his porch and watched Willy try to find a new place in the neighborhood pecking order. He came to pity Willy who had gone from great joy to depression because of one new boy in the neighborhood. Willy was now tolerated by the other children but continued to be the butt of cruel jokes administered by the new neighborhood leader. Willy was now on the same path that Robby had taken and his heart ached for Willy just like it did for Robby.

Without paychecks he couldn't make payments and when the bank took his house he moved into his trailer, planning to sell his art full-time. One night with his trailer packed and ready to go, he drove back to his old neighborhood. He entered Willy's room through an open window. Willy woke when he wrapped his hands around his throat and his face contorted horribly as he strangled him.

"I'm sorry for the pain, Willy, but it will be better soon," he whispered. "No more pain, Willy, no more forever."

Afterward, driving toward San Diego his emotions were a mix of joy and sadness. He was joyous that Willy would suffer no more but he was sad that he had waited so long to help the boy. He also remembered Willy's bulging eyes and protruding tongue as he helped him past the pain. He had to find a better way to help children and he had to help them before they knew the pain that Willy and Robby had known.

His ministry had started that way and he had helped many children since then but now Sinclair was a threat to his ministry. Worse, he suspected Sinclair was here to make sure his own daughter suffered into adulthood. He couldn't let that happen.

From his hiding place he could see Sinclair's house but Sinclair hadn't shown up yet. Waiting here was painful, since his need to minister was strong and with the Rose Festival Fun Center opening tomorrow he wouldn't have any more time to scout for children to help. He needed to get back on schedule and help those he had selected before it was time to move on.

Now he saw a man moving stealthily along the side of the road. The strange summer sky was bright but it was still too dark to see the man clearly. He knew it had to be Detective Sommers. The detective had come too soon. Sinclair hadn't returned to his hideaway yet.

As he watched, Sommers approached the house carefully, staying away from windows. When the detective was far enough away, he checked the road behind the detective—no police followed. The detective had come alone.

Detective Sommers was at the house now, disappearing around the far side. After a few minutes he appeared at the back, pausing by each window, peering inside. He continued across the back, looking in the windows, then continued around the other side to the front. Then the detective returned to the back and to the patio door where Sinclair entered and left the house. Sommers slid the door open—it had been locked the night he followed Sinclair to his hiding place. Nothing was going as planned.

The detective disappeared inside and he waited in hiding. Occasionally he saw the light of a flashlight flicker across windows. Minutes passed and the detective didn't reappear. Curious, now, he left his hiding place, shotgun in hand, and crept to the house, sliding along the wall to the patio door and looking in. From the patio he could see through the dining room into the living room and into the kitchen. The detective wasn't in either room. Puzzled, he was about to retreat to his hiding place when he saw the detective's flashlight. Detective Sommers came down the stairs. The detective came into the living room, alert, gun in hand. The detective squatted, looking at something on the floor, then stood, walking through the dining room, studying the floor with his flashlight. Still studying the floor, the detective walked toward the patio door.

Pulling his head back, he pressed against the wall, shotgun ready. The sound of the detective passed by the window. Now he was in the kitchen. Looking again, he saw Sommers studying the kitchen floor, squatting and looking at a scrap here and there. Then he stood, looking at the counters and cabinets—something caught the detective's eye.

From his hiding place he could see there was a piece of paper sticking out of the cabinet where Sinclair had kept his things. The detective opened the cabinet slightly, as if he were looking for a trip wire to a bomb. When he was satisfied it was safe, he opened it wider and pulled out two pieces of paper and started reading. While the detective read he puzzled over what to do.

Apparently Sinclair's secret stash was gone. The old man must have returned during the day, finding a new hideout. That made it harder to kill him. He didn't know where Sinclair had moved to but he did know where he would show up. Now he needed to decide what to do about the detective. Sinclair had left something in the cabinet and the detective was reading it. Without knowing what it said he didn't know whether the detective was a threat or not.

Crouching outside the patio door had cramped his legs. One leg was getting numb and he shifted slightly, trying to restore circulation. When he moved the barrel of the shotgun tapped the glass of the patio door. Sommers dropped the papers in a flash, bringing his gun up and aiming it with two hands. For a brief moment he and Detective Sommers locked eyes. Then he broke and ran.

His car was parked in the next development over and he ran for the trees separating the two projects. He heard the patio door slide open behind him and Sommers shout, "Police! Stop or I'll shoot!" He ran on, gambling the detective was bluffing. Sommers couldn't know who he was chasing and wouldn't risk shooting an innocent neighbor.

Even though he was a good-sized man and in good condition, Sommers was closing fast. He wouldn't make it to his car before the detective tackled him but he would reach the trees first. Reaching out with one hand he used a tree to stop himself, swinging around the trunk and bringing the shotgun to bear on the detective. The detective was quick and fired a shot from his pistol, the slug penetrated the trunk with a sharp *thunk*. He fired his shotgun a second later and the detective dropped into the thick weeds. He fired twice more to make sure the detective wouldn't be following and then ran for his car.

Driving away he realized that knowing the future had made him careless and that a simple tap on glass of a patio door had almost ended his ministry. He couldn't let that happen and he couldn't let Sinclair succeed either.

35

Split Decision

Friday, 7:50 A.M.

Kyle rang Sherrie's bell three times, then stepped back so she could see him from the upstairs window. When the curtain parted he could see Sherrie looking down on him. She stared long and hard and then the curtain closed. Kyle waited long enough for her to hand-walk down the stairs but she didn't come to the door. Kyle rang the bell again, this time waiting by the door and listening. Soon he heard "bump," "bump," "bump," down the stairs. Then the door opened a crack.

"Get away from my door or I'll call the police," Sherrie said.

"I've been shot. I need your help."

Sherrie opened the door wider and Kyle turned sideways showing his blood-soaked pants. Now concerned, Sherrie pushed the door open wide.

"What happened?" Sherrie asked, rolling back to let him in.

Kyle was limping and carrying his gym bag. He stopped in the entry hall, worried that he would stain her carpets with blood.

"Let's go into the kitchen."

"You need to go to the hospital," Sherrie said.

"I can't. They'll report the shooting if I do," Kyle said, walking past her into the kitchen.

"It should be reported," Sherrie argued, following Kyle.

Once on the linoleum floor, Kyle relaxed and sat in one of the vinyl-covered kitchen chairs, stretching out his injured leg.

"It's not bad," Kyle said.

"I'm taking you to the emergency room," Sherrie said.

"No," Kyle said. "I need to see this through. I know where the blue man is going to be, Sherrie."

Sherrie gave him another long look but Kyle had no idea of what was going through her mind.

"Take off your pants," Sherrie ordered.

Sherrie left while Kyle worked at getting his shoes off without bending over. Wincing from pain, he used his left foot to pry the shoe off his injured right leg. He had his belt unhooked and his pants unzipped when Sherrie came back with a first-aid kit. She shook her head when she saw him struggling to get his pants off.

"I'll do it," Sherrie said, pushing his hands away.

Then with a strong smooth pull, Sherrie pulled his pants down, Kyle wincing from the pain.

Kyle sat in the chair, letting her pull his pants the rest of the way off. His leg throbbed. Sherrie rolled to the sink and got a glass of water, returning to Kyle, dumping two blue pills from a prescription bottle in his hand.

"Take these," Sherrie said.

"What is it?"

"Painkiller," Sherrie said simply. "It's from my personal stash. Amputees get the good stuff."

Now Sherrie had cotton balls and peroxide out and was getting ready to attack his wound. She stopped with the cotton balls poised over his leg, studying the wound.

"Kyle, this is already scabbing. How long ago did this happen?"

"A few hours," Kyle said.

It was more than a few, since he had been shot around midnight. After that he had played possum, hoping the shooter would come back to make sure he was dead—he had no other way to find him. He had also hoped that the blue man might still show up.

"Your thigh looks like hamburger."

"It was a shotgun."

"Tell me what happened," Sherrie said, dabbing his leg with a cotton ball soaked with peroxide.

Kyle flinched when touched but the pain of the cleaning was negligible compared to the throbbing of his leg.

"I got a tip that the blue man was hiding out in a house. The caller said I should go after midnight if I wanted to catch him."

Sherrie looked up, clearly angry.

"So when you were here with me you knew about this and you didn't tell me?"

"It was an anonymous tip. We get a lot of them and most are bogus."

Sherrie cleaned his wound vigorously, Kyle wincing as she did.

"There was no one in the house but I found two more notes like those about the Martin girls and Wendy Kirkland. He left them to be found, Sherrie."

"He's done it before," Sherrie said. "Shut up and hold still for a minute. You've got something in your leg and I'm going to dig it out."

Kyle took a deep breath, steeling himself for the pain, but the pills from Sherrie's stash were working and the throb in his leg was quickly diminishing. Using a razor blade Sherrie opened the partially sealed wound, widening it until she could get tweezers inside. Kyle grabbed the arms of the chair when she sliced him and nearly broke the arms in half when she probed the wound. Then it was over.

"Hold out your hand," Sherrie said.

Sherrie dropped a bloody gray pellet into his hand.

Now she felt his wound, feeling for more pellets.

"That shotgun made a mess of your thigh, but the wound isn't deep."

"Sherrie, the notes aren't about something that's already happened, they're about tomorrow—today."

"Hold the gauze in place," Sherrie said, then pulled a long strip of tape from a round container. "Now he's warning you ahead of time?"

"Maybe or maybe he's passing on the responsibility," Kyle said.

"You think he called you and left you the tip so you would take over playing the Good Samaritan? Then why shoot you?"

"He didn't call me with the tip. It was a different voice."

"Then who?"

"Cradle Robber," Kyle said. "I think he wanted to kill us both."

"Did you see him?"

"Just eyes in the dark. I'd never be able to identify him but he moved like a younger man."

"Then they both got away," Sherrie said. "Kyle, why didn't you . . . you should have—"

"I know what you're trying to say, Sherrie. If I had brought a couple of officers with me, then we might have Cradle Robber in custody. Now children will die because I was thinking of myself."

"That's right. I know it sounds harsh but if it was Cradle Robber who shot you, then you had a chance to end this. You can't keep going it alone."

"I have to."

"You want to," Sherrie said.

"Yes, I want to and I need your help. The two articles are about two accidents that happen at the same time. I can't be at both and I need you to get to one."

"You have a whole police force at your disposal, Kyle."

"If the police get the time traveler, then my daughter has

no chance," Kyle said. "I know you think he has to be stopped but there's a chance he's here for some reason that won't create a paradox. If I help him then maybe he can help me."

"It's too disruptive, too dangerous."

"You don't know that for sure. Help me, Sherrie. If I can find him, then we'll know one way or another."

Sherrie finished bandaging his leg, chewing on her lower lip as she did. When finished she looked at Kyle long and hard.

"All right, I'll help, but I want to be there when we hear his story. I'm part of the decision, Kyle, or I go to the police myself."

"Agreed,"

"What do you want me to do?"

Kyle pulled the articles from his pocket.

Sherrie took the pages and read.

• Friday, 9 A.M.: On Friday morning fourteen-year-old Laticia Sternwell played hooky from school, telling her parents she didn't feel well. In reality she was planning to stay in her Gresham home to meet with her seventeen-year-old boyfriend, Patrick Menley. Patrick, who was a neighbor and friend of the family, decided to impress Laticia by showing off one of his father's shotguns. While showing Laticia how to load and fire the gun the shotgun accidentally discharged in Laticia's face, killing her instantly. A grief-stricken Patrick pled guilty to reckless endangerment and spent six months in a group home in Roseburg.

• Friday, 9:45 A.M.: It was multiculturalism day at James John Elementary School and the students were gathered on the playground to greet their special guests, the Hawaiian Riders. The Hawaiian Riders were in Portland for the Rose Festival parade and were making the rounds of elementary schools, showing off their brightly decorated horses, Hawaiian garb, and sharing with the students native Hawaiian folklore. The multicultural party turned deadly when four teenagers threw fire-crackers under the horses. Panicked, the horses bucked and kicked, one stumbling and falling onto the children. Michelle Winston and Evan Newbridge were crushed to death and five other children were badly injured. Two teenage boys, Nelson Naples and Ty Scolari, were arrested and convicted of manslaughter, serving seven years in prison. Two other teens involved in the crime, Vince Strong and Trent LePoer, died when they attempted to elude the police and their stolen car crossed the center line on Foster Road, crashing head-on into another vehicle, killing the elderly couple in the other car.

"I want you to go to the Sternwell house and make sure Laticia doesn't die."

"I figured," Sherrie said, but Kyle could see she was uncomfortable with the idea of altering the future.

"Laticia doesn't deserve what's going to happen to her," Kyle said.

"None of us deserves what we get—good or bad—it just happens, Kyle," Sherrie said, slapping her bare leg near the stump.

Then Kyle noticed he was staring at Sherrie's bare thigh and realized they were both sitting in their underwear. Sherrie's pills had killed his pain and seeing Sherrie wearing only a T-shirt and panties aroused him. He remembered the taste of her lips from the night before and the feel of her breast in his hand and he could feel his excitement growing. As if she sensed what he was feeling, and would have none of it, Sherrie spun her wheelchair and rolled out of the kitchen.

"If I'm going to make it to the Sternwell's in time, I have to get dressed."

Kyle stayed in the kitchen until he heard her thumping up

the stairs, regretting the lost opportunity of the night before. Then Kyle pulled his warm-ups from the gym bag and put them on. Then he took Sherrie's bottle of painkiller and stuffed it in his pocket.

36

Goals

His father kept the key to the gun cabinet under his bed, hanging on a hook screwed into one of the legs. Patrick had found the key years before while playing hide-and-seek with his brother, Dave. Working the key off the hook, he took it to the family room and unlocked the cabinet, swinging the heavy wooden doors open wide. There were six guns in the cabinet, four rifles and two shotguns. The two .22s belonged to Patrick and his brother. They were the guns their father had taught them to shoot with. They were both single-shot, bolt-action rifles with no scope.

"If you know what the hell you're doing you don't need more than one shot," his father had said when it was Patrick's turn to learn to shoot. Like his older brother Dave, now away at college, Patrick had developed good marksmanship and had graduated from the .22 rifle to a 30.06 and then to the bird guns—shotguns. The 30.06 was bolt action with a five-round magazine and no scope, the shotguns both double-barreled. His father had no tolerance with "idiots" who fired blindly with semiautomatic weapons and he bragged frequently he had never used more than two rounds to bring down any game animal. He expected no less of his sons.

Patrick was proficient with both the deer rifle and the shotguns and had hunted deer, elk, geese, and pheasant. He could kill Laticia with any of the guns but he selected a shotgun because he wanted to see what kind of mess it would make. The gun he pulled from the cabinet wasn't loaded, of course, his father was careful about that sort of thing. The shells were in a drawer at the bottom of the cabinet and he unlocked it with the same key. Patrick opened a new box of double aught shells and took out two. Breaking the shotgun open, he loaded both barrels and then snapped the shotgun closed.

"I'll do it just like you taught me, Dad," he said, giggling excitedly. "I won't use more than one round."

Patrick knew the school bus schedule since he rode it every day. The bus made its pickup at the corner at 7:40 A.M. If he was right, Laticia didn't get on the bus. She had left school early yesterday, claiming she was sick. He hoped she was sick enough to stay home one more day.

A few minutes ago Laticia's mother had left, keeping her schedule. Patrick watched as she got in her Volvo, leaving for work. Patrick went down his mental checklist once again, confirming that he had seen everyone but Laticia leave her house.

He thought about Laticia now, wondering if she would still be wearing her nightgown. He would like that. It would make it easier to look at her body after she was dead, even touch her if he was careful not to leave marks and if there wasn't too much blood. He would like to rape her first but she might fight him and leave marks he couldn't explain. Still, if the kill was clean he might be able to take a quick peek. He would choose another girl for rape, a stranger, but for murder his plan called for someone he knew.

"Rape" had originally been higher on his "Life Goals" list but he had bumped "Murder" up, reasoning that if something went wrong it was better to be tried as a juvenile for murder. As an adult you could get the death penalty for murder but only do a few years in prison for a single count of rape. So he put rape lower on his list but kept it ahead of embezzlement. He had selected accounting as an elective at his high school, beginning his preparation for embezzlement. After college he would work for a corporation, finding a position where he controlled the money. Then when the time was right he planned to take it and run. That was an adult goal, however. First came the murder.

Originally he planned to kill his best friend, Rob. He knew he couldn't kill someone he had a grudge against, since he would be an obvious suspect. As much as he wanted to kill one of the "popular" kids at school, he knew the only sure way to get away with murder was to kill either a stranger or a friend. Killing a stranger was the more dangerous option since you had to stalk the stranger, kill them, then get away without leaving telltale evidence. Killing a friend was easier since you could do it on familiar turf and the friend would cooperate, walking right into your trap. Rob had been the perfect choice for his murder, since everyone knew they were best friends. Patrick would have no reason to kill Rob. Only he knew that he didn't really much care whether Rob lived or died. Patrick was tired of Rob and ready to trade him in for a girlfriend and that girl was supposed to be Laticia.

He hadn't known Laticia was a tease but had recently come to see what she really was. She would smile at him when he wasn't looking, then look away when he would smile back. She led him on like that and when he responded to her teasing and touched her, she slapped his hand away. He had responded to her smiles again and a third time, each with the same result. That's when he had decided to switch from Rob to her.

As he planned for her murder, he realized it was better than killing Rob. If he planned it just right he would benefit from Laticia's death. With the right setup, friends and family would sympathize with him, rally round him, and support him. The more he thought about the plan, the better he liked it. Today, he would put the plan into effect.

The plan called for him to telephone Laticia so there would be a phone record to confirm that he and Laticia had spoken. That record would support his claim that they had talked before he went to her house. He would tell the police he called to be sure her parents weren't home. After he killed her he would make a panicky call to 9-1-1. When the police arrived he would make a tearful confession, telling them it had been an accidental shooting. If they charged him with manslaughter, he would plead guilty, again with tears. At best he would get probation and counseling, at worst, he would do juvenile time. Either way a dead girlfriend would get him more sympathy than a dead Rob ever would.

He took another peek out the window to make sure Laticia's mother hadn't forgotten something and returned home, then closed the curtain. It was almost time to go. Taking a towel, he slowly wrapped the shotgun.

37

Shotgun

Friday, 8:57 A.M.
The article describing Laticia Sternwell's death said she died around 9:00 A.M. Sherrie knew it was an estimate and prayed it was on the early side. Using the Sternwell and Menley last names from the article, Sherrie and Kyle had quickly located the correct Sternwell. There were only three listed in Gresham and only one on the same block as a Menley. Sherrie left immediately.

Once on I-84 she found she was traveling the opposite direction of most of the traffic pouring into Portland's core from the suburbs. Sherrie made good time, then the unpredictable happened and she got trapped in traffic backed up behind an accident. Inching along, she tapped her steering wheel and studied her watch. The minutes passed, eating into her safety margin, then eliminating it entirely. Another minute stuck in traffic and she wouldn't be at the Sternwell home in time. She was pounding the dash from frustration by the time she crept past the wrecked cars.

Now ignoring the speed limit she made up time, finding the nearest exit to Laticia's home and then counting down the street numbers as she searched for Laticia's street and house. The Sternwells lived in a twenty-year-old development, with five-thousand-square-foot lots and fifteen-hundred-square-foot houses. The trees were mature, the bushes overgrown. The cars parked on the street were Caravans, Hondas, and Toyotas. It was a middle-class neighborhood through and through. When Sherrie found the Sternwell home she was relieved there were no police cars or ambulances parked in front.

The Sternwell home was on Sherrie's left, so she parked at the curb across the street, then used the lift to get out of the van. The Sternwell home was one story and there was only one step to the front walk that Sherrie avoided by using her well-conditioned arms to muscle herself across the lawn. A teenage girl answered the doorbell, opening the door a crack, peeking out.

"Are you Laticia Sternwell?" Sherrie asked.

The girl in the door was short, maybe five feet tall and dressed in gray sweatpants and sweatshirt. There was a ring in her nose and three in each ear, as if she had reasoned if one earring was attractive, three would make her three times as attractive. It was teen-think. Laticia's hair was short and an unnatural black, her face round and her lips full. Sherrie thought she was trying too hard to be attractive. She also guessed teenage boys would like the look.

"Yeah, I'm Laticia. What do you want?"

The girl with the dyed hair and pierced body parts looked Sherrie over like she was a freak. While Laticia studied Sherrie's stumps, Sherrie noticed Laticia did not look well. Her eyes were bloodshot, her nose red and wet around the nostrils, and her face pale. The hairs went up on the back of Sherrie's neck. A girl with a runny nose and dressed in sweats wouldn't be expecting a boyfriend.

"Do you know a Patrick Menley?"

"Yeah, he lives over there," Laticia said, nodding vaguely to her left.

"I need to talk with you about him," Sherrie said.

"What for?"

The phone rang behind Laticia. Laticia hesitated, looking at Sherrie, listening to the ringing phone. Like most people, Laticia stereotyped her as a cripple and no threat.

"Come in while I get that," Laticia said.

When Laticia hurried inside, Sherrie rolled in and closed the door behind her.

"Hello, hello," Laticia said from the living room, then hung up the phone.

Sherrie rolled into the living room that was furnished with a green-flowered couch, matching chairs, and end tables with glass tops. A three-segmented mirror etched with flamingos hung over the couch.

"What's up with Patrick?" Laticia asked. "Is he in trouble or something?"

"Are you expecting Patrick?" Sherrie asked.

"Like, to come over here? No, why would he come here?"

"Isn't he your boyfriend?"

"God no! He's so creepy. He's always following me around, trying to put his hands on me. You know what I mean?"

"Actually, I kind of have the opposite problem," Sherrie said.

"On account of your legs, huh? Too bad, 'cause you've got a great body."

Sherrie smiled at her honesty but the hairs on her neck were still up and now a knot formed in her stomach. The article Kyle had found had been right about there being a Patrick Menley and a Laticia Sternwell who knew each other but they certainly weren't boyfriend and girlfriend. Laticia responded with honest revulsion at the suggestion they were. But if Laticia was honestly home sick and not skipping school to meet with Patrick, then how did the gun accident take place? The doorbell rang and Laticia left Sherrie to answer it.

"Patrick? What are you doing here?" Laticia said from the door.

"I came to show you something," Patrick said.

"I'm sick, Patrick—hey, what are you doing?"

Sherrie rolled toward the door but it was too late. Patrick

pushed himself inside and slammed the door closed. Laticia backed away as Patrick pulled a towel off the shotgun he was carrying. Now Patrick was giggling nervously.

"You shouldn't have teased me, Laticia. We could have been great together but you thought you were too good for me. Now you're going to get what you deserve."

Patrick raised the shotgun and leveled it at Laticia's face, cocking both hammers.

"Back into the living room," Patrick ordered.

"Put the gun down," Sherrie said, rolling into Patrick's view.

Seeing her for the first time, Patrick jerked the twin barrels of the shotgun to point at her. Patrick's mouth hung open in shocked surprise.

"You're not supposed to be here!" Patrick said, his voice becoming a whine.

"Put the gun down, you don't want to hurt anybody!" Sherrie ordered.

"You're ruining everything!" Patrick said, hysteria rising.

The shotgun was still aimed at Sherrie's chest. Patrick was flushed and perspiring and his breathing rapid. He was bordering on a panic attack. Sherrie could see that Patrick was unstable and what little sanity he had was dissolving right before her eyes.

"Put the shotgun down, Patrick. Let's talk about this," Sherrie said, rolling closer.

"Shut up! I have to think," Patrick said.

Sherrie continued to move closer until the shotgun was inches from her chest.

"You ruined the plan," Patrick said, the hysteria gone, replaced by rage. "I had everything worked out. It was going to be perfect."

"What was going to be perfect, Patrick?" Sherrie asked.

"Shut up!" Patrick screamed, his finger tightening on the trigger. "Shut up so I can think. I can make this work. I know I can if I only think it through."

Suddenly Patrick's face brightened.

"I know how to fix this," Patrick said. "You can't be here when the police come. Yeah, that's it. I just have to get rid of you before I call the police."

Patrick's calm was returning and his nervous giggle came back.

"Yeah, it will work if I get rid of your body," Patrick said, finishing with another giggle.

Laticia had been paralyzed with fear until now, her fingers pressed to her lips. Now she spoke, her voice quivering.

"I'm sorry, Patrick. I never meant to hurt you."

At the sound of Laticia's voice, Patrick's eyes flicked from Sherrie to Laticia, and he began to swing the barrels of the big gun back toward Laticia. Sherrie watched the barrel move across her chest, timing her move. Just as it cleared her left arm she lunged for the gun, her quickness and power catching Patrick by surprise. She grabbed the twin barrels with both hands at the split second it was pointed between her and Laticia and yanked on the gun. Patrick clamped down reflexively, his finger squeezing through the first trigger position, releasing one of the hammers. The shotgun discharged with a deafening roar.

Laticia screamed and ran for the front door, leaving Sherrie wrestling with Patrick, one of the barrels burning her hand. Sherrie had hoped to fire both rounds when she pulled on the gun but now still had to deal with a loaded weapon.

"You ruined everything!" Patrick screamed in rage.

Patrick took his finger from the trigger, then tried to pull the gun from Sherrie's grip, still underestimating her strength. Years of pushing herself in the wheelchair had given Sherrie a powerful grip and weight lifting made her more than a match for a pudgy teenage boy but without legs to brace herself she was nearly pulled from the chair, the barrel of the gun swinging toward her stomach. Seeing she was vulnerable, Patrick fumbled for the trigger, relaxing his pull on the weapon. Sherrie pushed the barrel sideways as he did, and pulled again, trying to discharge the other shell. Patrick had learned, however, and this time the gun didn't fire.

Now Sherrie pushed out with her upper legs to hold herself in the chair, bracing herself for Patrick's next move. He pulled again, trying to get the gun out of her grip. Still she held on and had the strength to keep the gun barrel away from her body.

Seeing she was too strong from him, Patrick suddenly changed tactics and pushed the gun forward, twisting as he did. With his mass Patrick pressed Sherrie back in her chair, then he released the gun, lunging at Sherrie, then reaching down and lifting her chair, dumped her sideways.

Still holding the gun, Sherrie tumbled out of the chair, rolling over onto her back. Pulling the shotgun up, she reached for the stock so she could turn the gun on Patrick. Patrick threw her chair to the side and jumped on her before she could, slamming the gun down onto her chest. Patrick was on top of her now, wrestling for the gun that was pressed between them with the stock on her chest and the barrel pressed against her abdomen. With his legs to brace himself, Patrick now had the advantage and Sherrie was losing the fight for the gun. Then she remembered she didn't have feet.

Holding the gun tight against her body with one hand, she felt for the trigger with the other. Patrick had both hands on the gun now, still pinning it between them with his body weight. Slowly Sherrie let Patrick win the tug-of-war, feeling the still warm barrel slide from between her legs across what was left of her left leg. When she was sure the end of the barrel was below her left stump she pulled the trigger through the second release, the hammer slamming into the brass cap of the shotgun shell.

The sound and heat of the blast shocked both of them and there were a few seconds when neither moved, Patrick still on top of her. Then Patrick's mouth opened, his eyes closed, and he began to whimper.

38

Playground

Friday, 9:30 A.M.
James John School was in North Portland in the community called St. Johns. St. Johns was one of the many small towns long ago annexed by Portland. The school's playground bordered busy Lombard Street and as Kyle drove by he could see hay bales set in a circle and the children gathering, ready to greet the Hawaiian Riders. The playground was fenced on three sides, the fourth side being the school. Kyle judged the distance between the fence and the hay bales, estimating how far boys could throw firecrackers, then turned left at the corner, driving along one edge of the playground. The school property was L-shaped and another playground was at a right angle to the first. As he turned left he passed the horse trailers parked along the curb. He could see the horses inside the fence, being saddled for their riders. The riders were putting the finishing touches on their native Hawaiian costumes, unaware of the pending tragedy.

Kyle passed the school, crossing over to the Safeway parking lot and hiding his car in the middle of a row. Then he walked to Lombard, coming back toward the school along the main street. On his first pass by the school he had noticed there was a café across the street and from its window he could see the two sides of the playground where the boys were likely to throw from. He also could stay hidden from Sinclair in case he showed up.

He bought a cup of coffee and then stood by the window watching the kids gather. Behind him he heard the waitresses whispering with the regular customers, curious about who he was. He ignored them.

Kyle could tell a lot about the style of the James John teachers by the way their classes came out to the playground. One class came out with the students following the teacher but spread out in an oval, talking and joking as they came, the teacher turning to speak to them briefly and the students laughing at what she said, then forming into a better line that almost immediately began to dissolve again. The next class walked single file, quiet, following a student leader while the teacher walked parallel to the line. A third class emerged in a sloppy line, following a student leader, while the teacher walked up and down the line scolding misbehaving children who would straighten up briefly, then resume their antics when the teacher walked away. Kyle had seen commanders with the same leadership styles and knew the first two kinds of leaders could be effective but the last teacher lacked the one essential element: respect.

The students were sitting around the ring now, leaving only an opening where the horses would enter. Kyle studied the fence lines, looking for Sinclair or for the teens. He saw neither. Then four young men passed directly in front of his window so close to him he didn't get a good look. He heard laughter outside from his left, then he saw them cross the street, walking toward the school along the fence. They were older teens, seventeen or eighteen, dressed in jeans and T-shirts. Kyle scanned the street for Sinclair—nothing. The teens were along the fence now, opposite the ring where the children were gathered—still no Sinclair.

Kyle saw the horses with their colorful riders lining up, ready to parade into the ring. Still Kyle waited, watching for Sinclair to show himself. The horses started forward now heading toward the ring. Excited, the children were loud enough now that Kyle could hear them inside the café. Picturing two children crushed under a horse, Kyle couldn't wait any longer. Leaving the café, he cut diagonally across the intersection to come down the street behind the teens. The horses were entering the ring now and Kyle could see the teens whispering, one digging into his pocket and pulling something out. The others laughed and egged him on. Kyle looked one last time for Sinclair but saw no one. He was about to stop the teens when he saw three of the Hawaiians hurrying toward the teens. They were big men, the smallest two hundred pounds, the largest nearly three hundred.

"You by the fence! What you doing?" the smallest of the Hawaiians yelled.

The teens turned with a start, one holding a lighter, another the firecrackers. Quickly the evidence disappeared into pockets and the teens took up tough-guy postures.

"Who the hell are you?" one of the teens demanded.

The Hawaiians squared off with the teens now, the three of them outweighing the four teens. The young males were holding their ground, trying to save face but they were spreading out. One inched up the block away from the Hawaiians.

"We know you got firecrackers," the smallest Hawaiian said.

"I don't know what you're talking about," said the biggest of the teens.

"Get away from the fence," the lead Hawaiian said, stepping close.

"Get out of my face," the teen said, but his voice wavered. "Where did you get that fag shirt anyway?"

His friends laughed at that, then the Hawaiian thumped him on the chest with the heel of his hand. The blow knocked the teen back a step.

"I said get away from the fence," the Hawaiian repeated.

Now the other Hawaiians stepped toward the other teens, the biggest facing off with two.

Kyle looked to the ring and saw the horses were all inside

now, parading around in a circle, the children wide-eyed and excited.

"Let's go, Vince," one of the teens said, pulling on the leader.

"No fag tells me what to do," Vince said, stepping back to face off with the Hawaiian.

Watching from across the street, Kyle couldn't see how the firecrackers would ever get thrown. Then it hit him. Sinclair had already been there. Holding his badge out, Kyle hurried across the street.

"Police," Kyle said. "Break it up."

The group turned toward Kyle, all eyes on his badge.

"We weren't doing nothing and these guys came along and started pushing us around," Vince said.

The other teens were nervous, avoiding eye contact. Only Vince looked Kyle in the face.

"Get out of here," Kyle ordered.

"We got a right to be here," Vince said.

"Get out of here now or I search you," Kyle said.

"I'm gone," one of the teens said, turning up the block. "Give it up, Vince. Not here, not now."

The others followed, Vince turning away last, giving the lead Hawaiian the finger as he did.

"How did you know they had firecrackers?" Kyle asked as soon as the teens were out of earshot.

"A man came by and told us he heard some boys talking about throwing firecrackers at the horses. Someone could have gotten hurt," the Hawaiian said.

"An old man in a coat and hat?"

"Yes."

"Where is he now?"

"He left."

"Walking or by car?" Kyle said.

"He was walking when I saw him last."

"Which way did he go?" Kyle asked, exasperated.

"Around that way," the Hawaiian said, pointing around the

corner toward where the horse trailers were parked.

Kyle took off running toward the Safeway parking lot, cursing himself for missing his chance. Reaching the lot, he ran along the rows of parked cars scanning for a man in a hat.

Two cars were pulling out of the lot on the far side and he ran toward the nearest, taking a chance it would be Sinclair. The brake lights went on, the car stopping at the edge of the lot waiting for traffic. Just as Kyle reached the car the brake lights went off, the car pulling forward. Kyle slammed his hand on the back of the car, the driver started at the thump and stopped. Kyle reached for the driver's door and yanked it open, finding himself staring into the face of a frightened woman. Kyle flashed his badge, then mumbled an apology. Turning away, he searched for the other car. He could see it up the street, turning onto Lombard and disappearing around the corner.

Sprinting to where he had left his truck he had his keys ready, jamming the key into the ignition as he slid behind the wheel. He slammed the gearshift into reverse, backing out of his parking slot. Then he shoved the gearshift into first and floored the accelerator. Tires squealing, he raced to the edge of the lot and out onto the street, following Sinclair. When he reached Lombard he skidded to a stop. There was an intersection to his left, with three different routes. He didn't know which road to take or even if the car he had seen come this way was Sinclair. Kyle pounded the steering wheel in frustration. Sinclair was his only chance for saving Shelby and he had just let that chance slip through his fingers.

39

Fun Center

Kyle was grim when he got back to the bureau, walking directly to his cubicle, hiding his limp. Those he passed on the way to his desk read his mood, wisely avoiding him. Only Mac would have ignored his hostile body language, coming directly to Kyle's cubicle to find out what was wrong. But Mac was in the hospital and Kyle was glad for the time alone. He was grieving the loss of Shelby again, even though she was long dead and buried.

Kyle had stopped by his house and changed clothes, taking two more of Sherrie's pills when he did. He pulled the bottle from his pocket now, popping the childproof cap off, shaking two blue pills into his hand. He studied the pills for a minute, then dumped them back in the bottle and returned it to his pocket. Pills were as bad as the booze.

Slowly he controlled the depression and began to think clearly again. He still had leads to Sinclair. Somehow he was linked to the house in Pumpkin Court. Thumbing through the yellow pages he found the real estate section. It took a half-dozen calls before he found the realtor developing Pumpkin Court. He had to talk to three people before a woman named Helen Burstyn had the information he needed.

"I'm Detective Sommers with the Portland Police. I need to know the name of someone who is building a home in Pumpkin Court."

"That would be Pumpkin Court Phase One," Helen said, as if she was beginning a sales pitch. "Three of the houses in Pumpkin Court are being built on spec and there will be a model available to tour by the end of June."

Helen's voice was low, almost gravelly. Kyle pictured a middle-aged woman with a cigarette hanging from her mouth, her voice ruined by a lifetime of chain smoking.

"This one is at the end of the first cul-de-sac, two-story, three-car garage, looks like it's sitting on half an acre."

"The smallest lot in Pumpkin Court Phase One is an acre, and all the lots are partially wooded," Helen said, again sounding like a commercial. "I know the house you're talking about. It's the first in the neighborhood. A California family is having it built. The Sinclairs. Very nice people."

It all made sense. If it was a future Robert Sinclair, Ph.D., who had come back to the past, then he would know the house he was having built would be weather tight and almost ready for occupancy. It would also be a safe place to avoid running into yourself, since he would know when he and his family would make the move to the Northwest. He would also have keys to the house.

"Do you know when the Sinclairs are going to be in Portland?" Kyle asked.

"Just a minute," Helen said.

Kyle could hear her talking to someone in the background. Then Helen was back on the line.

"Patty Sinclair and her daughter are already somewhere in the area and her husband is supposed to arrive today or tomorrow. Their furniture is being delivered today."

The move to Portland partially explained why the future Sinclair was here and not in California. Whatever he was here to change took place after his family moved north.

"You said the Sinclairs have children?" Kyle asked.

"I think just the one daughter," Helen said, then spoke to someone in her office asking them how many children the

Sinclairs had. "Yes, we think they have a daughter. She's about three or four I would guess."

"Do you have a work address for either of the Sinclairs?" Kyle asked.

Helen was cooperative, seemingly unconcerned about giving out personal information over the phone to a stranger even though he claimed to be a detective.

"We should have something here," Helen said. "Hold on." Helen was back in a minute.

"University of California at Los Angeles for Mr. Sinclair. There's nothing for Mrs. Sinclair. There's a home phone number too, but it's California. Would you like those?"

"No, thank you," Kyle said.

"Wait, here's a note. It says that starting at the end of June Mr. Sinclair can be reached at another number. This one's an Oregon number."

"I'll take that," Kyle said.

Kyle wrote the number down, then thanked Helen and dialed the Oregon number.

"Phoenix Systems," a woman answered.

"Dr. Sinclair, please," Kyle said.

"Dr. Sinclair will not be available until July first," the woman said after a brief pause. "I can give you his UCLA number if you wish."

"I understand that he and his family are going to be in the area this weekend, do you have a local number for him?"

"No, but I couldn't give out a personal number even if I had one," she replied honestly.

"What kind of company is Phoenix Systems?" Kyle asked.

"We're a software company," the woman said. "I'm new here so if you need more information I can connect you to our sales representative."

Kyle declined, then hung up. Kyle thought briefly, then pulled a phone book from his drawer and looked up stockbrokers. Picking an investment company by the size of their ad, Kyle called and asked to speak to a broker, telling the receptionist that he was interested in technology stocks. He knew unsolicited calls were distributed to the junior brokers but hoped by mentioning technology stocks whoever answered would be knowledgeable.

"Ken Horton, how can I help you?"

"My name is Kyle Sommers and I wonder what you can tell me about a company called Phoenix Systems?"

"I can tell you to stay away from it. They had an IPO last year just before their new Peacemaker operating system was set to debut. It was pretty successful—offered at sixteen and closed the first day over twenty-five. It was selling at thirty-two when they announced the first delay of Peacemaker. It's been delayed twice since then and now they have no announced roll-out date. If you still want to buy the stock you can get it for . . . let's see . . . two and a quarter."

Sinclair was a mathematician and Phoenix was a software company. Kyle couldn't understand how that combination could lead to time travel.

"What exactly is Peacemaker?" Kyle asked.

"It's nothing," Horton said, "because it doesn't work. The press handouts on it claimed it could rejuvenate old software and iron out incompatibilities between applications."

"How is that possible?" Kyle asked.

"As I understand it, Peacemaker reduces all programs to the binary level—below the programming language—and at that level identifies commonalities between different programs, then removes unused portions and substitutes compatible code that accomplishes the same functions. It basically rewrites old software to make it compatible with new—but that's all just theory because it doesn't work."

"Have you ever heard of a Dr. Sinclair?"

"Oh, yeah. He's their white knight. Peacemaker was based on his theorems but the code writers at Phoenix can't make it work. The management at Phoenix lured him out of UCLA by giving him a piece of the company. A big piece. They bet the farm Sinclair can save their bacon."

Kyle was silent, still trying to make the connection with time travel, but getting there from a mathematical model used to rewrite software was too great a leap.

"So are you still interested in Phoenix? I would be happy to recommend a couple of more promising companies."

"I'll think about it."

"Ask for Ken Horton when you call back."

"I will."

Kyle hung up, then dialed Portland State University and asked for Professor Murooko. The professor's voice mail answered and Kyle left his name and number and asked the professor to call. He had just hung up when Cassidy came in. She was in uniform but no other female officer looked as good in one as Cassidy did. She'd had the shirt tailored so it fit to her form and today she wore the skirt option, although Kyle was sure it was a few inches short of regulation length. She also wore navy-blue hose which wasn't a uniform option. Cassidy sat in the victim's chair, crossing her legs, her skirt well above her knee.

"I checked on Mac a minute ago," Cassidy said. "He's doing fine. They will send him home in a couple of days."

"Thanks, Cassidy, I haven't had a chance to call this morning."

"I called you last night but you weren't home."

"I was checking on a tip," Kyle said. "What did you call about?"

"I thought you might want to talk about everything that's happened—Mac getting shot, Art dying—most people want to talk when tragedy strikes that close to home."

"I'm okay, but thanks for the concern," Kyle said.

Now Cassidy recrossed her legs, brushing Kyle's legs as she did. It was more than accidental contact, the touch was deliberate and firm.

"I thought maybe we could go see Mac tonight together," Cassidy said. "Unless you're going with that other woman?"

"Other woman?" Kyle said, feigning ignorance.

"The woman in the wheelchair."

"Sherrie Nolan?" Kyle said, acting as if he knew a lot of women in wheelchairs.

"Yes, her," Cassidy said.

"I can't tonight, Cassidy," Kyle said, dodging the question about Sherrie. "The Cradle Robber case is heating up and I have to run down some leads."

Cassidy was staring at him intently and for the first time he saw how deep her feelings were for him. It made him uncomfortable.

Cassidy refolded her legs, brushing his legs again. Her message was clear; she was every bit the woman Sherrie was, and more—she had legs. Cassidy was more beautiful than Sherrie, with a perfectly sculptured face, proportional figure, and beautiful long legs. So why wasn't Kyle attracted to Cassidy? He doubted he would have performance problems with her.

"You have to eat, Kyle. We could eat together and then go see Mac. Better yet, let's see Mac first and then go back to my place. I can grill a couple of steaks."

The phone rang, saving him from turning Cassidy down.

"Just drop by and make sure Laticia Sternwell doesn't get accidentally shot," Sherrie said sarcastically when Kyle answered. "It wasn't an accident, Kyle. It was murder."

"What? Are you all right?" Kyle asked dumbly.

Cassidy was watching Kyle, listening intently. Kyle pressed the phone tighter to his ear to mask Sherrie's voice. Now he controlled his tone, hiding his concern.

"I'm fine and Laticia's not hurt, although she was crying hysterically the last time I saw her. Patrick's not so fine. Instead of shooting Laticia he ended up blowing his own foot off."

Kyle's eyes flicked to Cassidy who was still watching and listening. Kyle wanted to speak openly to Sherrie, to express concern and get the details but couldn't with Cassidy there.

"I may be in trouble, Kyle. I took off before the police

arrived. I wasn't sure you wanted me to explain why I just happened to show up at the right time in the right place. To tell you the truth I wasn't ready to tell that story myself. The police don't know who I am yet but it won't take them long to track down a woman with no legs. Someone might have noticed my van with the handicap tags."

"I have someone with me right now," Kyle said evenly, "could I call you back?"

"I'm on a pay phone at the Fun Center," Sherrie said.

"Good," Kyle said.

"Meet me where we bought the hot dogs," Sherrie said.

"That will be fine," Kyle said.

Kyle hung up and he faced Cassidy.

"Another Cradle Robber tip," Kyle explained.

"Promising?" Cassidy asked.

"You know how it is. You run down a thousand tips and maybe one leads to something."

"Sure," Cassidy said. Now she pressed her leg against Kyle again. "Call me about dinner."

"If I get free," Kyle said.

Kyle waited until he was sure Cassidy was in the elevator before hurrying to meet Sherrie.

Waterfront Park was filled with people now that the Fun Center was open. There would be fireworks tonight to celebrate the first full day of the Rose Festival but the rides were already operating, the carnival games busy ripping off customers, and the food stands selling greasy food as fast as they could cook it. The U.S. and Canadian Navy ships weren't all in yet but a destroyer and a tender were already docked. The ships tied up along the waterfront where the Fun Center was set up but sailors were seldom seen at the carnival, preferring instead the bars and strip joints deeper in Portland's core. The Rose Festival Association fought hard every year to keep the Fun Center family-oriented but it was a losing battle. Teens and young adults dominated the crowd even during the day and at night the Fun Center had a reputation for drunken rowdiness and fights. Two police officers had been beaten a couple of years back and one year a father was killed in front of his children by a stray bullet fired two blocks away. Portland had done some soul searching then but nothing had changed at the center and officers still hated being assigned to Fun Center duty.

Sherrie was finishing a hot dog when Kyle spotted her in the crowd, a can of Classic Coke held between her legs. Once again he shook his head in wonder over Sherrie. Nothing affected her appetite. She smiled when she saw him, something he hadn't expected, not after he had failed to make love to her, then endangered her life.

"It's easy, Sherrie, just drop by the house and stop a little shooting accident," she mocked again as he came up.

"I thought it was an accident," Kyle said apologetically. "The article described it as one."

"It wasn't," Sherrie said. "Push me and I'll tell you about it."

Kyle pushed as Sherrie held her Coke, alternately sipping and talking.

"Laticia wasn't expecting Patrick and she sure wasn't his girlfriend. You should have seen the look on her face when I asked if he was her boyfriend. I think that's why Patrick decided to kill her and make it look like an accident. He couldn't take the rejection. I was talking to Laticia about him when he showed up at her door with a shotgun, ready to shoot Laticia. He blew a fuse when he saw me. He said I screwed up his plan. This was premeditated all the way, Kyle. He was going to kill her and then claim it was an accident. Patrick had planned the perfect murder and he would have gotten away with it if you hadn't sent me over to Laticia's."

"You said he was shot?"

"We ended up wrestling for the shotgun. The gun went off and took off most of one of his feet. I haven't seen that much blood since my own accident."

Sherrie's voice wavered a bit, then came back strong.

"I put a tourniquet on his leg and then left. Laticia ran off somewhere—I think to a neighbor's. I hung around just long enough to make sure the police arrived and then got out of there. When they get Laticia calmed down she's going to give them a pretty good description of the legless woman who dropped by unexpectedly. Now, Mr. Police Officer, how much trouble did you get me into?"

"Did Patrick say he was going to kill Laticia?" Kyle asked.

"Said it and pointed the gun at her."

"Then you're going to be fine. Laticia's story will match yours and it was Patrick's gun."

"I left the scene. Isn't that suspicious?"

"You can get away with it," Kyle said.

"Because I'm a cripple?"

"Yes, because you're a cripple."

"Finally, I get something out of losing my legs."

Sherrie finished her Coke, then tossed the can into a trash bin and took over wheeling her chair.

"How long before the Gresham Police find me?" Sherrie asked.

"A couple of days," Kyle said. "If Laticia is coherent then they'll know you were a hero and not likely to shoot anyone else. It depends on the media, really. If it's a slow news day the local stations might play up the story of a handicapped heroine."

" 'Crippled Cripples Creep,' or some headline like that," Sherrie said. "How did you do with your assignment?"

"The horse didn't crush anyone but it wouldn't have happened anyway. Our Good Samaritan was there and tipped off the Hawaiians. They were confronting the teens when I got there. He got away before I realized what he had done."

"You think you lost your last chance to save Shelby?" Sherrie asked suddenly.

"He won't go back to his house and he didn't leave any

more articles behind. I don't know where to look for him."

"That means it's going to happen soon," Sherrie said, her voice low and ominous.

"What he came to stop?" Kyle asked.

"Yes. He didn't leave any more articles because the next tragedy is the one he came for."

"Sherrie, I know who the blue man is," Kyle said.

Sherrie listened as Kyle explained what he knew about Sinclair, his career and his new job in Oregon.

"I've heard of him," Sherrie said when Kyle finished. "He works in chaos theory. Cutting-edge stuff. But he's giving it all up to write software?"

"Sherrie, if it is him, have you noticed he's only helping children?" Kyle asked.

"Yes."

"Sinclair has a wife and daughter and they are in Portland somewhere."

"I see," Sherrie said. "It could mean that he's here because of something that happens to a child—his child."

Sherrie was silent for a few minutes, rolling along, chewing her lower lip.

"Kyle, do you have the strength to do the right thing if this is about Sinclair's daughter?"

"What is the right thing, Sherrie?"

"If she is supposed to die, she must die. If she is supposed to be disfigured like me, then she must be disfigured. No matter how horrible or tragic, you can't take away Sinclair's reason for coming back in time or you trigger a causality paradox that will be catastrophic. You believe that, don't you, Kyle?"

"I don't know," Kyle answered honestly.

"Then I'm sticking with you until this is over," Sherrie said.

"It may be over," Kyle said. "My only hope is that Cradle Robber knows where he is."

"But first you have to find Cradle Robber," Sherrie said.

"Something no one has been able to do. But I still have one lead."

They had reached the first of the two giant tents that held the vendors selling merchandise. Kyle directed Sherrie into the tent. The floor was matted grass and the tent smelled of wet hay. It had been an unusually dry year but the Rose Festival had a history of rain and the crowds at the Fun Center could quickly turn the park's grass into muck. Just inside the tent was a stand where a salesman was peeling carrots, getting ready to demonstrate an industrial-strength blender that could liquify vegetables. The salesman wore a mahogany-brown toupee that didn't match the graying hair on the sides of his head. Kyle spoke to the salesman who kept peeling as they spoke.

"Do you know the Santinis?" Kyle asked.

"Santini? They sell that redwood crap, right? They're in the second tent I think. Look way down at the other end," the salesman said, looking up from his carrot only briefly. "They didn't get a very good draw this year."

Kyle wasn't sure how the spaces in the tents were allocated but he understood why the salesman thought the Santinis hadn't fared well. The rides, most of the food stands, and the performing stage were all north of the vendor tents and the crowd would have to work south through two tents to reach the Santinis, giving virtually every other vendor a chance at the pocketbook of the potential customers. The blender salesman on the other hand had a good draw, right inside the entrance, getting the first shot at the passersby.

Finishing with his carrots the salesman stacked them next to a pile of celery stalks, a tomato, an apple, and two bananas. As Kyle and Sherrie moved deeper into the tent the salesman adjusted the microphone hanging around his neck, turned up the speaker, and began his spiel.

"Ladies and gentlemen, are you tired of paying exorbitant prices for vitamins and dietary supplements? Are you looking for a low cost natural alternative that tastes oh-so-delicious?"

Kyle and Sherrie passed stands with silver jewelry, leather goods, candles, hand-thrown pottery, and even a stand selling neckties made of wood.

"I bet Mac would like one of those," Sherrie said, stopping briefly to admire the ties.

The ties were made of small segments of hardwoods and came in a variety of patterns, created by using different woods and stains.

"It would be easier to clean than a real tie," Sherrie said.

They passed a stand where a computer would transfer your picture to a calendar or a mug. Two fidgety children were sitting in front of the camera while their mother reviewed snapshots displayed on a monitor. Mixed among the stalls selling crafts were food stands—jerky, Oregon jam, pickles. These stalls offered free samples and whenever Sherrie spotted a sample she cut through the crowd to get a taste. Kyle watched Sherrie sample boysenberry jam, venison jerky, lemon yogurt, and Kettle Korn.

They reached the end of the first tent and crossed a small open space to the next. There were two aisles in each tent, and they chose the left. Kyle was intent on finding the Santinis' booth, hurrying through the crowd, but Sherrie lagged behind, looking at the merchandise, sampling the foods. Sherrie's sampling irritated Kyle. He was tense, knowing he was down to the last chance to save his daughter. If the Santinis couldn't help, he had reached a dead end.

Then ahead, at the end of the tent, he saw a stall selling carved redwood.

40

Cradle Robber

Friday, 11:15 A.M.

"I'll take the one with the blue fairies," the woman said, her daughter bouncing excitedly on her toes.

The woman had selected one of his best-sellers and there were a hundred children along the West Coast who went to bed each night with a fairy scene just like it on their bedroom wall. His framed scenes were created with plastic, stretched in layers across the frame. The fairy scene had a layer of deep green plastic stretched across the bottom to represent grass and tree shapes in blues and bright greens along the side. A second layer held the fairies. The fairies came in a variety of colors and were glued to clear plastic that was layered behind the grass and tree layer. The fairies looked like they floated in midair. Scenes with pink and blue fairies were the most popular, then green and yellow. He stopped making scenes with red fairies because they rarely sold. The customers thought the red fairies were devils.

Taking the woman's check, he put her purchase in a bag, folding the paper bag to make a handle so the little girl could easily carry it. The girl smiled when she took the bag and he smiled back, sharing her joy. It hurt him to know what life had in store for her. Her address was on the mother's check so he could add her to his list but it was too risky. He never selected children who purchased his art. He would have to settle for knowing that his fairy creation would bring her a bit of happiness.

He was watching the mother and girl walk away when he spotted a wheelchair coming through the crowd. The amputee in the chair was an attractive woman, drawing the eyes of passing men. He recognized her. Now he found Detective Sommers a step ahead of her—alive. He fought the urge to break and run. It was possible their return was coincidence. He held his ground, head tilted to the side, keeping them in his peripheral vision while hiding his face as best he could.

The woman in the wheelchair was coming down his side of the aisle, ignoring those in her path, expecting them to get out of her way. His heart pounded and he wished he had his shotgun. With no other weapon he picked up one of the razor-sharp X-Acto knives he used to cut the plastic, holding it low, out of sight.

The detective looked focused and determined, eyes straight ahead. The woman's eyes, though, were busy, searching the stalls, taking in the merchandise but not stopping. They weren't shopping but if the detective was here on business, then why would he bring the crippled woman? Was she a police officer too? It was possible, he supposed, given the laws protecting the handicapped. Still, if she was a police officer, and they were after Cradle Robber, he expected they would have come with able-bodied officers.

As they approached his stall the woman angled closer, her eyes taking in his art, not really looking at him. He turned around as they passed, pretending to sort through the boxes of extra stock he kept behind him. After they had passed he stood, watching them as best he could as they moved toward the other end of the tent.

With the X-Acto knife still in his hand, he stepped into the aisle, following. He had to know what they were up to. Keeping a good distance behind, he watched them move to the far end of the tent, stopping at the stall run by the Santinis. He knew what kind of people the Santinis were. They could cause him trouble.

41

The Santinis

"I'm Myrtle and this is Floyd," Mrs. Santini said when Kyle showed his badge and introduced himself.

"This is Sherrie Nolan," Kyle said.

"So nice to meet you," the Santinis said in unison, glancing at Sherrie's stumps.

"I'll bet you have questions about someone working the fair, don't you?" Myrtle said.

"Yes, I do," Kyle said, surprised.

"This happens in just about every town we visit," Floyd said.

The Santinis sat in the back of their stall on lawn chairs crisscrossed with yellow and green webbing. The counters in front of their stall and along the sides were filled with redwood products, carved by Floyd. On one side there were rows of names cut out of wood. Sabrina, Sam, Sandy, Shane, Susan, and other "S" names, in one row, Ralph, Randy, Robert, and Ron on the shelf above. A white sign with red lettering advised that if you didn't find your name on any of the shelves, Floyd would carve your name for two dollars a letter. Floyd's workbench was to one side and held templates, two vises, and a router. Fresh redwood shavings littered the ground around the workbench, giving the stall a pleasant woodsy smell.

"There's a bad element that travels with the carnival folks," Floyd said. "Seems like the police are always looking for someone or another."

"Seems like they always come to us too," Myrtle said with a smile. "Don't know why, but they always come to us."

Floyd was looking at Sherrie now, the seventy-year-old man admiring her figure, then shaking his head when his eyes finally got to her legs.

"What happened to your legs?" Floyd asked abruptly.

"Car accident," Sherrie said.

Floyd held up his hands showing he was missing half of his pinky on his left hand and down to his knuckle on the middle finger of his right hand.

"Table saw," Floyd said, smiling broadly and showing yellowed teeth. "Hurts like hell when that happens, don't it?"

"Like hell," Sherrie said with a smile.

"Sheila Torres told me that you know everyone and everyone knows you," Kyle said.

"We've been around longer than most, that's true enough," Floyd said. "What can we help you with?"

"This is kind of vague but I'm wondering if there is someone working the West Coast fairs that has a thing for children. Someone who dislikes them or likes them too much? Probably a man and probably from California."

"Well, I'm not one to spread rumor, mind you," Myrtle said, her voice dropping to a conspiratorial whisper, "but I heard that Charlie Walker—he works the haunted house for Enchanted Amusements—he was arrested once for molesting the daughter of a woman he was living with."

"She wasn't molested," Floyd cut in. "She was seventeen when it happened and sleeping with him to get drugs."

"That doesn't make it right," Myrtle said.

"The girl didn't even press charges," Floyd said.

"I'm not looking for a child molester," Kyle said, "I'm looking for someone who either hates children or who has an especially soft spot in their heart for them."

"You couldn't hate kids and work fairs," Floyd said. "Kids are what it's about around here."

"Most people I know either like children or put up with them because they know the kids are a big piece of their business," Myrtle said.

"Eighty percent of what we sell is for children," Floyd said. "Maybe half the vendors in here depend on children as much as we do and of course the carnival rides are all for kids and teens."

"This person might have gone through a difficult divorce or separation. Maybe they fought for custody of the children and didn't get it," Kyle said.

"Or maybe they had a child who died tragically," Sherrie added.

"Mr. Norris was in a custody fight, wasn't he, Floyd?" Myrtle asked. "He sells knife sharpeners that look like slingshots—don't work that well, if you ask me."

"They weren't fighting to get the kids, they were fighting over who had to take the kids—she lost," Floyd said. "Two more obnoxious children you couldn't find."

"What about the Nagais? They lost a child to leukemia," Myrtle said.

"Doesn't sound like who I'm looking for," Kyle said, remembering the sketch Rhonda Benchly had drawn. He was sure Cradle Robber wasn't Asian American.

"What about Norman Patterson?" Myrtle said. "I don't know him well but I heard his boy committed suicide."

"How old was his son?" Sherrie asked.

"I'm not sure; maybe ten or eleven," Myrtle said.

"Has he been working the West Coast fairs?" Kyle asked.

"Sure, he started doing it full-time after his boy died," Floyd said.

"Was he in San Francisco a month ago?" Kyle asked.

"He was there and Pasadena before that," Floyd said.

"Any others you can think of?" Kyle asked.

"Nancy Miller's daughter got into drugs," Myrtle said. "She ended up prostituting herself to pay for heroin. Nancy swears she'll kill anyone she catches selling drugs to children."

"Nancy Miller is visiting her mother in Iowa," Floyd said.

"What about Brian Griffin?" Myrtle asked. "He left his wife and son."

"They left him," Floyd corrected. "He was sleeping with that woman that sells caramel apples and such."

"Wynona Nelson and Brian Griffin are having an affair?" Myrtle exclaimed. "You never told me that, Floyd."

"I'm not one to spread rumor," Floyd said with a smile.

"Anyone else you can think of?" Kyle asked.

"Not off the top of my head," Myrtle said. "I'll think on it some and see what I come up with."

Kyle handed her his card.

"The man you mentioned whose son had died—Norman Patterson," Kyle said. "Where is his stall?"

"Back that way, on the right," Myrtle said, standing to point. "He makes these darling scenes out of plastic. He sells a lot to young families. Mothers like that cutesy fantasy stuff for their children's rooms. If I could get Floyd to carve something like that we'd make a fortune."

"I don't do cutesy," Floyd grumped.

"I saw the stall," Sherrie said, turning her chair. "Thanks for the help."

"I'll call if I think of anything," Myrtle said as they left.

Sherrie led the way, scattering the crowd with her wheelchair, and Kyle hurried to catch up, reaching under his shirt, making sure his weapon was ready just in case.

42

Trail

As soon as he saw Myrtle Santini point in his direction he
knew it was over. He had been identified and sketches of his
face would be all over the evening news. Worse, they had
taken away his livelihood. He would lose his trailer and his
truck, his only source of income. His ministry was coming
to an end before it had really begun. There were still children
on his Portland list and many more across the country in
need of help, just like his son. They would suffer now because of that policeman and the cripple and because of Sinclair and the evil thing he had come to do. His ministry was
coming to an end but it was still his to decide how that end
would come.

Turning, he hurried through the crowd toward his stall,
finding two women looking at his art. He paused briefly,
smiling at the women.

"See anything you like?" he asked.

"Maybe, I'm still trying to decide," one of the women said.

"Take your time. I'll be right back."

Leaving the women, he hurried to the other end of the
tent. It was the opposite direction from his truck and when
he got to the exit, he turned the corner, walking back along
the side, merging with those walking along the waterfront,
hurrying, but not so fast as to draw attention.

43

Trailer

Friday, 11:25 A.M.

Sherrie led him directly to Norman Patterson's stall, Kyle pulling back on her chair before she could roll directly in to confront the suspect.

"We don't know if this is him or not," Kyle said. "Let's go slow and act like shoppers. I want a good look at him before we start asking questions."

"Fine," Sherrie said, starting forward.

Kyle yanked back on her chair again.

"Let me do the talking," Kyle said.

"Yank on my chair again and I'll break your arm," Sherrie said.

"Please," Kyle said.

"All right, you do the talking," Sherrie said.

Like hundreds of other couples at the fun festival, they strolled past the last stall before Patterson's, pretending mild interest in Patterson's art. Two women were in front of the stall, examining a colorful undersea scene. Pink, orange, and yellow seahorses were set against a background the color of sea foam. In the back of the stall Kyle could see a worktable with bits and pieces of plastic cut out and ready to fit into a frame lying on the table. There was no one behind the bench, and no one in sight that looked like they managed the stall.

"Excuse me, ladies," Kyle said. "Do you know where the man is that runs this stall?"

"I think he went to the bathroom. He said he would be right back," one of the women said.

Kyle and Sherrie exchanged looks, Sherrie still in the aisle, unable to squeeze her chair into the stall past the women. While Sherrie parked in the aisle looking at the same pieces over and over, Kyle shopped inside the booth, his back to the women, eyes staring through the framed scenes hanging around the sides, looking down the aisles for the man who might be Cradle Robber.

The women in the stall looked to be in their mid-thirties and talked like moms, discussing which of the framed sea scenes would go best in "Lindy's" bedroom. Lindy's mother was the taller of the two with dark hair—too dark to be natural—and a loud voice. The other woman's hair was blond, the part in her hair revealing her natural color. Five minutes passed and the women became impatient. Another three minutes and they were irritated, putting down the piece they were going to buy and walking out in a huff.

Now alone in the stall, Kyle looked more closely, finding a paper bag under the workbench. Kyle squatted, looking in the bag and seeing the remains of a lunch—fries and a piece of burrito. There were two foam coffee cups on the table, one still half full. Bolder now, Kyle looked at the piece Patterson was working on. It was a jungle scene, with leafy green vegetation along both sides. Pink and purple giraffes had been cut out and laid on the table, some ready to be glued to a clear plastic sheet that would hold them in place in the frame. Kyle picked up the clear plastic sheet and felt it—it had the same feel as the piece used on Peter Benchly.

"He knows we're looking for him," Kyle suddenly realized.

Sherrie rolled into the stall.

"How could he?" Sherrie asked.

"My face has been on TV. Maybe he spotted me when we passed here on the way in."

Kyle rushed out, pushing his way through the crowd, hurrying back to the Santinis. Sherrie rolled along behind, cursing people who didn't get out of her way fast enough. The Santinis were sitting as they had left them.

"Patterson's gone," Kyle blurted out. "Do you know where he's staying?"

"He's gone? He's not in his stall?" Myrtle asked.

"That's what gone means," Floyd said, taking over the conversation. "He's got a trailer out at Riverside Rest. That's where we're staying too—lots of the folks here are staying there. It's out on Highway 99 just south of King City."

Sherrie rolled up, catching the last of the conversation.

"I'm going after him," Kyle said.

"We'll take my van," Sherrie said.

"You can't—" Kyle began, but stopped, knowing she would call the department if he cut her out.

Together they hurried out of the Fun Center to Sherrie's van. With handicapped tags, Sherrie was able to park less than a block from the park. Sherrie drove, taking Interstate 5 through the city to the suburbs, then exited on Highway 99, driving through Tigard and into King City. Riverside Rest was easy to find, since there was only one river passing on the south side of King City and true to its name the trailer park had been built along its banks. Sherrie kept the engine running while Kyle jumped out of the van and hurried into the office, flashing his badge at a middle-aged man who appeared from the back room.

"I need to know where Norman Patterson's trailer is parked," Kyle said.

"Patterson, Patterson?" the manager said, typing a few commands into his computer. "He's here for the Rose Festival isn't he? I've got quite a few of them. Some of them have been coming here since we bought this place. Let's see, that was more than ten years ago." Then without taking a breath he continued. "Has he done something I should know about?"

"I just need to talk to him."

"If I should know about it you'll tell me, right?"

"Yes."

"He's in space 132. Go right at the fork and down the hill. He's around the far end where the road curves away from the river."

Kyle jumped back in the van, giving Sherrie directions. Using her hand controls, Sherrie guided them down the hill toward a row of RVs and trailers parked along the river. Trees sprinkled the bank behind the trailer park but most of the trailers had a clear view of the slow-moving Tualatin River. Sherrie slowed her van to a stop just as they reached the trailer parked in space 126. They could see space 132 just around the corner. A battered tan trailer sat in the space, there was no vehicle parked by the trailer. Kyle studied the trailer's windows—no movement inside. He watched the trailer itself too, trying to detect the slight rocking that someone inside would produce.

"How long do we wait?" Sherrie asked.

"He's not here. Pull up in front."

When Sherrie stopped Kyle was half out of the van before he remembered Sherrie couldn't just jump out and follow like Mac would have. Sherrie looked angry but it wasn't at him this time—she was angry at being less nimble than she once was.

"Go ahead. I couldn't squeeze my chair through the door of that trailer anyway."

Kyle approached the trailer cautiously, gun in hand. Even confident that Patterson was on the run, Kyle's experience kept him cautious. Kyle knew you didn't get killed when you were expecting it, you got killed when you weren't. Reaching the door he stood to one side and knocked, then shouted, "Police, open the door!" As he expected there was no response. He also knew that with a trailer this size there wasn't a back door Patterson could flee out of. He knocked again and repeated his shout, then tried the handle. It wasn't locked and he opened the door throwing it wide, keeping back out of sight. When the door slammed shut he pushed it open again and held it. Crouching, he leaned in—no one was in sight and there was precious little room to hide. The door opened into what served as the living room, the space continuing to his right for a few feet. A small couch and a chair were the only contents. To his left there was a kitchen with a short corridor on the other side. A dirty green carpet covered the floor and continued into the hallway. There were Tupperware dishes in the kitchen sink crusted with food and a box of Cheerios and a half loaf of Wonder bread on a small table bolted to the wall. Kyle crept down the hall, finding a small bath with a toilet, sink, and the smallest shower he had ever seen. The trailer ended in a bedroom with a double bed. The bed wasn't made and there were men's clothes on the floor.

Replacing his gun in his holster, Kyle retraced his steps, looking for something that would put him on Patterson's trail again. On the kitchen table, propped against a set of pig-shaped salt and pepper shakers, Kyle found a note. If there had been any doubt left that Patterson was Cradle Robber, the note erased the last bit of it. He searched the rest of the trailer, finding nothing that would lead him to Patterson. The only pictures he found were of a little boy; Patterson's son, he assumed. Then he returned to the van where Sherrie was waiting, engine running.

"Well, what did you find?" Sherrie asked impatiently.

Kyle handed her the hand-scrawled note. Sherrie read, "If you want Sinclair, be in the parking lot of the Washington Square Embassy Suites Hotel at 10:00 on Saturday morning."

"He wants us to catch Sinclair?" Sherrie asked.

"Yes," Kyle said.

"Why? If Cradle Robber wants to continue killing children he can just change his pattern."

"Maybe he doesn't understand that. Maybe he thinks that

Sinclair can come back from the future again. Or maybe his murders follow some obsessive pattern that he can't change," Kyle said.

"You won't ask anyone in your department for help, will you?" Sherrie asked.

"I'm going to call this in now," Kyle said. "We know who Cradle Robber is and soon the whole world will know. He won't be able to hide and we took away his source of income."

"I'm talking about the note. About the Embassy Suites. You can't go alone."

"I have to do this myself."

Sherrie sighed but he could see the sympathy in her eyes.

"Then, remember your promise. We go together and decide together what to do," Sherrie said.

"I remember," Kyle said.

Now Sherrie's face hardened.

"Kyle, I won't let you do this without me. I will call your captain or the chief of police or whoever I have to call to stop you."

"I know."

Then Kyle called the bureau, asking for a forensics team and officers to secure Patterson's trailer. He had already entered, so he didn't bother asking for a search warrant. Patterson's flight from the Rose Festival would have to suffice for probable cause. Riverside Rest was outside the Portland city limits, so the Washington County Sheriff's Office would have to be contacted and involved. As soon as the calls were made, Sherrie made him promise to meet her for dinner and to visit Mac, then left.

As police and deputies began arriving, Kyle organized them, detailing some officers to cordon off the area around the trailer, then sent others to interview the manager and neighbors. Danforth arrived thirty minutes after Kyle had called it in, immediately taking charge. Kyle briefed Danforth about how he had found Patterson—the Santinis, Patterson's presence in the cities where Cradle Robber had struck, the visit to his stall, the fact that Patterson ran. Danforth was skeptical but had no other leads. Kyle didn't mention Patterson's note or Sherrie Nolan. Danforth failed to notice Kyle didn't have a car.

As soon as Danforth began ignoring Kyle he borrowed a car, returning to the bureau. When he got to his cubicle he found the message light on his phone flashing furiously. He ignored the flashing red triangle. He felt like his life was coming to a crossroads where choices would have to be made and it frightened him. Kyle didn't know how Cradle Robber—Patterson—and Sinclair had become intertwined, but whatever they had put in motion was coming to a head tomorrow and he would know then if he would ever get Shelby back.

The phone rang and he answered it automatically, regretting it as soon as he said "hello."

"Detective Sommers, this is Professor Murooko," a man on the line said. "You called me earlier this afternoon."

Kyle had little interest left in talking with the professor but asked his questions anyway.

"Thanks for calling back, Professor. This is going to seem off-the-wall to you but if you could help in any way I would appreciate it."

"Sure, sure, anything I can do to help," the professor said.

"Professor, I'm still working on that case where knowing something about theories of time travel might help."

"I gave you the three possibilities but I can fill in the details a bit if you like," the professor offered.

"I think we can rule out the theories involving spaceships. What I'm dealing with is pretty down to earth."

"Unfortunately, the other theory of time travel operates on a subatomic level."

"The one that involved tachyons?" Kyle said.

"Tachyons, yes," Professor Murooko said.

"There's no way to send something bigger back through time?"

"Not unless you could get the larger object to act like a tachyon."

"And there's no way to do that."

"Oh, there's always speculation on how to do that sort of thing but no one is working on it—you can't get funding for that kind of research. It's too speculative."

"Do you know of a Dr. Robert Sinclair?" Kyle asked.

"Certainly. I've read his papers. He might have won a Nobel Prize."

"Might have?" Kyle probed.

"He left academia to go into business—a software company, I believe. I heard he's moving to Portland, actually. Is he connected to what you're investigating in some way?"

Kyle couldn't risk Murooko tipping off the young Sinclair of what was going on.

"It's not about him, it's about his theories," Kyle said quickly. "I know his theories are being applied to software development but do they have anything to do with time travel theory?"

"I suppose they could . . . in a way. Sinclair's mathematical models predict the order within disorder and disorder underlies everything including time."

"I'm sorry, that's a bit confusing," Kyle said.

"Try explaining it to undergraduate students," Murooko said. "In its simplest form it goes something like this. Our conception of the universe has moved from a Newtonian model, where cause and effect can be predicted by using certain fundamental laws, to a quantum conception where at the most basic level of the universe prediction is impossible. Today, instead of nice and neat Newtonian laws that can be mathematically modeled, we find that underneath it all is chaos—ultimately the universe is built on disorder. Once we accepted the fact that in the quantum universe there is no order at the subatomic level, we were left wondering how order manages to emerge from chaos. That's where Dr. Sinclair and his theories come in. Dr. Sinclair put two pieces into that puzzle. First, he demonstrated mathematically that disorder is necessary for order to exist—does that make sense to you?"

"No," Kyle admitted.

"Try thinking at a macro level—a human level. We don't allow relatives to marry and have babies since cross-breeding of near relatives leads to birth defects. But breeding across diverse peoples produces a hybrid that minimizes birth defects and the result is healthier babies and the human race is better off."

"But they control the breeding of animals to produce certain traits," Kyle argued. "More milk production, faster race horses, dogs with specific traits."

"True, but the rate of genetic disorders is high in animals bred that way. They have to periodically introduce new bloodlines to reduce the accumulation of recessive defects."

"So the disorder that lies behind our universe—the chaos at the subatomic level—reduces defects in our universe."

"That's Dr. Sinclair's theory," Professor Murooko said.

"How does that get to time travel?"

"It's his second puzzle piece that might do that," the professor suggested. "Dr. Sinclair also learned to mathematically mimic chaos and to predict the order that emerges from it. Understanding how order comes from disorder would be the first step to controlling those forces. Control the forces that are the fabric of our universe and anything is possible, even time travel."

"How likely is that? It sounds like science fiction," Kyle said.

"Not very likely, but virtually every technological innovation predicted in science fiction has come to be. Satellites, computers, lasers, space travel, organ transplants—all were forecast by science fiction writers."

"What's the lag time?" Kyle asked. "How long between the forecast and the actual creation?"

"Twenty to thirty years on average, I would guess," Professor Murooko said. "But time travel was predicted more than one hundred years ago."

"Thanks for your patience, Professor," Kyle said. "Good luck with getting tenure."

Murooko chuckled and said, "Don't worry, I can handle Professor Lipke."

Kyle hung up, realizing that knowing more about the theory of time travel didn't help him with his decision.

Kyle heard Harding's deep voice out in the office. Kyle kept his head down, hoping Harding didn't know he was back. He didn't want to face him again until it was over. With the identification of Cradle Robber, Harding would be busy interfacing between Danforth and the chief. Since Danforth had Kyle's report, Harding had enough information for now. Later would come the tough questions.

Kyle listened to Harding's voice recede. Relieved he wouldn't have to face Harding, Kyle was about to slip out when Cassidy suddenly slid into the victim's chair.

"Nice work in identifying Cradle Robber, Kyle. You did what three other police departments couldn't."

"I got lucky," Kyle said.

"Danforth's taking credit for it," Cassidy said. "He's referring to you as a 'member of the task force.' "

"I don't care."

"People need to know you broke the case. The media barbecued you, Kyle. This is a chance to get your reputation back. Come with me to the trailer park. The local stations are setting up remotes at Riverside Rest. The networks will pick this up for the national news. I can get you interviewed; make sure you get credit for your work."

"You're the one who should do the talking, Cassidy. You're good at this."

"They won't ask you about your problems, Kyle. I can make sure of that."

"I really have to finish my report—Harding wants it. Besides, we don't have Cradle Robber yet. When we do maybe I'll take you up on the offer and get myself on TV."

Cassidy nodded, but didn't leave.

"It looks like I won't be able to see Mac with you," she said.

"Maybe some other time," Kyle said.

Still Cassidy did not leave.

"Kyle, we received a bulletin from the Gresham Police," Cassidy said softly.

Kyle tried to keep his face impassive.

"According to the GPD, a woman in a wheelchair was involved in a shooting this morning."

Cassidy paused but Kyle didn't volunteer anything.

"A boy was badly injured, Kyle, and the GPD wants to talk to the woman involved."

"The woman in the wheelchair shot the boy?" Kyle asked.

"It's not clear who shot whom, Kyle. You know how the early stages of an investigation go. There's a lot of confusion at first. A teenage girl witnessed what happened and claims the woman in the wheelchair saved her from being killed but the GPD never got to talk to the handicapped woman. She left the scene before they arrived."

"And you think because Sherrie Nolan is handicapped that she might know the Gresham woman?" Kyle asked.

Cassidy sighed, shaking her head.

"Kyle, I came down here as a friend. I don't know what's going on and you don't seem to want to tell me. That's fine. You can play this any way you want; that's up to you. I just thought you should know all the metropolitan police will be looking for a handicapped woman in a white van."

Cassidy stood to leave, sad, not angry.

"Thanks, Cassidy," Kyle said.

Cassidy stopped half out the cubicle, standing in profile, reminding Kyle how beautiful she was.

"You're welcome," Cassidy said, then was gone.

Kyle waited for her to get down the elevator and then left. He wasn't going to risk getting called into Harding's office or having another officer make the connection between the GPD bulletin and Sherrie's visit to Kyle. There would be plenty of time for explaining when it was over.

44

Embassy Suites

Friday, 6:15 P.M.

The note Patterson left in his trailer told Kyle to be in a hotel parking lot at ten the next morning. Kyle planned to be there and didn't want anything to interfere so he avoided contact with his department. It would be a long night and Kyle found he didn't want to spend it alone.

Sherrie picked up Kyle insisting that she drive to dinner and to see Mac. Kyle worried briefly about getting caught in Sherrie's van, since the Gresham Police would be systematically tracking down vans registered to the handicapped but decided it was a small risk. It could take a week to find her.

Kyle planned to meet Sherrie downstairs, since there were four steps up to the front porch of Mrs. Pastorini's old home, so the sound of the door buzzer caught him by surprise. Kyle hurried downstairs to find Sherrie on the sidewalk talking to Mrs. Pastorini. His landlord had rung the bell.

"He's been walking the floor at night," Mrs. Pastorini was saying. "I can hear him up there pacing back and forth, of course he won't tell me what's bothering him."

"He's not exactly open with me either but I'm working on him," Sherrie said.

"I don't want to be worked on," Kyle said.

"This is a private conversation," Sherrie said.

Kyle could see Mrs. Pastorini taking the scene in, studying the body language and the inflection in their voices.

"Don't worry about Kyle," Sherrie said. "I've been working my way through that tough-guy detective shell of his. I'm just about to learn what makes him tick."

"And you'll share . . ." Mrs. Pastorini prodded.

"Every little detail with you," Sherrie finished.

"I've got to get you two apart," Kyle said. "Let's get something to eat. I'm starving."

Kyle wasn't ready for Sherrie and his landlord to become friends.

Sherrie said good-bye to Mrs. Pastorini, then rolled to the driver's side of her van, hauling herself in and letting Kyle collapse the chair and stow it in the back. Mrs. Pastorini watched the whole process from the sidewalk, intensely interested. She waved good-bye to Kyle as they pulled away.

With the Rose Festival in full swing, they agreed to stay away from the downtown restaurants and negotiated briefly over where to eat.

"How about Newport Bay," Sherrie suggested.

"I don't like fish," Kyle said.

"They serve chicken and steak."

"You can still smell the fish," Kyle said.

"I can't believe you live in salmon country and don't like fish," Sherrie said.

"I like tuna fish."

"That canned stuff?"

"It's fish," Kyle said.

"If you say so," Sherrie said.

"What about the Sports Page?" Kyle offered.

"No one talks in a place like that, they just watch games on the big screens."

"Maybe we can get them to tune one of the TVs to a musical," Kyle said. "Then we can get to see a real live bar fight up-close and personal."

"What about one of the McMenamins' pubs?"

"A pub?" Kyle said.

"Oh, sorry," Sherrie said.

Kyle realized he'd been so absorbed in the case he hadn't thought about drinking for days but he wouldn't risk visiting a bar.

"How about Mexican food?" Kyle suggested. "Chevy's?"

"Tex Mex is okay but how about Jose's over on Broadway near Lloyd Center."

"Never heard of it," Kyle said, "but if you like it I know one thing for sure."

"What's that?" Sherrie said, already preparing to make a turn that would keep them on the east side of the Willamette River.

"They serve generous portions."

Sherrie's right arm whipped out, thumping him on the shoulder.

"I meant it as a compliment," Kyle said quickly.

"If you want to compliment a woman you talk about her proportions, not her portions."

"Well, your proportions are generous too," Kyle said.

Kyle half expected another slap on the shoulder but this time Sherrie kept her eyes on the road, smiling.

Jose's was a short drive from Kyle's house and Sherrie had them there in minutes. It was a small restaurant a few blocks from Lloyd Center, the largest shopping mall in Portland. Kyle had passed the restaurant dozens of times but never noticed the nondescript building. The "JOSE'S MEXICAN RESTAURANT" sign was professionally painted but there was no fancy neon, just a floodlight to light the sign at night. There was no parking lot either and the customers had to park on the side streets and walk. Sherrie parked a block and a half off of Broadway and let Kyle get her chair from the back. Then she rolled alongside of him back to the restaurant. Inside Kyle found the decor to be as plain as the exterior. There was a lounge to one side—a tavern really—with three video poker machines lined up against one wall. A gray-haired man sat at one of the machines, alternating between sipping a beer and feeding quarters into the machine. There were eight tables in the restaurant and six of them were oc-cupied, Kyle taking that as a good sign. There was a cash register just inside the entrance, with four folding chairs for customers waiting for a table—another good sign, Kyle thought, reasoning that a bad restaurant would never need a waiting room. There seemed to be only two waitresses, a teenager and a middle-aged woman. The resemblance be-tween the two women was striking, the younger a thinner version of the older. Mother and daughter, Kyle decided, and the restaurant family-owned. A boy came out of the kitchen then and began bussing one of the empty tables. He was younger than the teen waitress and Kyle guessed he would be a brother or cousin.

The older waitress smiled in greeting and nodded at Sher-rie as if she knew her. Without asking she walked to a table by the window and took away one of the chairs, making a place for Sherrie. Then she took two plastic menus from a rack by the cash register and walked them to their table. The plastic tablecloth had a red checkerboard pattern and there was a plastic flower in a glass vase to one side, surrounded by a collection of condiment bottles. There were three kinds of hot sauce, all labeled in Spanish. A crusty ring surrounded the top of each bottle just below the cap. Kyle took a bottle and picked off a piece of crust.

"You've eaten here before?" Kyle said.

"Yes."

"And you came back?"

"A little dried hot sauce won't hurt you, Kyle. Trust me, nothing could live in that sauce."

After surveying the menu, Kyle decided to sample widely in the hope of finding something he could eat. He picked one of the combination plates. Sherrie asked for the same combination. Both ordered iced tea to drink. When the wait-ress was gone Kyle found himself staring across the table at Sherrie with nothing to say. She was a beautiful woman and with the table blocking his view of her missing legs, he found it easy to want her. As he looked at her, he remembered embracing her and the taste of her kiss. Under his stare her face flushed and a slight smile came to her lips. He imagined she shared the feeling and the memory.

The waitress came back with their drinks, a basket of warm tortilla chips, and a dish of salsa. The food broke the mood and they sampled the chips. The salsa was thick with chunks of peppers and tomatoes and left Kyle's mouth burning.

"What happened between you and your wife?" Sherrie asked with her mouth full. "Did she blame you for the death of your daughter?"

"At first, but I think she finally came to see it as an accident. Our marriage was over by then. She didn't bother to wait for the divorce to find another man. On the day I moved out she told me she was sleeping with her boss. I guess she didn't think I was hurting enough."

"I don't know her," Sherrie said, "but she must have been hurting as much as you."

"I know that now but then I thought she was deliberately cruel. She put the house up for sale as soon as the divorce was final and moved in with her boss—Lawrence Kenneth Quimby, III. He's in insurance—a vice president with an office in one of the big downtown towers. She was his executive assistant but quit after they got married. They had a baby six months ago."

"Having a family on the rebound," Sherrie said. "I wouldn't recommend it as the best way to cope with grief but then I'm not the poster child for healthy coping."

"She had another girl but I've never seen her," Kyle said. "Not many people have. She's overprotective of the baby. Aldean has a nanny and the baby is never left alone. They rarely take her out of the house."

"What does her V.P. Quimby the Third think of this?"

"It's his second family and I don't think he was ready to start all over again. Aldean was supposed to be his trophy wife; someone to show off at corporate parties, travel with, feed his ego. I think he indulged her with the baby. They named the baby Helen after his mother."

"What about his other children? Do they live at home?"

"The boy was living at home when they got married but Quimby threw him out. He and his sister are both grown. He's a cocaine addict. Quimby's paying his rent on an apartment in Eugene. The boy is supposed to be working on his degree at the University of Oregon but he really moved out to get away from his father. He picked Eugene because it's the easiest city in Oregon to get drugs in. His sister didn't turn out much better. She had two abortions in high school before Quimby sent her to a boarding school in Virginia. She graduated but never came back to Portland. She lived with her mother in Santa Barbara for a while and now is living with an actor in Los Angeles. He's had a couple of bit parts on TV—two soap operas and a dog food commercial. The dog got more lines than him."

"You know a lot about the Quimby family," Sherrie said.

"I did a little investigating," Kyle said, embarrassed. "Aldean and I have history, Sherrie. We fell in love, married, and started a family together. If I had left half an hour earlier the night of the accident, Shelby would be in kindergarten and we might even have a second child. With just a little more care that night I would be sitting around a kitchen table with Aldean and my children instead of here with you. That future never happened but I still care about what happens to her."

"If I hadn't been drunk I might have been quick enough to get out of the way of the car that crushed my legs, Kyle. I might be married too with a family of my own instead of being a crippled old maid with nothing to look forward to but a long lonely life. Fate screwed both of us, Kyle. We have a right to be pissed off but we can't change what has happened, we just have to find a way to live with it."

"Can't we?" Kyle said.

"We shouldn't," Sherrie said.

The waitress arrived with the food, spreading it in front of them. Familiar with chain restaurants, Kyle expected the plates to be sizzling hot and his burrito, tamale, and taco to be glued together with melted cheese and smothered in guacamole. Instead the refried beans were in a small bowl and his burrito, tamale, and taco lined up neatly on the plate. Sherrie started with the taco, choosing one of the hot sauce bottles with an orange crust around its top, pouring a generous portion. Kyle took the bottle from her when she finished but Sherrie stopped him before he added it to his food.

"That's like eating lava, Kyle. Unless you like it really hot I'd recommend one of the others."

"If you can eat it, I can eat it," Kyle said.

Kyle poured the hot sauce on one one end of his taco and then took a small bite. He had the taco only half chewed before the pain started. The sauce was liquid fire in his mouth and he gulped iced tea, swishing it around trying to dilute the pain.

Sherrie laughed at him, then took a huge bite of her taco. Lettuce and tomato chunks showered onto her plate. Kyle waited for her to reach for her water but she never did, taking a second bite when she had swallowed the first. With the pain nearly gone, Kyle tried the other end of his taco. The shell was homemade just like the chips and had the same oily taste. The filling was warm and the vegetables fresh. Kyle chewed slowly, pushing the contents around in his mouth. The flavor was odd, nothing like Tex-Mex. He decided he liked the flavor.

Sherrie was a serious eater and even though they had been in an intense conversation she now concentrated on her food. Sherrie finished her food first, watching Kyle polish off his order except for the end of the taco with the hot sauce.

"You told me what happened to Aldean but what about you, Kyle?" Sherrie asked as soon as she was finished.

"You know part of it," Kyle said. "I didn't take it any

better than Aldean—worse in some ways. She found a way
to start over. I never did. After Aldean left me I started drinking—I'm not blaming her. I was already drinking pretty
heavily but held back a bit because I was still trying to work
it out with Aldean. But once she left I didn't have any reason
to be conscious. When I was awake all I could think about
was the accident and when I slept I'd find myself back in
the car, reliving it over and over. The booze kept me from
dreaming—kept me from thinking. Pretty soon I started
missing work and used up all my sick leave and more. Captain Harding cut me some slack but I abused it. Finally it
got so bad that I started hallucinating."

"Seeing your daughter?" Sherrie asked.

Kyle nodded.

"I remember the first time it happened. I was in bed—
drunk—and the door opened and Shelby was there. She was
wearing a pink nightgown and asked me to read her a story."

Kyle paused, eyes in a blank stare.

"I fell getting out of bed. I was too drunk to stand. When
I managed to crawl to the end of the bed she was gone."

"You must have been terrified," Sherrie said.

"No. I was relieved. Reading her stories at night was one
of my best memories of Shelby. When she asked me to read
her a story I knew she wasn't angry at me for killing her."

"You didn't kill her, Kyle. It was an accident."

"I was driving, Sherrie."

"But you didn't mean to."

"I killed her," Kyle said flatly. "I saw her several more
times, mostly when I was drunk but then one day I was
driving to work and she appeared beside me, sitting in her
car seat. She was covered in blood and begging me to help
her."

"You hadn't been drinking?"

"I was hungover but not drunk. This time it scared me and
I lost control. I rear-ended a minivan. I was afraid I was

going insane. I told the department psychologist about seeing Shelby and eventually Captain Harding. I went into therapy but I couldn't stop drinking so Harding put me on medical leave and I checked into a residential program in Spokane. I was there three months."

"And the hallucinations?"

"Gone, unless the blue man, Cradle Robber, and you are the biggest hallucination yet."

"And the drinking?"

Kyle leaned forward, taking Sherrie's hands.

"I was drunk the night Carolynn Martin was killed. I haven't had a drink since."

After that moment of honesty they talked of other things for a while; memories of childhood, attending the Grand Floral Parade, how they chose their careers. Then it was time to visit Mac and they split the check and the tip. Kyle picked up a matchbook on the way out, planning someday to bring Mac to Jose's for lunch.

When they got to the hospital they could hear Mac's nurse giggling from halfway down the corridor. She was still giggling when they entered. The nurse was young and pretty and looked fresh out of nursing school. Her cheeks were flush and her mouth open as if they had caught her in mid-laugh. Mac looked better. Color had returned to his face although he wasn't back to his normal cherubic red. He was more animated tonight and wiggled his eyebrows at Kyle, pleased he'd been found entertaining a young woman. The nurse excused herself immediately, promising to check on Mac later.

There was a food tray on a table in front of Mac and he pushed the rolling table to one side. Kyle noticed the food was almost gone, except for a little applesauce. It looked like the meal had been Salisbury steak, peas, and potatoes. There was a meal card next to the tray and Mac had marked it, indicating his meal selections for the next day. He had picked a turkey sandwich for lunch and chicken breast for dinner, eating as much meat as he could while he was out of his wife's control.

"What does that nurse have that I don't have?" Sherrie asked, rolling close to Mac's bed.

"More in some places, but less in others," Mac said, wiggling his eyebrows.

Sherrie laughed, reaching out and squeezing Mac's shoulder, letting that substitute for a hug.

"You two are still together?" Mac asked in mock surprise. "You know what you call two people who go places together, don't you? A couple."

"I'd call it a car pool," Sherrie said.

"Oh, that's what it is? A green thing. I know Kyle's a tree hugger from way back. You can tell that by the Greenpeace sticker on the bumper of that V-8 four-by-four he drives. Deny it all you like but you two are spending a lot of time together."

"She's helping with the case, Mac—remember man-in-the-hat—the Good Samaritan? The case we were working on?"

Mac ignored Kyle.

"He's clearly in denial, Sherrie. Tell me what's really going on between you two."

"I'm consulting on the case, Mac. That's it," Sherrie said.

"Right," Mac said.

"Don't jump to conclusions," Sherrie continued, "just because a couple of people eat a few meals together, go out to dinner, watch a few movies, and make out on the living-room floor, it doesn't necessarily mean anything. We're just working together on a case, right, Kyle?"

Kyle's face was hot from embarrassment.

"Tell me more about the making out part," Mac said.

"I think we've identified both the Good Samaritan and Cradle Robber," Kyle said to change the subject. "The blue man playing Good Samaritan may be Robert Sinclair. There was a fingerprint on the first note he left."

"Have you picked him up?" Mac asked.

"There might be two of them," Kyle said, finding it hard to express what he once thought impossible. "I think Sinclair has come back from the future, so there is a younger Sinclair somewhere on the road between Pasadena and here and an older Sinclair in Portland."

"Time travel?" Mac said, surprised to hear it coming from Kyle. "You finally opened up your mind. You say there are two of them and you can't catch one?" Mac asked.

"I think I know where the older one is going to be," Kyle said. "I got a tip from Cradle Robber."

Now Kyle had Mac's full attention.

"Since Cradle Robber was working his way up the West Coast, we guessed he had to be supporting himself some way and came up with a list of jobs that might move him along the coast. With the Rose Festival going on we thought he might be someone with a traveling show or one of the vendors. We were checking for likely suspects when one of them bolted—a man named Norman Patterson. We found this note at his trailer."

Kyle handed Mac the note. Mac read it, his eyes wide by the time he reached the end.

"How does Cradle Robber know who Sinclair is and how does he know where he's going to be?" Mac asked.

"I caught Cradle Robber—Patterson—sneaking around Sinclair's house. He might have picked up a clue there."

"But how did Cradle Robber find Sinclair's house? Come to think of it how did you?"

Kyle told Mac the whole story, leaving out only the part where he was wounded. Sherrie lifted one eyebrow when he skipped the shooting.

"I don't like this, Kyle," Mac said. "If a serial killer asked me to be at a certain place at a certain time, that's the one place I wouldn't be. He's setting you up."

"It's a setup, all right, but not the kind you're thinking of," Kyle said. "He wants me to stop Sinclair. If the notes we've been getting from Sinclair are to be believed, he's stopped Patterson from killing more than once. Patterson may be afraid of him or just tired of him interfering. Whatever the reason, Patterson wants me to catch him so he can get back to being Cradle Robber."

"But if this Patterson is Cradle Robber, then why didn't he just disappear?" Mac asked. "He can buy a bus ticket to Florida and be killing his way up the East Coast in less than a week."

"He may think that Sinclair will follow him to wherever he goes, so he wants to end it here and now," Sherrie said. "But I think there's more. I think he's still here for the same reason Sinclair is here. Sinclair is here to change the past, Cradle Robber doesn't want it changed. He's using Kyle to stop Sinclair. If that doesn't work, he'll do it himself."

Mac looked thoughtful for a second and then spoke with a tone he rarely used—serious and compassionate.

"Why are we trying to stop Sinclair? He's the anti–Cradle Robber, leaving living children behind him."

"This is going to be hard to accept, Mac, but by saving those children he could end up killing them anyway and many more people," Sherrie said. "He's changing the past and creating an energy difference between the old future and the new one. That energy is building up like pressure in a boiler and you know what happens when the pressure exceeds tolerances."

"But boilers have escape valves," Mac said.

"And the strange weather may be that release valve—dry lightning, static electricity, ionizing radiation causing the northern lights. But if the pressure is too great an escape valve won't be enough," Sherrie said.

Mac pulled at his hospital gown.

"Just when you need me most I go and get myself shot," Mac said. "I'd be there for you if I could, buddy."

"I can handle it."

"Take backup," Mac said. "Don't do it alone."

"It's not a trap, Mac," Kyle said. "Cradle Robber isn't gunning for me."

"Don't go alone," Mac said.

"He won't be alone," Sherrie said.

"Good. You take care of him, Sherrie. I don't want to break in a new friend."

"Maybe you could find someone who hasn't heard all your recycled jokes."

"That hurt, Kyle," Mac said, feigning chest pain.

"Kyle, I'm surprised at you. Mac was shot," Sherrie said.

"Kyle's got a mean streak, Sherrie," Mac said. "It's better you learn it now. Did I ever tell you about the time he locked me in the back of a police car with a drunk he knew was going to hurl?"

"No!" Sherrie said in mock horror.

"It's true," Mac said. "I was pounding on the window, screaming for help, when that drunk barfed all over my shoes. You wouldn't believe the stink."

"He's lying," Kyle said. "He climbed in the back of that car to get out of the rain. I got soaked while he stayed dry."

"Yeah, but at least your shoes were clean. I had to pick the little pieces of barf out of the eyelets with a toothpick."

Mac started into another story of alleged cruelty by Kyle and while he was head to head with Sherrie, Kyle slipped Mac's meal card into his back pocket. Kyle let Mac finish, then interjected a bit of reality. When it was time to go, Mac admonished Sherrie to stay close to Kyle, then Mac and Sherrie reached out to each other, managing as much of a hug as a wounded man in a hospital bed and an amputee in a wheelchair could.

Outside at the nurses station, Kyle changed Mac's meal card to all vegetarian choices, then turned it in.

"You do have a mean streak!" Sherrie said.

On the way down in the elevator, Sherrie commented on

how good Mac looked and about how quick his recovery
was for a man of his age and condition. Kyle grunted a
response now and then but Sherrie could tell his mind was
somewhere else and stopped her chatter. When they reached
the lobby, Kyle stopped by the information desk asking
which room Willie Mendez was in.

"Mendez?" Sherrie said. "Wasn't he one of the boys that
shot Mac?"

"That was his brother, Alberto. This is the one that was
tarred and feathered."

They rode up to Willie's floor with a man and two kids,
the little boy holding a silver balloon that said "It's a girl,"
and the little girl holding a vase of flowers. There were bags
under the father's eyes and he had a day's growth of beard.
The kids looked happy until they noticed Sherrie's legs, then
they stepped closer to their father.

Willie Mendez's door was open. Willie was in bed, his
body covered by a sheet but held away from his skin by
frames over his legs and chest. His face was pink but not
burned. His neck was an ugly red beginning just under his
Adam's apple continuing down his body where it disappeared under the sheet. A teenage girl sat in the only chair
in the room, talking to Willie. She was a pretty girl, with a
round face and black hair and eyes. She wore black slacks
and a blue tank top. A gold cross dangled from a chain. Even
sitting down Kyle could tell she was short. She smiled at
Willie while she talked and kept the smile when they entered,
even when she glanced at Sherrie's legs.

"Are you Willie Mendez?" Kyle asked.

"Yes. You're a cop, aren't you?" Willie replied. "I seen
you on TV. You were in the garage when my brother was
shot."

"Detective Sommers," Kyle said.

The girl lost her smile now and studied Kyle warily.

"I'm his sidekick, Sherrie," Sherrie said, rolling up close
to the bed. "The sidekicks never get introduced."

The girl was smiling again, put at ease by Sherrie.

"Linda Roquet," the girl said shyly.

Kyle started at the girl's name, realizing she was mentioned in the note received from Sinclair. She was supposed to have been killed in the drive-by shooting.

"I came to say I'm sorry about your brother," Kyle said. "We went to the Domino Garage to head off a gang war, not get in the middle of one. It wasn't what we wanted."

Kyle expected anger from Willie but Willie's eyes were glistening as if he were about to cry.

"Nobody wanted it," Willie said. "Alberto was doing it for me because of what they did. If I hadn't let them take me he wouldn't have gone gunning for them."

Linda took Willie's hand.

"I never wanted your brother to die or Nick Bletson or any of the others in that garage," Kyle said.

"He doesn't blame you," Sherrie said, touching Kyle on the arm.

Kyle could see concern in her eyes and Kyle realized he hadn't been listening to Willie. The boy held no grudge and felt no malice toward Kyle, yet Kyle couldn't help but apologize.

"Is there anything I can do?" Kyle asked.

"No," Willie said. "Linda talked to my teachers. School was almost over anyway and they said I can make up the work I missed. I won't be able to walk with my friends at graduation but I'm going to get my diploma."

"That's good news," Sherrie said.

"Willie's going to be a CPA," Linda said proudly.

"I said I was thinking about it," Willie said, embarrassed.

"There's always work for CPAs," Kyle said.

"Yeah," Willie said.

"How bad are your burns, Willie?" Sherrie asked.

Willie shrugged.

"He hurts pretty bad," Linda said. "The doctors wanted to give him morphine for the pain but he wouldn't take it. They got him on something else that isn't as good. He doesn't want to get hooked on drugs. They don't let drug addicts become CPAs you know?" Linda said.

"No, they wouldn't," Kyle said. "Accountants handle the money."

"That's right," Linda said. "Accountants are important."

"Are you going to have scars, Willie?" Sherrie asked bluntly. "I can't see the rest of your body, but it looks like your pretty face was spared."

"He's good-looking, isn't he?" Linda asked.

Willie was embarrassed, quickly changing the subject.

"I'm going to have some scars but the doctor said I probably won't need skin grafts," Willie said.

"If there's anything I can do, call me," Kyle said, holding out one of his cards.

"I got a special place where I'll keep it," Willie said.

"Take care of him," Sherrie said to Linda. "That's what sidekicks do!"

When they were out in the hall and out of earshot, Kyle said, "Sidekick? You could never be second banana to anyone."

"No, but Linda could."

"I thought you were a feminist!"

"Only if that means letting women choose what's right for them. She and Willie would be good for each other."

They reached the lobby again, passing the woman at the information desk for the third time. When they were out on the sidewalk Sherrie paused.

"Would you like to go back to my house?" Sherrie said. "There's nothing we can do until morning anyway. Maybe we could watch a movie and eat ice cream? I've got a half gallon of Almond Roca in my freezer."

"Actually, I got us a hotel room," Kyle said.

Sherrie's eyes went wide. She looked honestly surprised but happy. Kyle explained quickly.

"The room is at the Embassy Suites. Sinclair is smart and

won't show up without knowing what he's getting into. I thought if we spent the night at the hotel your car would be in the parking lot when he comes to check it out. We would also get to look over the layout before whatever is going to happen, happens."

Kyle thought Sherrie might be disappointed that he hadn't booked the room to seduce her. Instead, she was cordial and gave him a slight smile.

"We could stay up all night watching movies, eat ice cream, whatever you want to do," Kyle said.

Kyle mentioned staying up all night deliberately so that Sherrie wouldn't expect something he couldn't deliver. She seemed to accept the limits.

"I'm normally not the kind of girl that does this sort of thing but I'm willing to make an exception in this case."

"Great," Kyle said.

"On one condition," Sherrie added.

"What's that?"

"I get to pick the movies."

"Musicals?"

"What else?"

Sherrie not only picked the movies but the snacks, buying microwave popcorn and the largest box of Junior Mints Kyle had ever seen. When they passed a 7-Eleven on the way to the Embassy Suites, she had Kyle buy two Big Gulps—Classic Coke for Sherrie, Diet Coke for Kyle. Washing down candy with liquid sugar was more than Kyle could stomach.

Nothing embarrassed Sherrie and she insisted they carry the movies, Big Gulps, popcorn, and Junior Mints into the lobby while Kyle registered. Passersby, and the clerks behind the desk, studied them with furtive glances.

"Do you need help with your luggage?" the desk clerk asked, looking at the junk food in Sherrie's lap.

The other clerks working the desk smiled.

"We'll manage," Kyle said, taking the key card.

Before going to their room they toured the main floor. The

lobby was triangle-shaped and open to the top, eight stories above. Glass elevators were set to one side and a pool in one corner. There was a restaurant and bar and meeting rooms. Sherrie and Kyle had already walked the outside of the building, studying the parking lots. The note told him to be in the parking lot but there were two lots. The rear lot was largest, the few spaces in the front lot used for guests checking into the hotel. There were three exits from the hotel property, two from the back lot. The traffic past the hotel was heavy when they arrived but then it frequently was. The hotel was only two blocks from the busiest shopping mall in the state and right across from a freeway entrance. Although the traffic in the area was heavy anytime the mall was open, the easy access to the freeway made a quick getaway possible nearly anytime of the day.

Satisfied he knew the hotel inside and out, they went to their room on the fourth floor, Kyle using the key card to open the door and Sherrie pushing the door open wide. The room was as advertised—a suite—larger than the standard hotel room with a living room, small kitchenette, and a separate bedroom and bath. There was a hutch with a large television, VCR, and DVD player. Sherrie set the drinks on an end table by the couch, tossed him one of the packages of microwave popcorn, then put the movies next to the television and studied the controls.

Kyle started the popcorn in the microwave, then went to the window that looked out toward the shopping mall and the freeway. There was nothing to be seen but he couldn't help but look. Cradle Robber and the time traveler were out there somewhere, heading toward each other on a collision course, both of them knowing what was going to happen in the morning. Somehow Kyle needed to wrest control, to shape the future and reshape the past, but without knowing what was coming it was impossible to plan.

The sound of the popcorn faded to a few pops a second and Kyle returned to the microwave, passing Sherrie who was sliding out of her wheelchair onto the couch, then lowering herself to the floor. The popcorn was hot enough to burn his fingertips and Kyle pulled it out gingerly. The fanfare from one of the movies began as Kyle used napkins as pot holders to carry the popcorn, sitting next to Sherrie on the floor.

The first movie was *Blue Skies*, a black and white musical starring Fred Astaire. For some reason Kyle couldn't quite follow, Fred Astaire's character was impersonating a Russian. It was really a love story interspersed with songs and dances, as all musicals were, but Kyle thought the music easily forgettable, recognizing only one tune.

They finished the popcorn before the movie was half over. When it was gone Sherrie scooted closer to Kyle, lifting his arm and leaning against him. They spent most of the night like that, watching one movie after another, eating popcorn and candy. Kyle slept off and on but whenever he woke Sherrie was wide-eyed and focused on whatever was playing.

Sherrie ordered breakfast at six the next morning, selecting generously from the room-service menu. Kyle shuddered when he signed the bill. Kyle ate sparingly but Sherrie ate her portion and much of his. By 7:15 A.M. they were in Sherrie's van parked midway between the two rear exits, the van backed into a parking slot. Kyle could see both parking lots from where he sat. The next few hours passed slowly, both of them tired but too tense to be drowsy. Occasionally a pedestrian would cross the lot and Kyle would tense, studying them until they were gone. Three times couples came from the hotel and got into cars, driving away. Five men in suits arrived, parking and going into the hotel. When Sherrie announced it was "five to ten," the tension notched up to a new level, their eyes busy, studying every car on the street. A minute later two young men dressed in jeans and black denim jackets came down the block. They were smoking joints and laughing. They passed, ambling along the sidewalk paralleling the hotel, oblivious to the world.

"Behind us, Kyle!" Sherrie said a second later. "I can see him in the rearview mirror."

Kyle didn't turn, instead he waited for the man Sherrie saw to pass. A few seconds later he saw a man wearing a hat and overcoat—the old version of Dr. Sinclair—slipping between two cars parked a few rows over. He was moving fast. The key to controlling the past and the future was only a few steps away and Kyle still hadn't decided what to do. Sinclair was walking away from them now, angling toward the front of the hotel. Stepping from the van Kyle called to the mathematician.

"Dr. Sinclair!"

Sinclair froze in place, then turned. Half his face was hidden by his wide-brimmed hat but the exposed half had a distinct blue tinge. Kyle and Sinclair stood face-to-face, neither speaking, neither moving, both unsure of what to do next.

45

Destiny

The traffic on both sides of the Embassy Suites was picking up with early morning bargain hunters flocking to Washington Square, the Target, or the electronics stores down the street. Even more cars roared by on Highway 217, only a block from where Kyle faced off with Sinclair, yet Kyle was so focused that he heard none of the car engines, truck air brakes, or the friction roar of rubber on pavement. Instead, he was tense, ready to reach for his weapon, dodge, or attack, whatever was necessary to bring the man under control. What he hadn't expected was Sinclair to scream.

"Nooooooo!"

The "no" was loud and long, then suddenly Sinclair turned and ran toward the front of the hotel. Kyle was after him before Sinclair had a full step, closing on the old man like a lion on a crippled antelope. Sinclair wasn't an athletic man and even if he had been a twenty-year-old in his prime, Kyle would have run him down. He tackled Sinclair before he reached the far edge of the parking lot, the old Sinclair going down hard, his hat knocked from his head. Stunned by the fall, the old man lay still for a few seconds. Then his senses returned.

"No, you have to let me go! You don't understand!"

Sinclair was flailing wildly now, in full panic mode, and Kyle struggled to control him without hurting him. He had

Sinclair on his back and was holding him there, trying to keep him from rolling over. The man's long coat was thick and difficult to hang on to. Reaching around to get past the coat, Kyle shoved his hand inside, trying to grip his shirt or belt. Instead there was a buzz and a mild electric shock as he touched Sinclair's chest. Wrestling for a new hold, Kyle snagged Sinclair's left arm, trying to bring it around behind where he could twist it, using the pain to bring the man under control. As he brought the arm up his back, Sinclair suddenly switched tactics, rocking violently sideways. Kyle had his legs spread wide, however, and rode out the rock, then pulled up on the arm again.

"Stop struggling," Kyle said.

"Let me go! Please, it's not too late," Sinclair pleaded.

"Put your other arm behind your back!" Kyle ordered, getting ready to cuff Sinclair.

Suddenly Sinclair rocked again, pulling his right arm from underneath his body. There was a revolver in Sinclair's hand. Kyle released the left arm and lunged for the hand with the gun. Sinclair was so desperate to be free that he pushed the gun up on his back, aiming it blindly in Kyle's direction, ready to risk wounding himself. Kyle saw the hammer pull back and jammed his left hand between the hammer and the chamber. The hammer released, the webbing between his thumb and index finger taking the blow, the firing pin puncturing his skin. The gun didn't fire and now Kyle pulled Sinclair's arm up on his back violently, the man yelping with the pain.

Wrenching the gun free, Kyle threw it sideways, sending it skittering under a car. Now Sinclair was a wild man again, with the kind of strength and determination Kyle had only seen in the insane. Sinclair ignored the pain Kyle dished out and there was no other way to control him without a stun gun or another officer to help. Kyle had only one tool left. With a quick move he wrapped himself around Sinclair, slipping his right arm around the older man's neck, pinching his neck in the crook. It was a choke hold and against department policy.

With his wind cut off, Sinclair ceased his violent thrashings and concentrated on trying to free his breathing passages. Kyle's right arm was locked in place with his left and Sinclair had no chance of prying Kyle from his neck. Now Sinclair pounded at the arm and then reached over his shoulder trying to gouge one of Kyle's eyes or scratch his face. Kyle expected the moves and countered each, keeping his head down to protect his eyes. Sinclair finally managed to get some of Kyle's hair and would have pulled it out by the roots if he had had a few more seconds of oxygen but it was too late. With his brain oxygen starved, Sinclair began to lose consciousness.

Timing the release of a choke hold was critical. If you released too soon the perpetrator could be on you in a flash, turning the tables. If you choked too long the perpetrator would die and there would be hell to pay in the department followed by suspension or firing. But if you held it just long enough, the perpetrator would begin to twitch, his arms and legs jerking, his body flopping around. Police called it "doing the chicken," and Sinclair was just beginning to twitch when Kyle released his hold, hearing a long healthy intake of air followed by gasping and wheezing. Before Sinclair could resume his struggle Kyle had him handcuffed and lying on his stomach. Sherrie rolled up next to him just as he finished.

"I thought you were going to kill him," Sherrie said.

Sinclair regained some control over his breathing and the fog cleared from his mind. Suddenly he began to struggle again.

"Let me go! You must let me go! I have to help her!"

"Calm down," Kyle said. "Help who?"

"My daughter, Naomi. They're going to kill her!"

"What?" Kyle said, panic rising in his chest. "Where?"

"Around the front. Now! Please help her!"

Without hesitation Kyle was up and running toward the corner of the hotel.

"Don't do it, Kyle!" Sherrie screamed after him.

Kyle ignored her, running at a full sprint, rounding the corner of the building recklessly, heedless of whatever danger he might find on the other side. "They're going to kill her," Kyle heard over and over in his mind.

Kyle drew his weapon as he ran. He heard the squeal of tires as he came around, seeing a green Ford Explorer leaving the parking lot at high speed, forcing its way recklessly across the lanes of traffic, turning toward the freeway entrance. A woman was picking herself up from the pavement, head bleeding, sobbing. She was short, maybe five feet two, brunette, dressed in white shorts and a T-shirt with UCLA emblazoned on the front. When she saw Kyle's gun she flinched, looking terrified.

"Police," he assured her.

Relieved, she staggered toward him, pleading with him.

"They took my daughter! They took Naomi."

She was dizzy from the blow to her head and Kyle held one arm, steadying her.

"Who took her?" Kyle asked.

"Two men. I just put her in the car. They stole it!"

Kyle looked over just in time to see the Explorer cut around a lane of oncoming traffic and disappear toward the freeway entrance ramp. In the backseat of the Explorer he could see a child's car seat.

A couple came out of the hotel, staring at Kyle's gun and then at Patty Sinclair, pleading with Kyle, blood streaking her hair.

"I'm a police officer. Call 9-1-1 and ask for police and an ambulance," he ordered the man. "Stay with her until the ambulance gets here," Kyle ordered the woman. Then Kyle lowered Patty Sinclair to the ground, waving the woman over to take care of her. Kyle raced back around the hotel. Sinclair was lying where he had left him, Sherrie parked next to him.

"Get the van started," he shouted to Sherrie.

Sherrie hesitated only a second, reading correctly that he would go without her if she argued. Kyle unlocked the handcuffs.

"They got your daughter. Where can we find them?"

"Oh, my God, no!"

Sinclair was sobbing now and oblivious to Kyle.

"Not again, I'm so sorry, Naomi, I tried, I did my best."

Kyle pulled Sinclair to his feet, confused. Why wasn't Sinclair rushing to the van. Half carrying him, Kyle took him to the van, pushing the crying man into the back, then hurrying to the other side to grab Sherrie's wheelchair and toss it in the back with Sinclair.

"Get to the freeway heading west," Kyle said as he climbed in next to Sherrie.

"What's going on?" Sherrie asked, even as she pulled out of the parking slot directing her van toward the exit.

"Sinclair, where are they taking her?"

Paralyzed with remorse, Sinclair responded slowly.

"I . . . don't . . . know!" he said.

"You have to know, you knew about the other children," Kyle said.

"The carjackers—Ryerson and Butler—never remembered where they left her," Sinclair said.

Sherrie had them on the street now, waiting out a light and cross traffic. Kyle wished he had a police car so he could clear a path with the siren.

"What happened to your daughter?" Kyle demanded. "If you want to save her you have to tell me quick."

There was no hope in Sinclair's face.

"Patty—my wife—was carjacked when she came out of the hotel. She had just buckled Naomi in the backseat when they hit her on the head and took the car. They were drug addicts, high and out of their heads."

Kyle remembered the two pot smokers walking down the sidewalk.

"They didn't want Naomi, just the car, so they drove out into the woods and tied her to a tree, planning to call the police and tell them where to find her. They were so stoned they forgot to call. They left my little girl tied to a tree in the woods. Left her to die all alone."

"You know Ryerson's and Butler's names. They must have been caught. Where? What were they doing?"

"The police find them in Boise three days from now," Sinclair said. "It won't matter, they won't remember where they left her. They tried, I think they honestly tried to remember but they just couldn't do it. They led search parties through the woods for six days but they never found my Naomi. I searched two more weeks and every weekend for a year but . . ."

Sinclair's voice trailed off, his mind's eye turned inward thinking of the fruitless search and the horror of his baby's last few days on earth. Sinclair was old, graying, skin loose and wrinkled, shoulders slightly bent forward but not old-old yet. When Kyle had wrestled with him, he found he was still a powerful man. But now, thinking about his daughter's pending second death, he looked ancient, his life energy totally spent in a rescue attempt that had taken him across time only to fall a minute short.

Kyle knew Sinclair was a kind man, tenderhearted and compassionate. If he had been a selfish man he would have hidden out in his house, waited until today to come to the Embassy Suites and save his daughter. But the pain of his own daughter's death sensitized him to Cradle Robber's victims and to the other children he had tried to save. Kyle knew that kind of compassion grew out of one's own pain; he had felt it himself. He was feeling it now.

"They haven't had time to leave her anywhere yet!" Kyle said, nearly shouting at Sinclair.

Pulling his cell phone from his jacket pocket, Kyle punched in the bureau's number.

"Kyle . . ." Sherrie said, her voice trailing off.

He turned, catching her eye just before she accelerated through the intersection, making the turn toward the freeway entrance. He knew what she wanted to say. She wanted to tell him not to interfere and that little Naomi Sinclair had to die to save others—to save the city of Portland, if Sherrie's worst fears were realized. But she couldn't bring herself to say it, not with a grieving father sobbing on the floor behind them and not with a little girl in the hands of a couple of drug-fogged carjackers.

Sherrie guided the van down the freeway, quickly picking up speed. Kyle alternated between giving information to the dispatcher, and dragging it out of Sinclair who still failed to see any hope of saving his daughter. Painfully, Kyle confirmed the year and model of the car Patty Sinclair had been driving and got the California license plate number. Kyle also directed the dispatcher to relay the information to the State Police in case they made it out of Portland. The most logical route to Boise would be Interstate 84 through the Columbia River Gorge. That would narrow the search considerably but Ford Explorers were nearly as common as pickup trucks in Oregon. California plates almost as common.

"You said the carjackers led you to where they thought they left her. Where was that?"

"Out toward Scappoose along Highway 30. They took some old logging road into the woods, walked her into the trees and tied her there."

Sinclair dissolved into tears again and Kyle knew it would be a few minutes before he could get more information.

Scappoose was north of Portland along the Columbia River and if the carjackers were heading in that direction they would either have to travel out the Sunset Highway and cut through the west hills, or connect to Highway 30 in Northwest Portland. It was unlikely Sinclair knew which route the carjackers took, so Kyle guessed and directed Sherrie toward Northwest Portland.

Sherrie drove without speaking, weaving in and out of traffic while Kyle spoke again to the dispatcher, asking them to contact the State Police and the Scappoose County sheriff and tell them to watch Highway 30 for the Explorer. Kyle knew it wasn't more than a day's drive to Boise and he suspected the carjackers would find someplace to hide out for a couple of days before driving the stolen car across a state line. First, however, they would get rid of their unwanted passenger.

Kyle kept his phone to his ear for much of the trip out of the city, talking to the dispatcher, other detectives, and sheriff's deputies. When they were out of the city, past St. Johns, the last northern suburb, Kyle focused on the road, studying every green vehicle they passed. In the back, Sinclair was calmer now, peering out the windows, a flicker of hope still alive.

They reached Scappoose in forty minutes, then turned back, Sinclair studying every side road, trying to remember which one the carjackers had guided the search parties up.

"They took us up a dozen of these and there were multiple branches. It could be any of them or all of them. I can't be sure."

"Pick one," Kyle ordered in frustration.

"Take the one near the golf course," Sinclair said.

Sherrie turned west off of Highway 30 on a two-lane road that climbed past a golf course, winding into the hills. There were homes sprinkled in the low hills, ranging from older homes with rusting automobiles parked in their side yards, to new estates with large houses and manicured lawns. Some of the homes reminded him of his father's "farm." They passed several roads that branched off, most with mailboxes indicating they were driveways. Finally Sinclair directed them down a branch that quickly turned from pavement, to gravel, to dirt and took them into the forest. Oregon forests are dominated by evergreen trees, Douglas firs keeping the state green year-round. Because it was late spring, the shrubs and deciduous trees mixed among the firs wore the bright green of fresh growth and wildflowers were sprinkled generously along the sides of the road. No one in Sherrie's van noticed the beauty around them.

Sherrie worked the hand controls of her van expertly, driving as well as anyone with legs. The road was rough and she was forced to keep the speed low to keep them from being slammed around the interior. A mile down the road they came to a fork where Sherrie stopped, waiting for directions.

"Which way?" Kyle asked impatiently.

"I don't know—left, try left!" Sinclair said.

The left fork climbed higher into the hills, finally emerging into an old clear-cut. From the size of the regrowth Kyle guessed the clear-cut was five years old. Kyle directed Sherrie to turn around, taking them to the other fork. The dirt road deteriorated quickly into two ruts, which they bumped over for twenty minutes. Finally, Kyle ordered Sherrie to turn around.

"Those carjackers wouldn't go to this much trouble to get rid of the little girl," Kyle explained.

They tried two more roads, having no better luck. As they were coming back from the most recent try, Kyle realized that Sherrie was silent, no longer arguing with him and actively looking for side roads. He realized she was cooperating because she thought he would fail to find Naomi. She wanted Kyle roaming the hills, looking for a car he would never find.

Kyle got back on his cell phone and contacted the county sheriff, asking him to organize a search party, telling him they might have taken the girl into the woods and tied her to a tree. Thankfully, the sheriff didn't ask him how he knew. The sheriff assured him he could have a search party organized within an hour.

They searched back roads for another forty-five minutes with no luck. By now it was midafternoon and the kidnappers had had plenty of time to dump Naomi or hide the Sinclairs' Explorer in a garage where they would never find it. If they had managed to pull into the woods and tie her to a tree, the only hope of finding her was a massive ground search. Even knowing they had failed to find Naomi the first time it happened, Kyle clung to the hope that this time would be different.

They met the search party at the Dairy Bar Drive-In on Highway 30. The parking lot was filled with four-by-fours, four-wheel drive pickups, and off-road vehicles. Hunting, fishing, and camping were popular in Oregon, so rounding up a posse equipped for searching rough roads was easy. Deputy Coolidge had been given charge of the search party. He was in his thirties, tall and weathered, the look of a man who spent more time outdoors than in. He was dressed in tan from head to toe, a regulation uniform, shiny badge on his chest. He wore reflective sunglasses, looking every bit the Hollywood image of a deputy. When Sinclair saw the deputy he gasped and then shrank into the back of the van.

"I know him," Sinclair said. "I mean I will know him. He shouldn't see me."

"I'll stay with him," Sherrie said to Kyle.

Kyle left them in the van. Deputy Coolidge's speech was crisp and to the point, wasting few words and none on greetings.

"We've got enough vehicles here to cover every back road between here and Highway 26 in a few hours," Coolidge said. "If they don't find that California Explorer, it's not there."

Coolidge repeatedly referred to the Sinclairs' Explorer as the "California Explorer."

Like many Oregonians, Coolidge disliked Californians whom they viewed as invaders from the south, driving up property values and bringing big-city crime with them.

"If they did take the little girl into the woods like you think, it won't be easy to find her," Coolidge said. "We've got search and rescue teams, explorer scouts, and tracking dogs on the way. We'll set them to combing the woods on both sides of the roads."

"They're in a hurry so they won't take her more than a few yards off the road. Just enough so she can't be seen," Kyle said. "I wouldn't search more than a hundred yards in from the road. Not on the first pass."

"Sounds right," Deputy Coolidge said. "I've broken the searchers into teams and assigned them to roads. I've got Forest Service maps but even those won't show the logging roads. Don't worry, most of the men here have hunted in those hills and know the roads that aren't on any map."

Coolidge was more confident than he had a right to be but Kyle found it infectious. Leaving the deputy to send out his teams, Kyle had Sherrie drive the van to the other side of the drive-in while he checked in with the Portland dispatcher, making sure there had been no news on the location of the carjackers. The dispatcher relayed a message from Danforth, demanding that Kyle check in with him. Kyle ignored Danforth's request.

Kyle got three cups of coffee from the drive-in and returned to the van to wait. Kyle stood outside the van, the door open, swallowing two more of Sherrie's pills. Sinclair stayed in the back, looking out the windows, clearly agitated. Sherrie stayed behind the wheel, seemingly relaxed. After a while she tried to coax information out of Sinclair.

"How much energy did it take to send you back?" Sherrie asked. "A thousand megawatts? I've been trying to estimate it but I don't know enough about the parameters."

Sinclair ignored her.

"Ten thousand megawatts?"

"Ludicrous," Sinclair said.

"So more than a thousand but less than ten thousand megawatts."

"Five thousand megawatts," Sinclair said.

"Is that a lot?" Kyle asked.

"Nearly five times the output of Bonneville Dam," Sherrie said. "How did you pull that much power? You must have had your own reactor? Fission? Fusion?"

Sinclair returned to ignoring her. Sherrie tried another tack.

"I think I understand the blue cast to your skin. It's the result of ionized nitrogen, right? That gives off blue light."

Sinclair looked at Sherrie with new respect.

"That suit under your overcoat. It's a superconductor, isn't it? Is the nitrogen in the fabric liquid? You're surrounded by an energy field for a reason, aren't you?"

Sinclair refused to confirm Sherrie's speculation.

"How do you control for the space-time relationship? Let's assume you came back twenty years in time. If you simply displaced yourself in time without controlling for the movement of the Earth in its orbit and the movement of the sun which pulls the solar system with it, you would find yourself floating in space. So how did you direct the time displacement? A focused energy beam to a point in space where the Earth was twenty years in your past?"

Sinclair snorted, then turned to Sherrie.

"Absurd."

"Which part? Can't you direct the beam that accurately?"

"There is no beam," Sinclair said derisively. "You don't have to direct the object being displaced to maintain its relationship with other matter. Time and matter are intricately linked in the quantum substrate. They can't be separated, at least not yet."

"But if you can't separate matter and time then it wouldn't be possible to come back in time," Sherrie said.

Sinclair had an ego and Sherrie had pricked it.

"But I'm here!" Sinclair said. "I found a way when no one thought it could be done. My colleagues didn't even know what the project was really about."

"Tachyons travel back in time," Kyle pointed out.

Both Sinclair and Sherrie looked at Kyle in surprise.

"Yes they do. But tachyons aren't matter," Sinclair said. "At least not always."

Sherrie chewed her lip, thinking, staring out the window of the van. Sinclair let her think.

"If you can't separate matter and time, then you had to find a way to influence the bond between matter and time," Sherrie said.

Sinclair was back to staring out the window. Sherrie continued thinking and chewing on her lip. Kyle returned to the drive-in and came back with more coffee. Sherrie declined the coffee. Sinclair accepted a second cup. After a few minutes Sherrie spoke again.

"You must have realigned the bonds between matter and time. Yes, that must be it. If the connection between this coffee cup and this second could be captured then I could reconnect the coffee cup with a previous second. When that connection was made the cup would travel back one second in time."

"I told you the bonds cannot be broken. As the bonds between time and matter are weakened the energy necessary to complete the separation approaches infinity in much the same way that an object approaching the speed of light requires an infinite amount of energy. Therefore the speed of light cannot be achieved and mass and time cannot be separated."

"But you're here," Sherrie repeated.

"Am I?" Sinclair asked.

Now Sherrie chewed her lip again, looking away, turning her empty coffee cup in her hand, creating indentations with the nail of her thumb.

"That accounts for the arrow of time?" Kyle asked.

Sinclair spoke to Kyle like a man explaining to a child.

"Yes. Matter and time are linked and time only flows in one direction. That connection also accounts for entropy which is the change from order to disorder."

Kyle didn't understand but didn't have the patience for a lecture.

"That can't be right," Sherrie said, turning to face Sinclair again.

"As an object approaches the speed of light time slows relative to objects that are stationary. Time is not a constant . . . or . . ."

Sherrie trailed off, thinking.

". . . or time is constant and mass is the variable."

"Of course mass isn't a constant," Sinclair said.

Kyle gave Sherrie a puzzled look.

"Imagine riding up the first hill on a roller-coaster," Sherrie explained. "Built into that hill is a ratchet that the cars move over. There's no danger of slipping back because every foot or so the ratchet engages a new rung. You can only move forward but not back. Think of time as the coaster track and us as sitting in the coaster car. We can move slow or fast relative to the track depending on other variables like hills and valleys. We can move forward in time at different rates but the coaster never goes backward."

"And you can't jump out of the coaster and run back down the hill?" Kyle asked.

"No," Sherrie said, slightly amused.

Then Sherrie lost her smile.

"That's it, Kyle," Sherrie said. "You can't jump out because you have a seat belt on. But if you were tied to the car with a rope you could get out and run back a short distance before you ran out of rope and the car towed you along with it. You can't untie yourself but you can lengthen the bond that keeps you with the car—lengthen the rope. That's how you did it. You lengthened the bonds between an object—you—and time. You're still tethered to your time line."

"Very good but not right," Sinclair said. "I couldn't add to the bonds, the best I could do was stretch them."

Now Sherrie was quiet, thinking. What Sinclair had said meant little to Kyle.

"But then you can't stay in our time," Sherrie concluded. "You'll return to your own time when you drop below the energy threshold necessary to stretch the bonds."

"It's inevitable," Sinclair said. "And it will happen soon."

Kyle was still trying to understand the implications when Deputy Coolidge began shouting at him. Word had come over the CB. The California Explorer had been found.

46

Missing

According to the searcher who radioed in on the CB, Sinclair's Explorer had been found lying on its side a hundred yards off a nameless dirt road. To find that road the searchers positioned guides at each turn from Highway 30. Sherry followed Deputy Coolidge who followed the guides. Sherrie kept a discrete distance to hide Dr. Sinclair and the fact she was handicapped. She worried the deputy had read the bulletin from the Gresham Police.

The road they were following was nothing more than a narrow path bulldozed through thick underbrush, Douglas fir lining each side. After a slow mile of bumping and sliding, dodging the biggest holes, they rounded a bend and found the narrow road choked with four-wheel drive vehicles. The searchers had congregated to see for themselves what they had been looking for. With the road blocked, Sherrie stopped at the outer edge of the makeshift parking lot, pulling her van as far off the road as she dared. Sinclair leaned between the seats, looking intently through the windshield.

"It didn't happen this way," Sinclair said, his tone a mix of hope and confusion. "They caught Ryerson and Butler in Boise. They were still driving our car and it wasn't damaged—not like this."

"You came to change things," Kyle said.

"But I didn't do anything," Sinclair said.

"I don't see how our actions could have changed this," Sherrie said. "We haven't done anything to alter this piece of the time line. I'm sure of that. Ryerson and Butler carjacked the Explorer just like in the original time line, so it should be playing out the same way. Somehow the time line has been altered."

"That's good," Kyle said.

"No," Sherrie said. "It has to play out the same way as before or the consequences will be catastrophic." Then turning to look over her shoulder at Sinclair, she said, "Isn't that right, Doctor?"

Sinclair's face was pressed to the window, searching anxiously. He was looking for his daughter even though the CB radio report had said nothing about finding her. He had heard Sherrie, though, and kept his face turned away as he answered.

"Changes can be safely made in a time line," Sinclair said, continuing to look for his daughter.

"Small changes," Sherrie said. "What about a causality paradox?"

Sinclair didn't answer, his face still turned to the window.

"Dr. Sinclair, what would be the energy release from a paradox where someone removes the reason that brought them to the past?" Sherrie asked. "Have you run the math?"

"There are too many variables," Sinclair said, continuing to avoid Sherrie's eyes.

Kyle ignored the exchange. He didn't want to know who was right.

By now Deputy Coolidge had worked his way among the four-by-fours and was out of his car and surrounded by a group of men in flannel shirts. Deputy Coolidge listened to what the men were saying, his head turning from man to man as each took a turn. When each man had spoken two or three times he turned and looked back to their van. Kyle reached for the door handle just as he saw the deputy turn and walk toward them.

"He shouldn't see me," Sinclair moaned, shrinking farther back.

"Why?" Sherrie said. "Meeting you before he meets your younger self can't be as catastrophic as what you're planning."

Sinclair hid in the back of the van, ignoring Sherrie.

Kyle intercepted Deputy Coolidge, who turned as he approached. Kyle fell in beside him, following a herd of men in flannel shirts across a small clearing.

"You said there were two carjackers?" Deputy Coolidge said, looking over at Kyle, sun glinting off his mirrored glasses.

"That's right."

"And a little girl was in the vehicle when it was stolen?"

"Did you find her?" Kyle asked.

"No."

The Explorer was on its side and they approached its underside. By the tracks left in the clearing, Kyle could see someone had tried to drive the Explorer across a small gully but the ground was soft and the vehicle had slid sideways and then tipped. Kyle knew any four-wheel drive should have easily handled the terrain, telling him the driver was either incompetent, panicked, or stoned.

"There was no one in the car," Deputy Coolidge said, stepping aside to let Kyle inspect the interior.

The windshield was cracked, spiderwebs running so thick through the glass that it was nearly opaque. Kyle leaned over the vehicle, looking inside but finding nothing in the front except floor mats, a box of tissues, Tic Tacs, and a map of the city of Portland. In the back Kyle spotted a child's blanket and a Beanie Baby shaped like a puppy. There was also a car seat still strapped tightly to the backseat.

"They tell me there are two bodies back in the woods," Deputy Coolidge said abruptly.

"What? The little girl?"

"Two adult males."

"Show me," Kyle said.

Deputy Coolidge and Kyle followed three men in flannel shirts into the woods. Fifty yards in they found the bodies. Two men in jeans and black denim jackets lying on their stomachs. Kyle recognized the clothes of the pot smokers he had seen at the hotel. There were bullet holes in the back of their heads. It looked like an execution. Kyle was mystified. He knew that finding the Explorer was a long shot but he expected if they did get lucky and find the car the carjackers and Naomi would be with it.

"Are you sure there were only two carjackers?" Deputy Coolidge asked. "Someone killed these men and it sure wasn't the little girl."

"She must be around here somewhere," Kyle said. "They might have tied her to a tree."

"Tied to a tree? They've done this before?" Deputy Coolidge asked.

"Something like that," Kyle said.

Kyle realized how peculiar this must seem to Coolidge.

"We need to organize a search," Kyle said, but the deputy was already in action, shouting orders to the volunteers.

Deputy Coolidge set up the search in the shape of a spoked wheel, the searchers walking into the woods along one of the spokes and then folding toward the next spoke, searching the space between. The ground was uneven and the undergrowth thick. The searchers had difficulty keeping the pattern as they forced their way through the brush. Kyle worked with one of the groups and soon understood how difficult it was to search natural terrain. There were stretches where the undergrowth refused to be parted. Kyle was forced to skirt large sections. Naomi could be lying in one of those sections hidden under a wild rhododendron and never be found.

Hours passed as the spokes of the search pushed deeper and deeper into the woods, the wedges between became greater, taking more time to search. The terrain became steeper on the west side, slowing the search in that direction.

Deputy Coolidge redistributed his searchers, shifting more to the west.

Someone arrived with bags of hamburgers and coolers of pop and beer. Searchers began breaking, refreshing themselves but slowing the search. The afternoon passed without finding Naomi.

Searching through the brush with the others, Kyle reviewed their actions and how history might have been changed. Kyle couldn't see how anything he or Dr. Sinclair had done could have altered what happened to his family. Because Kyle had interfered, Sinclair had been stopped from helping his wife and daughter and Kyle had arrived too late. If anything, Cradle Robber's note taking Kyle to the Embassy Suites had kept history on the right track since Kyle had kept Sinclair from saving his daughter. There would be no causality paradox because Naomi had been kidnapped just as before. But from that point the scenario unfolded much differently. Some factor Kyle hadn't accounted for had altered the time line and once again Naomi was missing. Then Kyle realized there was only one other person who knew when and where the carjackers were going to strike—Cradle Robber.

Kyle raced through the brush and past Deputy Coolidge to Sherrie's van. Kyle reviewed everything he knew about Cradle Robber, searching for some clue as to where he might take Naomi. Cradle Robber's trailer wasn't safe, especially after leaving Kyle the note. He could take her into another part of the woods to kill her but he could have killed her here. He could take her to a motel to smother her in bed but it wasn't Cradle Robber's style. He liked to kill children at home, in their own beds. With that realization there was a flash of lightning and a peal of thunder so loud Kyle's ears hurt from the pressure wave. Flinching, he looked up seeing nothing but hazy sky. Quickly forgetting the lightning, Kyle waved and shouted at Sherrie, telling her to get the van started. Kyle had one last chance to save Naomi and one last chance to save his daughter.

47

Naomi

Sherrie hesitated when Kyle directed her to take them to
Pumpkin Court. Her hands rested on the controls briefly before she started the ignition, clearly reluctant. As she maneuvered the van around to align with the ruts in the dirt,
there was another flash and crack of thunder.

Kyle had never been at ground zero where the lightning
flashes and the thunder were simultaneous. The explosions
of sound were terrifying. Leaning forward Kyle studied the
sky, seeing no storm clouds. In the back, a nervous Sinclair
stared out the windows.

The pace Sherrie set frustrated Kyle. The ruts they followed were barely passable, the suspension of the van being
tested even at Sherrie's speed. The road improved with each
junction, Sherrie adjusting her speed to the condition of the
road. Impatient, fists clenching and unclenching, Kyle barely
kept quiet as Sherrie took them out of the hills and onto
Highway 30 turning toward Portland, accelerating to the
speed limit, then creeping over until she was only five miles
per hour above.

"Faster, Sherrie. You don't have to worry about the police."

Sherrie took the van to ten miles over the limit. Kyle desperately wanted to take the wheel but the controls were designed for an amputee and unfamiliar to him. Even more

difficult would be getting control away from Sherrie. So Kyle gritted his teeth and suffered in silence.

Taking Cornell Road, she drove into the west hills, slowing to a crawl as she negotiated the hairpin curves, one of which was posted at five mph. After a painfully slow climb, they crested the last hill for the short run to Highway 26. There were only two intersections between them and Highway 26 and then Pumpkin Court. The first intersection was ahead, the only car in sight crossing the intersection. As they approached the light ahead changed to green and Kyle's right foot pressed the floor as if it were an accelerator. Sherrie kept her speed constant. Eyes riveted on the green traffic light, Kyle judged whether they could make it to the intersection before the signal turned. It would be close but they could make it if only Sherrie would accelerate. Unconsciously, Kyle leaned forward, his body rigid. They were almost to the intersection when the light switched to yellow and Sherrie braked hard, bringing them to an abrupt stop. Kyle turned on Sherrie, furious.

"Give me the wheel!" Kyle demanded.

Sherrie turned to him, speaking softly.

"I understand how much you hurt, Kyle, but I can't let you do this."

With both hands Kyle reached for Sherrie, grabbed her arm, and tried pulling her from the seat. Sherrie grabbed the steering wheel, holding herself in the driver's seat. Kyle couldn't budge her, so he tried to get his arms around her waist to drag her off the seat. She countered, grabbing his right wrist while his left arm snaked past the small of her back.

Unable to move her, Kyle dropped his hand to her hip and pulled, feeling her bottom slide across the seat. Realizing she was losing the fight, Sherrie let go of Kyle's wrist and slapped him across the head, the palm of her hand cupping his ear. Nearly rupturing his eardrum, a sharp stab of pain cut from his inner ear deep into his brain. He yelped and jerked back. Then he lunged at her again, trying to get in close so she couldn't cuff him.

With his head buried against her chest, Kyle took a beating while he worked his arms around her, then lifted and pulled, feeling Sherrie come free. She stopped pounding his back and grabbed the steering wheel with both hands. Kyle managed to pull her to the edge of the seat but Sherrie's powerful grip kept him from dragging her all the way off. It was a stalemate with Sherrie clinging to the steering wheel and Kyle unable to move her the rest of the way out of the driver's seat. Kyle was about to give up when a shadow covered them and Kyle looked up to see Sinclair leaning over the seat, prying Sherrie's hands from the steering wheel. When she was free, Kyle pulled her from the driver's seat and with Sinclair's help dragged her into the back of the van.

Sherrie was cursing now, Kyle climbing into the driver's seat and Sinclair into the passenger seat. A horn sounded behind them but Kyle wasn't sure which hand control was the brake and which the accelerator. Kyle shifted the car into Park, then squeezed one of the controls, the engine rpms increased. A car passed them, the passenger giving Kyle the finger. Shifting back to Drive, Kyle looked up to see the traffic light was red again. Looking both ways he saw no one coming so he squeezed the throttle and the van chugged forward. Tentatively he accelerated, getting the feel of the hand accelerator.

"You can't do this, Kyle," Sherrie said, pulling herself between the seats. "People are going to die."

"You don't know that!" Kyle said.

They were approaching the second intersection. There was cross traffic and two cars waiting at the light ahead of Kyle. As Kyle felt for the hand brake, the light turned and the cars in his way began to move. Kyle slowed just enough so he wouldn't rear-end the car in front, then accelerated through the intersection as the cars ahead of him picked up speed. As he accelerated, Sherrie crawled between the seats, reaching for Kyle's cell phone. Sinclair realized what she was after and snatched the phone away, throwing it out the window.

"Kyle, you can't trust him," Sherrie said. "You saw the lightning! You've seen the night skies. Have you ever seen anything like it?"

"Many times," Kyle said, watching the oncoming traffic, looking for a gap big enough for him to risk passing the car in front of him.

"Lightning from a clear sky in spring in Oregon?" Sherrie said.

"It happens," Kyle said.

"Never," Sherrie said. "Haven't you noticed? The lightning has stopped! Look at the sky now, Kyle!"

Concentrating on the hand controls and the freeway entrance they were approaching, Kyle didn't look at the sky. Instead he studied his mirrors, then timed the turn between the cars in the oncoming traffic. Cutting through a space he normally would never risk, Kyle shot across and down the ramp, accompanied by angry honking. Once he was merged with the traffic on Highway 26 he finally looked at the sky and was shocked. The sky was tarnished, looking like the smog-choked skies of Los Angeles in summer. Kyle hadn't seen a sky like this since before Oregon banned field burning. The grass seed farmers burned their fields in the fall sending up choking clouds of brown smoke. Back then some nights at his father's farm had been unbearable. There was no sitting on the deck those nights. This sky was different, though, because there was no smell to the air, just a slowly deepening gloom.

"The lightning was just the beginning, Kyle. There's an energy buildup because of the causality paradox you are creating."

"You don't know that."

"Kyle, whatever we change today has already happened in the past of those in Dr. Sinclair's future. Linear time is a human perception, part of the psychological universe. The past and future coexist in the physical universe."

Kyle was watching the exits while Sherrie argued with him from between the seats. The exit taking him to Pumpkin Court was only a couple of miles away. Among the cars traveling in the opposite direction on the other side of the divider he noticed some had turned their lights on. It wasn't even seven o'clock yet. The sky continued to darken, nearly all the blue gone now, replaced by a deepening brown.

"If what I'm going to do has already been done, then why hasn't the explosion taken place yet?" Kyle said.

"Because you haven't reached the critical moment. Just what are you planning to do?" Sherrie asked.

"I'm going to save Naomi from a horrible death," Kyle said.

"Are you?" Sherrie prodded. "You have doubts, Kyle, I can see it in your face. As long as you have those doubts there's a degree of uncertainty. Once you act you remove all doubt and then the paradox is created and that's when it will happen. All this," Sherrie said, indicating the darkening sky, "is just the buildup. We won't survive the main event."

Sinclair had been silent in the passenger seat, listening intently to the argument. Now he joined in.

"No! She's not right. The lightning *is* the energy release. Lightning has always served this purpose and we just didn't understand that! It's just a lightning storm, that's all. They happen all the time. Isn't my daughter's life worth a storm or two?"

"You can't trust him, Kyle. He'll do anything and say anything to save his daughter. You can't trust yourself either for the same reason. That's why you agreed I would be with you. Listen to me, Kyle! Believe me!"

They were at the exit now, Kyle taking it at full speed.

"Look at the sky now, Kyle!" Sherrie said.

Kyle looked up to see a chocolate-brown, as if the air was thick with dust particles gathered from a thousand square miles. Most of the cars had their lights on now. Scattered clouds were forming, dark and threatening. Most striking of all was the glowing streak that undulated above the horizon. Looking like a long green ribbon, the streak in the sky shimmered as it continually changed shape.

"It's the aurora borealis," Kyle said.

"Not in these latitudes," Sherrie said. "It's like the northern lights because it's caused by charged particles in the atmosphere. Where's all that energy coming from, Kyle?"

Kyle tailgated the car in front of him now, more confident in using the hand controls. Turning left off the exit he stayed a half-car length behind the car in front of him all the way to the entrance to Pumpkin Court. Only when he turned into the development did he pause, looking again at the sky. There were multiple ribbons in the sky now, undulating, glowing brighter against the darkening sky.

"Kyle," Sherrie said, reaching up to touch his arm.

He shook off her touch and he squeezed the throttle, the van moving forward.

"You're doing the right thing," Sinclair said.

"We'll soon know," Kyle said.

They followed the road toward the Sinclair home. The workmen were gone for the day, the homes under construction deserted. As they rounded the curve they could see Sinclair's newly finished home and Cradle Robber's truck parked in front.

Kyle squeezed the brake hard when he saw the truck, surprised that Cradle Robber wasn't trying to hide. As soon as the van lurched to a stop Sinclair opened his door and jumped, running toward his home, his long coat flapping behind him.

"Stop!" Sherrie shouted.

Kyle squeezed the throttle and shot forward, passing Sinclair and reaching the house first. Pulling his gun he got out of the van, keeping low. Pausing at the front of the van, he peeked around the grill and studied the house. Suddenly Sinclair ran past, straight toward the front door. Gun still in his hand, Kyle chased him down, tackling the old man in the front yard. Sinclair went down hard but immediately tried to wrestle himself free. Kyle held him down despite the electric shock he received every time his hands touched Sinclair's bare blue skin.

"Let me go to her!" Sinclair shouted.

"Shut up!" Kyle said. "There's still a chance he doesn't know we're here."

Sinclair calmed down. Kyle spoke softly to him.

"Stay behind me and don't do anything stupid. If I don't tell you to do it then it's stupid, you understand?"

Sinclair nodded. Then the two of them got to their feet and Kyle led them to the protection of Cradle Robber's truck. Creeping along the driver's side, Kyle checked inside, finding it empty. By now Sherrie had managed to get her wheelchair out of the van and rolled up behind them. Kyle didn't bother to order her to stay behind. Then with an old man and a crippled woman as his backup, Kyle trotted to the front door, motioning the others to the other side. Then Kyle tried the knob, finding it turned and released the catch. Kyle pushed the door open slowly, keeping his back to the wall, peering around the corner into the house. The carpet layers had been there since his last visit and the movers had come from California. There was furniture and cardboard boxes stacked everywhere—dozens of places for Cradle Robber to hide.

Sinclair was edgy, ready to rush into the house. Kyle motioned for Sinclair and Sherrie to stay and then picked a large carton halfway between the front door and the stairs and ran for it. He made it to the carton, keeping his back to it while he checked the living room behind him for Cradle Robber. When he was sure he wasn't going to get shot in the back he turned and peered over the carton, scanning and listening—he saw and heard nothing.

Besides the living room and dining room on the first floor, there were the kitchen, family room, den, pantry, and bathroom. There was also an attached three-car garage. All had been filled with boxes and furniture. Normally it would take fifteen minutes of cautious searching before they could move to the second story. With Naomi's life on the line Kyle couldn't wait that long. Sinclair couldn't wait at all.

Sinclair rushed into the house, shouting for his daughter, running from room to room. Kyle called to the panicked father but it was no use. Within a minute he had circumnavigated the first floor and came back past Kyle and then ran up the stairs.

Sherrie rolled up next to Kyle just as Sinclair hit the stairs. Kyle started after him but then stopped, realizing Sherrie couldn't easily follow and he couldn't keep his gun ready and carry her up the stairs.

"Go after him," Sherrie said.

Sinclair's mad rush around the main floor had convinced Kyle that Cradle Robber wasn't lying in wait for them on this floor, so he left Sherrie and hurried after Sinclair who was still shouting his daughter's name. Suddenly the shouting stopped. At the top of the stairs Kyle went into a crouch, his gun held straight in front of him, his left hand steadying his aim. Cautiously, he worked down the long corridor that split the second floor in two. There was a large bonus room at the far end and open doors on both sides of the hall— three doors on the left, two on the right. Peering in the first bedroom, Kyle saw a headboard, bed frame, and a mattress leaning against one wall. There was a dresser and boxes labeled "NAOMI'S ROOM" in black marker. Kyle stepped in, quickly sweeping the room, finding nothing.

There was an end table and two chairs in the hall and Kyle skirted these. The next door was on his left and there was nothing in the room except boxes labeled "EXTRA BEDROOM." The next door on the left was a bathroom connecting to the bedrooms on either side—it was empty. Next on the right came the master bedroom, filled like the others with boxes marked "MASTER BEDROOM." Kyle could hear sobbing as he approached the door. Squatting, he leaned in. There was a queen-size mattress on the floor, Sinclair sitting on it, his overcoat tight around him. Naomi was cradled in his arms, her body limp. Kyle didn't rush straight to Sinclair, instead he checked the bathroom, then the walk-in closet and then closed the double bedroom doors. No Cradle Robber. Kyle knelt beside Sinclair.

Naomi was still, her limbs limp, her right arm hanging over the cradle created by Sinclair's arms. Her hair was brown, cut short, almost boyish, her skin the translucent pink of children just out of infancy. Naomi looked to be three years old, just like Kyle's Shelby. She was dressed in pink-and-white-flowered shorts and a matching sleeveless top. Kyle could easily picture Shelby wearing it. Tears dripped from the corners of Kyle's eyes, some for his own daughter, most for Naomi.

"I'm sorry," Kyle said, touching Sinclair's shoulder. "We were too late."

"No, she's alive," Sinclair said, looking up, eyes liquid with tears of joy. "She's alive but I can't wake her."

Kyle knelt and put an ear close to Naomi's mouth, hearing the girl's tiny breaths. Feeling for a pulse he found it slow but regular. The little girl's forehead was cool and damp. Naomi was alive but Patterson had drugged her. Whatever he had given her was potent.

"There was no explosion, not even lightning," Sinclair said with obvious relief. "I did calculate the energy release. I thought it would be half a kiloton," Sinclair said, laughing nervously. "This means Sherrie was wrong—I was wrong."

"Maybe," Kyle said soberly. "Or maybe this isn't over."

Urging Sinclair to his feet, Kyle opened the bedroom doors and then ordered Sinclair to wait while he checked the other bedroom and the bonus room at the end of the hall. With his Naomi safe in his arms Sinclair was ready to take Kyle's orders and stayed where he was told. Then, cautiously, Kyle led them back toward the stairs, covering each doorway they passed as if Cradle Robber could suddenly burst from one. Only when they reached the stairs did he allow himself to relax a bit, letting his gun arm dangle at his side. Straight ahead off the landing at the top of the stairs was a decorative, octagonal window. Kyle saw the sky was still a deep brown. The shimmering streaks of green light had coalesced, forming a spiral with arms curving around the bright glowing center. It was beautiful but if it was over, why was the sky still shimmering?

With Sinclair slightly ahead, Kyle followed him down, still watching the sky through the window. A third of the way down the stairs Kyle realized Sherrie wasn't where he had left her. Then he saw her rolling out of the small foyer the front door opened into. Walking behind her with a shotgun leveled at the back of her head was Cradle Robber.

48

Decision

Psychologists call them flashbulb memories. Memories so powerful you never forget even the smallest detail, created instantaneously as a result of trauma. Assassinations like Martin Luther King Jr.'s, or disasters like the space shuttle *Challenger*, all fixed indelible images in people's minds. Seeing Cradle Robber's shotgun pressed against the back of Sherrie's head was just such a moment for Kyle. If he lived, he would never forget the sights and sounds around him. There was the smell of new carpet and new paint, the sound of Sinclair's gasp, and the look on Sherrie's face, determined and fearless. Kyle knew Sherrie would sacrifice herself to save them. She hated being a cripple and was ready to die.

Cradle Robber yanked back on Sherrie's hair like a rider on a horse's reins. Sherrie stopped rolling forward, her face red from anger and humiliation. They were out of the foyer now, ten feet from the stairs. Kyle and Sinclair, still holding the sleeping Naomi, were halfway down the stairs. Kyle looked to Sherrie, seeing her flick her eyes upward repeatedly, signaling something.

"Put Naomi down," Patterson said in a conversational tone, as if he didn't care if Sinclair obeyed or not.

Kyle's gun was in his hand at his side, hidden from Patterson's view by Sinclair and Naomi. Sherrie shielded Patterson to mid-chest making a shot at him risky. Kyle also noticed the ease with which Patterson handled his weapon. The serial killer held a pump shotgun and stood twenty feet away. With that weapon an experienced gunman could fire off a round every two seconds, almost as fast as a semiautomatic.

Patterson held his fire, Kyle realizing he didn't want to shoot Naomi. He preferred to kill children gently. The barrel of Patterson's gun hadn't been sawed off so the pellet spread would be minimal at this distance but there was still some risk to Naomi.

"Put Naomi down," Patterson ordered in the same even voice, this time lifting the shotgun from the back of Sherrie's head to shoulder level, aiming the weapon over Sherrie's head.

"I can't," Sinclair said, drawing Naomi tight against his chest, lifting her face to his, pressing his cheek to hers. "I can't ever let her go again."

Patterson's answer was a shotgun blast that caught Sinclair in the legs. There was no warning, no explanation of why he had become a child killer or why he had gone to such pains to kidnap Naomi Sinclair. Patterson simply fired.

Sinclair's left leg crumpled, and he collapsed with his daughter still clutched to his chest. Sinclair turned as he fell, landing on his back, Naomi cushioned against his chest. Even as Sinclair was falling, Kyle heard the well-oiled action on the shotgun as Cradle Robber pumped another shell into the chamber. Kyle reacted instantly, raising his arm and firing high to miss Sherrie but to catch Patterson in the head. It was too small a target. Kyle missed, the bullet passing the killer's left ear, creating a spray of dust as it passed through the Sheetrock behind him.

Everyone in the room was awash in adrenaline and every muscle was tensed. Reaction time would determine who would live or die. Kyle had survived the gunfight with the Brotherhood of the Bloody Rose because he had been quick and kept low. With Patterson he had been quick enough to get the second shot off but Patterson would fire the next round, the barrel already aimed at Kyle's chest. Then an instant before Cradle Robber fired Sherrie's arms shot up and shoved the barrel of the shotgun high, the blast tearing through the ceiling, showering Kyle with dust and pieces of Sheetrock.

Sherrie tried to hold the shotgun but the hot barrel burned her hands and Patterson twisted it free. Still shooting high, Kyle fired once, twice, three, four times over his head, bringing each shot lower, trying to get a head shot without risking Sherrie. The child killer broke and ran, keeping low, Sherrie rolling to the side at the same time to get out of the line of fire. With Sherrie clear Kyle fired three more rounds as Patterson ducked around the corner into the foyer. Kyle held his fire now, listening. He heard the front door open but kept the gun aimed, expecting a ruse.

Sherrie rolled to the stairs, lowering the side of her wheelchair and dropping to the floor, crawling up the stairs to where Sinclair lay, head down, his daughter clutched to his chest. His trouser legs were shredded, the left worse than the right, both bleeding. The new beige carpeting on the stairs was soaked with his blood. While Kyle held his shooting pose, Sherrie reached Sinclair and felt Naomi, checking her for wounds.

"Please, is she hurt?" Kyle heard Sinclair ask.

Sinclair's voice trembled as he fought against the pain.

Kyle backed up the stairs, watching the spot where he had last seen Cradle Robber, finger tight against the trigger.

"She's not wounded," Sherrie said. "But she's barely breathing. I can hardly feel a pulse. We've got to get her to a doctor—"

Sherrie checked herself in midsentence, realizing that getting Naomi medical help was the one thing they couldn't do.

Then the front window imploded, shards of glass and shotgun pellets spraying around them. Sinclair convulsed as if he had been hit, but the spasm was from shock.

"Save my daughter," Sinclair said, releasing his grip on Naomi.

Kyle fired the last round from his clip through the shattered window, then expertly released the spent clip and inserted his spare. He was down to his last nine rounds. Then he saw the end of Patterson's shotgun appear at the corner of the foyer and he fired two rounds to drive him back. Patterson responded by blowing three softball-size holes in the wall next to Kyle. It was time to retreat.

Squatting, Kyle scooped Naomi under one arm and backed up the stairs, while Sherrie hand-walked after him. Pausing at the top, he lay Naomi in the hall and then covered the bottom of the stairs. Sinclair lay where he had fallen, the blood on the carpet coagulating, changing from crimson to a deep scarlet. Suddenly there was a boom from Patterson's shotgun and pellets rocketed past Kyle's head. Patterson had fired blind to drive Kyle away from the top of the stairs, nearly getting a lucky kill. Kyle squatted now, leaned out, and fired a round down the stairs, careful not to hit Sinclair. Patterson returned fire, showering Kyle with shredded Sheetrock. Sherrie sat behind him, back to the wall. Kyle heard movement, looking out he saw Patterson at the corner of the stairs. Kyle fired three quick rounds, trying to end it once and for all.

There was a lull then, Kyle wondering if he had killed Cradle Robber. After a minute he risked a look. He saw no one but Sinclair, bleeding on the stairs. Kyle studied the ground floor. There were too many moving boxes, the light dim. Then there was movement. Kyle fired first, then ducked for cover, Patterson pumping round after round through his shotgun. Kyle studied the hall behind them as they kept their heads down, protecting Naomi with their bodies. There were many boxes but he doubted there was a weapon in any of them—Sinclair was a college professor. Kyle was down to two rounds and no escape route. Kyle could go out a window and jump off the roof, maybe even carrying Naomi, but he would have to leave Sherrie. He wouldn't do that.

"Sherrie, we're in trouble," Kyle said. "My nine-millimeter is no match for his shotgun and I'm almost out of ammunition."

Cradle Robber fired twice more up the stairs, the wall at the top shredding.

"We could try talking to him," Sherrie said. "Stall him. Someone might have heard the shots and called the police."

"This is the only finished house in the development," Kyle said, keeping his voice low and his tone even. "There's nothing but undeveloped land around us.

"I can hold my fire, make him come slowly, but if we do Sinclair and Naomi are going to die," Kyle said. "Sinclair will bleed to death and Naomi's so heavily sedated she'll never wake up."

"Maybe they should die, Kyle," Sherrie said after a pause. "Naomi did die. At least this is a better death for her than being tied to a tree and dying of thirst."

"I can't accept it, Sherrie. I'm sorry. I've tried but I just can't let another little girl die. There has to be a way to save her and prevent the causality paradox."

Another shotgun blast interrupted them, this one closer as if Cradle Robber knew their position.

"Back down the hall," Kyle ordered.

Sherrie dragged herself down the hall to the end table left in the hall by the movers. Kyle held his position until the corner just above him exploded from a near miss. Kyle fired once more down the stairs and then picked up Naomi and retreated to Sherrie. Looking down at legless Sherrie and then at the end table in the hall. Kyle noticed the table had a small compartment with a sliding door. Kyle checked his load, finding one last round.

"How small a space can you fit into?" Kyle asked.

"What?" Sherrie said, confused.

"Could you squeeze into this?" Kyle said, patting the end table.

"Maybe. Why?"

Kyle slid the door open, revealing a space two feet wide and three feet high. Sherry pulled herself to the opening but paused, looking doubtful. Kyle picked her up, helping to fold her in half so that her back was against one wall, the stumps of her legs tucked up at the top of the other wall. It was a tight fit but she was in.

"You have only one shot, Sherrie," Kyle said. "You've got to do it without warning and you'll have to shoot him in the back. Can you do that?"

Sherrie nodded, her lips tight.

Kyle wasn't sure she could. Sherrie was an ordinary person with a healthy amount of human compassion. She would find it hard to take a life without warning. But if they were to have a chance she would have to kill him from an ambush.

"No warning," Kyle reminded her.

Kyle cocked the gun, then handed it to her. Then he slid the cabinet door closed, leaving a half-inch crack for her to peek out. Then he picked up Naomi and hurried to the large room at the end of the hall and lay her in an empty closet. Checking her breathing, he felt only a slight whisper of a breath on his cheek. Then Kyle slid the closet door closed and went back to the door to the hall, leaning out far enough so that he could see the top of the stairs and so that Patterson would see him.

Minutes passed and nothing happened. Kyle knew the minutes were precious to Naomi and to Sinclair. Time was on Patterson's side and he was using it. More time passed and Kyle saw nothing. He was about to risk a walk to the stairs when he saw Patterson peek around the corner at the head of the stairs and then jerk his head back. A minute later the head was back, this time lower, as if he was lying on his stomach. This time Patterson spotted Kyle and again pulled back. Kyle waited, exposed, until Patterson appeared again, firing at Kyle. Kyle ducked back into the bonus room, counting to ten, then kneeling and peeking again. The lack of

Kyle's return fire told Patterson what he needed to know. Patterson was no fool, however, and would come slowly. When Kyle peeked again he saw Patterson dart from the left side of the corridor to the right, hiding in a doorway, the shotgun aimed at Kyle's position. When he saw Kyle's head he aimed and fired, Kyle rolling out of the way just in time to save himself from a face full of hot lead.

Now Patterson was just across from the end table where Sherrie hid. Kyle feared he would spot Sherrie through the small opening in the sliding door. Risking his own life, Kyle stood, then jumped across the doorway to the other side, drawing another blast from Patterson's shotgun.

"If you're trying to get me to waste ammunition, it won't work!" Patterson shouted to Kyle. "I have boxes of it in my pockets."

As if to illustrate, Kyle heard the sound of the shotgun being reloaded.

"You're out of ammunition, aren't you?" Patterson shouted. "Or maybe you're saving a last shot or two. What's that automatic hold? Nine rounds?"

Kyle risked a peek, seeing Patterson behind the end table where Sherrie hid, the shotgun resting on top, aimed at Kyle's doorway.

"Patterson! Why are you murdering children?" Kyle shouted, trying to distract the killer.

"They call me a murderer but the real murderers are people like you and Robert Sinclair and all the others in this world that can't take the time to spend a few minutes with a lonely boy. You kill the spirit. Not all at once, of course, that would be too kind. Instead you use slow torture, the death of a thousand little cuts, until there's not enough spirit left to keep a person going."

"You're lonely?" Kyle asked.

"I'm not talking about me!" Patterson roared. "I'm talking about children. I'm talking about my Robby."

The tone of Patterson's voice communicated the depth of

his feelings for his son. Kyle could feel the tenderness when he used his son's name.

Kyle looked down the hall again. Patterson still used Sherrie's cabinet for cover, but now his head was down, eyes glazed, lost in some memory. Kyle needed to get him away from Sherrie.

"Did something happen to Robby?" Kyle asked.

"Don't use his name! You have no right. You have no idea of the hell he went through."

"Went through?" Kyle said gently. "Did your son die?"

"I told you, people like you killed him."

"Suicide?" Kyle asked.

"It was murder."

"So you're getting even," Kyle said. "Murdering other people's children? Spreading the pain. Is that what you're doing? Spreading the pain?"

"Preventing the pain! I'm the cure not the disease. I get to the children before the world goes to work on them, beating them down. They're happy the day I send them from this world."

"You suffocate them, Patterson. It's a horrible death. Those children fought you, clawing at the plastic you pressed against their faces, trying desperately to live. It takes minutes to lose consciousness like that, and there is more suffering packed into those few minutes than in most children's lifetimes."

"That's a lie!" Patterson shouted. "They're surprised, that's all. I admit that, but then they go to sleep."

"You're lying to yourself," Kyle said. "Those children suffered at your hands. Suffered horribly."

"Shut up!" Patterson shouted.

"Robby must be proud of his old man. A child killer— Cradle Robber."

"Don't use my son's name!" Patterson shouted. "He would be proud of me. He loved me. He would understand."

Kyle looked again while Patterson was shouting, seeing

he was still behind the cabinet. As he spoke, he leveled the shotgun on Kyle's doorway and stepped from behind the cabinet, his face red with rage, his lips speckled with saliva.

"I helped those children. They would thank me if they knew the pain I saved them from."

Patterson was staring right at Kyle's partially exposed head but didn't shoot. He stepped forward now, coming slowly, either confident Kyle was out of ammunition or so enraged he didn't care.

"Children are happy, outgoing, trusting. Know any adults like that, Detective? Know any adults who aren't cynical and suspicious?"

He was past the cabinet now, still coming, eyes locked on Kyle's head. Kyle watched Patterson's hand for any sign that he was about to fire. Then behind Patterson the cabinet door moved, the sound covered by Patterson's loud ranting.

"In my mind I can still see each child I helped. Playing, laughing, singing silly songs, finding joy in the feel of sand through their fingers or mud between their toes. But it wouldn't last. It can't last because people won't let it. We can't stand to see someone else's happiness because we're jealous. We won't let them have something we don't have."

The cabinet door was half open now and Sherrie's arm appeared, unfolding, straightening, aimed up at an angle, the pistol in her hand.

"I saved them all from the pain Robby went through and now they're somewhere else, in a better place, playing with my Robby and they're just as happy as the day I sent them on their way. I'm going to help as many as I can and not you, or that time traveler, or the cripple is going to stop me."

It was the last line of Patterson's speech and Kyle moved. The shotgun fired a split second later, the door frame where his face had been exploding into a shower of wood splinters. Pellets pierced the wall, burying into Kyle's right arm and side. There were splinters in his cheek and forehead and he hurt from head to waist despite Sherrie's painkillers. Kyle hit the ground and lay still, letting the pain subside. Then he heard his pistol fire.

Quickly getting to his feet Kyle leaned against the frame and looked around. Patterson was standing there, his back to Kyle, his shotgun held in his limp right hand. There was a hole in the back of his jacket, blood soaking through the fabric. The wound was right of his spinal column, high enough on his back that Kyle couldn't be sure Sherrie's shot had caught a lung. Even if she had, it would be a slow death wound. Patterson's blood would dribble into his punctured lung, slowly drowning him in his own vital fluid. That would take time, time Patterson could use for killing.

Looking past Patterson he could see Sherrie pulling herself out of the cabinet, dragging herself away from Patterson. Slowly, Patterson was bringing the shotgun up but his right arm was quivering as if the nerves had been damaged and he had only partial control. Reaching over with his left arm Patterson helped his right arm lift the heavy weapon, steadying it on Sherrie. Sherrie was about to die.

Kyle was running down the hall before he knew he had acted. Kyle tested his right arm as he ran, finding he could move it as long as he clamped his jaws tight, grinding his teeth.

Sherrie was still dragging herself away in a desperate attempt to reach a doorway where she could get out of the line of Patterson's aim. Patterson was tracking her, taking one unsteady step after another. Kyle could see his left arm move as he worked the shotgun's pump action, a spent plastic shell casing ejected from the side, making a soft, harmless, clacking sound as it bounced off the wall to the carpeted floor. Then Kyle heard the sound of the fresh round loaded into the chamber.

Afraid he was two steps short of saving Sherrie, Kyle launched himself at Patterson in a desperate attempt to take him down. He hit the serial killer in the small of his back just as he pulled the trigger, the shotgun roaring and belching a cloud of lead pellets that would reach Sherrie in a tight little swarm.

Kyle's tackle took Patterson to the floor, Kyle landing on his legs, one arm still around the killer's waist. Now, like a trapped and wounded bear, Patterson found new reserves of strength. Insanity gave his struggle a feral quality, Patterson growling and snarling. But Kyle had his own pathologies to draw on and he kept his grip, keeping Patterson pinned beneath him, crawling up his back, reaching for the shotgun. The gun was under Patterson, the barrel visible over his left shoulder. Kyle reared up, punching Patterson in the ear with his left fist. Kyle felt a bone in his hand break from the power of the blow but it momentarily stunned Patterson, and he went limp. Using his good left arm, Kyle reached under Patterson's armpit and lifted and rolled him, then lunged for the gun. Patterson was only half over when he recovered from the blow to his head, reaching back for the shotgun. Kyle was on it now, though, and used his body to block him from the gun. Kyle tried to pull the gun up to where he could use it but Patterson used Kyle's tactic, jumping on his back, trying to pin him to the floor. Kyle still had the gun and enough strength to keep one knee under him and move the gun up.

Scratching and clawing, Patterson's attack was wild and uncoordinated and Kyle knew as long as he could take the abuse being heaped on his back, shoulders, and head, he would win control of the gun. There was a sane Patterson somewhere in the Cradle Robber persona, however, and it took momentary control.

Patterson stopped the attack, pushing himself to his feet, letting Kyle get up on both knees and pull the gun from under him. Kyle expected Patterson to flee or, worse, retreat to the bedroom where Kyle had secreted Naomi but instead Patterson attacked again, kicking Kyle between the legs from behind. Kyle's groin exploded in pain, shooting to his extremities, temporarily paralyzing him. Seconds passed before he could even gasp from the pain, realizing he was vulnerable to another kick. Moving sideways just in time, he took the next kick in the right buttock, the added pain insignificant. Then Patterson grabbed the shotgun, nearly wrenching it from Kyle's grasp. Kyle reared, twisting, pulling with all his strength. The gun was ripped from the killer's grasp, Kyle whipping around, the gun slipping from his grasp, flying down the hall. Kyle began to get up, to go after the gun, but Patterson kicked him in the side, Kyle's breath exploding from his body. Kyle collapsed.

Curling into a fetal position, Kyle readied himself to take more of Cradle Robber's kicks but they didn't come. Instead, Patterson staggered toward the gun, the bullet in his chest weakening him second by second. Kyle looked to see Sherrie pulling herself along the floor, trying to beat Patterson to the shotgun. His legs gave Patterson the advantage, so Kyle reached out, slapping Patterson's left foot as he passed. Kyle had enough strength to push Patterson's left foot behind his right, Patterson tripping and sprawling flat. Then Patterson's head came up and he found himself face-to-face with Sherrie and the race for the gun was on.

Using his forearms, his legs ineffectual, Patterson crawled toward the gun, Sherrie coming from the other side. Kyle reached out with his right arm but he had little strength, and found it hard to grip Patterson's trousers as he wriggled toward the gun. In desperation, Kyle rolled toward the killer trying to get his body up over his legs. He managed to get kicked in the face as Patterson moved away. Now with his left hand, he slapped out, grabbing an ankle, holding tight. It slowed Patterson briefly as he kicked himself free. Now Kyle struggled to his knees but once there he saw the race was over. Sherrie had the shotgun pointed at Patterson's face.

"Don't move," Sherrie said.

Patterson froze, his face no more than two feet from the barrel. Then he put his head down on the carpet, resting, thinking, weighing how much his life was worth. Now his head came up.

"Ever kill someone?" Patterson asked. "Ever shoot a man in the face with a twelve-gauge load?"

"No, but yesterday I blew the foot off a teenage boy and I'll blow your nose into your brain if you move," Sherrie said coldly.

Then as if she had practiced the move, Sherrie pulled the slide back, ejecting a shell and moving a fresh one into the chamber. The sound of the mechanism froze Patterson in place.

Patterson had managed to pull one of his knees up under him but now he stopped, Sherrie's response not what he expected.

Kyle was on his knees, trying to get to his feet. Patterson heard him, turning to look back, focusing on Kyle only briefly, then glazing over. Kyle knew Patterson had made his decision but as Kyle shouted a warning, Patterson turned and lunged for the gun. Patterson's arm was outstretched, reaching when Sherrie pulled the trigger. His thumb and half his hand were torn away, the rest of the pellets ripping into his throat and upper chest. He didn't die instantly, but the blood quickly pooled around him, gurgling sounds coming from the hole in his throat as he tried to breathe.

Half crawling, half walking, Kyle reached Sherrie whose head was on the carpet, tears flowing down her cheeks.

"I didn't want to kill him," Sherrie said.

"He wanted to die, Sherrie. He didn't give you any choice."

"I didn't want to kill him," she repeated. "I didn't want to shoot Patrick either. They didn't give me any choice, Kyle. There was no other way."

"I know, Sherrie. You did what you had to do. No one will blame you."

Kyle stroked her head, then helped her move away from the pool of blood that was spreading through the carpet. Propping Sherrie against the wall, he said, "I'm going to check on Naomi and Sinclair."

Struggling to his feet Kyle found it hard to walk, his groin hurting as much as his arm and side. His head throbbed in perfect synchrony with his heart, one stab of pain for each beat. Leaning against a wall as he walked, slowly Kyle made his way back to the bonus room where he had left Naomi. There were holes in the walls from Cradle Robber's buckshot but none had touched the closet and he found her inside, just as he had left her, oblivious to the dead and wounded spread through her new house. Her breath was shallow and her heart beat slow and weak—she was almost dead.

Kyle brushed the little girl's bangs off her forehead, studying her delicate features. Hair color, eyes, facial features, all were different from Shelby's, but when Kyle looked at Naomi he saw his daughter. She had been peaceful like this at the end. When Kyle's jeep left the road, Shelby had been injured and begged her daddy for help. Slowly blood loss dulled her senses and she became drowsy, falling to sleep, closing her eyes to the world like she had every night since she had been born, never to open them again. The little girl lying on the floor in front of him was dreaming her last dream too.

Crying now, Kyle scooped Naomi up in his arms, wincing from the pain in his right side, letting his left side carry the little girl's scant weight.

Sherrie had left Patterson's body and Kyle heard her thumping down the stairs toward Sinclair. At the end of the hall he looked out the octagonal window and saw the bright glowing spiral was dissipating, elongating, resembling the northern lights again. He understood. Naomi would die that night and Sinclair would have his reason for coming back in time. Kyle heard Sinclair's voice a second later.

"You're alive!" Sinclair said through gritted teeth. "Naomi? Is Naomi hurt?"

"I have her," Kyle said, coming down the stairs.

Sinclair reached for his daughter but Kyle motioned to Sherrie to sit against the wall and handed Naomi to her. The

Kyle pulled Sinclair down the stairs, leaning him against a wall and checked his legs. The blood flow had stemmed, although moving him had created more seepage. When Kyle touched the bare skin through the holes in Sinclair's pants, Kyle felt the tingle of the mild electric shock. Kyle wondered if whatever gave Sinclair his blue glow wasn't helping to stem the blood flow. Then Kyle took Naomi from Sherrie and gave her to her father who cradled her against his chest, sobbing with relief. As Sinclair pressed his cheek against his daughter's forehead, Kyle saw her flinch reflexively from the mild shock, the blue glow spreading to her forehead.

"Thank you," Sinclair said. "Thank you for saving my daughter."

Kyle said nothing because he knew she hadn't been saved. Looking through the high window he could see the sky was lighter now, the light dissipating as if it was the little girl's life force. Soon there would be no glowing light and Naomi's voice would be forever silent. Sinclair continued to rock his little girl, happy, oblivious. Kyle looked at Sherrie who nodded slightly, telling him he was doing the right thing.

"No!" Sinclair suddenly screamed. "She stopped breathing. Help me. She stopped breathing!"

Kyle didn't move.

"Help me! I said she stopped breathing. What's wrong with you? How can you stand there?"

Now Sinclair lay Naomi on the floor and tried to get into position to give her mouth-to-mouth resuscitation. His badly mangled legs made it impossible, however, and he nearly passed out from the pain. Still he lay next to her, pushing himself up with one arm, trying to pinch her nose and blow in her mouth at the same time—he didn't have the strength and nearly collapsed on her.

"Please, I can't do it," Sinclair begged.

Unconsciously, automatically, as if controlled by a deeper, more feeling part of his mind Kyle stepped toward Sinclair and Naomi.

"No, Kyle!" Sherrie said.

"I can't do this, Sherrie. I can't watch another little girl die."

"Do you think it's easy for me to just sit here? But it has to be this way!"

"Please," Sinclair begged, trying to breathe into Naomi's mouth.

Sinclair needed his arms to support his body so he couldn't pinch Naomi's nose closed. His breaths exhausted uselessly.

"She's only three," Sinclair said. "She doesn't deserve this. She's my baby."

Kyle took another step knowing each second he hesitated took Naomi closer to death and further away from her father's arms.

"You were a father, how can you let this happen?" Sinclair asked.

"I am a father!" Kyle said. "And I won't let it happen—not again."

With that Kyle stepped toward Naomi and as he did the house shook from another peal of thunder.

49

Little Girl Lost

Saturday, 8:19 P.M.

The sky was darkening again, the atmosphere ionizing to the point of glowing but no one in the Sinclairs' new home was watching the sky. Sinclair was lying next to his daughter, trying to stay conscious and bear the pain of his badly wounded legs. Sherrie was hand-walking across the floor toward Kyle, begging him to stop, while Kyle was bent over Naomi, alternating between mouth-to-mouth resuscitation and compressing her chest.

"One, two, three, four, five," Kyle counted softly, then pinched her nose and blew in her mouth. "One, two, three, four, five," he continued and then puffed again.

"Kyle, you can't do this!" Sherrie said, sitting next to him and pulling on his arm.

Brushing her arm away angrily, Kyle continued with his resuscitation.

"One, two, three, four, five," Kyle said, then puffed again into the little girl. "Get to the highway," Kyle said. "Flag down a car. Call for an ambulance."

"You'll kill us all if you do this, Kyle. Let her go. For everyone's sake, let her go."

The room was darkening fast, the thunder peals loud as if they were right above them. Like before, the storm built to a crescendo, then faded away.

"It's building up again, Kyle," Sherrie warned. "Stop before it's too late."

"No," Kyle said, continuing his routine. "Get help."

"I won't," Sherrie said.

Now Kyle looked to the front door, judging how long it would take him to sprint to the truck, drive to the road, and flag down someone with a cell phone. It was impossible unless someone took over for him, keeping Naomi alive. Kyle looked to Sinclair, wondering whether he might manage to keep Naomi alive long enough for him to get to help. Then he remembered that Naomi's skin had turned blue when Sinclair touched her.

"She doesn't have to die!" Kyle said suddenly. "Please, Sherrie, there is a way to save her and the city. Take over for me!"

Sherrie hesitated but then pulled herself over, performing resuscitation.

Kyle turned to Sinclair stripping off his long coat, the man grimacing as Kyle turned him and tugged the coat off.

"What are you doing?" Sinclair demanded.

Underneath the coat Sinclair wore a tight-fitting suit of a dark gray fabric. The surface was covered with bumps from head to foot and was textured, with ripples running in all directions, interconnecting the bumps, as if there were large veins just below the surface. Wrapped around his chest was a wide band, gray like the fabric, but made of something hard. More of the same material ran down his legs into his loose-fitting pants. There were controls on his chest and five tiny lights, all of which glowed green.

"We put the suit on Naomi," Kyle said. "Send her to the future."

"It won't work," Sinclair said. "If you try to take it off I'll be pulled back to my present."

"Then can you take Naomi back with you?" Kyle asked.

Sinclair looked confused, hesitated, and then said, "I don't know—maybe."

"Yes or no!" Kyle demanded. "It may be her only chance."

"Let me think—the returning mass must be within ten percent of the sending mass—fifteen percent at the max."

"She might weigh forty pounds," Kyle said.

"More like thirty," Sherrie said as she pumped Naomi's chest.

"Is it possible?" Kyle demanded again.

"Maybe, maybe—I can't think!" Sinclair said.

"Strip everything off of him," Sherrie said.

Kyle pulled off Sinclair's shoes, socks, and pants, Sinclair moaning when Kyle had to tug the pants away from his wounds because the blood had dried, gluing the material to the skin with scabs. Finally there was only an old man in the skintight gray suit. There were holes torn in the legs of the suit where the bullets had ripped through.

"There are holes in your suit," Kyle said.

"Touch my feet," Sinclair said. "What do you feel?"

"I got a shock," Kyle said.

"Then it will be all right but we need to have a full charge. Take me to the kitchen."

With his wounds, Kyle didn't have the strength to carry the old man so he dragged him around to the kitchen. Under Sinclair's direction he found a power cord in his coat pocket and plugged the pigtail in a socket prepared for a range while Sinclair plugged the other into the plate on his chest. Sinclair touched the plate on his chest and an image formed in midair, a foot from Sinclair's chest. The image coalesced into a data display.

"Strip everything off of Naomi," Sinclair said. "Every bit of mass matters."

Kyle left Sinclair and hurried back to Sherrie and Naomi. He didn't know how effective their resuscitation efforts were and knew that the sooner they got her medical attention the better chance she had of surviving. Kyle relieved Sherrie while she took Naomi's clothes off. Then Kyle shouted to Sinclair.

"We're ready here."

"There's another problem," Sinclair said.

Cursing, Kyle let Sherrie take over again while Kyle hurried back to Sinclair.

"Even if this works, she'll still die," Sinclair said. "I did this on my own. No one knows I'm here. When I return, I return to the second I left. No significant time has passed while I was here so there's no one in my time to help me."

"Help will be there," Kyle said.

"How do you know?" Sinclair said.

"Because I'll be there," Kyle said. "Tell me when and where."

Kyle pulled his notebook and pen from his back pocket, handing it to Sinclair.

Sinclair smiled in gratitude, writing down the information and handing it back.

"Are you ready?" Kyle asked.

Sinclair studied the numbers floating before his face and then punched the controls on his chest. One of the green lights flashed five times and then turned steady red.

"Bring her to me, now!" Sinclair said.

Kyle hurried to Sherrie and Naomi, waiting until Sherrie blew one more breath into her lungs, then lifted her, favoring his left side. Naomi was pale, peaceful, and looked like a sleeping child. Hugging Naomi to his chest he carried her to her father. There were only two green lights left on his chest plate when Kyle got there and as he handed Naomi to Sinclair one of the last two lights flashed and then turned red. Handing Naomi to her father Kyle felt the last of the pain from Shelby's death uncovered, and then as if by saving Naomi he was saving his own daughter. The agony he had kept buried left him, leaving a hurt that he would always have but a hurt he could live with.

Sinclair spread his daughter out on his chest, draping her legs around his sides. The blue color slowly spread over Naomi's naked body, covering her completely. To Kyle the blue was pale, barely distinguishable and he worried that Sinclair wouldn't be able to take her back with him. With Naomi on his chest, the last light was covered so Kyle did not see it begin to flash. Then Sinclair looked at him one more time and said, "Thank you." Suddenly he and Naomi were gone. Kyle was sucked forward in a rush of air that filled the space Sinclair and his daughter had occupied.

Kyle stared at the place where Sinclair and Naomi had been, wondering what was happening now in their present. Had they been able to save her? Unfortunately, the last chapter of their story wouldn't be written for another couple of decades. Then Sherrie was next to Kyle, reaching out to him. He took her in his arms.

Epilogue

Kyle had picked up another tailgater, this one an impatient family in a minivan. Kyle pulled his pickup as far onto the shoulder as he could, then signaled them to pass. When they were safely by, Kyle took the lane again, then resumed his search. Once he thought he would never forget the place where Shelby had died but now worried he wouldn't find the spot on the first pass. Kyle rounded the next corner and instantly recognized the stretch of road. There was the steep embankment to his right, the row of trees beyond that, the fields to his left. In his mind's eye he could see the deer appear as it had that night, jumping in front of him, the bone-crushing thump as he struck the animal, throwing it to the side of the road. The rolling came next, the roof crushing in on him and unconsciousness.

Kyle pulled the pickup over, stopping where the jeep had rolled over the embankment. There were no skid marks left and even the section of the embankment that had given way showed no scars. The Jeep was long gone, of course, and even the bits and pieces of glass and chrome from the wreck were covered by grass and ferns.

Kyle got out into the August heat, taking the cross from the back of the pickup and a sledgehammer and walked down the steep embankment, estimating where the jeep had come to rest. Using the sledge he beat the point of the cross deep into the ground. Standing back he surveyed his work. On the vertical axis of the cross it read "BELOVED" and on the crosspiece it read "SHELBY N. SOMMERS." With luck the cross would stand for a few years until the wood rotted and a strong wind knocked it over. Kyle wouldn't replace it. He wouldn't let a cross by the side of the road become an obsession. Besides, there was a permanent marker in the cemetery where Shelby was buried.

The cross he had erected couldn't be seen from the road. Only the occasional pedestrian or bicyclist would be likely to see it, but he would know it was there. Even when it had fallen and decayed away, he would still picture it down the embankment, out of sight, memorializing his lost daughter.

Now Kyle pulled a wad of folded papers from his pocket. On the pages were taped the "notes" left behind by Sinclair when he tried to save children. Kyle had pieced together the complete article from clippings he found after Sinclair returned to the future. Kyle read the article again.

The Oregon Chronicle

In My Opinion
Cassidy Kellogg

THE ROOT OF PORTLAND'S PROBLEMS

Portland's economic and social problems can be traced to one horrifying week of violence.

Personal tragedy can traumatize a person and change them forever, but can a city be traumatized? Can one week in the life of a century-old city do more to change its course than the other five thousand weeks combined? Some say Portland had such a defining week; one terrible week when the residents who were proud of the "big city" they had built came face-to-face with the dark side of urbanization. It was a week of senseless death, gang violence, and spree killing. Worst of all it was the week the child serial killer known as Cradle Robber came to Portland.

• Sunday, evening: A pickup full of teenagers was run off Highway 26 by an angry motorist. The teens had mooned Nicholas Dawson, the driver of a sport utility vehicle and in one of the worst cases of road rage in Oregon's history, the enraged Dawson slammed his car into theirs, sending them into a concrete support for an overpass. In the fiery crash that ensued, Mark Nielson, Geni Marsh, and Winnie Young were killed. Nathan Myers was paralyzed, and Kim Lee and Leah Carson badly burned. Nicholas Dawson, father of two boys, is serving a thirty-year sentence in the Oregon State Correctional Facility.

• Sunday, night: Twin teenagers, Carolee and Carolynn Martin, cut through Pier Park on their way back from a friend's house and stumbled into a group of drunken teenage boys gathered for a kegger and a little "wilding." By all accounts the primarily middle-class boys had limited their previous wilding to drinking and vandalism, but with Carolee and Carolynn the boys sank to new depths, raping and murdering the girls. Tried as adults, five boys served three to eight years for the crime. The ringleaders, Enrico Cortez and Marcus Jennings, were convicted of murder and executed by lethal injection after three years on death row. Nancy Martin, the murdered girls' mother, was present at the execution. Two days after Cortez and Jennings were executed for the murder of her only children, Nancy Martin was found in her bathtub, her wrists slit. A note taped to the bathroom mirror read simply: "I'm going to be with my babies."

• Monday, early morning: The serial killer called Cradle Robber announced his arrival in Portland by entering the Janelle and Raymond Kirkland home in North Portland and suffocating their six-year-old daughter. Janelle Kirkland put Wendy to bed at 8:00 P.M., Wendy holding a stuffed Winnie the Pooh and listening to a Winnie the Pooh CD. Janelle Kirkland checked on Wendy at 8:30 P.M. Raymond Kirkland checked on Wendy at 11:00 P.M., as he went to bed. Wendy was a restless sleeper and her father remembers that he found Wendy sleeping sideways in her bed that night and had to turn her to get her head back on the pillow. Sometime after the parents were asleep, Cradle Robber cut through the double-pane glass of Wendy's bedroom window and entered. According to the medical examiner's report, something was pressed against Wendy's nose and mouth and Wendy was suffocated. The coroner estimated it took two minutes for Wendy to lose consciousness and another two to die. The next morning Janelle Kirkland found her daughter dead, a blue baby rattle resting in her hand.

• Monday, morning: Sandy Brown was walking her seven-year-old daughter, Marissa, to Tom McCall Elementary School when they were struck by a truck. It was the start of a big week for Marissa because she was going to be "Special Person of the Week," which meant it would be her turn to lead the class line to lunch and recess and to bring something for show and tell every day. On Friday, Marissa could bring a special guest, and at the end of Marissa's special week her father was coming to sit in the big rocking chair with the class gathered around and tell them stories about when Marissa was little. But Marissa's father never sat in the class rocker, or told the baby stories. While Marissa and her mother waited for a walk signal, a delivery-truck driver suffered a heart attack and lost control, running up onto the sidewalk, killing her mother and crushing Marissa. One of Marissa's legs was amputated that day but Marissa never knew since she never regained consciousness. Three days later she was declared brain-dead and her father made the difficult decision to end life support. Four days after the decision, her lips cracked and her tongue swollen, the body of the little girl who never got to be Special Person of the Week died.

• Monday, evening: Two children drowned in a freak accident when their mother left them alone to run to the store to get milk for dinner. While she was gone the children drowned in the family's spa. Police speculated the children were playing or fighting on the deck by the spa when they fell in. Six-year-old Nick and four-year-old Christy were found by their mother headfirst in water. The mother, Millie Sadler, and a neighbor tried to revive the children but they were pronounced dead by the paramedics. Four days later at the funeral for her children, Millie Sadler suffered a miscarriage.

• Wednesday, early morning: Cradle Robber found his second victim in Peter Benchly, the six-year-old son of Rhonda and Lawrence Benchly. Like Cradle Robber's other young victims, Peter was found the next morning, smothered and holding a toy baseball bat. The second Cradle Robber murder hit the city hard and the public lost faith in the police. After the Wendy Kirkland murder the public prayed that the police could stop Cradle Robber but after the Peter Benchly murder a feeling of helplessness set in and the parents were reduced to hoping the murder spree wouldn't touch their own families.

• Wednesday, morning: After a night of car thieving, members of the Brotherhood of the Rose gang liked to gather in front of Alberto Mendez's house to flirt with the neighborhood girls on their way to school. It was this moment that members of the Psychlos chose to deliver a message to their rivals for the Portland stolen car market. Eight gunmen in two cars opened fire while they dumped the body of Willie Mendez. Willie, Alberto's brother, had been tarred and feathered. Drunk and reckless, the Psychlos gunfire cut down one of Mendez's gang members, Paco Nobles, as well as a teenage girl, Linda Roquet, a four-year-old boy, Kelly Grant, and a three-year-old girl, Teresa Nunez. The attack set off a gang war in which four more innocent bystanders would be gunned down as well as Willie Mendez and most of the Brotherhood. The war ended six months later when Alberto Mendez killed rival gang leader Nick Bletson, wiping out the last of the Psychlos. Alberto Mendez is serving three consecutive life sentences.

• Thursday, early morning: Cradle Robber's third victim, Wyatt Newcombe, was found in his bed, suffocated like Wendy and Peter. Unable to have children, Marissa and Edward Newcombe had adopted four-year-old Wyatt only the year before. Wyatt was the Newcombes' pride and joy, neighbors said, and the Newcombes doted on their son, nearly to the point of spoiling him. Wyatt survived the car accident that killed his parents and sister, to find a second chance at happiness with the Newcombes. Cradle Robber took that second chance from him.

• Friday, 9 A.M.: On Friday morning fourteen-year-old Laticia Sternwell played hooky from school, telling her parents she didn't feel well. In reality she was planning to stay in her Gresham home to meet with her seventeen-year-old boyfriend, Patrick Menley. Patrick, who was a neighbor and friend of the family, decided to impress Laticia by showing off one of his father's shotguns. While showing Laticia how to load and fire the gun the shotgun accidentally discharged in Laticia's face, killing her instantly. A grief-stricken Patrick pled guilty to reckless endangerment and spent six months in a group home in Roseburg.

• Friday, 9:45 A.M.: It was multiculturalism day at James John Elementary School and the students were gathered on the playground to greet their special guests, the Hawaiian Riders. The Hawaiian Riders were in Portland for the Rose Festival parade and were making the rounds of elementary schools, showing off their brightly decorated horses, Hawaiian garb, and sharing with the students native Hawaiian folklore. The multicultural party turned deadly when four teenagers threw firecrackers under the horses. Panicked, the horses bucked and kicked, one stumbling and falling onto the children. Michelle Winston and Evan Newbridge were crushed to death and five other children were badly injured. Two teenage boys, Nelson Naples and Ty Scolari, were arrested and convicted of manslaughter, serving seven years in prison. Two other teens involved in the crime, Vince Strong and Trent LePoer, died when they attempted to elude the police and their stolen car crossed the center line on Foster Road, crashing head-on into another vehicle, killing the elderly couple in the other car.

• Saturday morning, 10:15 A.M.: Patty Sinclair, wife of Robert Sinclair, president of Phoenix Systems, and their daughter, Naomi, had just left the Washington Square Embassy Suites Hotel when they were attacked. Patty and her three-year-old daughter were staying at the hotel while their new home was being finished and their belongings delivered from California. After buckling Naomi into her car seat, Patty was clubbed unconscious by two men who robbed her and stole the car with Naomi still in the backseat. Ira Ryerson and John Butler were apprehended three days later in Boise, Idaho, still driving the Sinclairs' car. Ryerson and Butler admitted they had taken the girl into the woods and tied her to a tree, planning to tell authorities where she could be found, but they were high on crack, and forgot to call. Too stoned to remember accurately, neither Butler nor Ryerson could lead the police to Naomi and after a massive two-week search the police gave up. Robert and Patty searched for another month but never found their daughter.

Cradle Robber continued killing for two months, then left Portland to mourn its dead. Portland became a "big" city that June, with fearful, distrustful residents hiding in their homes, never learning their neighbors' names. Evening and night were turned over to the predators, the parks abandoned to muggers, drug dealers, and gangs. Taxes were diverted from parks and beautification to police and prisons, the City of Roses becoming the antithesis of its pre Cradle Robber self.

The old-timers remember Portland from the days before Cradle Robber, remember what Portland was, what it could be again, but what kind of miracle could ever turn the City of Roses back to what it was before Cradle Robber came to town?

Cassidy Kellogg is anchorperson for the Channel 7 Evening News. Ms. Kellogg was the Communication Officer for the Portland Police Department at the time of the Cradle Robber murders.

Sinclair had prevented some of the deaths mentioned in the article but not all, and others died who would not have died if Sinclair had not come back to save his daughter. Was it worth it? Were the lives saved more valuable than the lives sacrificed? Kyle supposed that Sinclair would think so since he had his daughter back, but Kyle still mourned for his Shelby. Once he would have done anything, sacrificed anything, to get his daughter back, but ultimately he couldn't put other parents through what he had gone through.

Striking a match, Kyle held the corner of the pieced together article and lit it, letting flames engulf it entirely before dropping it and letting it burn itself out. The week described in the article never happened, at least most of it, and because of that all the coming weeks would be different for those families—and for him. Kyle ground the ashes into the ground. With a last look at Shelby's cross, Kyle climbed the embankment and got back into the pickup. It was another fine August day, hot and dry and nearly two weeks since the last rain.

Kyle had three cars backed up behind him when he

reached Grandpa's farm. Sherrie's van was parked tight up against the garage door where she could get out easily and up the newly built ramp to the house. Kyle and his father had spent six weekends modifying the house so Sherrie had access to both levels, although she had to go outside to get from one level to the next. The ramps were all new redwood and decorated with flower boxes, benches, and decorative lighting. Kyle admired their work, remembering the planning they had put into the project. It had been his father's idea, suggesting it right after he and Sherrie had returned from their honeymoon. Sherrie wanted to help at first but then she realized this wasn't just a remodeling project, it was a chance for father and son to renew old bonds.

Taking the ramp toward the back deck, Kyle smelled the steaks cooking even before he made the turn and walked up the ramp. His father was at the barbecue.

"About time, Kyle," his father said. "Sherrie couldn't wait any longer and made me start the steaks. Police work hold you up?" his father asked hopefully.

"No, I'm just late."

The patio doors opened and Sherrie and his mother came out, his mother greeting him with a hug. There was small talk then, his father probing for more police stories, his mother asking Sherrie about her training for the Portland Marathon. They talked like that, passing in and out of the house, carrying out salads, fruits, drinks, and place settings. Finally, the steaks were done and they sat down to eat, Sherrie setting a pace the others couldn't match and outlasting them as well. There would be watermelon for dessert but that would wait until later, after the sun had gone down.

Now sitting on the porch, they enjoyed the late evening shaded by the house as the sun settled behind the horizon. After the conversation ran its course, Sherrie turned to Kyle and spoke softly.

"Is it time to tell them?" Sherrie asked.

"Time to tell us what?" Kyle's mother wondered.

"I'm pregnant," Sherrie said.

Kyle's mother's face exploded with joy and she bent over, hugging Sherrie in her chair.

"Seems right," Kyle's father said simply.

"Yes," Kyle said. "Feels right too."